A PASSAGE IN BLACK

OMAHA BOUND ENTERTAINMENT

About Cullen Bunn

Cullen Bunn is best known as the writer of graphic novels and comic books. He has written THE SIXTH GUN, THE DAMNED, HELHEIM, and THE TOOTH for Oni Press; HARROW COUNTY for Dark Horse;THE UNSOUND and THE EMPTY MAN for Boom! Entertainment; UNHOLY GRAIL and DARK ARK for Aftershock! Comics; and REGRESSION for Image Comics. He also writes titles such as X-MEN BLUE, DEADPOOL KILLS THE MARVEL UNIVERSE, and MONSTERS UNLEASHED for Marvel Comics.

He also wrote the middle reader horror novel, CROOKED HILLS.

All writers must pay their dues, and Cullen has worked various odd jobs, including Alien Autopsy Specialist, Rodeo Clown, Professional Wrestler Manager, and Sasquatch Wrangler. He has also been a Career Consultant, Product and Project Manager, IT Manager, and Director of Marketing. He made up at least a few of those jobs. He was unqualified for all of them.

Cullen grew up in rural North Carolina, and the locale influences much of his work, but he now lives in the Missouri Ozarks with his wife and son.

And, yes, he has fought for his life against mountain lions and he performed on stage as the World's Youngest Hypnotist. Buy him a drink sometime, and he'll tell you all about it.

www.cullenbunn.com
@cullenbunn

About Tim Mayer

Tim is a freelance illustrator whose credits include "Prophetica", "The Anywhere Man", and "Oldguy: Superhero". He has also designed book covers for the sci-fi novel series 'The Surface' and EAB publishing's "Midnight Circus" (2013-14).

When he's not hunched over a drafting table, he teaches for the Art of Imagination program at Ollie Webb Center, Inc.

timmayerart.com
@timthemayer

A PASSAGE IN BLACK

&

OTHER STORIES

BY

CULLEN BUNN

A Passage in Black & Other Stories copyright 2017 by Cullen Bunn.

Published by OmahaBound. www.OmahaBound.com

ISBN-10: 0-9886313-3-4
ISBN-13: 978-0-9886313-3-5

All stories originally published elsewhere are credited after the text.

This collection of short stories
is dedicated to my Dad,

Roman Franklin Bunn,

who could spin a story like
nobody's business.

Foreword by Cullen Bunn

There's a filing cabinet in my utility room. It's old and dented, purchased some time ago at an antique mall, and it is stuffed overfull with folders full of all the short stories I've written over the years. Within that filing cabinet are tales of ravenous zombies and haunted bicycles and Ozark howlers and evil wizards and ice cream trucks filled with the corpses of the recently deceased. There are unfinished novels and incomplete stories and rambling essays. Some pages are typed out with an old school typewriter, some are printed on perforated printer paper, and some are handwritten on loose leaf notebook pages. Some of these stories were submitted to various magazines over the years. Some of them were critiqued by classrooms full of aspiring writers. Some were simply shoved into a folder and filed away almost as soon as they were finished.

Every now and again, I open that filing cabinet and shuffle through those crumpled, faded old folders. I admit, some of the words written on those pages embarrass me more than a little. But there's something special about them, too, at least to me. Looking through those files, I so easily recall the joy... the pride... I felt in the crafting of those tales. I was writing stories, sometimes with publication in mind, sometimes for a grade—but always to be read and (hopefully) enjoyed.

A few of those stories have been reprinted in this collection, along with many others I've written over the years. In this book you'll find tales of demonic machines and terrible curses, hillbilly vampires and testicle festivals dedicated to the elder gods. Horror and dark fantasy have always been my preferred playgrounds, and that is evident in this tome. The creepy crawlies run rampant herein, and they all serve the same dark purpose: to entertain and thrill and scare.

In a way, sharing these stories is a lot like digging through that filing cabinet, only this time around, I'm being a little more selective, and I've got you—the reader—to take the journey along with me. I'm quite proud of many of these yarns. Others don't hold up quite as well. But I love them all for one reason or another, and I feel like they help to form a kind of shadow world of my own creation.

If you are only familiar with my comic book work, you're in for something altogether different. Something twisted and dark and fun and surprising. There are dark corners to be explored, and once you're done, you'll have a better idea of who I am as a writer.

Before I go, I should take a moment to thank the people who helped make this book possible. Tim Benson, who ran the show in terms of design and printing; Tim Mayer, for the awesome illustration work; Jeremy Morong and Aaron Stueve for editorial reviews, and Tyler Crook, who painted an amazing cover for our special edition.

And you, of course, the reader.

Not to compare you to a rusty antique filing cabinet, but you also remind me why I do what I do.

I hope you get a kick out of these tales of terror.

Cullen Bunn
2017

Book One

Why Sing the Sirens   15

Wide is the Way, Broad is the Gate   23

The Storm Children   35

Come Again, Halloween   47

Cold Snap   57

Still Waters   61

Creeping Stones   73

Tomorrow, When the Demons Come   81

Beneath Black Boughs My Darling Slumbers   93

The Caller from the Void   107

For Her Love   113

Cry of the Machine   127

The Feast of Crows   149

Remains   157

Book Two

School for the Dead   193

Dance, Dance Upon the Night of the Ball   207

The Last Night of the Fair   217

Piasa Dreams   231

Great Balls of Ire   245

Killer Frog Blues   289

A Passage in Black   297

Pappy's Deep Fried Deep Ones   309

Witching Eyes   311

Blood Feud   327

Bonus Stories

Slaves to the Wheel   381

Someday Dolls   391

Gallows   397

WHY SING THE SIRENS

(A TALE OF AHMEN'S LANDING)

Reaching the end of the narrow, sand-swept road, Mitchell swung the car into a parking lot nestled amid the dunes. With the windows down, he heard the hiss and rumble of waves breaking upon the nearby shore, smelled salt and the lingering taint of low-tide on the air. The paved lot was crowded—too crowded for a night in the middle of the off-season. The vehicles lined up alongside Mitchell's Honda Civic were empty, seemingly abandoned, windshields reflecting the blackness of a clear sky speckled with stars.

The car idled while Mitchell listened to the end of a Van Halen song on the radio. Summer music. Local stations played the stuff all year round, as if trying to coax the warmer months back a few days early. The cab was lit by the greenish glow of the tuner and digital clock. Eleven forty-five.

Hell of a time for a beach party, he thought.

Cutting the engine, he grabbed his windbreaker from the passenger seat, and stepped out of the car. He heard no sounds of celebration—only the steady rush and retreat of the surf somewhere beyond the sandy hills—but he detected the faint smell of a bonfire, and his nose led him in the direction of a footpath cutting through the dunes.

Sand shifted underfoot as he climbed the track through the ridges. Dry patches of wild buckwheat and tangled beach grass rustled in the breeze, whispering secrets. Closer to the beach, the vegetation thinned, and the wind shaped wavering patterns into the barrier sands.

From the crest of the dunes, Mitchell saw a blazing fire, around which at least three-dozen people assembled, sitting upon gnarled driftwood logs, roasting hot dogs or marshmallows on sticks, talking, laughing. White sand, marred by dimpled footprints, stretched towards a shoreline pebbled with shells, smooth stones, and driftwood. Frothy white waves licked at the beach. Beyond the ceaseless ebb of the tide, all was rumbling blackness, the ocean at night.

Descending the hill, he heard someone call his name. Barry stood near one of many coolers placed strategically around the fire. He waved Mitchell over.

"Mitch! I was hoping you'd make it!" Barry clutched a Miller Light in his hand, even though a painted sign at the edge of the path read "No Glass Containers. No Alcohol."

Mitchell shook his co-worker's hand and nodded towards the bottle. "Got one of those for me?"

"Plenty of them, man, plenty. Party's just getting underway." Barry opened the cooler, pulled out a couple of icy bottles, holding them in one hand by the necks. He passed one to Mitchell. The other he handed to a beautiful, dark-haired woman. She wore snug beachcomber pants and a sleeveless white blouse that showed off both her figure and her deep tan. She was barefoot, her toes digging playfully in the sand.

"Mitch, I'd like you to meet my wife, Leslie."

Mitchell wondered how Barry, with his receding hairline and protruding beer belly, had ever attracted such a lovely lady.

Maybe there's hope for me yet, he mused.

Mitchell had only agreed to come to the party after being promised the opportunity to meet a few single ladies. Meeting people was difficult enough, especially in a new town, so the bonfire sounded like a good idea. To hear Barry tell it, the party was just about the best way to meet a girl in Ahmen's Landing.

"Nice to meet you," Leslie said. "I haven't seen you around here before, and you don't have that bleary-eyed look of a local yet. Been living in the Landing long?"

"Only a couple of months, actually. I just took a job with Phillips Industries."

"Don't let him be so modest." Barry laughed and clasped a hand on Mitchell's shoulder. "Old man Phillips practically begged Mitch to take the job. If you believe the hype, he's going to single-handedly revitalize our sales department."

"Is that right? Well, congratulations."

"Thanks." His face flushed. Somehow Barry's compliment came off as if Mitchell himself were bragging. "I guess it's pretty nice of Mr. Phillips to sponsor this party, huh? And he does this once a year?"

"Like clockwork," Barry said. He raised his bottle, and everyone around him joined him in a toast.

"The sea gives, and the sea takes away."

"So, you're here alone?" Leslie asked. "No wife? No girlfriend?"

"Uh, no. I'm flying solo, I guess."

Flying solo. Didn't that just sound stupid. This, he thought, is why I should never speak to women.

"Well, I can't imagine you'll be single for long." Leslie touched his arm lightly.

"A cutie like you—you're bound to get snatched up."

Mitchell didn't know what to say. Was Leslie flirting with him? Surely not with her husband standing right there.

"I'll let you boys talk." Leslie gave Barry a quick peck on the cheek, and winked at Mitchell. "Try to have a good time tonight, okay?"

She made it sound as if her heart might break if he didn't enjoy himself, as if she would do anything to ensure that he had a nice time. He shook the thought from his mind. Still, Mitchell couldn't help but watch Leslie as she sauntered away to mingle with some of the other partygoers. If Barry noticed, he didn't complain.

"So, what do you think, buddy?" Barry asked.

"I think you're a lot luckier than you deserve to be."

"No argument there."

Mitchell admired—but couldn't completely understand—Barry's attitude. If he had been married to a woman like Leslie, he would have been insanely jealous if she flirted with another man ... if another man looked at her the way Mitchell had looked at her only seconds earlier.

"Hey, let me show you around," Barry said.

Mitchell recognized a few guys from work, and he smiled and shook hands with their wives and girlfriends—all lovely. He didn't know most of the partygoers, though, and Barry introduced him to almost everyone, sharing with each how Mr. Phillips had named Mitchell his personal champion in the sales department.

As he mingled, Mitchell started to notice something odd.

He glanced around the beach.

He saw a group of married couples laughing and drinking around the bonfire.

Nearby, a man and woman were making out as if one of them were about to board a departing flight to some far off place.

Another couple stood in each other's arms at the edge of the shore, watching the tireless motion of the tide.

He saw one man was crying, while another tried to console him.

He met no single women. All of the ladies he met were breathtaking, but they all accompanied someone. The only single people at the party, he realized, were himself and several other men.

"What kind of party is this? I thought you said—"

A billowing sound rolled in with the crashing waves.

A mournful trumpeting.

Barry smiled.

"What is that?" Mitchell asked.

An excited chatter passed through the crowd. A few people took tentative steps towards the water, then backed away, as if unsure whether to go towards the sound or flee from it.

Barry walked towards the gathering crowd.

"Hey!" Mitchell called after him. "What's going on?"

The bonfire guttered as a salty wind whipped past. Flaring cinders flew into the air, sweeping into a whirlwind like dancing fireflies.

A line of men gathered across the beach, standing side-by-side, like breakers awaiting an onslaught of tidal force.

The women assembled in a different group, closer to the shoreline. They discarded their shoes and sandals in the sand, strode out into water. The surf lapped at their ankles.

Mitchell joined the men.

Bits of seaweed uncoiled from the depths, rolling across the sand with the next wave, slithering and grasping the ankles and calves of the women.

The women started to disrobe, shimmying out of their pants and skirts and underwear, pulling shirts off over their heads, helping each other unfasten their bras. They demonstrated no modesty before the watching men.

What the hell—

The bellowing continued.

"What's going on?" Mitchell asked.

The waves swelled and crashed upon the beach. The sound beyond the shore continued, a deep resonance racing through the waves and quivering beneath the sand. Mitchell thought he might have seen something moving out in the darkness, something large rising—uncoiling—in the depths and bobbing in the choppy water like an impossibly large channel marker.

The women, their clothing like discarded skin in the lapping waves, dashed into the water. Leslie was among their number, her perfect figure just one among many. The water must have been freezing, but they didn't hesitate. They waded against the current, then dove down into the water, vanishing beneath the black surface.

The trumpeting peaked and receded, swallowed up by the sound of the tide.

The hint of movement in the distance slipped away, as if the floating shape had slipped beneath the surface.

The pale forms of the swimming women appeared, coming up for air, then disappeared as they dove down again.

"What am I seeing here?" Mitchell asked. "Somebody answer me!"

The waves rumbled.

Minutes ticked by. The waves whispered to them. A nervous shuffling passed like an unvoiced thought through the group.

The bonfire crackled in the wind.

Suddenly cold, Mitchell wrapped his arms around his body. What had happened to them? Where were they?

"Over there!" someone in the crowd shouted, and a thrilled gasp passed down the line. Several men ran for the shore.

18

The air carried a strange, arousing smell.

He took a step, following the men, then another. By the third step, his curiosity and a strange, mounting sensation of desire, fueled him to a run.

A woman lay upon the sand. She lay on her side along the shore, covered in streamers of kelp and patches of sand, cast out of the sea. Surely she was dead, drowned ... but she took a gasping breath, coughed out a mouthful of water.

"Who is it?" one of the men asked.

"Anyone know her?"

One of the men knelt beside her naked form, turned her head and brushed her wet, matted hair from her face for all to see.

"It's Carol Freeman," someone called.

A man broke through the group and fell to his knees beside her, scooping her into his arms and crying, "Oh, thank you, Lord, thank you."

"Another one!" someone cried.

And now dozens of figures appeared along the shoreline, sprawled in the sand like cast up debris, and with each rushing wave, more figures rolled limply out of the water. Men scurried this way and that, examining the women and calling out names to worried husbands, fiancés, and boyfriends.

Mitchell's skin tingled. His breath came in ragged gasps. His heartbeat quickened.

A pale figure washed up directly in front of him.

The undercurrent threatened to pull her back into the depths.

Mitchell stumbled towards her.

The girl was perfect, her olive skin glistening wetly, her hair thick and dark, her body toned but shapely. Mitchell did not remember seeing her at the party, although he would have certainly remembered her.

Barry walked up behind him as he held the girl close, savoring the wetness of her body, the warmth.

"Who is she?" Mitchell asked.

"Who knows?" Barry shrugged. "She's for you, man."

Before another question could slip past Mitchell's lips—

She opened her eyes, looked at him, and smiled.

The sound of the pounding surf filled his senses, as if he were sinking below the ocean waves, being swallowed down by the cold, dark waters, sinking into her deep, dark eyes.

He leaned down to help her to her feet, and she threw her lithe arms around his neck and raised herself into an embrace.

"She'll make you happy," Barry said, slapping him on the back. "You just make sure you bring her back every year on this night and everything will work out fine."

Mitchell's mind was clouded by the intoxicating touch of this beautiful creature, by the smell of her skin.

"You hear me, man?" Barry asked. "Every year at this time."

"What—"

Mitchell stopped himself, then nodded.

He threw his jacket over her shoulders. He did not ask her name, not yet—he didn't know if she even had a name, if she could even talk.

While most of the women were back, now dressing upon the shore, some of the men who had come with wives or girlfriends now stood alone, clutching the discarded clothing of their mate.

Some of the men, like Mitchell, who had come alone, now accompanied beautiful, unclothed women.

He saw the crying man, still staring out into the sea, still weeping.

"That's how it happens sometimes." Barry's eyes glistened. "Sometimes they come right back in, sometimes they vanish for a year or maybe more."

Mitchell realized that Leslie was nowhere to be seen.

"Oh, God," he said. "Barry, I'm sorry."

"That's the way of things," Barry said. "The sea gives, and the sea takes away. I just have to trust—"

"Barry! Over here!" Someone called from down the beach. "It's Leslie!"

Barry's face lit up and he dashed towards the cry. A group stood around a figure recently cast up from the ocean's depths.

Leading his companion gently, Mitchell went to see what was happening.

"I've never seen this before."

"What does it mean?"

"A blessing! A blessing!"

Barry leaned over his wife's slowly stirring form. He looked up, and his expression was mixed awe, revulsion, excitement, and horror.

Leslie's belly was swollen with the child she carried.

The women looked upon Leslie curiously, tilting their heads, then raised their faces towards the night sky. In unison, they emitted a screeching chitter, not unlike the cry of dolphins.

Cries of joy.

From the vast darkness of the ocean, a proud bellowing answered.

"Why Sing the Sirens" was originally published on Horrorfind.com (2004).

"Why Sing the Sirens" takes place in the fictional town of Ahmen's Landing, North Carolina. The Landing was the setting for a failed "shared world" experiment I tried with several other writers. While the experiment was a colossal flop, the town of Ahmen's Landing is a place I return to every now and again. "Why Sing the Sirens?" started out as a much longer piece titled "The Sound in the Shell." That's a novella (or maybe a novel) I may return to at some point in the future.

- CB

WIDE IS THE WAY, BROAD IS THE GATE

The memory of the healing woman—and the day we took my sister to her—haunts me.

I was thirteen years old and lived, as I do to this very day, in the town of Spivey's Crossroads. Back then, the woods grew thick and dark around the scattered, squat houses and struggling farmland, and legends of witches and ghosts—"haints," my father called them—were commonplace. After the day's chores were done, old-timers gathered around hearths to spin yarns of the devil's business, black magic, and other more frightening things. They told of the Quarry Spook Light, bobbing above black waters on lonesome nights; the skeletal remains of Pullman Bridge and the echo of a murdered woman's heartbeat that could be heard there when the wind was still; and the Bleeding Gallows Tree, where blood-soaked spirits of hanged men dangled from creaking ropes to gibber confessions to passersby.

As a boy, those legends made my blood run cold as creek water.

The healing woman's name was Sadie Montcrief, and she was as much a part of local folklore as spectral lights and devilish apparitions. In her youth, she had been a midwife and, because no doctor lived within miles, she was asked to minister to all manner of ailment. Rumors circulated that she treated her patients without aid of teas, salves, or poultices—that her very touch cured disease and mended bones. The townsfolk decried Sadie for her witching ways, for they had never heard her utter a prayer, and surely anyone who could perform such acts without calling upon the Good Lord was in league with those things that prowled the darkest places. Driven away by gossip and blatant threats, Sadie secluded herself deep in the forest, far from well-worn walking trails, where few people traveled for fear of becoming lost. Still, some folks sought her out, seeking remedies for themselves or their families, but only after medicine failed to bring about a cure, and prayers went unanswered.

Over the years, of course, the old ways and traditions have been forgotten, as have the legends of the healing woman. I remember her story, though, and the part I played in what became of her.

Memory is her ghost, tormenting me.

* * *

Recent thunderstorms had turned the earth into a mire that sucked and pulled at my hiking boots. Oak, hickory, and short-leaf pine trees hugged the narrow path. Tangled branches, still damp and dripping, grew into a heavy canopy overhead, and a patchwork of light and shadow crawled across the ground. A chill wind whipped through the trees, and I hunched over, shielding myself from the cold. Winter would come early this year, I thought, and it would likely be a bad one, bitter days marking time between sleet and snow.

Up ahead, my father trudged along, leading the way. Plumes of frost enveloped his head with each labored breath. He carried Sarah, wrapped snuggly in a hand-stitched quilt, close to his chest. My sister stirred fitfully. Her thin, pale fingers flexed against Dad's shoulder. She mumbled in her sleep, but I couldn't understand—or didn't want to understand—the words.

She had not awakened in more than two months.

An image played through my mind—

Finding her upon the banks of the creek, her face spattered with drying mud, her mouth gaping, and her eyes open but unseeing.

I shivered, not because of the cold, and tried to shake my thoughts clear.

The ground dipped and rolled. We crossed fallen, moss-covered trees and skirted winding creek beds. Patches of thorny brush laid siege to the trail, snagging our pants, scratching our exposed skin. The woods were silent, save for the sound of our passing and the distant song of Sparrow and Towhee.

My legs and arms ached. We had been walking since first light, seldom stopping to rest. I lugged an old apple crate full of canned vegetables and preserves. The jars rattled against each other. The goods grew heavier with every step.

The areas I knew—hollows where I hunted squirrel, the muddy swimming hole, and the brook where I skipped rocks on lazy afternoons—seemed a distant memory. The air smelled of rich, earthworm-ridden soil freshly turned for a crop, but I couldn't imagine anything wholesome growing in this place. The trees were twisted and clustered together in gnarled tangles, the trunks knotted with fat, black growths and veined with pale vines. It was easy to envision moldering spirits wandering through the thickets. I hoped our business with the healer would be quickly finished. I didn't want to be caught in the woods after nightfall, when the darkness was as thick and sticky as tree sap, and the sweet smell of honeysuckle was redolent of decaying funeral wreaths.

We pushed through a tangle of briars, and I saw a tiny, run-down cabin nestled at the bottom of a deep, sloping trench. The gray timber frame was buckling, and the roof sagged on the verge of collapse. Climbing weeds and runners might have been all that held the cabin together.

"I'll need you to go first, Bobby," Dad said. "Be careful. It looks right treacherous."

The breakfast my mother had prepared before we set out—thick slab bacon, eggs, and toast—churned uneasily in my stomach.

We descended the hill. Dad clutched Sarah tightly with one arm and leaned on me with the other. Muddy sheets of leaves and twigs sloughed down the hillside like boiled skin off the bone. I snagged my foot on a swollen root, stumbled, and nearly dropped the wooden crate. Upon my shoulder, Dad's grip tightened, as if he would rather risk falling himself, along with Sarah, than let me take a spill.

I felt a stab of guilt.

Creeping back through the woods, once the screaming had stopped—only after I thought it might be safe again.

As we reached the bottom of the hill, the cabin door creaked open, and a woman hobbled onto the front stoop. Whether she had heard our approach or somehow expected our arrival, I couldn't guess. Her skin was dark and deeply wrinkled, and her gray hair was pulled into a tight bun. She leaned upon a bone-white cane as gnarled and bent as her own wiry frame. I've never seen anyone who looked so old. Her eyes, though, were bright and piercing, so pale blue they might have been white, and she quietly looked my father and I over before her gaze settled on Sarah.

Dad started to speak, but the old woman cut him off.

"What's ailing her?"

"We don't rightly know," Dad answered. "She just took sick, all of a sudden. We found her like … this."

She nodded and limped down from the porch to examine my sister. She pulled the quilt away from Sarah's face, touched her forehead with the back of her hand. "You'd best bring her inside, Jacob." She used my father's name like he was an old friend. "Be quick about it."

We climbed the steps—the wood groaned under our weight—and entered the cabin. Sadie followed us in, closing the door behind her, and her walking stick tapped shakily upon the scuffed hardwood floor.

The cabin was small, cramped, and dusty. A black potbelly stove squatted in the corner, the nearby walls dirty with dark streaks of ash. Alongside the stove was a rickety rocking chair, a hand-me-down blanket draped over one arm. A little, two-person table stood nearby, next to a pie safe. Metal bowls, pots, and skillets hung upon pegs on the wall. To our right, a door stood open, revealing a bedroom.

"Through there, Jacob." Sadie jabbed her cane towards the open door. "Put her on the bed."

Dad carried Sarah through the door, leaving me alone, just for a minute, with the old healing woman. "Put that box over yonder," she said, "by the pie safe."

I kept my eyes downcast, not wanting to meet her stare.

My father returned to the room. Even though he no longer carried Sarah, his shoulders still slumped as if a great burden weighed down upon him.

"Who was it that found her?" Sadie asked.

Dad nodded towards me.

"That right?" She impaled me with her gaze. "Where'd you find her, boy?"

"By Cedar Creek." My voice trembled. A knot uncoiled in my belly like a nest of snakes. "She played there sometimes."

"Down by the old mill?"

"Yes, ma'am."

She clucked her tongue. "Children ought to know better than to play there. What happened to her?"

"When I came to fetch her for supper—" The lie scratched its way from my mouth. "—I found her like that."

I wanted to tell the truth.

I wanted to but couldn't.

I remembered . . .

The creek hissing like whispered secrets.

Sarah humming one of our mother's favorite tunes as she scoops mud pies along the bank.

I cast a line into the water, drive my stick pole into the damp earth, lay back, and stare up at the clouds. There is no better way to spend an afternoon when chores are finished and the fish aren't biting.

I close my eyes.

Sarah's tune is different than our mother's, I realize, but only slightly, and still soothing.

The droning of crickets rises from the weeds, working into the back of my mind.

"Bobby?"

Sarah stops humming. I hear her only distantly, the sound of the crickets consuming her voice.

"Bobby!"

I open my eyes.

She whispers, "There's a man over there."

The crickets fall silent.

Standing, I ease over to my sister's side, following her gaze into the brush. For a minute, I see nothing. Then, the afternoon sun glitters in the eyes of a man peering at us from the foliage. I see only his eyes, deep and dark, and he must be crouching down, like a mountain cat stalking prey.

"Who's there?" I ask.

The eyes blink.

No answer.

I take Sarah's hand. Her fingers are caked with slimy mud and grit. I gently pull her to her feet.

"Don't go, children." The voice is musical. "Don't you want to play?"

"Do we know you?" I ask, my voice unsteady.

The man leans forward, and I see his long, lean face. He is clean-shaven and fine-boned, but his flesh is covered in patches of soot, like he's been washing in an ash pail.

He smiles.

As the grin splits his face, the crickets and katydids start screeching again, and they don't hush until his lips slide back to cover his needle-point teeth . . . .

He steps out with the crickets screeching up a storm—but only when he smiles—and strolls down to the bank, and he is as naked as the day he was born, covered in dirt and soot. "I have something to give you, children. You like presents, don't you?"

Sarah stands.

He reaches out for us, moving faster than I would have thought possible. We almost stumble over each other, scrambling away from him.

And we run, snapping through brambles, but he chases us, and I hear him crashing through the woods behind us. Limbs slap us in the face. Roots snare our feet.

"Run, Sarah!" I cry. "Run! Don't stop!"

He's right behind us. A spindly, soot-covered arm shoots out of the brush, snatching Sarah by the neck and yanking her back. She screams, and the crickets and katydids scream right along with her. She cries my name, but I keep running, trying to get as far away as possible. I look back, but see only the rustling of the weeds and bushes.

I run until my legs are too weak to carry me farther. I collapse, covered in sweat, panting for breath. In the distance, I hear the hint of Sarah's cries. I close my eyes. I want to go back, want to stop what is happening to her, but my legs won't work, not until it is over and there is nothing left to do but stagger back to find her there in the mud.

Tears burned in my eyes.

I didn't cry because of what happened to my sister, but because of my unwillingness to tell the truth, my shame at what I had done. I couldn't tell my father I had abandoned Sarah the way I had.

"It's all right, child. She'll be all right." Sadie reached out to comfort me. Instinctively, I pulled away, as if her touch was poisonous.

"You'll help her, won't you?" Dad asked.

Sadie nodded, but she didn't take her narrowed eyes off me. "It will take time. You might want to gather some wood for the stove. It will likely get a mite cold before morning."

My hopes of making it home before nightfall drained away.

"I'll be with the girl when you come back inside," Sadie said. "If I need you, I'll call for you. This door stays closed and you stay out here until it's done."

Dad offered a short nod in agreement. "Come on, son."

Chopping firewood was hard work. The wood was thick and heavy. The axe was rusty and dull. Dad and I took turns with the axe, one splitting logs from the woodpile while the other searched the weeds for kindling.

I wanted to tell him about what happened to Sarah, hoping he'd understand why I had abandoned her to the soot-covered stranger. I couldn't force the words out, though, and instead I asked him about Sadie.

"How does she do it? Heal people, I mean."

"I reckon I don't need to understand it." The axe fell. Wood splintered. "As long as it helps your sister, what does it matter?"

"She scares me."

"That's nothing to be ashamed of." Dad left the axe embedded in a half-split log, straightened his back, and fished his old yellowed handkerchief from his pocket. "As long as you don't let fear get the better of you."

"But I heard she can heal folks because she's got the devil's touch."

"I've heard that, too, I reckon." He mopped the sweat from his brow. "But before you climb into the pulpit, you should know that you might have died if not for that old woman."

"Me?"

"You were just a baby, sick with the Fever, when I brought you here. Your whole body was covered in awful blisters, and we couldn't get your temperature down, no matter what we tried. I didn't expect you to live another week. Sadie, she healed you, though, and it was the damndest thing. When she came out, she carried you in her arms, and you were just fine, the blisters gone, the fever easing off. But as I watched, the rash appeared across Sadie's hands, neck, and face. Blisters opened up on her skin. It spread quickly. Then, just as fast, the signs of the Fever faded, and she was just fine again. It was like she had taken the sickness out of you and into her own body."

A flock of black birds burst from nearby trees and took flight as if disturbed by a gunshot.

I stood quietly, humbled by my father's words. Dad was a good man, a God-fearing man, and if he trusted Sadie with Sarah's life, then I should have given her the same courtesy. I should have been thankful for her healing—

A shiver raced down my spine.

She took the sickness into her own body . . .

"Dad—"

"Let's head back in." He brushed past, carrying an armload of wood. "I think this should be enough."

Night seeped up from rotting tree stumps and out from beneath stones.

Shadows trickled into the house, pooling in the corners, then spilling out around us. A couple of flickering oil lamps beat back the darkness, and the glow of cinders through the stove's vent painted the room in red splashes.

Through the bedroom door, I heard Sadie shuffling about, sometimes murmuring. I sat in the rocking chair, still, as darkness settled into the house. My stomach growled. Suppertime had come and gone. I was starving, but I didn't want to think about eating, not there in the cabin with that wormy, earthy stink lingering in the air.

Dad hunkered in the corner, his knees drawn up, supporting his arms. He stared at the door, expecting it to swing open at any moment.

We waited.

In the bedroom, something fell over, crashed to the floor.

Sadie cried out.

My muscles tensed, and I started to rise.

"Let it run its course," Dad said.

The healer screamed again, her voice filled with shock and pain.

Dad's mouth was set in a resolute grimace. No matter what happened, no matter what he heard, he would not interfere.

Another scream, but this time, it is Sarah who cried out, frightened and confused and surprised.

Dad winced.

Their shrieking formed a chorus, rising, cutting me to the bone, trailing off to whimpering moans, then mounting again to a frightening disharmony.

"Was it like this?" I asked. "When she healed me, was it like this?"

He shook his head.

Again, I felt the urge to tell my father what really happened at Cedar Creek. I started to, there in the dark, between the cries of my sister and the old woman, but I caught myself.

His eyes gleamed in the low light.

The screams stopped—finally—and silence rushed in to fill the following moments. Wood popped in the stove. The house creaked, settling. I held my breath in dreadful anticipation.

Sadie's weak voice, like a whisper, came from the other side of the door, calling for my father. "Jacob . . . Jacob."

Dad rose and threw the door open. I hurried behind him.

In the room, Sarah lay peacefully upon the bed. In the lantern light, I saw that the color had returned to her face. She woke as we approached. She rubbed her eyes, as if waking from an afternoon nap. "Daddy? Bobby?"

My father fell to his knees beside the bed, scooping my sister into his arms and hugging her. Her expression was one of confusion, but within seconds she returned his embrace. He sobbed, "Oh, baby girl," over and over.

Next to the bed, upon a wooden hope chest, lay a tattered copy of the Holy Bible.

A rattling gasp drew my attention to the corner. Sadie leaned against the wall as if she had no strength to rise. I tugged on my father's sleeve and pointed to the old woman.

"Sadie?"

As he released my sister, she looked at me curiously. I wondered how much she remembered.

Sadie's chest rose and fell with her shallow breathing. "She'll be just … fine."

"Are you all right?" my father asked.

She tried to pull herself into a seated position. Her movement reminded me of an animal with a broken back. "I-I'll be fine. That just took more out of me than I would … have expected."

"Bobby, let's get her to the bed."

Together, we tried to help her stand. Her dress was soaked through with sweat. I pulled, trying to lift her to her feet.

She shrieked.

Her body tensed and convulsed. She hacked and coughed. I drew my hand away and stumbled back.

"Sadie?" my father said.

"What's wrong with her?" my sister asked.

Bloody spittle speckled Sadie's lips.

Sarah started crying. She pulled the bedclothes up around her.

"Hush up now," Dad told her.

Sadie's eyes closed, and milk-white froth spilled from her mouth. Her body thrashed about. Her bones popped.

"Help me hold her, son."

We tried to calm her, but she squirmed in our touch.

Suddenly, her eyes snapped open and she grabbed at me, snatching a handful of my shirt and tugging me close. I tried to pull away, but she was stronger than I thought.

"What's wrong with me?" she hissed. "What happened to that girl?"

I grabbed at her sweat-slicked, withered forearm, tried to pry her free.

I heard my father hollering, Sarah crying in the background, but Sadie's gaze burned into my skull like a brand.

"Tell me," she spat.

"He drug her off into the woods," I cried. "He drug her off and I could hear her screaming for help, but I was scared."

"What are you talking about, boy?" my father asked.

Sarah wrapped her arms around her knees and rocked back and forth.

"I didn't want to see, and I didn't go back until she stopped screaming, until

I was sure he was gone."

Sadie shuddered, and her hand fell slack, releasing me. She fell back, her eyes rolling up, as she started to breathlessly pray.

"What are you saying?" Dad asked me.

Sadie gasped and slammed back against the wall. She opened her eyes and looked at my father. "You get out of here, Jacob, you hear? You take your children and you go—go and don't never come back."

"But..."

"Ain't nothing you can do, not now."

"I won't just—"

But he never finished the sentence.

Something like water, only thick and syrupy, washed across the floor, soaking into our pants legs, lapping at our boots. I hopped to my feet, stepped back, but Dad remained at Sadie's side, trying to determine where the fluid came from.

In the valley between her legs, her dress was soaked.

She gasped. Her stomach suddenly puffed up and swelled. She clasped her hands protectively over the bulge, whether to protect it or to hold it back, I couldn't tell.

I heard a meaty chittering sound, a sticky, slimy sloughing.

Hunching over, she coughed.

"What's happening—"

Something crawled out from under the dress—a bloated, slimy thing, like a blood-gorged tick.

Sadie shuddered as more viscous slime splattered the floor, and another one of those things scurried out, leaving a glistening track on the hardwood. Wriggling, fleshy umbilical cords trailed behind the creatures. They had no eyes upon their fleshy gray bodies. They scuttled upon too-thin, insect-like legs, crawling towards me, then inching back, sensing my presence.

Sadie drew in a tremulous breath and spoke to us again, for the last time.

"Run."

One of the creature's jumped at my father. He fell backwards, scrabbling through the birthing fluid, swatting the thing away. The umbilical cord snapped loose and the creature plopped against the wall, landed on its back, its legs twitching, righted itself, and skittered after us again.

Sadie spasmed and twitched. She slid down the wall. Drool dribbled from her chin. Another of those things pulled itself from her body. Another, then another.

Dad jumped to his feet. One of the creatures bit his boot, tearing some of the leather away. He cursed, stomped it. He shoved past me, scooped Sarah into his arms, and ran for the door.

Now, more than a dozen of the tick-like creatures crawled upon the floor. I stood, stunned, watching as some of the creatures started chewing away at the old woman's body, while others scrambled at me, their flabby, dripping bodies suckering apart, almost splitting in two to reveal rows of razor-sharp teeth and black, writhing tongues.

"Bobby! Come on!"

One of them bit into my leg. I reached down and tore it off.

I turned and limped out of the room. Dad stood in the front door. He cradled Sarah in one arm. She bawled in terror. In his other hand, he held a lantern.

I rushed past him. He hurled the lantern into the room. The glass hood shattered, and flames darted across the old wood. Dad slammed the door.

He did not say a word to me, only walked past, vanishing into the woods, taking my sister with him.

I stood at the edge of the clearing, watching the cabin burn. Heat washed across my body in waves. My eyes watered in the clouds of smoke drifting like fog around me and billowing into the night sky.

The old, rotted structure burned quickly, the roof starting to sag and collapse in fiery wedges. Shapes moved in the flame—fat, bloated shapes skittering about, sizzling like bacon grease, blackening and popping. The cries of the creatures were awful, painful, high-pitched keens, dozens of deathly screeches.

I never heard Sadie scream, and I thought she might have been too far gone to feel pain. For that, I felt blessed.

In the distance, my father called to me.

Wind slipped through the veil of smoke, and it sounded like a sigh.

* * *

That was nearly sixty years ago, and now I'm an old man.

As often as I could help it, I've lived a quiet, uneventful life here in the backwoods and hills where I grew up. Many things have changed in all those years. The collection of houses once scattered about the region has grown into a full-fledged town, complete with fast food restaurants and chain department stores. Faces in the crowd don't look familiar anymore, and folks seldom take the time to greet their neighbors like they used to. I keep to myself mostly.

But even though much of the forest has been chopped down to make way for "development," the pines still grow thick and dark in places, and ghost stories are still popular with local children.

The patch of land upon which Sadie's house had stood is still scorched and desolate, as if the earth cannot heal itself, and the air around the place smells faintly of ash and smoke. Locals say the devil himself once spent the night on that unholy spot, and that's how it came to be burned.

I know the truth but, like I said, I keep to myself.

Sometimes, on late fall afternoons, with the insects calling from the tall grass and milkweed, I think of the soot-covered man my sister and I met so long ago. I reckon he still wanders these parts from time to time, visiting Cedar Creek near the ruins of the old mill, searching for someone to play with. Maybe, like me, he thinks back on those days and wonders where the time has gone. Maybe, now that my days are growing short, he'll call upon me, sit for a while, and reminisce about the part I played in what happened to Sadie.

Even now, I hear the wild song of the crickets and katydids.

And I can't help but wonder why he's smiling.

"Wide is the Way, Broad is the Gate" was originally published in DARK LURKERS (2004).

Many of my stories are firmly rooted in a tradition I like to call "backwoods horror". What can I say? I grew up in the country. I explored deep woods and spirit-haunted ponds and old tobacco barns. I heard more than my fair share of ghost stories, all of which inspired stories like this. With this story, I wanted to start off telling one kind of tale (a moody, spooky story) and then turn it on its ear (and tell an icky monster yarn).

- CB

THE STORM CHILDREN

In the dim lamplight, Grandpa Grant's face looked almost skeletal, all bone and shadow. As he spoke, though, with the children huddled close, his eyes gleamed, as if the light had decided to swim within them. His voice calmed the children, and little Stevey, only three, crawled into the rocking chair and onto the old man's lap.

Rain pelted the windows, pouring down the glass in thick, rippling sheets, and lightning ripped bright gashes in the pitch-black sky.

Frightened, Stevey buried his face in the crook of his grandfather's arm and shivered. Thunder boomed, closer now, ever closer, and window glass rattled in the pane. Jenny and Samantha, sitting with their legs crossed on the floor, jumped, scattering the pieces of the puzzle they were working on. The puzzle had been intended to distract them from the storm, but the storm would have none of it.

The oldest of the four children, Kenny, stood in a corner and rocked back and forth, back and forth, quietly.

"Don't you worry about that old storm," Grandpa Grant said. He turned his attention away from the children and stared out the window as he spoke. "It's just pitching a little fit, wailing like a baby. That's all."

Outside, wind thrashed through the trees, and the branches clawed and scraped at the sides and top of the house like bony fingernails. The children—except for Kenny—shuddered at the sound.

From across the room, Beth watched her father entertain the children. She held a cup of coffee in her shaking hands and listened to the stories—stories she had heard before, she supposed, when she herself was a child. It struck her how quickly the years slip by, how easily the stories were forgotten. It didn't seem that long ago that she had sat on his lap and listened to his tall tales. Now she had four children of her own, and her father would never be simply "daddy" again. Now he was Grandpa Grant.

"The storm will pass soon enough," the old man continued, "taking its thunderboomers and lightning with it. You'll see. Everything will be just fine. And if you sit real quiet, you might even be able to hear the storm children out there playing in the rain."

"Who are the storm children?" Samantha asked, chewing nervously on a strand of her dark hair, a bad habit she might never outgrow.

"You see," Grandpa Grant answered, "folks around these parts say that when we lose a child in a storm, he or she might come back on nights just like tonight. That's why the storm's pitching such a fit, because its children got away and are out playing."

Beth looked down, urging her hands to stop trembling.

Her mother—Grandma to the children—hissed. "Grant!"

"What?" The old man looked up. "I just—" His eyes strayed to Beth, and his mouth fell slack. "Oh. Oh, Beth. I'm sorry. I didn't mean to . . ."

"It's all right, dad." She placed her coffee cup aside. "No harm done."

"It's the storm," he said. "I guess it's got us all worked up a little. I wasn't thinking."

"It's all right," Beth said, but even she could hear the icy edge in her voice.

Sitting on the floor, Jen looked back at her mother. "What's wrong?" She was eight and almost too smart for her own good. "Did Grandpa do something wrong?"

"No, honey, he didn't."

Beth knew that the little girl didn't believe her. Jen wasn't old enough to remember her brother, Kenny, before the accident, before the change. The change—that's what the family called it, and wasn't that just a nice and clean way of explaining something they didn't understand and didn't like talking about? No one could explain how Kenny survived the accident with only a few scrapes and bruises when all of the other children had died.

Nor could anyone—not any one of a dozen specialists—explain why he could no longer function on his own, why he couldn't speak, why he couldn't eat or go to the bathroom without assistance, why he seemed so empty.

The school bus driver had been going too fast, especially for the weather—that much Beth understood—and it was a miracle that any of the passengers survived. She should have been thankful, or so her friends and family members said, but sometimes she just didn't have the energy for thankfulness.

She suddenly felt as if she might vomit, and if she did, she wondered if she'd see the color of her shame. Even after five years, she still held onto so much anger and guilt. She had blamed her husband for not sending Kenny to a private school, like they had wanted, but those were leaner times, before his business had taken off. She had blamed herself for not picking him up after school, but she had her hands full with the girls at the time, and riding the bus wasn't so bad, after all. She had blamed the bus driver, of course, but he was dead and she found no relief in the act. She even, at times when her nerves were shot, blamed Kenny for his condition.

But she knew where the real blame lay.

The storm.

The storm had glazed the road and obscured the driver's vision. The storm had prevented the brakes from taking hold on the wet pavement. The storm had sent the bus careening into the wrong lane, right into the path of oncoming traffic.

The storm had brought on the change.

Even now, years later, a storm struck Beth not as an act of nature, but as something more, something dark and hungry that had taken her son away—

"When will daddy get here?" Samantha asked.

"Not for awhile, sweetie." Beth forced a smile. "He has a lot of work to finish before he can leave the city."

"I doubt he'd be able to get to the house anyway." Grandpa shook his head, set Stevey on the floor beside his sisters, and walked to the window. "Way it's coming down out there, the creek's bound to have flooded the road by now."

"I hope he's not out driving in this," Grandma said. She busied herself, checking flashlight batteries, pulling dusty candles from drawers, just in case power failed. "Weather like this, he'd be wise to wait it out."

"Don't worry about him." In fourteen years, Beth had never known her husband to leave anything to chance, and it wouldn't be that unusual for him to miss another weekend visit to her parent's anyway. "He'll be fine."

The lights flickered as thunder grumbled in the distance.

Kenny rocked back and forth in the corner, his expressionless features coming into the light for but a moment before vanishing again into shadow.

"What do the storm children want?" Jen asked, challenging her grandfather's story.

"Oh, they just want to play, but when they come, the storm follows, seeking to grab them back up."

Grandma gave the old man another dirty look and clapped her hands together to get the attention of the children. "I think it's about bedtime."

"But I'm not tired," Jen answered, looking over her shoulder at her mom for some sign of sympathy.

"Sorry, kiddo." Beth nodded towards the stairs. "Up you go."

Jen muttered under her breath as she and her sister followed their grandmother upstairs.

"Don't pout so," Beth called after them. "Look on the bright side. By the time you wake up, the storm will have passed."

Grandpa Grant hoisted Stevey into his arms. "Let's go, boy. Time to get some shut-eye." The child giggled. The old man had a way of making even sleep sound adventurous. He looked over at Kenny, then to Beth.

"I'll get him," she said.

She approached her son, who continued to rock where he stood, completely unaware of the world around him.

"Let's get you to bed," she said, but gave up on speaking to him further. What was the point? Her words might as well be drowned out by the thunderstorm.

* * *

Jen sat up in bed as thunder rolled across the top of the house, threatening to peel the roof away, reach in, and snatch her and her brothers and sister away. The chandelier hanging in the center of the room rattled. She always had trouble sleeping while visiting Grandma and Grandpa's. She wanted to sleep, too, because she hoped that the storm would be over when she awoke. If she were lucky, her father would have arrived, too. She crawled out of bed—the hardwood floor felt dusty under her bare feet—and looked out the window.

A low blanket of slow-moving clouds blotted out the stars and the moon, and lightning jumped back and forth through the darkness.

Jen wondered if her father was caught in the storm, if there were other kids, back home maybe, who were awake in bed right now, waiting for the storm to pass. Black clouds stretched across the sky as far as she could see, and it wasn't hard to imagine that this storm was as big as the world.

"Rain, rain, go away," she whispered, finding little comfort in the words, "come again some other day."

But she didn't want it to come again. She wanted it to go away and never come back.

In the bed next to hers, Samantha lay, wide-eyed. "Maybe the storm's coming for us," she said. She held the covers up over her mouth, and her voice was muffled. "It might be coming for the storm children, like Grandpa said, and if it doesn't catch them, it might come for us."

Lightning flashed, frightening shadows into corners. Jen peered out the window, and her mouth fell open in surprise. In the distance, she saw movement. Several child-like figures took flight across a hilltop, running, running, running as lightning streaked after them, and the lightning, forking and splintering, took on the shape of a grasping hand.

She hopped away from the window as if she had been slapped across the face.

Samantha sat up in bed, clutching the covers to her chest. "What? What is it?"

But Jen couldn't answer. Her mouth worked, opening and closing, but only a startled gasp found purchase. A queasiness roiled in her stomach, and she wondered if this is what Kenny felt like, wanting to speak but unable to do so, and she thought for a dreadful second that the lightning and thunder and rain had somehow stolen her voice.

"Mama!" Samantha cried. "Mama!"

Jen stepped cautiously towards the window again. In the darkness, the trees dotting the hillside swallowed up the figures, but when lightning flashed, tearing the darkness open, she saw them, dancing and running, playing in the storm.

The door flew open, spilling light into the room.

"What's wrong?" Her mother came through the door, panic in her eyes.

"Jen saw something," Samantha blurted.

"Jen? What is it? What's wrong, honey?"

"Out there," she said, finding her voice again. She pointed a shaky finger towards the hillside.

Beth eased her daughter aside, holding her shoulders, and leaned down to peer out the window. A flash of lightning colored her face blue. She touched the glass, leaned closer.

"Who are they?" the little girl asked. "Do you think they're—"

Beth turned away from the window, fear crawling across her face.

"I-It's nothing." Beth's features calmed. She brushed the hair from Jen's face. "There's nothing out there."

"But—"

A blast of thunder warned the girl not to argue.

"Go back to bed, baby," Beth said. "You . . . just had a nightmare. That's all."

Jen crawled back into bed, pulling the thick covers up, and glanced over at her sister. Samantha lay quietly, and Jen hated her for not coming to her defense, hated her for being too afraid to look out the window. Beth, smiling sadly, watched them for only a few seconds before stepping into the hall and pulling the door closed.

Darkness.

Jen listened, and the storm growled, angry with her for revealing its secrets.

The rain came down harder now. Wind howled. Thunder chased lightning. Lightning sizzled in the darkness. In the distance, masked by the sounds of the storm, Jen imagined that she heard what might have been children laughing and singing.

She looked over at Samantha, who was already asleep.

Still, she could not sleep. She rolled on her side so she did not have to look out the window. She closed her eyes, squeezed them tightly shut, but still she imagined the storm watching her, flowing up to the window and staring at her, rattling the latch, trying to force its way in—

Outside her room, she heard movement, the shuffling of feet across the hardwood floor, the hiss of clothing. The stairs creaked. The front door opened. Wind swept into the house.

"Mama?" she said, but there was no answer.

The little girl sat up, but didn't dare get out of bed again. Who, she wondered, was going out in this weather?

* * *

Beth led her son into a torrent of wind and rain. His grasp was weak, and she checked herself, afraid she might break his fingers if she gripped his hand too tightly. He wouldn't complain, she knew, even if she was hurting him. Rain stung her face, slicked her hair and skin. Her clothes were soaked and heavy. Kenny, too, was drenched, even though he wore a red rain slicker over his pajamas, and his hair dangled before his expressionless eyes.

Mud tugged at Beth's feet as she pulled her son through the darkness, leading him up the hill and towards the forest where she had seen the storm children dancing.

That was what she saw, wasn't it? What else could it have been?

Lightning snaked through the clouds, carving a zigzagging grin in the night.

A gust of wind whipped past her, so strong it almost knocked her off her feet, and she saw the tops of trees, bending almost to the point of snapping.

She felt like she was living in one of her father's stories as she approached the hill. A hint of fright jumped through her body as she saw perhaps a dozen figures, all hazy outlines in the rain, dancing, moving in slow motion, their high-pitched, singsong voices chanting in an eerie rhythm.

Beth stumbled towards them, dragging Kenny along behind her, thinking how insane she must be. But as she drew close, a curtain of rain fell before her, and the force of the wind pushed her back. A spray of water blinded her, and she held her free hand before her face.

Her vision cleared.

And she saw that the storm children surrounded her.

* * *

Jen hated the basement, and when her grandmother had pulled her out of bed, suggesting that the family might be safer downstairs, dread filled her. There were scorpions in the basement—nasty, pale scorpions skittering out from between cracks in the wall and from under boxes. She knew that she needed to wear shoes in the basement, but Grandma did not give her time to put them on. Once she had stepped on and been stung by a scorpion, and she remembered how it burned. What she remembered more, though, was the way the tiny creature, broken and oozing from its shell, twitched and spasmed as it tried to get at her, wanting to sting her again and again.

She thought of the storm, raging outside, and how it only grew stronger, more furious, as the storm children eluded it.

Patches of mildew crawled along the basement walls. Cobwebs covered dozens of stacked boxes. Along the wall, an old lawnmower leaked oil, forming a glistening stain upon the floor, and in the corner a tattered broom was propped next to the washing machine and dryer.

Water dribbled down the walls, pooled on the concrete floor. Jen saw a snaking stream of water oozing towards her, reaching for her, and she stepped away, afraid to touch it.

Upstairs, Grandpa Grant stood at the front door, calling for Beth and Kenny. The sound of the wind consumed his voice.

Grandma held Stevey in her arms, rocking him, as she paced back and forth.

Thunder boomed. The single, bare bulb fluttered, dimmed, dangerously close to dying out, and Jen held her breath, because she knew that if the light went out, the scorpions waiting in the shadows would come scurrying out of hiding for them. Another crash of thunder, and the bulb sprang back to life, washing the walls in a dull glow.

The storm, Jen thought, was playing games with them.

A door opened at the top of the staircase, and Grandpa Grant rushed down to join them. His clothes were wet.

"Where's mama?" Samantha asked. "Where's Kenny?"

Grandma and Grandpa looked at each other in silence. Grandma started weeping softly.

"Nothing to worry about," Grandpa Grant said, unconvinced. "We're safe down here."

But even as he said it, the light faded, and darkness devoured them.

* * *

The storm children circled Beth and Kenny, staring with blank, expressionless eyes, but also smiling gleefully, and the effect reminded Beth of a doll, grins and giggles, but no soul. Wet strands of hair hung down in their faces. Their clothing clung to their bodies like wet tissue. Wisps of spectral fog rose from their bodies, writhing slowly, dissipating into thin air. They regarded Beth, their heads tilting curiously, and then they looked at Kenny.

Beth grabbed his hand more tightly.

"This is my son," she said, drawing in a deep breath, tasting salty water on her lips. She was unsure if these children understood or not. "I . . . I believe he might be with you."

The children, moving in unison, turned their attention back to her. Their skin was pale and slightly bloated, and Beth imagined that they had perhaps been underwater for a long time.

"He's with you," she continued, "but you can see he's not like you. He's not—"

Dead, she almost said, but the word caught in her throat.

41

Wind shrieked. Lightning jumped down to the earth. The hair on her arms stood on end.

"Please." She raised her voice to be heard over the storm. "I want him back."

Pellets of ice struck her face, leaving stinging red welts upon her flesh. Thunder rumbled, loud and constant, as if something large—something behind the storm—had awakened.

The children turned from her. They giggled and squealed and sang their song as they danced away, mud spattering their pale legs, moving like ghosts.

"Give him back!" Beth cried, chasing after them.

Her foot twisted in the mud, and a knife of pain stabbed at her. Kenny's fingers slipped from her grasp, and she tumbled down the hill into a rippling pool of cold, gray water. She struggled to her hands and knees. She saw Kenny standing at the top of the hill. Behind him, clouds pooled, gathered, and contorted; roaring and whirling; reaching down with a twisting funnel to touch the earth.

"Oh God," she cried, struggling to climb the hill, slipping and sliding in the wet earth. "Kenny! Get down, baby! Get down!" But the sound of the rushing air drowned out her voice, and Kenny wouldn't have responded, even if he heard her.

The wind and rain writhed in a chaotic cyclone, tearing trees from the ground and tossing them aside, churning the earth and spitting debris into the air.

As Beth reached the top of the hill, she saw the tornado ripping over the ground towards her. She stood dumbstruck as the storm children danced nearby. They reached up as toddlers might reach for a parent and were sucked into the torrent.

She grabbed Kenny, swept him into her arms, and threw herself back down the hill just as the screaming tornado might have torn them both apart. She covered his face with her arms as the winds buffeted her and debris scratched her skin. She risked glancing up and saw the tornado pass over her, spinning sluggishly, and the currents flowing around the inner wall of the funnel looked like the writhing bodies of children.

She forced her eyes down. Sobbing, she clung tightly to Kenny.

The wind passed and took some of the rain with it. She lay very still, shivering, weeping. With the sudden passing of the storm, the night seemed too quiet. The storm was gone, racing off and vanishing into the night.

Beth didn't stir for several seconds, afraid that even the slightest movement might upset the delicate peace around her.

What had she been thinking?

She had almost gotten Kenny—and herself—killed.

Kenny shifted against her. She looked up in stunned silence and saw her son looking back at her.

"Mama?" he said softly.

* * *

Downstairs, in the darkness, Grandpa Grant whispered, "I think the worst of it has passed." He turned his flashlight towards the ceiling. Tiny dust motes whirled in the beam of light.

"Maybe we should stay down here a while longer," Grandma said.

"What about Beth?"

"What could have possessed her? Why would she go out there?"

"I don't know." His voice was drawn tight.

"Is Mama all right?" Jen asked.

"I'm sure she is," Grandma said, but she did not sound sure.

Little Stevey mewled softly.

"I'm going to take a look around," Grandpa said. When Grandma grabbed his shoulder, he patted her hand and moved it aside. He walked up the creaking wooden stairs, pulling the upstairs door open. As he ascended, taking the flashlight with him, shadow poured back into the basement.

"I don't want to wait down here anymore," Jen said.

"Me either," Samantha said. "We don't have to stay down here anymore, do we? The tornado's gone."

Grandma looked upstairs, then at the children. "I suppose it's all right," she said, and they followed her up the stairs.

A branch had pierced the kitchen window, carving a jagged scar across the front of the refrigerator, showering glass and water over the kitchen floor. Shattered dishes covered the counter.

Grandpa walked through the mess, heading for the front door.

"Be careful," he warned. "There's broken glass all over the place."

Grandma shook her head at the ruin and drew the children close.

Grandpa opened the front door.

"Lord almighty!"

Snapped limbs covered the yard. The barn had been torn asunder and lay split open like the ribcage of a massive skeleton. An old rusted swing-set lay on its side, twisted, and a cement birdbath was smashed into chalky pieces. As they looked over the yard, they saw two figures approaching.

Beth and Kenny, dripping wet and covered in scratches, bruises, and cuts, stumbled towards the house. Beth was crying. Crying and smiling at the same time.

"What were you thinking?" Grandpa asked as they reached the front porch. "You could've gotten yourself killed."

But Kenny looked at him and spoke.

"Grandpa?"

The old man looked at Beth, a dozen or more questions forming on his lips, but she was shaking her head, unable to answer, unsure herself of what had happened, except that she had managed to bring her son back.

Carrying little Stevey, Grandma led Jen and Samantha towards their mother. When Beth saw them, she started crying anew.

"Girls," Beth said between joyful sobs. "Come say hello to your brother."

Samantha took a step towards her brother, looked down shyly and giggled, but Jen could not even look at the boy.

"Don't act like that Jennifer," Beth said. "This is your brother."

But the girl turned and ran away, going upstairs to the bedroom and curling into a ball upon the bed, shivering. She could not explain how she felt. She could not find the words.

She listened to them, downstairs, talking for hours, asking question after question, listening to Kenny's answers, and then laughing and crying and sometimes a mixture of the two.

Much later, as they all went back to bed, her mother stopped in her room as she tucked Samantha in. "Jen," she said. "I know this is strange for you. I know. But you have to try. Your brother has been through something very traumatic. Do you know what that word means?"

Jen nodded.

"Well, if you do, you know that he needs our help and understanding. Samantha did her best to get along with him. I need you to do the same. Can you do that?"

Jen nodded again.

"Good." Her mother kissed her on the forehead. "Get some sleep. We can start over in the morning."

Jen lay awake for some time, considering what her mother had said. She wasn't exactly sure why she had reacted the way she had, treating her brother like a stranger. But in a way, that's what he was, she supposed, a stranger. She had never known him in any other way. Still, she resigned herself to be nicer to him.

With the storm gone, she realized exactly how tired she was, and her eyelids grew heavy.

Later, she was roused from sleep by a flickering light filtering into the room. She did not rise, but saw the door creaking open, a narrow sliver of light growing across the floor, climbing the bed, and touching her face. Her sister remained asleep, breathing deeply, steadily. As the door swung open, she saw Kenny standing in the hallway, watching her.

His eyes were narrow and gleamed like silver. His hair and skin looked wet, damp footprints trailed off behind him, and water dripped off his body and pooled at his feet.

And Jen might have cried out for her mother if fear hadn't clutched her throat, choking her silent. She didn't know what her mother had brought in from the storm, but it wasn't her brother. A light rain speckled the window, sending undulating shapes crawling across the floor, walls, and ceiling.

The boy smiled.

In the distance, new thunder bellowed.

And in the water pooling at the imposter's feet, the reflection of a little boy, lost and alone in the storm, screamed.

"The Storm Children" was originally published in DARKNESS RISING (2002).

This is an older story — one of the oldest that I'll allow to see print — but it holds a special place in my heart. You'll find that I write about storms... and about people vanishing... quite a bit. Both of those things stir a sense of dread in me. In the middle of a violent storm, I can't help but think that the world has turned against me... that it's out to get me. As for the fear of vanishing, I've always been terrified of abductions... of what happens to the helpless soul once they are carried off to God knows where. When I was a young boy, I witnessed an attempted abduction. The would-be victim (a boy who was about my age) got away, and my parents helped him. I'll never forget the look of terror — the purest incarnation of any emotion I've ever seen — on the boy's face.

- CB

COME AGAIN, HALLOWEEN

The last day of October brought with it the promise of winter, lurking just beyond tomorrow, or perhaps the next day, its frosty breath rasping through brown and gold leaves, rushing through dark alleys and long-deserted roads, distant still, but drawing closer, closer.

It brought memories—memories of trick-or-treating and fanciful costumes; rubber-masked goblins creeping through bushes and hiding behind leafless trees; ghost stories and pumpkin-carving; and the taste of candy corn and Tootsie Rolls on her tongue as she knocked on door after door in search of sweets.

Memories. Nothing more.

There had been no Halloween, not for her, not for years.

Her name was Jessica, but her brother had always called her Jesse or Jess, and she liked the way the nickname sounded. Some of the boys at school laughed at her and called her "Messy Jesse" for no other reason than she was a girl and they were boys. Those same boys would one day forget their childhood jibes and compete for her affections. None of this mattered to her, nor would it ever.

She stood by the living room window, her face nearly pressed against the cold glass, her breath spreading across the pane like a writhing spirit and then quickly evaporating. The sun had begun to set and the sky was a mottled mixture of red and darkening gray. Streetlights flickered to life, and dull pools of illumination spread along the sidewalk, beating back the encroaching shadows. Upon the porches and steps of neighboring houses, grinning jack-o-lanterns glowed, awaiting the chance to lure trick-or-treaters like moths to a candle. Paper images of skeletons and witches and snarling black cats were taped upon doors and in windows.

The porch of Jesse's house was undecorated.

"Come away from the window, sweetie," her mother said. The house was dark—there would be few lights turned on tonight—and the woman passed like a shadow from room to room.

Jesse pouted.

Today at school, her class had a party. Some of the parents brought in tiny bags of mixed candy and cupcakes frosted to resemble ghostly faces. Most of the kids and many of the parents wore costumes. Even the teacher, Mrs. Brewer, wore a bent witch's hat. But Jesse, who wore her everyday school clothes, sat at her desk quietly. She gazed sadly at the untouched ghost-faced cupcake staring back at her from her desktop while her classmates shared spooky stories and sang "Stirring and stirring and stirring the brew."

Her mother had not attended the party.

"Come on, young lady," Mom said. "Don't make me tell you again."

"Why can't I go out tonight?" Jesse asked, looking over her shoulder. "Can't I, just this once?"

"I'm not going to argue. Now, come away from the window."

"But—"

"Jessica!" Anger sharpened Mom's voice. "Don't you dare talk back. Not tonight. Not tonight of all nights."

Jesse took one last look at the neighborhood. Down the street, a group of children dressed as ghouls and vampires and fake blood spattered zombies rounded the corner. They laughed and cheered and clutched at reflective plastic bags half-full of candy. Behind the group, following in the shadows, an adult kept watchful eye. Parents always accompanied their children nowadays, ever since—

Jesse drew the blinds and slinked to the couch.

"What would you like for dinner, sweetie?" The anger had vanished from her mother's voice, replaced by the hollow desperation that always set upon her with the passing of summer and the approach of October.

"I'm not hungry," Jesse said.

"Nonsense. You have to eat something."

Tomorrow, Halloween would be over, leaving behind tales of candy and pranks and frights—all of which Jesse would miss. She thought about her brother, Josh, and felt a stab of sadness. He had spent weeks planning his costume, planning his pranks, planning just the right route for the best trick-or-treating. But Josh was gone now, and one night, just a few years earlier, he had taken Halloween away with him.

"Why don't I make grilled cheese sandwiches?" Mom asked. "How would that be?"

Jesse did not answer. In her mind, it was the last Halloween, back when Josh was alive and loved the holiday more than anything.

* * *

Josh wore a red and white striped sleeveless shirt and tattered black jeans cut into ribbons just above the knee. A bandana was tied around his head, and he had used black makeup to give himself a stubbly beard. A patch covered his left eye, and a five-and-dime plastic cutlass was tucked into a sash around his waist. All afternoon, he stomped around the house shouting things like "Avast there!" and "Shiver me timbers!" and "Aaargh!"

Jesse chose to dress as a fairy princess in a frilly white dress and a plastic tiara studded with brightly colored gemstones.

"Would you look at the two of you?" Mom smiled and clapped her hands together with glee as her children modeled their costumes. She did not hate Halloween, not yet, but she would before the night was over. She grabbed the instant camera. "You both look so great. All right, Josh. Give me your best pirate sneer."

"I'll make ye walk the plank." Josh bared his teeth. "Aaargh!"

The flash flooded the room. The camera buzzed and spat out a print.

"Now you, little princess," Mom said.

"Aaarrrggh!" said Jesse, doing her best to imitate Josh's snarling grin.

Mom snapped the picture and they all laughed.

"All right, Josh." She put the camera aside and fanned the developing photos. "Where are you going tonight?"

"Probably just a few blocks over," Josh said, already over-eager to get out on the streets.

"But you're not crossing the bridge, right?"

"No, ma'am."

"Promise?"

Josh rolled his eyes and nodded. He stepped towards the door with Jesse quickly following.

"Hold on, you two." Their mother went to the closet and pulled out two jackets. "It's cold out tonight. You're going to need these."

"But, mom," Josh said, "it doesn't go with my costume. Pirates don't wear jackets."

"Princesses don't wear jackets, either," Jesse chimed.

"They wear jackets tonight. It's either the jacket or no trick-or-treating." Mom winked. "Your choice, matey."

Reluctantly, Josh shrugged into the jacket. Jesse giggled and waved her wand at her mom's nose as she was helped into the coat.

"Take care of your sister," Mom said. "And be careful."

Josh rushed towards the sidewalk with Jesse chasing after him. The night was alive with the laughter of children. The wind whipped at them.

They visited all of the neighborhood houses in rapid succession. Doors opened. Neighbors oohed and aahed over their disguises. Mrs. Beechum, two doors down, gave them each a handful of pennies, but Jesse didn't think that was much of a treat. Mr. Clark at the end of the block tried to scare them when they knocked on the door; he jumped out from around the side of the house wearing a gorilla mask. They laughed at how silly he looked. The goodie bags quickly filled with treats. Jesse couldn't wait to get home and tear into the candy.

But Josh wasn't done.

He took his little sister by the hand and led her to the narrow, concrete bridge that spanned the deep trench dividing their neighborhood from Slocum Street.

"We're not supposed to go there," Jesse said. "Mom said so."

"Mom doesn't have to know. Besides, we'll get the best candy over there. Promise."

As they crossed the bridge, Jesse looked down into the trench. A strip of water rushed beneath them. Two bed-sheeted ghosts stared up at them, their ragged eye-holes deep and dark.

"What are they doing down there?" Jesse asked.

But Josh was too busy telling her how he often got whole candy bars—not just bite-sized pieces—from the people on Slocum Street. They knew how to celebrate Halloween. The houses were well-decorated, entire yards converted into graveyards or haunted mazes.

"Prime pickings," Josh said.

Dark forms rushed back and forth across the street. A Frankenstein's monster watched from the shadows. Spooky horror movie music and ghostly sound effects played on boom boxes from front porches.

At one of the houses, Jesse and Josh were invited inside. In a darkened room they were asked to reach into several bowls. "Feel those" the resident intoned. "Those are eyes," and "reach into this bowl of guts." In the final bowl, they found candy. They thanked the resident for the scare and the treats, then continued on their way.

"Were those really guts and eyes?" Jesse asked.

"Nah," said Josh. "Peeled grapes and cold spaghetti."

They passed a yard covered in toilet paper. It hung in wispy tendrils from fence posts and cascaded from tree limbs, gently undulating in the breeze.

Somewhere, not too far away, Jesse heard a car's roaring engine. She jumped at the sound.

Up ahead, across the street, a screen door snapped shut, and a group of giggling children—a cowboy, a cat, and a boy in a bloody hockey mask—dashed along the sidewalk. "They're giving out Snickers and Skittles!" one of the children called.

Josh clenched his sister's hand tightly. "Come on."

Josh stepped off the sidewalk.

Jesse paused, only for a moment, to adjust her tiara. When she looked again, Josh was bathed in shimmering light.

A horn blared.

Tires shrieked in an attempt to find purchase.

Josh's hand was ripped from hers. She felt as though her arm might tear from its socket. She was yanked off her feet, skinning her knees on the sidewalk, and her wand clattered to the ground.

The car slid to a stop.

Along the street, doors flung open and people rushed out of their houses.

The spooky music, the artificial screams, seemed so loud.

"Are you all right?" a man asked, kneeling to help her to her feet.

Several people gazed down at her. The headlights of the car lit their faces. The emergency flashers glowed, then faded into darkness, then glowed again, and the faces of the people in the crowd bore looks of shock and terror.

My costumes not scary, she thought. Why are they looking at me like that?

Her knees stung. She saw gravel embedded in her skin.

The music was so loud.

"Josh," she said. "My brother."

Someone gasped and choked out, "Oh God."

Voices rose from the crowd, a weird choir.

—Oh, dear. Oh, dear.—

—Don't touch him. Don't move him.—

—Where did he come from? Did anyone see?—

Jesse thought she heard a ghost wailing in the distance, its sorrowful cry riding a current of cool wind through the trees. As the sound drew closer, it took on a rhythmic, steady cadence. An ambulance rounded the corner. Its lights pulsed.

A man stepped out of the crowd, waved towards the ambulance.

She could not see her brother—too many people teemed around him—but she saw blood spreading across the pavement, black and sparkling over the rough asphalt. The blood inched towards her, reaching out for her. She took a step back. Her breath hitched, and she started to cry. Tears blurred her vision, and the sorrowful faces of the men and women took on the twisted aspect of leering goblins.

* * *

Jesse and her mother ate dinner—grilled cheese sandwiches and soggy, oven-baked French fries—in silence. They sat upon the living room couch, TV trays balanced on their laps, just as they did every night, but the television was off.

A trio of long shadows passed across the living room window.

Jesse's mother tensed and held her breath as they passed.

"It's just kids," Jesse said.

Mom smiled weakly as she stood. She gathered the plates—they rattled in her hands—and took them to the kitchen. She scraped off the remainder of the food, ran hot water over the dishes, and left them soaking in the sink.

"I have a headache, Jesse," she said, returning to the living room. "I think I might lie down on the couch for a few minutes. Are you all done with your schoolwork?"

Jesse nodded.

"Why don't you go to your room and play for a while before bedtime?"

"Yes, ma'am."

Jesse glanced at the window. The shadows were gone. Only darkness awaited outside. As she walked to her room, she passed the hall closet. The door shook gently in the frame.

Her imagination?

No. The closet door rattled, as if something on the other side sought release, tapping and knocking, soft but persistent. She looked towards the living room. Her mother was already stretched out on the couch. Quietly, she opened the door and peered inside.

Old shoes were piled upon the floor. A vacuum cleaner leaned in the corner. On a shelf above the coats, several boxes of photos teetered on the verge of falling over. Jesse wondered if those Halloween pictures might be found within.

She saw her brother's jacket, the one he had worn on Halloween night. She wondered why her mother had insisted on keeping the jacket. She stood on her tiptoes and pulled the garment down. The hanger clattered against the rack. Jesse flinched, but thankfully her mother did not hear.

Hugging the jacket close, she crept to her room.

She looked the jacket over. It had been washed several times, but the bloodstains could still be seen, deep in the weave of the fabric. The fabric smelled of dust and heavy detergent.

She swept her hair back over the collar as she tried the jacket on. She looked at herself in the mirror. The jacket engulfed her, hanging almost to her knees and swallowing her hands in the folds of the sleeves. She turned from side to side, regarding herself.

The house creaked.

A branch scratched against the roof.

Outside, children laughed. Distantly, someone called "trick or treat!"

Halloween called to her.

She waited until she was certain that her mother was asleep, then she tiptoed out of the house, bundled in her brother's coat and carrying a pillow case.

The steps she took as she walked along the house were familiar, becoming second nature as she traipsed up one walkway after another, knocking on the door to draw people out, begging for candy or promising mischief. Some of the people greeted her strangely, not recognizing her costume, but she didn't let that bother her. They cheerfully tossed handfuls of brightly-wrapped candy into the bag. One of Jesse's neighbors dropped Life Savers into the bag and looked nervously to the street, asking, "Are you all alone out here?" Jesse only shrugged and pranced to the next house.

As she approached the bridge to Slocum Street, she met a group of children she knew from school. She saw no pirates or fairy princesses among their number. Some of them carried flashlights with plastic jack-o-lanterns or witch's heads over the lenses, casting orange and green glows over the street. A few grown-ups, like shadows, followed them. One of the girls, Maggie, said, "Hi, Jessica. Are you getting a lot of candy?"

Jesse smiled and nodded.

She recognized one of the grown-ups as Mr. O'Brien, who lived down the street and had a daughter in Jesse's class.

"Would you like to come with us?" Mr. O'Brien asked.

"No, thank you," Jesse said.

"You should have an adult with you," he said. "Where's your mother?"

"She's not feeling well."

"What are you supposed to be?" one of the children asked. He adjusted his latex monster mask by pulling at the eyes.

"Don't be silly," said Maggie. "She's a ghost."

"Oh, yeah."

One of the children said, "We don't mind if you come with us." He looked at the others, seeking approval. "Do we?"

"No," the monster said. His voice was muffled under the gruesome mask. "Why don't you?"

"I don't think so, but thank you." She nodded towards the darkened neighborhood across the bridge. "I'm going over to Slocum Street."

Mr. O'Brien grimaced. The children gasped and whispered to each other.

"Don't go there," one of the children said.

"No, don't," said another. "It's haunted."

"I know," Jesse said. With that, she started across the bridge.

Beneath her, the creek bubbled, choked with brush and mud. She looked down, half expecting to see those bed sheet ghosts. If she did, she would call out to them to see what they were up to. She saw no one, though.

Slocum Street was quiet and dark. No costumed children ran from house to house. No sounds of laughter could be heard. The porch lights at each house were out. The neighborhood her brother had described as "prime pickings" now resembled something out of her mother's ideal vision of Halloween. Trees lining the street loomed overhead, casting deep pools of darkness, a patchwork carpet of moonlight and shadow over the pavement. There were no other trick-or-treaters, and a shrill wind swept past.

She walked up the sidewalk to the first house. Her bag was full of miniature candy bars and raisins and apples. The porch steps creaked beneath her feet. She knocked on the door and waited.

"What are you supposed to be?" asked the pinched-faced woman who answered the door. The words sounded forced, out of practice.

"I'm my brother," Jesse said.

"Oh, what a scary costume."

With that, the woman tossed something into the bag, said "Happy Halloween," in a whisper, and pushed the door closed.

At each house, Jesse was greeted with gasps of dread or titters of nervous delight, and as she made her way to the final house along the street, the pillowcase grew heavy, so much so that she could not pick it up off the ground, but instead let it drag along the pavement behind her.

She paused a moment before approaching the last house on the street. The yard was not made up to look like a cemetery, but Jesse felt a nibble of fear in her stomach. A familiar-looking car, unused and partially covered with a tarp, waited beneath the carport. She walked up and knocked on the door.

"Go away," came a voice on the other side "I don't have anything for you."

Jesse stood still on the porch for a few seconds, then knocked again, rapping the door twice.

"Please," said the shaking voice. "Leave me be."

But Jesse knocked on the door once more and cried, "Trick or treat."

The door creaked open, just a bit, not enough to see inside.

"Trick or treat!" Jesse said.

The door creaked open another inch. Jesse opened her bag and held it out. From inside the house, an arm emerged, dropped the prize into the bag, and then quickly withdrew. The door slammed shut and the voice said again, "Leave me be."

Jesse turned and skipped back to the sidewalk, the bag bouncing along behind her. She tested the bag's weight. The pillowcase was heavy and wet. She flung the bag over her shoulder so it would not drag the ground. Smiling, her work done, she walked home. The moon grinned down at her, and dried leaves skittered along in her wake.

When she got home, she quietly opened the front door. Her mother was still sleeping upon the couch, and neither Jesse's movement or the rush of cold air from outside roused her. Good. Jesse took off her brother's coat and draped it over the arm of the couch, just below her mother's feet. She knelt down in front of a nearby chair and emptied the overstuffed bag. The spoils of her night's work spilled across the floor. She quickly organized the candy into neat piles of chocolates and chewing gum and licorice. Into another pile she placed the oranges and raisins and apples. The third pile was set aside for those dark, wet things she retrieved on Slocum Street, those things that did not belong to her at all.

After she completed this task, she rose and tiptoed across the room. She flipped the light switch beside the front door, and the porch light flared to life. She waited.

* * *

Later, the knocking woke Jesse's mother.

She sat up quickly, as if startled from a nightmare. Jesse sat in the chair across from her, kicking her legs playfully and nibbling on a miniature Snickers bar. She smiled.

Someone knocked at the front door.

"Who could that be?" her mother asked. She squinted at her wristwatch. "It's much too late for trick-or-treaters."

The front door rattled as the pounding—steady and strong—continued.

"What is this?" Mother asked. "Some kind of joke?"

She rose from the couch. Her legs were shaky and unsteady. She looked at Jesse as if seeking an answer in the little girl's eyes.

Jesse grinned, her mouth smeared with gooey chocolate, and said only, "Happy Halloween."

"Don't say that, Jesse. You know I don't like it when you—"

The door shook as if it might come off the hinges. Jesse's mother jumped and turned towards the door, holding a hand to her chest to calm the panicked beat of her heart. She took a step and kicked candy across the floor. She looked down, her eyes following the path of candy as it rolled and spun away.

Someone pounded on the door.

And she saw the candy corn and Tootsie rolls, the oranges and the tiny red boxes of raisins.

Pounded.

And she saw those things that Jesse had gotten from Slocum Street, lying on the floor, waiting.

Waiting for the trick-or-treater lurking on the front porch.

Dark, glistening blood soaking into the carpet.

Pounded.

The door shivered.

And she screamed.

"Come Again, Halloween" was originally published in Sinisteria Magazine (2004).

To me (and most likely to you) it's obvious that this yarn is a kind of love letter to both Bradbury and W. W. Jacobs. I still like it a great deal. Halloween is my favorite time of year, and the holiday features in a number of my short stories.

- CB

COLD SNAP

This is the sound of Hell:

The clicking of sleet upon the roof of the car and against the windshield. Wind rushing along the deserted road, howling, moaning. The dull thumping and hissing of the wipers, now caked with ice. Keys rattling on the chain as the ignition is turned, turned, turned desperately. The grind of the car's engine—metal against metal—screeching, sputtering. And the baby—oh, God, the baby—crying as she shivers in the car seat, crying for food, for warmth, but—oh, God—not crying as loudly as she had been only a moment before.

And every sound followed by a thought I cannot shake:

I'm going to die here. I'm going to die and so is my baby. We're both going to die because of what I've done.

I try the ignition once more, my fingers bruised I've gripped the key so hard, my hands numb from the cold—the cold, so bitter and sharp that it's almost solid, filling the car, drowning me as I breathe it in. I turn the ignition again and again—so hard that it surprises me that the key doesn't snap in two. A feeble red light on the dash flashes SERVICE ENGINE SOON. Shivering, I hold my hands to my face, breathe on my fingers, trying to warm them, but even my breath seems frigid as a cloud of frosty air escapes my lips.

The baby cries—she sounds so weak—and I shrug out of my fleece jacket, letting the air snap at me, and cover her with it, tucking the cloth around her small form.

"It's going to be all right, Wendy," I whisper, knowing she doesn't understand. She doesn't understand any of what's happened in the past few hours. "Everything's going to be all right."

She coughs and struggles in the seat.

And she looks so pale, her flesh like the snow, only her tiny hands and face are stained a mottled red.

She's so cold. So cold.

Ice coats the windshield, freezing the wipers in place.

A distant signal comes through the radio, fading in and out. "A winter storm ad . . . the freezing . . . several more . . . later this morning . . . road crews working . . . are slick . . . advising . . . to stay . . . warmth . . ." And then it is gone, consumed by the static.

Come on . . . Come on . . .

I urge the engine to crank as I turn the keys one last time. Nothing. Too late. The car's had it. I pushed it too hard, trying to get as far away as possible, far away from—

I look down to the floorboard, where my pistol lies, where I tossed it. The barrel looks black in the darkness, glistening slightly, caked with blood, a few blonde hairs stuck to the metal.

The baby wails. She is shaking. Why won't she stop shaking?

I know that if we stay in the car, we are going to die. Reaching over, I unstrap the baby from the car seat. I will not let her die here. I press her close to my body. I cover her face with the scarf and make sure she's bundled tightly. I shove against the door and it comes open with the brittle crack of ice.

We are out in the middle of nowhere. I kept to the back roads, trying to avoid running into anyone, especially the police, and I have no idea where the nearest gas station, rest stop, or house might be. But I don't have a choice. The storm was battering through the car, trying to get at us, and sooner or later it would have succeeded. At least this way there might be a chance.

I can hear the baby's muffled crying as I start to trudge away from the car, away from the fading headlights. Snow and ice fill my shoes. I can't feel my toes, fingers, or nose. Plumes of frosty, labored breath writhe around my head. I press the baby closer to my chest.

If only they hadn't tried to keep the baby from me—my ex-wife and her new boyfriend.

The bastard . . . the bastard could have had her for all I care . . . stepped right in and took my place . . . but not the baby . . . I wouldn't let him have the baby . . .

But I never meant to hurt anyone.

That's not true, though, is it? Otherwise, I would have left the gun at home, left it in my sock drawer and gone unarmed.

My feet crunch through the snow and ice. Wind blisters my face as I glance around, seeing no sign of the car, only a haze of whipping snow, and the trail of my footprints, slowly filling, vanishing, swallowed up by the snow.

The tingling at my fingertips and toes tells me that frostbite is settling in. I clutch the baby closer to me, staggering, almost falling, but pressing on.

Keep moving . . . keep moving . . .

Against me, the baby stirs, only slightly, and I can't be sure if it is actual move-ment or just my imagination, but I know one thing for sure—she's cold, so cold, and I can't shake the thought that I'm not carrying my daughter at all, but instead carrying a shank of chilled meat against me.

The wind whips the snow into phantom shapes, figures gliding around me, reaching for me, and their touch numbs my body.

I walk for what seems like a lifetime. The road vanishes under the blanket of ice and snow. I can't feel my legs, and I hardly notice that they are no longer working until I crash down to my knees. I can't stand, can't walk, can't crawl. I want to scream, to cry for help, but the sound won't come, as if silenced and trapped by the ghostly cloud of freezing breath.

I fall to my side, hoping I don't crush my daughter against the frozen ground. I'm so tired. I can't stand the thought of walking any farther. The cold doesn't even seem that bad anymore.

My vision blurs, and I wonder if its possible that my eyes are freezing.

Large flakes of snow, like the feathers from an angel's wings, float down around me.

In the distance, I hear the rasping of footsteps through the ice. I raise my head . . . and wonder at first if the snow is not playing more tricks on me. Several figures approach, hunched over against the cold, their shadowy forms covered in ice and rain. They surround me, looking down on me as I try to ask for help, and they reach for me, pulling the baby from my stiffening arms, and I think for a few dreadful seconds that they might be saving only the child, leaving me out here to die. They whisper, but I cannot make out the hissing words. They lift me to my feet, and just beyond a rise of snow I see a darkened house.

Dry laughter escapes my throat. Funny how I hadn't noticed the house, and it was so close. My laughter is the last sound I hear before weariness overtakes me and the world vanishes from my sight.

I awake sometime later—how long?—on a tattered and filthy couch that smells of damp earth. The room is furnished only by the couch. The floors are dirty, stripped of carpeting and wet. A stink rises from somewhere in the house. It is warm, though, and somewhat comfortable. The memory of the cold lingers painfully on my skin. I lay still for a few minutes, letting the warmth of the house soak into my body, before I realize that the baby is no longer with me.

I rise from the couch, stagger across the room, and look out the window.

I can see for miles.

And all I can see is snow, a vast plane of ice glittering coldly in the moonlight.

I stumble from the room, into a winding labyrinth of hallways. Water trickles down black walls, pools along the baseboard, and a slight draft filters through the hall, the storm trying to break in. Wet, muddy footprints leave a stained trail across the floor. I follow the footprints, and despite the cold I feel a sweat breaking out across my forehead.

Ahead, flickering light fills a room, and a wave of almost oppressive heat flows towards me. I step into the room, where several dark figures gather around a glowing hearth and whisper to one another.

The smell and the heat assault my senses. I stagger back into the wall, covering my mouth to keep from vomiting. The figures turn to face me, and for the first time I notice their black, shark-like eyes, their overly large mouths full of chattering, needle-pointed teeth, their skin blackened, frostbitten, and flaking away. Beyond them, I see the fire, the fire that heats the house and seeps into my bones like some kind of disease.

I fall to my knees.

The figures come at me, shuffling across the floor, but I cannot take my eyes from the fire, even as they grab me with long, spidery fingers.

I cannot take my eyes from the tiny, blistered body in the heart of the flame.

This story jumped into my head pretty much fully formed as I drove home from work in the middle of a freak ice storm. It's a story that I don't think I'd be able to write now. As a father, I'm kind of mad at myself for ever writing it.

- CB

STILL WATERS

Some folks deserved to die, my daddy once told me, but some deserved to live, not because they were good people, but because the longer they lived, the longer they could be made to suffer. At the time, this philosophy seemed simple enough, the way many of the things my daddy said seemed simple. He was an uncomplicated man and prone at times to mean-spiritedness. What I came to realize, though, is that sometimes it's hard to tell who deserves to live, who deserves to die, and who should have never been born at all.

* * *

Standing on the front porch, I watched Mr. Hennessey's car pull into the gravel roadway leading to our house. A shiver crawled through my body—a shiver, even though it was so hot you might have believed that the earth itself had cracked open to vent the furnaces of Hell. I suppose I should have expected a visit from him, after everything that had happened, but I can't say that I was ready to deal with him. I wished my brother or my daddy were home, wished I were not alone, as I watched the car slowly approach.

Gravel skittered from under the tires, and a layer of chalk gray dust settled onto the car's black paint as the engine died. The door screeched open, and the driver hopped out. Balding and red-faced, Mr. Hennessey wore a white short-sleeved shirt and a wide, crooked tie. His gut hung over his belt, and yellowish stains spread out from under his arms. Tiny whirlwinds of dust swirled around his legs.

He may not have looked like much, but Mr. Hennessey was probably the richest man in the entire county. He owned a new and used car lot in town and, rumor had it, had his stubby fingers dipped into a number of other area businesses. Like most rich folk, he was the subject of a lot of gossip when his back was turned. I didn't know whether I believed the gossip or not, but I knew for sure that I didn't like him.

"Hello, Betty," he said. He smiled, and his feet crunched in the gravel as he approached.

"My daddy's not here right now, Mr. Hennessey." I regretted it as soon as I spoke. The words hung in the air, and I wanted to pull them back into my mouth. "He'll be back later. Tonight sometime."

"Actually, Betty, I came to talk to you." He fished a handkerchief from his pocket and dabbed his forehead. The smile—a fake smile if ever there was one—flashed across his mouth again. "Awful hot out here. You think I could come inside?"

I didn't really want to let him in, but I knew my daddy would have been awful angry if he found out I hadn't shown a visitor, especially Mr. Hennessey, who owned the title to Daddy's truck, some hospitality. "I guess that would be all right," I said.

The screen door creaked and snapped shut as Mr. Hennessey followed me inside, wiping sweat from his nose and upper lip with his handkerchief. "Don't seem like summer's ever going to end, does it?"

"Guess not," I answered.

"I tell you what," he said. "I sure could use something cold to drink."

He followed me into the kitchen, where I poured ice and dark red Kool-Aid. Mr. Hennessey grabbed up one of the glasses, slurping the Kool-Aid down.

"So you wanted to talk to me?" I said.

"Yes." He set the glass on the counter. The ice cracked and popped. "Yes, I do."

He drew in a deep breath, taking time to figure out how to ask his question, but I already knew what he was going to say.

"You've talked to her, haven't you?" he asked, nodding, trying to prompt an answer. "Haven't you?"

"What are you talking about?"

("Betty . . . . Can you hear me? Are you listening?")

"Please," Mr. Hennessey said, "you can tell me."

I sipped my Kool-Aid. It tasted too sweet, too sticky, for such a hot day. "Ain't nothing to tell."

("I need to tell you something. I need you to listen.")

"I really don't know what you're talking about." The lie, like the Kool-Aid, tasted sweet. "Maybe—"

Before I could react, he reached for me, grabbing me by the shoulders and almost jerking me off my feet. His nails, which were in need of clipping, dug into my arms. I dropped my glass, and Kool-Aid splashed against my leg, across the floor.

"You tell me." Anger filled his shaky voice—anger and desperation. "Don't try to hide what she's been telling you!"

I opened my mouth, tried to force out an answer.

"Tell me." A bead of sweat rolled down his forehead and pooled in the thick hairs of his eyebrows. His voice softened. "Please. I have to know."

In that instant, he appeared suddenly weak.

"You got no right to grab me like that!" I slapped his hands away. "You got a question for me? Ask nicely if you want a straight answer."

The color drained from his face. He stepped back, wiping his palms on the front of his shirt. You'd think it was the first time anyone—let alone a thirteen-year-old girl—had stood up to him like that. I like to believe that maybe it was. He pulled at his tie, cleared his throat, and asked me, real nicely, to tell him what the ghost of his dead wife had said to me.

And that mean streak I inherited from my daddy must have gotten the better of me, because I just smiled prettily.

But I didn't answer.

* * *

I never liked it when my brother, Charlie, and his best friend, Eddie, called me a tomboy. I ain't saying it ain't true. I'm just saying I never liked it much when somebody pointed it out. Those two were always running off, trying their best to leave me behind, laughing and hollering, "We don't need no girls following us around, especially no tomboys!" But I always managed to keep up with them when I wanted. Sometimes, I thought they let me catch up, but only put on a big show of complaining. Maybe they didn't mind having me around so much after all.

Eddie's granddaddy once told me, "Don't you mind that boy ribbing you, girl. That's just a young boy's way. He don't know how to tell you that he's sweet on you."

"That's not true," I had said, blushing, mad at myself for being embarrassed. "He don't like me."

The old man laughed and said, "Well, I've been around for too long not to know when a boy fancies a girl."

"If that's so, then why don't he just tell me?"

"Maybe he's shy. Or maybe he's scared--scared of what you can do."

Eddie's granddaddy had been dead for three months when he told me that.

You see, for as long as I can remember, I've been able to talk with dead folk. Not long dead, mind you, but dead all the same. Why they picked me, I couldn't say. My daddy told me it ran in the family. My mama, God rest her soul, could do it, and while it skipped my grandma, I heard that my great grandma could do it, too. I guess most folks, like Eddie, were a little scared of me, but they accepted me just the same. Folks were always asking me to pass on some final message to their dead relatives. What nobody really understood, though, was that I couldn't do a thing unless the ghosts or spirits or whatever you wanted to call them came to me. Most of the time I just faked it.

I wasn't sure how Mr. Hennessey knew that his wife had been talking to me. Maybe he was taking a wild guess. I was nervous, though, since he was certain that I had talked with her, and that meant that he was also certain that she was dead and not just run off like local gossip suggested.

Of course, she hadn't told me much, except for where her body was hidden.

* * *

"You mean you know where she is?" Charlie asked. "You know and you ain't told anybody?"

"I just told you, didn't I?" I said. "Besides, who else am I supposed to tell?"

"You could tell Daddy."

I shook my head. "You know better than that. Daddy would tell me to keep my mouth shut about it, because it would only cause trouble."

Charlie, Eddie, and me sat in the tall, dry grass behind the crumbling barn, like we did near about every afternoon, trying to figure out how to spend the rest of the day. Even in the shadow of the barn, the sun beat down on us, the air was stagnant, and it was so hot that I didn't want to breathe, didn't want to draw the heat into my body. I had told them about Mr. Hennessey's visit and that I had been talking to his dead wife, and that had started my brother and me arguing.

"I don't see why I have to tell anybody." I plucked a blade of brown grass from the front of my shirt. "It'll pass soon enough and I can forget all about it."

"If she's dead," Charlie said, "if she's been killed, somebody ought to know."

Eddie, who had been listening quietly, shifted uncomfortably. "You think . . . Mr. Hennessey . . . killed her?" he finally asked in a soft, worried voice. I felt a little sorry for Eddie, because some kids made fun of him because he was too skinny and he stuttered sometimes. "I mean, I heard she ran off with a Bible salesman or something like that."

"It weren't no Bible salesman," Charlie said. "I heard it was that fella who comes around every few weeks selling frozen meat. Don't really matter what I heard, though, not if Betty's been talking to her, because that means she ain't run off. She's dead."

"So you think Mr. Hennessey killed her?" Eddie asked again.

Charlie and me looked at each other, trying to figure out just how to answer. Then Charlie whispered. "I wouldn't go around saying that if I were you."

"Why not? If he killed her we should tell someone, the sheriff maybe." But all the conviction drained quickly from Eddie's voice. "Shouldn't we?"

"Well, we couldn't tell the sheriff." Charlie picked up a stick and tossed it into the grass angrily. "Him and Mr. Hennessey are good friends. He'd probably throw us in jail just for gossiping."

"Look," I said. "I don't know if he killed her or not. She didn't tell me that. She only told me where her body was."

"Well, why should she tell you that?" Eddie asked.

"I don't know. Maybe she wants somebody to find her."

"I got an idea." Charlie's features grew crafty. He was half joking, but half serious, too. "Why don't we go look for ourselves. We could go take a peek at the body, see what it looks like, then decide if we should tell someone."

"How's looking at the body gonna tell us anything?" I asked.

"Well, we'll know if we should tell someone or not if she looks . . . ."

"Looks what?" Eddie asked.

"I don't know. Murdered, I guess."

I shook my head.

"You can stay here if you want." Charlie smiled, daring me, daring me not to go. "You'll probably only get scared. But me and Eddie are going. Right, Eddie?"

Eddie swallowed and nodded.

Brushing the dirt off his knees, Charlie stood. He looked at us, expecting us to jump up at his lead, then waved us away in disgust, turned, and walked off. Eddie watched him for a second or two, then scurried after him.

I muttered under my breath, tossed the blade of grass to the ground, and followed.

* * *

Dust had settled onto the surface of the lake, glittering like dirty glass. The trees surrounding the clearing were dry and bare, offering little shade.

"You sure this is it, Betty?" Charlie walked along the edge of the lake and peered into the murky water. He kicked a few pebbles down the bank, and sluggish ripples spread over the lake's surface. "I thought dead bodies float."

"Don't you think somebody would have found her before now if she was just out here floating?" I asked.

"Maybe not." Charlie shrugged. "Nobody ever really comes out here. Fishing's no good, and the water's mostly too nasty for swimming."

Kneeling on his hands and knees, Eddie leaned in close to the water, as if he could see all the way to the bottom if he stared hard enough. "I heard the water's pretty deep. Maybe she's tied to a stone or something. That would keep her from floating."

Charlie looked back at me, as if I had the answer, but all I could do was shrug.

"Well, that ain't a half bad idea." Charlie stood by Eddie's side and both of them stared at the water. "I bet old Mr. Hennessey just tied her mutilated body to a big rock and tossed her in."

"M--Mutilated? You think he mutilated her?"

"Sure. I bet he nearly cut her to pieces."

Eddie grimaced.

"Really only one thing to do," Charlie said, sitting in the grass and tugging at his shoes and socks and tossing them over his shoulder.

"What are you doing?" I asked.

"The only way I know to see if she's down there is to go check." He pulled his pants down and kicked them off his legs.

"You're going swimming in there?" Eddie's face was pale and pasty. "There's a dead body down there."

"It ain't like I'm going alone." Charlie's voice was muffled as he pulled his tee shirt over his head. "You two are going with me."

"Oh no, I'm not," I said.

"What? You ain't scared, are you?" Charlie stood up, wearing nothing but his underwear, and stepped cautiously towards the water.

"I'm not scared," Eddie said. He sat down on the muddy bank and carefully untied his shoes. He looked over his shoulder at me. "Could you turn around, Betty?"

"You ain't got nothing I want to see," I said. "Besides, I'm going with you."

* * *

The water was colder than I expected, and I had to catch my breath when I stepped into it. Charlie had already waded out to where the water came up to his hips, and Eddie, shivering and wrapping his arms around himself, wasn't far behind. The water was so murky that I couldn't see my feet. Mud squished between my toes, and underwater weeds scratched at my legs.

"This water stinks," Eddie said, wrinkling his nose.

I waded farther out. My underwear and shirt clung to my skin.

"You be careful," Charlie said. "There's a steep drop off over here. The water's probably a lot deeper than you think."

"This ain't a good idea," I said. "We should just go home."

Eddie looked at my brother hopefully. He didn't want to stay, either, but he wouldn't leave unless Charlie agreed.

"I'm not going anywhere until I see that body. If you want to go, I'm not stopping you."

"I want to see it, too," Eddie said.

"Good." A victorious smile crossed Charlie's lips. "I'm gonna dive down here, see if I can spot anything. You two wait right there for just a minute."

As Charlie started to lower himself beneath the water, I heard a soft, whispering voice, a voice from somewhere below.

"Betty . . . . "

"Charlie!" The name jumped from my mouth. He glared at me angrily. "You be careful."

And then, just like that, he was gone, this time without so much as a splash.

It was as if the lake had gently swallowed him down. I stood, shivering, staring at my rippling reflection on the surface of the cold, murky water.

"Betty," a voice urged. "My baby . . . ."

The words were muffled, distant.

"Please . . . my baby . . . ."

Suddenly, Charlie surfaced, spitting water and calling excitedly. "I found her! I found her! You're not going to believe this!"

* * *

Sunlight barely pierced the inky water. Bits of white debris floated around me, as if somebody had spilled milk into the lake. A few bubbles bobbed towards the surface. Spiny weeds writhed in the stirring mud, reaching out for me.

Charlie swam down into the darkness. Eddie tugged at my arm. His face looked swollen, he had taken such a large breath of air. He motioned for me to follow and kicked after my brother.

"Betty," the voice said, more clearly now.

Charlie pointed towards a large shadowy form that I thought at first to be a pile of rocks. As I drew closer, though, I realized that it wasn't a pile of rocks at all, but a car. I felt my lungs straining, telling me I needed another breath of air, but I didn't want to turn away yet.

A thin layer of grayish white slime coated the windshield, but I could make out a form sitting in the passenger side seat. Mrs. Hennessey, still and quiet, her eyes and mouth wide open, her blonde hair writhing around her face. Swimming closer to the windshield, I saw ropes tied around her forehead, wrists, and waist, binding her to the seat.

"Betty . . . ."

Mr. Hennessey had trapped his wife in one of his old junkers, driven it out to the lake, and rolled it in, where he hoped no one would find it. I imagined the car slowly filling with stinking water. I imagined Mrs. Hennessey screaming, choking, drowning.

She seemed to be staring right at me.

My lungs wouldn't last any longer, though, and I started swimming towards the surface. Eddie, too, swam away from the car. But Charlie waited, treading water in front of the car windshield.

"Betty, wait."

The voice sounded frantic.

"My baby . . . my baby . . . ."

I looked down at the car. Charlie still looked through the windshield, and I could tell that he was so scared of what he saw that he couldn't move.

Through the windshield, I saw something . . . moving, squirming like a nest of eels slithering out from under the seats, slipping against the cracked glass—not from under the seat, I realized, but from inside Mrs. Hennessey's body.

"My baby's hungry!"

The slithering mass surged against the windshield, settled back down for only a second, then surged against the glass again.

Charlie, finally gaining his senses, kicked hard for the surface, his mouth open, white frothy bubbles exploding from his mouth.

A garbled scream chased after him.

The thing in the car surged against the glass one last time, and the glass gave way, shattering in a cloud of bubbles and slime and glittering shards, spreading out, away from the car before being pulled back through the broken windshield by a kind of suction. The wriggling, eel-like tentacles rolled out of the cloud, long and bloated and curling, and in the pale, fleshy mass, I saw what might have been an infant's face, only if an infant was born in pieces.

I broke the surface of the lake coughing and screaming. Nearby, Charlie was swimming for shore. My eyes burned, and snot ran thickly from my nose.

Confused, Eddie bobbed in the water nearby. "What's wrong?" he cried. His nose ran also—ran snot and blood—and red blisters covered his face.

"Get out!" was all I could manage as I swam for shore.

Charlie hit the shallow part of the lake, got to his feet and half stumbled, half ran for the bank, where he collapsed and crawled through the mud and kept crawling until he was well away from the water.

As I got to the bank, he jumped up and helped haul me out of the water. His hands, his arms, his face were covered in blisters. As I collapsed to the ground, I realized how badly my skin burned and itched.

I looked over my shoulder, and a feeble gasp escaped my throat.

The lake was silent and still, with only a few bubbles breaking the surface.

"Where's Eddie?" I asked.

But Charlie didn't have an answer.

We waited by the lake, lying on the muddy shore, hoping Eddie would reappear, but knowing he would not. We waited until the foul water had dried from our burned skin and the sun had faded to a bruised glow in the sky.

We started walking home as the crickets began their nightly song.

* * *

Several days later, when I felt up to leaving the house, I called upon Mr. Hennessey. I knocked on the door, but he didn't come to the door right away. I wondered if maybe he was hiding inside, hoping I would leave. When he finally opened the door, he looked down at me, and he looked ashamed and small and sick.

"I was expecting you." He pushed the door open. "Come in."

We sat for a while in the living room, across from each other, not saying a word, unsure of what, exactly, to say, both afraid to speak first.

He couldn't bear to look at me, and his eyes strayed to a picture on the mantle – a picture of him and Mrs. Hennessey, smiling, looking happy. I knew I looked pretty awful, like I had been roasted over a fire, my skin red and peeling, my eyelids swollen, my lips cracked. Charlie, still back home in bed, was much worse off than me. He could hardly see—and the doctor said that he wasn't sure if his vision would ever clear—and sometimes his hands shook so badly that he couldn't hold anything.

And Eddie—

I thought of Eddie, and I felt tears burning my eyes.

"What was it?" I asked finally.

Mr. Hennessey looked up, started to speak, then fell silent and only shook his head.

"You don't know, do you?"

"All I know is that it wasn't right, that thing inside her. I could see it, sometimes, when she was sleeping, moving inside her stomach, and I knew I couldn't suffer it to be born into the world. But she wouldn't hear of it. She wanted to have it. She wanted that thing in her body."

I glanced at the picture on the mantle.

"Are you going to tell anyone?" Mr. Hennessey asked.

I shook my head. "We're not telling anybody. Who would believe us? Eddie's parents, they believe he ran away, and I guess that's for the best. Sometimes it's better not to know the truth."

"I'm sorry, Betty. I really am."

And I believed him, not that it really mattered.

"Eventually," I said, "somebody will find her."

"I know." He looked at his hands, clenched tightly in his lap. "I know they will."

I started to ask him what he would do when the truth was discovered, but decided that I didn't want to know, that I didn't care.

"You . . . you understand, though, don't you?" he said. Worry crept into his voice and he looked desperate for me to understand. "It wasn't mine. It couldn't have been. I couldn't have put that . . . thing inside her."

I nodded, even though I wasn't sure if I understood or not, wasn't sure if I could ever really understand. I stood, walked towards the door. I didn't know why I had come in the first place, didn't know if I had accomplished anything. Mr. Hennessey followed me to the front door.

"Betty, wait." He grabbed my shoulder. I hissed in pain as his fingers brushed my blistered skin, and he quickly drew his hand away. "What if that thing gets out of the lake? What happens then?"

"I don't think it will," I said. "I think it's dead."

He didn't say another word, just watched me walk away. As I reached the sidewalk, I heard his door close.

I didn't hear from the ghost of Mrs. Hennessey ever again. But another voice called to me, and I knew it was that baby, dead, starved to death at the bottom of the lake, but still calling me, trying to draw me back into the dark, cold water.

And the sound of it cut me to the bone.

Because it sounded like Eddie.

"Still Waters" was originally published in Darkness Within (1999).

This is definitely the oldest story in this collection, and it shows. If nothing else, though, "Still Waters" shows where I was headed as a writer even in those early days. Some of the elements — in particular the "haunted" pond — show up in some of my other stories. This tale and "Remains", which appears later in this book, are siblings, I think. If you and I went to North Carolina together, I could lead you straight to the pond described herein. Is there a car at the bottom? I always heard there was.

- CB

CREEPING STONES

If she did not know better (and she did because she was, after all, a practical and rational young woman) she would have sworn that the headstones were moving closer to the house. While the stones had been, just yesterday at the bottom of the grass-covered hill, nestled alongside rosemary and honeysuckle, now they appeared to be . . . closer, as if they had slid through the ground, making their way slowly, ever so slowly, up the gentle slope towards the gardens behind the house. They were closer today than they had been yesterday, and closer yesterday than the day before. She knew this because she had watched the small cemetery with an almost morbid fascination for several days.

She shook her head at her own naiveté. Surely the stones were no closer. Her memory did not serve correctly. She did, in fact, know better, she told herself, and that meant she was imagining things, as her husband suggested, or—

Or she had lost her mind.

Watching from the upstairs window, she silently urged the stones to move, to move while she watched, so that she could have some assurance that she had not taken leave of her senses. Any sign would do—a bit of loosened mortar falling to the ground or a tall sprig of grass twitching at a marker's passing. She knew, however, that while she watched, nothing would happen, and when she looked again, in the morning perhaps, the stones would be closer to the house, an inch or less in all likelihood, but closer nonetheless. It was as if they waited for a time when no one watched to proceed on their strange pilgrimage, as if they were trying to sneak up on the house, and on the town beyond.

Past the small cemetery, the sun had long finished its descent below the horizon, its color bled into the surrounding gray, fading into shadow and mist.

And her reflection, ghost-like in the window glass, stared back at her piteously as she waited for something that might never happen . . .something that might very well be the product of her imagination.

It was a slow, tedious progression, the journey of the stones, but what were the headstones of the dead if not patient?

She turned from the window as she heard footsteps—her husband's footsteps—in the outer hall. She allowed the curtains to fall back into place and smoothed the fabric with a stroke of her hand.

The dark oak door creaked open, and light from the hall beyond flooded into the dimly lit room, spilling over the floral wallpaper and matching chairs, glinting off the heavy gold mirror hanging above the fireplace, and illuminating Meagan's face.

Matthew wore his dark suit and carried his cane under his arm, which meant he would be going into town tonight. He entered the room quietly, and shadows pooled beneath his heavy brow, banishing his expression to darkness. Meagan did not need to see his features, though, to know that he wore a mask of disappointment. Without a word, he crossed the room, setting his cane aside and laying his topcoat along the curling arm of a chair. He glanced towards the window—the only window in the house overlooking the cemetery. The long, deep green curtains rustled gently back and forth. With a sigh, he turned his eyes towards his wife.

"At it again, are you?" he asked.

She looked down, touched the lace collar at her neck.

"What am I to do with you?" he asked. "Why must you let your imagination run away with you?"

"But I'm not imagining it. See for yourself."

"The stones have not moved."

"But you haven't even looked. How could you know?"

"Because they have never moved. I have looked out that window hundreds of times. But I've never seen what you want me to see."

"Look again, husband, will you?"

Shaking his head in defeat and smiling slightly, he pulled the curtains aside and, as moonlight spilled across his face, stared out the window.

"What do you see?" Meagan asked. She anxiously clenched her hands into tight fists.

The curtains fell as Matthew turned away.

"What did you see?" she asked again.

"I saw the gardens, the pavilion, the fountains, nothing more." He sighed. "Haven't I tried to be a good husband? Haven't I built a beautiful home for you? Haven't I offered you every luxury? Why obsess yourself with these fantasies?"

His words stung, but she saw a hint of concern crease his face—a hint of fear in his eyes—and she knew that this time, when he looked out the window, he had seen something, something he had not seen all the times before.

She settled back at the realization, then reached out to touch his arm. "You

know."

"Don't try to pull me into this fantasy girl! I'll not hear of it again. If I must brick every window in this house, I'll not hear of it again!"

Seldom did he raise his voice to her. His lack of control, the brief loss of his beloved composure, only cemented her belief that he had seen something different than when he had looked before . . . or something that he had seen before to which he would not dare admit. Still, Meagan thought better of pressing the issue.

"You're right, of course." She smiled weakly and looked, ashamed, at the floor. "I am certain that I am only letting my imagination get the better of me."

He gently touched her cheek, raised her head so that he could look upon her.

"I did not mean to be curt. You know how I worry. It is not good for you that you get excited over nothing."

She nodded, smiling slightly, and looked briefly back to the closed curtains.

He turned away from her, started towards the doorway, and gathered his coat and cane. "I must go."

"Why?" she asked. "Why this time?"

"Ah, girl, you're too curious for your own good, aren't you? I'm expected in the village. A meeting has been called."

"Take me with you."

"Such affairs are not for young ladies. You would find yourself quickly bored. You should rest. I'll send Elizabeth in with something to help you relax."

With that, he turned—turned a little too hastily she thought—and left the room, the sound of his footsteps receding down the hall.

Bored? she thought. She would have gladly suffered a little boredom surrounded by the stodgy old town council if it meant getting out of the house, even for just a little while.

Once more, she looked towards the window, took a step towards it, then turned away, steeling her courage. She did not have to look. She had seen the evidence in her husband's eyes, heard the truth in his voice.

The headstones were moving closer. She was sure of it.

But for what purpose?

* * *

Matthew's cane clicked upon the cobblestones as he moved along the street, holding his topcoat at the collar to keep out the evening breeze. A light mist clung to the air, and a chill wind swept past. There would be a heavy fog tonight, he realized, and winter would quickly set upon the village in the coming days.

Behind him, his house overlooked the village to the east, much as it overlooked the cemetery to the west. Along the street, the shops were closed, the shopkeepers having locked their doors at sunset. Some of the apartments above the shops were lit, and he noted more than one set of drapes being slowly drawn closed at his passing.

What had happened here? He wondered. Once, the townsfolk had greeted him warmly as he passed. Now, they shunned him, even feared him, and for what reason?

The stones. They blamed him for the stones.

And were they not just in the accusation? Possibly, but they had to understand there was no other choice, not for him, and he would set things right if they only gave him time, even if it took all of his power to do so.

He thought of Meagan and his spirits warmed a little. Ten years his junior and already his wife was more stubborn than he. Perhaps he should tell her the truth. Perhaps she was ready. But not yet. When she was stronger.

Ahead, he saw the town hall, and through the tall stained glass windows he saw the movement of many figures. Even as he climbed the steps he could hear the murmur of conversation through the doors. It would be a crowded meeting. He had known it would be. Drawing a deep breath of the damp air, he pushed open the door.

Indeed, a large crowd of men had gathered, and they turned their attention toward Matthew as he entered.

Several men—Tarkin and McAllister and Owensmith among them—gathered around a table, deep in heated conversation. Tarkin leaned with both hands braced against the table, McAllister shifted uncomfortably in a wooden chair, and Owensmith shook his head vigorously as he argued his point. They looked up as Matthew approached.

"And there he is," Tarkin said, loudly, showing off for the crowd. "The man of the hour. And here we were beginning to wonder if you would bother to come at all."

"Stay yourself, sir." He nodded towards the large clock upon the wall. The pendulum clicked back and forth. "It is not yet meeting time, and I have never been absent from this council. Besides, I doubt that you could start this gathering without me."

"Quite so," said McAllister. He smiled, always the gentlemen. "But now we are all here. I feel certain that everyone willing to brave the night air is here already. I see no reason why we cannot get started."

Matthew nodded.

Never one to hesitate, Tarkin set in immediately. "The stones, they continue to draw closer to the village and, despite your promises to the contrary, you have done nothing about it. How long will you continue to deny this problem?"

"I deny nothing."

"We are . . . concerned," McAllister said. "Of course, you understand."

"Of course. You have every right to be concerned. I am concerned about the stones, as are all of you good people. Yet I tell you, do not let panic best you. I am working on turning the stones back. You must give me time."

"There is no time!" Tarkin jumped to his feet. "The stones are almost upon us as we speak." He turned to the crowd. "What will happen when they reach the village?"

This brought frantic whispers from the townsfolk.

"Calm yourselves." Matthew raised his hands to them. "You all know that I have never failed you. Mr. Forsyth—" He pointed to a man in the crowd. "—when your crops would not grow, didn't I purge the blight from them? And Mr. Rothchild—" He motioned to another grim-faced man. "—when your son lost his sight, didn't I restore it? You must believe me. I will find a way to turn the stones back."

"You already know the way," said Owensmith, that and nothing more.

Matthew turned. "That . . . is not an option."

"Do you presume to speak for the entire village?" Tarkin asked. A smile crawled across his face. He was trying to lure him into a trap.

"In this—" Matthew's voice dripped venom. "—I am the only authority."

An undercurrent of threat flowed with Matthew's words, and the smile faltered upon Tarkin's lips. Again, whispers danced through the crowd, now tinged with fear.

"This is something you cannot possibly understand." Having heard enough from the council, he made ready to leave. "I will solve this dilemma in my own way."

With that, he turned, striding out of the hall and into the night.

Had he waited, he would have heard McAllister ask, "What if he cannot do what he claims?"

And he would have heard Tarkin answer, "It has already been dealt with."

* * *

As soon as he stepped inside, Matthew realized that something was terribly wrong. He sensed it in the stillness, the darkness, of the house, the way the shadows slithered along the smooth plaster walls.

"Meagan?" he called out, but received no answer.

He tossed his coat and cane aside and strode through the house. Racing up the creaking stairs, he threw open the bedchamber door and found the room empty, the bedclothes undisturbed.

Where was she?

He called her name once more, and felt dread uncurl in his stomach when, yet again, he received no answer.

After a moment's hesitation, he dashed to the study, certain he would find her there, staring out the window, fixated on the stones.

78

He should tell her.

But the study was empty, although the green curtains were drawn open. A tray of uneaten food and a full bottle of wine from the cellar sat upon the desk. On the floor lay a piece of folded vellum.

As he grabbed the note from the floor and unfolded it, he felt a presence behind him. He turned expectantly.

"Meagan—"

Grayson, his aging manservant stood in the doorway, his shoulders slumped, his face ashen and grim.

"What is it?" Matthew asked.

"Sir, I am sorry." His voice quivered as he spoke, afraid of the anger he might provoke. "I am only an old man. I could not stop her."

"What is it? What has happened?"

Grayson swept a strand of white hair from his eyes. "I did not know she would be given the note, sir. You must believe me. I did not know what Elizabeth was about."

* * *

In her darkened quarters, a young maid curled into a ball upon a simple bed and wept at her own treachery.

* * *

Cold sweat beaded upon Matthew's forehead as he unfolded the note. His fingers trembled. It took all of his willpower to force his eyes towards the page. He might have guessed what the delicate handwriting said before he ever read a word.

They are coming for you.

With an anguished cry, he threw the note aside. He turned and pushed open the window.

Down the hill, he saw her, his darling Meagan, descending through the fog towards the grave markers. Her gown, the color of mist, flowed over the ground.

He leaned upon the windowsill, calling her name.

* * *

In town, councilman Tarkin woke screaming from a dream of an innocent girl, a girl vanishing into the night like . . . .

Like smoke.

His wife, in bed beside him, stirred.

"You have doubts, don't you?" she asked. "Doubts that you did what was right."

Tarkin shuddered as the memory of the dream faded. "I did what had to be done. The stones were coming for what he took from them."

He settled back down, staring out the window.

Fog swirled slowly outside. Winter would come early this year.

* * *

Whether or not she heard her husband's cry, no one would ever be sure. But Meagan looked back over her shoulder and smiled sadly before continuing her journey amongst the stones, becoming one with the mist, and vanishing into the shadow.

Within a week, the stones had returned to their original location.

"Creeping Stones" was originally published on Horrorfind.com (2003).

This is definitely a dark fantasy yarn more than a horror tale (if there is really a difference). I used to live across the street from a very old cemetery, and I'd often have nightmares about the stones moving closer and closer to the apartment complex while I slept. The last time I checked, the apartment complex had been leveled, but the cemetery was still there. By now, the graveyard might have expanded into the lot previously occupied by the apartment building. In that way, life might imitate art.

- CB

TOMORROW, WHEN THE DEMONS COME

"What we do today doesn't matter," Marco said, the preamble to a mantra I had heard time and time again. "Nothing matters. For tomorrow, the demons come."

"Don't tell me that." I tried not to let pain show in my voice. "I don't want to hear that. I don't believe it . . . and neither do you."

A smile played across his lips. He looked at his hands for a few seconds, and the smile slipped away, leaving in its wake a hint of disgust. Disgust at me? I wondered, pathetically, hating myself for feeling so doubtful and weak, like a schoolboy in the thrall of a crush. Or was he disgusted with himself? He pressed his palms against his chest. Wiping his hands on his tee shirt, he pulled the wash-worn fabric tight against the muscles of his chest and stomach. Crimson patterns stained the shirt at the passing of his fingers, the bloody outline of his hands smeared down his belly, melting towards his crotch.

"Is that it?" I asked. "Is that all you have to say to me?"

Still, he ignored me, tilting his head curiously from side to side as he examined the blood on his shirt and the pinkish discoloration of his hands, the bright veins of red running through the creases of his flesh.

"How do you do it?" I pleaded.

The smile returned, and he looked up, held me in place with his stare.

"Is it that important to you?" His voice was little more than a whisper. "Do you really need to know my every secret? Do you really want to know how it is that I live with myself?"

A snake of fear uncoiled in my belly. He was turning my own words against me, taking my curiosity and twisting it into something sad and pitiful, needy and obsessive.

He reached out for my cheek, and I jumped at his touch. I had barely noticed him move across the room. His fingers seared my skin. The smell of his body—rich and meaty and delicious—washed over me. I turned my mouth towards his hand, but he pulled away.

"You don't want to know everything, now do you? Where's the fun in that?"

I blinked, unable to speak. He had drugged me, poisoned me with his touch, with the memory of his past caresses, with the promise of more to come.

I shook my head. "No."

"Good." He turned from me, walked across the room and shrugged his scuffed leather jacket on over his bloodied tee shirt. He looked over his shoulder at me as he pulled open the door. What might have been love, or perhaps triumph, gleamed in his eyes. "I'm going out for a while. I'll be back before long, but don't wait up for me. Go to sleep."

And he was gone.

I rushed to the window, hoping to get some hint of his destination. He moved along the sidewalk, hunched over to fight back the chill night air, but still somehow graceful. Frosty breath plumed in small clouds around his head. He seemed to be talking to himself, maybe bitching about me—

Stop it, I told myself. Don't think like that. Ever.

Marco turned a corner and vanished into shadow.

He would not be back for several hours. I was alone. I paced about the creaking, unkempt house for a while, trying to keep my mind occupied, but tormented by the anger and doubt and confusion spinning in my head. My thoughts drifted again and again back to Marco.

And to the locked room.

Marco owned a massive, decaying house downtown, the kind of house that a "working class Joe" might dream of one day restoring but would never be able to afford to renovate. But Marco's parents had left it to him when they died, along with enough money that their son would never need to hold down anything so banal as a steady job. I lived with him in the house. I had complete run of the place, except for a single locked room upstairs. That chamber was forever denied to me. At times I wanted to enter, even though I knew very well that Marco would have hated me for it.

Finally—thankfully—exhaustion overcame me, and I crawled into bed, pulling the silk sheets around my body, drifting to sleep surrounded by the scent of Marco's sweat.

* * *

"Nothing matters. For tomorrow, the demons come."

I always assumed the phrase was nothing more than a way to shut me up, or a contrived defense or justification for the things he did to people. Not to me, mind you. He never hurt me, not physically, not intentionally. I was one of the lucky few he allowed to share his life. There had been a half dozen or so in the years before he met me, and I never considered what had happened to them, how it came to pass that they stepped aside to make room for me. Perhaps Marco simply grew tired of them, the way he would eventually grow tired of my company. Perhaps they had each in turn were lead to the locked room.

I remember the night I met him. I was twenty-three years old, little more than a frightened boy—shy and unaware. He was beautiful and pale, his blonde hair teased into spikes, an oversized white dress shirt hanging from his lean frame. He seduced me with his jaded eyes and gentle touch—me, virgin territory to him. His every word spoke of thrills and dangers. He was charming and cunning and wise, and he captured me, enslaved my imagination.

To say he ravaged me wouldn't be completely true, but it wouldn't be a lie either. He ravaged everyone. Everyone he spoke to, everyone he glanced at across a smoke-filled room, everyone he brushed up against on the metro. He ravaged them all in some way, men and women, gay and straight. He tore into their minds, their thoughts, their dreams, and left little pieces of himself, shrapnel memories of his passing, behind to taunt them.

God, I hated him, but I loved him, too.

He made love to me. He brought me to heights of pleasure I had not known before, and I gladly followed him into depths of depravity unlike anything I had ever seen or heard or felt. He went down on me in public places, movie theaters, bus stops, and dance clubs. He held me close and read poetry to me from dog-eared paperbacks as he fucked me.

He told me fairy tales.

Late at night, when outside the sirens shrieked and gunshots echoed along seldom-traveled streets, he pulled me against the heat of his body and told me such beautiful stories, tales of creatures personifying twisted human emotion. Greed, with his many grabbing hands; Love, whose beauty was so terrible that she drove those who looked upon her mad; Lust, with wiggling tongues sprouting from his mouth, nostrils, eyes, and ears. And Jealousy—how I loathed her—clad in tangled, living vines, torturing her victims with their own imaginations. All these creatures had a place in his stories. He shared the tales with me in the same way a parent might tell a bedtime story to a restless child.

We drank too much, got stoned. We sipped Absinthe and shot Jack Daniels, depending on our moods and the day of the week. We pushed ourselves to the limits of alcohol poisoning and held each other when we were trembling and sick. We smoked weed and dropped acid and shot up, and together we expanded our thoughts, our horizons . . . or maybe we only succeeded in dulling our senses, even for a little while. The end results didn't matter. They were all the same to Marco.

We shared lovers—men, women, girls, or young boys. Nothing as base as gender mattered in Marco's bed, where the scent of rose petals clung to the air and every sensation was of heat and pleasure and longing.

But when we were done, he always sent me away. This was the unspoken rule between us. He did not need to tell me to leave, but his eyes commanded me. I would wander from the room, and he would take our lovers away, take them to the locked room, and there the screaming would start.

He wouldn't let me watch. I was forbidden to enter. I suppose that's how I knew that he loved me.

"You don't want to find out if you have the stomach for this," he once said. "You don't ever want to know."

So I lurked outside the door sometimes and listened and jacked off and when I grew weary of the screams I retired back to bed or crashed on the soiled living room couch. Sometimes I stayed awake long enough to hear the screams change to cries of delight or pleas for help or gurgling sobbing. Sometimes, listening to Marco's playthings, I used a razor to scratch spiraled patterns into the flesh at the back of my hand, letting the blood bead along the tiny white trails of torn skin.

Often, that bitch Jealousy appeared to tease me, bringing her tongue close to my wounds, but never quite suckling the blood away before turning and laughing and dancing into the ether.

Afterwards, Marco would emerge from the locked room, covered in blood, out of breath, and carrying himself as if a burden had been heaped upon his shoulders.

He would leave then, storming out into the night, only to return sometime later. When he returned, his mood was almost always brighter, some might even say cheery. It was unsettling and frustrating. Where did he go and what happened to affect him so? I never asked, no matter how bad I wanted to, and he never volunteered the information.

There were times when I wanted to leave him. Once, while watching the evening news, I saw a picture of a young boy that Marco had brought home flash across the screen, and I considered calling the police. But as afraid as I was of Marco's depravity and the things he did behind the door to the locked room, I was more afraid of losing him.

It turned my stomach, but I started to look forward to visits from new lovers. For months, Marco would bring no one, then he would bring someone new each night for a week, a new and different taste or texture to enjoy, a new cry in the night. That I know of, Marco used no criteria other than a moment of whim in choosing who he would bring home, and I worried that he might one night bring home someone who he shouldn't, someone who might hurt one or both of us.

Sometimes, he would call to me from upstairs, and I would find him standing outside the locked room, a bundle wrapped in garbage bags and packing tape at his feet. Together, we would drag the body downstairs and out to the car, stashing it in the trunk. We'd drive out to the landfill and dump the body, all the while talking about books or music or something equally pointless. Once the body was abandoned to the waste, Marco did not mention them again.

* * *

This was our life for the two years I lived with Marco. We lived and loved and reveled in our own depravity. We might have gone on like that forever—I was beginning to think that Marco might very well live forever, and I would have lived with him. But sooner or later, everyone falters, everyone stumbles.

I stumbled late one autumn afternoon. I was not lured by the embrace of another. Marco and the strays he brought home were more than enough to satisfy my sexual appetite. But my curiosity, especially when it came to the secrets of the locked room, got the better of me.

Marco was out, I assumed buying cigarettes and booze, maybe trolling for an evening's pleasure, and I found myself standing at the door to the locked room. I allowed my eyes to creep over the door, noting every imperfection of the wood, every nick and scratch, the way the door hung just a few centimeters crooked in the frame. I imagined that the other side was scoured with scars left behind by clawing, desperate fingernails. Sweat beaded on my upper lip. I wiped it away, licked it from my fingertips as I considered the contents of the room beyond. I believed myself ready for whatever I might find, for whatever horror or god or devil awaited in the room. Nothing I found would change my feelings toward Marco. I belonged to him completely, but I needed to know everything about him, and only two secrets eluded me—the contents of the locked room, and the purpose and destination of his journeys in the early mornings following his activities in the chamber that waited for me to enter it like a lover.

My hand strayed to the doorknob. What would be the harm in testing it? I knew it was sealed, but the thrill of doing something forbidden tempted me.

My fingers brushed the cold metal knob.

My palm closed around it.

Ever so slightly, I turned—

"What are you doing?"

Marco's voice startled me, and I spun around. He stood in the hallway, watching me. He drew a long breath from one of his cigarettes. The scent of cloves hung around him like a halo. The hollows of his cheeks and the dark circles beneath his eyes made him look like something dead.

"I—I was—"

He didn't wait to hear my explanation. He only shook his head and walked away.

"Marco, wait."

He did not face me, but only raised a hand to silence my protests.

I didn't follow. I didn't try to further explain my indiscretion. A dreadful assurance filled my heart.

Marco would be leaving me.

I knew then and there that I had one chance, just one chance to prove my worth to him—or maybe I needed to prove it to myself.

* * *

I found her at the Skin Trade, a trendy little bar on the landing, one of those places where yuppies go when they want to get a taste of the darker side of life. College kids in Polo shirts and Dockers crowded around a chain-link protected stage to stare at a bad Marilyn Manson cover band.

Her name was Kimmy. At least, that's the name she gave me. She was gorgeous—thin, pale, blonde—and there was an air of innocence about her. Marco would like that. She couldn't have been more than 20, but her fake ID had served her well, and she was well on her way to being totally trashed by the time I approached her. She had watched me from across the bar, and I used the veil of smoke between us to hide the mixture of lust and venom in my eyes. She was talking to some guy, a wannabe goth in black jeans and mascara, dancing with him occasionally, but all the while her bleary eyes returned to me as I slouched against the bar, knocking back shots of vodka, waiting, biding my time. When her companion staggered off to the john, I approached her. She looked me up and down, and a pouty smile formed on her lips. I stepped in close, leaning on the table and whispering in her ear.

"That your boyfriend?" I asked, but the words were not my own. I recognized a chilling familiarity in my voice, and the question was whispered in just the right tone to coax the answer I wanted.

"He's an ass," she said, matter-of-factly, shrugging and wrinkling her nose as if the thought of him was distasteful.

"You didn't answer my question."

She shrugged.

"Do you want to get out of here?" Again, the words were not mine, but this time I recognized the phrasing. I sounded like Marco. For a second, this realization shocked me, and doubt welled up inside me. Quickly I tried to grasp what it was that I had lost. I grabbed her hand—gently. "Well, do you?"

She nodded, meekly, but her hand tightened in mine, and I pulled her away from the table. As we pushed our way through the crowd, she looked back, once, and maybe she caught a glimpse of her boyfriend.

It was the last she would ever see of him.

She was indeed twenty, an art major, but taking a semester or two off to earn a little extra money by working full time at a floral shop. This she told me as we took a cab back to the house, all the while the cabby, a dark-skinned man with darting eyes and shaky hands, watched her in the rear-view mirror. Kimmy dreamed of one day working as a commercial artist for ad agencies. She had grown up in a small town, and she wanted to make her parents proud, she wanted to one day have a family of her own, and she hoped that she hadn't hurt Nick, her date for the evening, too badly. Most importantly, she wanted me to know that she had never, ever done anything like this before, and I believed her.

I, on the other hand, only wanted her to be quiet. I did not need to hear about her life. I did not want to. For a second, as I listened to her tell me about her roommate, a dear girl named Stephie, I looked out the car window and saw Doubt, the filthy thin beggar, panhandling along the sidewalk. I placed my hand upon her leg. Her skin was cool and smooth. The cabby craned his neck to see if I was copping a feel up her skirt.

"Shhhh," I whispered. My voice was heavy. "We'll be there soon."

She remained silent for the rest of the ride.

When we walked into the house, and she saw Marco lounging on the couch, she tensed and shot a glance at me. He was stretched out, reading from his tattered copy of Byron, sipping from a glass of dark wine.

"Kimmy," I said, "I want you to meet a friend of mine."

I saw a hint of surprise on his face. He was impressed with me, I could tell. He pursed his lips and tossed the book onto the coffee table. He rose and crossed the room like a ghost, extending his hand to Kimmy. She shivered but offered him her own, which he kissed, ever so lightly.

"Can I get you something to drink?" he asked.

And she was ours.

Later, we gathered in Marco's bedroom, his silken sheets slick with our sweat. Marco knelt at the head of the bed, his perfect body shimmering in the candlelight. He cradled Kimmy's head in his lap, and she grasped handfuls of the sheets and looked up at him through a haze of passion as I wrapped my arms around her thighs and kissed and licked at the warmth between her legs. She gasped and cried out and moaned, and I crawled up her body, thrusting into her. All the while, Marco held her head forcing her to gaze up at him, and he asked over and over.

"Is this love? Is this love?"

I wasn't sure if he was asking her or me, but I saw the way she looked up at him, the way she reached up to touch his face, and I knew that her trembling and whimpering was for him—him!

That bitch Jealousy tittered at me from the corner of the room.

I shoved into her, faster now, wanting to hurt her, and my own sweat ran into my eyes, blinding me. Kimmy begged for more, wailed with increased pleasure. I looked to Marco, but his face was a twisted blur.

"Is this love?" he asked.

When we were done, the three of us lie coiled around one another, still, panting, the closeness of our bodies warming us in the cool night air.

"She's asleep," Marco said.

I was nearly asleep myself, but his voice roused me.

"It's time for you to go," he said to me.

I sat up. "No. Wait. I thought—"

He silenced me with a kiss, leaning across Kimmy's body to press his lips against mine. When he pulled away, he said, "go."

I could hear her—Jealousy—lurking in the shadows, giggling.

"No. I . . . I want to go with you . . . with her . . . to the locked room."

"I've told you before," Marco said. "That's not allowed."

He touched Kimmy's porcelain cheek. She sighed softly and stirred in her sleep.

"Marco," I said, "please. Just this once."

He looked up at me and muttered, "I said, go!" with such venom that I could only stagger off the bed and out of the room.

Never had I heard such sweet passion . . . or such horrid torment . . . as I heard from the locked room that night.

When silence had once again shrouded the house, I lay upon the couch with my eyes closed, pretending to be lost in blissful sleep. But as I heard Marco come out of the room, gather his jacket, and leave through the front door, I jumped up, threw on a pair of jeans, a tee shirt, and leather boots, and followed.

I kept my distance, stayed just close enough that I wouldn't lose sight of him. He walked past packs of people staggering out of bars, passed hooting whores and brightly lit peep show windows. He did not stop, did not even look up, until he reached a small, poorly lit storefront.

The sign out front was written in bold Korean lettering, and I could not make it out. The windows were dark, painted on the inside and dirty. My reflection twisted in the glass. The buildings on either side were dark and deserted, the doors and windows boarded up. Shadows poured off the derelict buildings and flooded toward the storefront, only barely beaten back by the single bare bulb that fizzled near the door.

Marco stepped inside.

I waited for a few seconds, steeled my courage, and followed him.

The interior room was bathed in a dim red light. Almost suffocating heat clung to the air. I saw no sign of Marco, but an elderly Korean woman waited for me behind the counter. She beckoned, and as I stepped towards her, she smiled and asked in broken English, "Wash your troubles away?"

"I followed someone here."

"Wash your troubles away, yes? Twenty dollars." She pointed to a doorway covered by a beaded curtain. Beyond, a cloud of steam writhed.

I put my money on the table. The woman smiled and pointed to the doorway again while sliding the crumpled twenty off the counter and into her pocket.

I stepped through the curtains.

A heavy wave of heat rolled over me. Before me lay row after row of shallow, steaming pools of water. Buckets and towels were lined up along the far wall. The pools were all empty, save for the last. Through the vapor, I saw Marco, naked, basking in the steaming bath with his back to me.

I stepped closer, intending to speak, intending to reveal myself, but as I did, I noticed something strange about the water in which he lay.

Images seemed to dance through the water.

Here was a reflection of Kimmy, screaming, slashes across her once-beautiful face.

This was quickly washed away and replaced by the image of my own face, crying out in passion.

Then, a young boy, crying for his mother, purple bruises over his frail body.

I looked to Marco, who was asleep or in a kind of trance, then back at the images roiling in the pool.

Another young man, weeping and mewling as Marco led him to the locked room.

Suddenly, I realized how Marco lived with himself, lived with the atrocities he inflicted, because somehow the bath was washing away his shame, washing away his remorse, washing away his inhumanity.

Marco stirred, on the verge of waking. I stepped away from him, hoping the shadows and the steam might hide me. He emerged from the bath, the last of his guilt dripping off his body and forming strange, rippling images in the pool. Did he see me? I could not be sure. Nor did I care. The bath held my fascination now.

I glanced at the doorway. The beaded curtain swayed gently, the strands clicking against one another. I saw no other sign of Marco.

I was alone, save for the quickly changing images lapping at the tiled sides of the bath.

Trembling with excitement, I disrobed. I stood above the pool and watched memory after memory play itself out upon the water's surface, but the images vanished so quickly.

I slipped a toe into the bath. The water was warm, soothing.

I checked the door once more. I couldn't believe that Marco had failed to see me. But if he had spotted me, he did not return.

Shuddering, I slipped down into Marco's bath. Every part of him washed over me. I bit my tongue to avoid crying out at the feeling of ecstasy. Tears ran down my face as Marco's memories invaded my pores.

I ducked my head beneath the surface and drank, drank it all in, drank all of Marco into me, every part of him. I drank more of that steaming water than was humanly possible, gulping down all the evil, terrible thoughts that Marco had washed away. I drank it down, lapped it up, like a lover's juices, and the bitterness of it intoxicated me.

Finally, having drank my fill, I passed out.

I am not sure how long I lay unconscious in the bath. It seemed an eternity, an eternity plagued by dreams—no, nightmares—that were not mine. I lay there for at least a day, quite possibly more, and when I awoke I found myself in a different room. I lay upon a cold stone slab. My back stung, feeling raw, as if I had writhed against the rough stone during my fitful sleep. A gauzy shroud covered me; it felt like a spider's web as I pulled it away.

Who had brought me here?

At the foot of the slab, I found my clothes, neatly folded. I dressed quickly.

I staggered weakly from the bathhouse. The old Korean woman was not to be found. The place was empty, the pools drained. It looked as if the place was closed, or as if it had never been opened at all.

It was early, the sun only just starting about the task of burning the night's fog away. The city was only now waking, and I passed only one person on the walk home.

A young black man, he did not look up as he passed. He walked quickly, his hands shoved into his jacket pocket. I detected Marco's meaty smell, and the coppery tang of blood, clinging to him.

I turned as he walked past, and the hair at the back of my neck stood on end. I quickened my pace. By the time I reached the house I was almost out of breath from running.

When I entered the house, the smell of blood was even stronger. I rushed upstairs, to the bedroom, where I found Marco.

He was naked and pale—oh, so pale—and he lay upon his silk sheets stained crimson. His throat had been slashed open, and it looked as if his head might fall off if I so much as touched his body.

As I had feared, he had brought the wrong person home to play.

Had Marco seen me in the bathhouse?

Surely, he must have.

And he had brought this man home, perhaps at the urging of a green robed whore.

I fell to my knees.

This could not be happening. I would not lose him, not now that I understood him so well, so much better than he understood himself.

I don't know what brought me to do what I did then. Perhaps it was some dark urging from the thoughts and dreams and fears that I had consumed.

I rammed my fingers down my throat.

I gagged, and stomach acid flooded my mouth, and I wanted to scream as I felt something tear at my insides and claw its way out of my stomach, up my throat. It felt as if it might rip me open, and chunks of flesh—maybe my own, torn away from my stomach lining, maybe something else—spilled from my lips, spattering the floor. I wretched and choked and wretched again, and the vile stream poured from my mouth, as my body emptied itself of Marco's memories.

I couldn't look, couldn't turn my eyes towards the putrid thing that must have

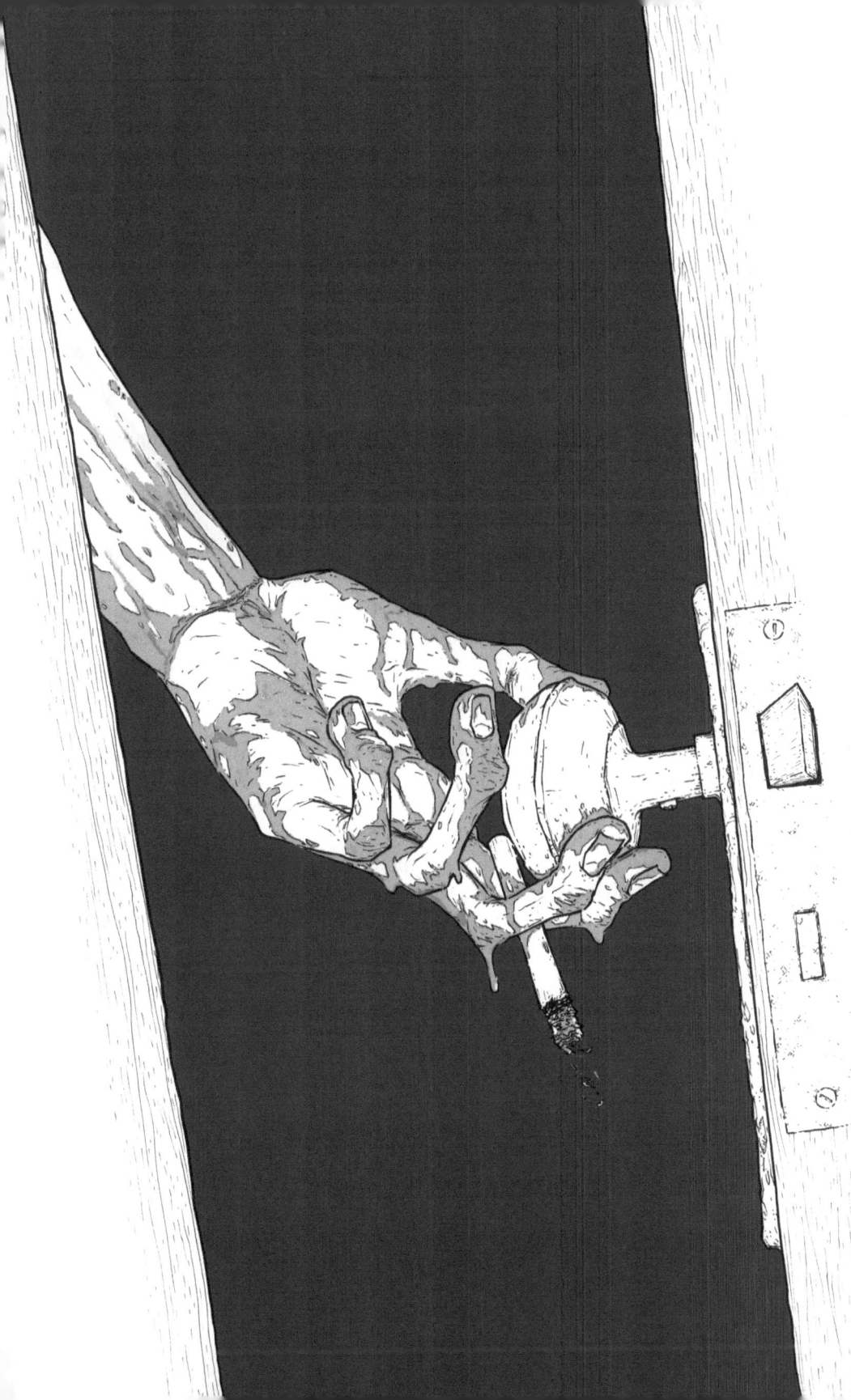

lain beside me. I squeezed my eyes shut, and tears blazed hot trails down my cheeks. My throat burned, and acid tingled in the back of my mouth. The smell—God the smell—was sickening, a mixture of vomit and rose petals and Marco's meaty stink. I could not look, but I heard something moving, something flailing about painfully on the hardwood floor, and soon enough a rattling, raspy breath, an inhuman gasp. And it cried out, this thing lurking beside me, this thing I had brought into the world but—like a shamed mother—could not look upon, and its cry was that of an infant, an infant born of washed away sin, and it was the most unnatural sound I have ever heard.

I could not look.

I staggered to my feet, all the while turning my head from the whipping, spindly thing, lying in a pool of bile. My stomach felt as if it had been ripped inside out. My chest felt as if my ribs might snap through my skin, tear open my heart. I was distantly aware that I had pissed myself, and warmth spread down my legs. Bracing myself along the wall, I stumbled down the hall, to the locked room. My fingers closed upon the dented, brassy handle. I turned the knob.

A dry laugh caught in my throat. The door had never been locked at all.

I only barely crossed the threshold before collapsing, crashing to the bare floor, grunting like an animal as I pulled myself into this room that had been denied to me for so long.

Darkness enshrouded me.

I thought, in those last few seconds before I lost consciousness, that I saw Jealousy and Fear and Exile watching me from the shadows, but they were not real, they were only figments of my imagination, and save for these phantoms the room was empty.

From the hallway, I heard the wet flapping of bare feet against the hardwood floor, but I did not have the strength to turn.

I closed my eyes.

And waited for the demon to come.

"Tomorrow, When the Demons Come" was originally published in
LIKE A CHINESE TATTOO (2007).

This story marked a distinct change in my approach to short fiction. It's darker, meaner, and weirder than a lot of the stories that came before it. It, along with "Remains", is one of my favorite short stories in this collection. This story started with the main character, Marco. He's not a character I wanted messing around inside my head for too long, so I quickly wrote this yarn to get him out of my skull and onto the page.

- CB

BENEATH BLACK BOUGHS MY DARLINGS SLUMBER

A lie, I believe, often proves more powerful than the truth. This story starts with a lie—a lie passed down in my family from generation to generation—but it ends, here, now, with the truth, and while a lie can be more powerful, the truth is almost always more frightening.

* * *

My name is Edward Porter. I have lived most of my life in Cove Point, a small village along the North Carolina seaboard. Seldom have I strayed far from its salty, sea-sprayed air, clouds of swooping and crying gulls, and churning tides.

Since the Cove is situated near Morehead City, Atlantic Beach, and Harker's Island, it is an ideal spot for a stopover during a tour of the Outer Banks, and the bed and breakfast trade is lucrative. During the warmer months, the Cove lures in tourists with its scenic beaches, boardwalk boutiques, and antique shops. Griffin's Calabash on Main has been recognized nationally as one of the best places to go if you have a taste for flounder and hushpuppies, and people have been known to drive for hours to dine there. Some local folk only grudgingly accept the tourist commerce, but it has never bothered me. I mind my own business, and I'm happy to take walks along the beach with my wife, take the boat out every now and then, and help my daughters search for shells in the sand.

I've always known that I belonged here . . . even after everything that happened.

In college, I discovered, quite by accident, my talent for spinning tales and putting them on paper. While taking a creative writing class, I penned my first stories centered around North Carolina folklore that my father shared with me at bedtime and ghost stories children told around crackling campfires— legends of the Maco light, the ship of fire, and the Devil's Tramping Ground. To my surprise, a few literary journals and small magazines started accepting my work.

I established something of a name for myself in the small press with my tales of spectral ships and confederate ghosts. After graduation, I moved my family to Cove Point, where I took a job covering local sporting events for the paper and wrote flowery articles for travel magazines in my spare time. In the evenings, after the girls had been put to bed and my wife had fallen asleep watching Letterman, I spent hours hunched over the word processor, hammering out new works of fiction. My stories started appearing in a few high-circulation magazines, and the exposure both opened new doors for me and fueled my creativity. I finished and sold my first novel, a thriller concerning legends of lost pirate treasure that met with some success. When my second novel, a ghost story concerning the lost colony of Roanoke Island, was published, I was able to move my family out of our cramped apartment and into a small but respectable house overlooking the beach.

My wife, Helen, adjusted quickly to life in a small town. She spent her time taking care of the girls and tending a struggling garden in the back yard. Helen and I met when we were both freshmen, when she had been a dedicated, ambitious architecture student. Our relationship yielded two daughters and a marriage for which neither of us had been prepared. I sometimes worried that we had started our family while we were both too young, that Helen had felt pressured into sacrificing her career. On occasion, I asked if she ever regretted her decision to marry me. She always smiled—a beautiful smile that my daughters had inherited—and said, "Not once."

By this time, of course, I had forgotten the lie and the events that had led to its telling. The mind will work to protect itself from the truth, shuffling memories into the subconscious or fogging the past as needed. Some fragment of the truth remained, I suppose, the stirring of which often woke me shuddering from nightmares.

I did not fully remember until the storm willed it.

* * *

The first squall of the season blew through in early May. From the house, I saw fishing boats bobbing up and down in the chopping water. Gulls, fighting against the rising winds, hovered against a backdrop of darkening clouds. Living in Cove Point, you learned to accept that storms sometime sweep in from the ocean without much warning. Modern technology had come a long way since the days when old-timers had predicted storms by spotting sundogs or analyzing the flight patterns of gulls, but every now and again, a squall slipped in virtually undetected and set up shop for a bit. This was a minor squall, though, and I convinced Helen to walk down to the beach with me to watch the storm blow in.

"What about the girls?" she asked.

"The girls will be fine." I took her hand and led her along the winding path that cut through the grass-covered dunes down to the beach. "We won't go far."

A cutting wind whipped past us, and I wrapped my arm around Helen and drew her close. Over the water, clouds tumbled and rolled over one another, changing colors from white to gray to deep indigo, like mixing paint. The waves whispered and sighed and grumbled as the water swelled in frothy crests and spilled over onto itself.

Helen leaned against me and said, "It's beautiful."

I barely heard her as I stared out over the water. The hiss of the waves crept into my thoughts, spoke to me in a furtive voice. Memories flooded my mind, suddenly, violently, and I stood, still, shocked, as all of it—the truth, the lie—came rushing back to me.

"Edward?" Helen tugged at my arm. "Are you all right?"

But I might as well have been a million miles away.

* * *

I was too young to remember when the storm took my mother. As a child, I could sometimes picture the way she looked, but only for a few seconds at a time, and the images would fade from my memory completely as I grew to adolescence.

I remembered my sister, though, and the night the storm came for her. I remembered the way the wind battered our tiny home, slapping against the windows, trying to tear the walls away, screeching as it sought to rip open the house to get at us. I remembered sitting up in bed, huddling with the covers pulled around me, watching as lightning streaked like white fire through the sky, washing the walls of my bedroom in a painful glow. I remembered jumping every time thunder boomed, rattling the walls. And, most of all, I remembered thinking that the storm was not an act of nature at all, but something like an animal, starving, angry, thrashing about and roaring for food.

Earlier that day, a policeman had come to the house. He wore a yellow slicker, and his hat, which he grabbed onto when a gust of wind threatened to take it, was wrapped in clear plastic and beaded with water. He greeted my father pleasantly—everyone knew each other in the Cove—but his smile was false, hiding worry, and behind him the sky looked as if it might rip open at any moment. He told my father that a hurricane was coming—a bad one—and they were asking people to leave the area, as the danger would be great. But my father only thanked the man for his concern and said, "We'll be staying here, I think."

Later, I asked him why we couldn't leave, why we couldn't seek shelter, and he told me only that, while he couldn't explain, one day I would understand.

"When you're older," he said. "When you're ready."

And so I lay awake that night, listening to the storm attack our home.

When my sister, in the next room, started screaming, I leapt from bed. The wind sounded like a freight train blaring through the house, but the sound of my sister's terror pierced my heart like a shard of ice. I might have stood, immobilized by fright, for several seconds, but when my quivering muscles started working, I ran towards her shouting. Before I took more than three steps, the door swung open, and I saw my father standing in the darkened hall, blocking my path. His face was a grim mask, and he pushed me back into the room, stepped inside, and closed the door.

I started to protest, but I knew he would have none of it. Another cry came from my sister's room, and I tried to force my way past my father, but he grabbed me and hurled me back, towards the bed.

"Let it pass, son," he said.

Another peal of thunder shook the house. Something swept past my window. I could not see it clearly—it moved so fast. Still my sister screamed.

"Daddy!" she cried. "Daddy help me!"

The entire house quaked on its frame, as if it might explode into splinters under the force of the storm.

"Help me!" my sister shrieked. "It's got me! Daddy, it's got me!"

Her pleas sent a shiver down my spine. My father sat beside me on the bed and put his arm around me. In the flash of the lightning, I saw tears in his eyes.

The next morning, my sister was gone.

After the storm took my sister, my father told me the lie, the same lie his father must have told him. Maybe he didn't intend to deceive me. Maybe he thought that he spoke the truth. More likely, though, the loss of his wife and daughter had stripped away his strength to break the cycle of deception that had entrapped my family for so long.

"I don't know why this happens to us," he told me, and as he spoke I thought he looked older—withered beyond his years. Perhaps it was the burden of the lie that weakened him so. "I don't expect you to understand, not yet anyway, but I want you to know that I've only done what I had to do, what every man in our family has had to do. It is the nature of our curse."

Curse. The word struck me.

"The others know about it, I suppose." My father looked down at his hands as he spoke, as if he was too full of shame to look me in the eye. "They have to know, don't they? The rest of the village, they know that when the storm passes, it takes our wives, our daughters . . . but they don't speak of it out of fear that the same thing might happen to them. What could they do anyway? They could no more fight this than we can."

"Why don't we move away?" I asked.

"If we flee, the storm would chase after us. It would only come farther inland until it caught us, and then it would take much more than its share. So much more. No, we wait here, as we always have. We give the storm what it wants from us, and it returns to wherever it came from."

96

And yet all of this was but the preamble to the lie.

That night, I found myself unable to sleep. I lay in bed, thinking of my father's story, jumping at the creak of the settling house, dreading the day that the storm would come to take my own wife, my own daughters. Suddenly, I found myself weeping for the loss of my sister. As I wiped stinging tears from my eyes, I heard movement outside my room, a shuffling. I rose from the bed and peered into the hall in time to see my father standing in the foyer, donning his coat and hat. Fear washed over me, as he opened the front door and stepped out into the night. I wondered if he, too, was leaving, never to return. I grabbed my shoes, tugged them onto my bare feet, and followed him.

He walked slowly, with his shoulders stooped, and I followed. The road curled blackly through the hills and sparse woods. He led me to a spot beyond the dunes, where the forest grew thick and the scent of pine was heavy. High school kids sometimes came out to the woods to get drunk or high, and they told stories of ghosts haunting the woods, dead pirates seeking lost treasure, confederate soldiers whose wounds had cost them their lives. Shadows loomed over me, and I felt as if those ghosts were staring down at me, waiting for the right moment to snatch me up.

After a while, I saw a light shining through the trees up ahead, and I ducked down as my father strode towards the glow. I approached carefully, trying not to make a sound, because I knew that if my father caught me spying on him, he would be angry enough to frighten even the forest ghosts away.

In a clearing I saw a small shack that looked as if it might fall in upon itself at any minute. I wondered how such a building could survive a storm like had blown through. A light flickered through a small window beside the front door. I could see the shadow of movement inside, and, without so much as knocking, my father threw open the door and entered.

After several minutes, I crept closer. Sneaking to the dirty window, I peered inside. I saw my father speaking to a woman. How beautiful she was with her dark skin, dark eyes, dark hair. They talked for some time. I couldn't make out the words, but I could tell that while the woman remained calm, my father spoke excitedly, almost yelling at times. I thought more than once that he might hit her. And then, the argument stopped. The woman smirked at him, placing a hand upon her hip as she muttered something. My father seemed to grow tired, weak and slouched, as if he had lost the will to fight. He stepped towards the woman, embraced her, started kissing her mouth and pawing at her.

My stomach knotted in revulsion as I watched my father tear at her clothes, squeeze her body close to his own, but the look on his pale, sweaty face—

He looked as if he wanted to scream in terror.

And as he pushed her back against the wall, ripping open her blouse and kissing her breasts, she looked up, towards the window, and smiled at me.

I turned away from the shack and rushed home.

Much later, when my father returned, he opened my bedroom door and stood there, staring at me. In the shadows, I could not read his expression. His voice quivered, ever so slightly, as the lie crawled its way from his throat.

"It's over," he said. "The curse ends with me."

He never brought it up again, but sometimes he looked at me in the strangest way. I didn't recognize it then, but now I know that he was trying to judge if I believed him or not. The lie, I now realize, was too much for him to bear. The summer I turned eighteen, my father suffered a massive heart attack and died.

* * *

"Is everything all right?" Helen asked me one morning over breakfast.

"Everything's fine." I shrugged. "Why, shouldn't it be?"

"It's just that you've been acting strange. I don't know. Distracted."

"I'm sorry." I leaned back in my chair. A cool morning breeze flitted through the open window, playing with the gauzy curtains. "I've just been having a little trouble writing lately, that's all."

"Well—" she leaned close behind me and wrapped her arms around my neck— "I'm going to take the girls down to the beach. Want to come?"

"No. I better not. I'm just going to stick around. Try to write something."

"Your loss." She kissed my cheek and pulled away.

Smiling to myself, I finished breakfast, placed my dishes in the sink, and returned to my office. From my desk, I could see the rising dunes and the deep blue waters beyond—a distracting view that I couldn't really afford. I had wiled away hours watching the beach when I should have been writing, but the view was a luxury I endured.

I spent the next half hour trying to kick-start a story revolving around the Cape Lookout lighthouse and the ghosts that only appeared in the lonely beam of its light. Nothing seemed to come out the way I wanted, though, and eventually I shut down my word processor and spent several minutes absently browsing through my bookcases, thumbing through a few paperbacks, then putting them back.

The rekindled memories of the curse played in my mind. How could I have forgotten? Had my father ever really told me of such things? Or had it been only a dream? I could not be sure.

A knock at the front door startled me.

When I answered the door, a wave of strangeness washed over me, and I took a step back. The woman at the door looked exactly like the woman I had seen my father with so long ago—only it could not have been her, for she looked as if she had not aged a day.

"May I come in?" she asked, and she stepped inside, brushing against me, before I could answer.

"Who are you?" I asked.

"You know who I am." Her accent was heavy, high tide lurking behind her words. She strolled casually through the house, regarding the furniture, the pictures upon the wall, the knickknacks on the shelves.

"I'm afraid I don't—"

She turned towards me then, and her eyes held me in place. She stepped towards me.

Standing close.

I could smell her skin, her hair, and the faint clove scent of her breath.

She watched my mouth as she spoke.

"I've come to offer you a warning," she said. "The same warning I brought your father. The curse remains unbroken. What your father suffered, you will suffer now."

"I don't know what you're— "

She shook her head and touched a finger to my lips to shush me.

"You don't have to believe me. I didn't expect that you would. But you will." A smile curled her lips. "Soon enough."

She slipped away from me, and for a second, I wanted to reach out and draw her back.

"A storm comes," she said as she turned to the door. "Don't try to hide from it. Don't run."

I forced myself to look away from her body and glanced out the window. Down the beach, I saw Helen leading the kids back to the house.

"Don't worry," the woman said, looking over her shoulder. The smile still lingered upon her lips. "She'll never know I was here. And when you're ready, you know where to find me."

With that, she was gone.

And she was right. Helen never guessed that the woman had been there.

And I never told her.

* * *

That night, I woke from a dream of the woman's embrace. I jumped up in bed, gasping for air, the memory of her heated touch playing through my mind.

"What's wrong?" Helen asked drowsily. "Bad dream?"

I nodded.

She brought her hand to my bare chest. "Oh, you're burning up."

I grabbed her fingers, perhaps a little too forcefully. Helen gasped. I pressed her hand to my chest and she fell silent. I pulled her close.

What frightened me most was the certainty—the complete faith that the woman had, indeed, told the truth—and the serenity in knowing that this was my fate, the fate of my family, the fate that had clouded my memories and drew me back to the Cove.

* * *

The storm struck the next week, howling in over the waters to the east, offering no warning save for a slight change in the wind, a discordant clinking of the wind chimes. Clouds rolled across the sky out of nowhere.

Helen, who had been tending the garden in the back yard, rushed inside. "Have you looked outside?" she asked. "Has the weather report said anything about a storm?"

I shook my head and joined her at the door. Already, sheets of rain slapped against the screen. Lightning crashed down as a blackness, like nightfall, slid over the churning waters.

"It's a bad one, isn't it?" Helen asked.

"There would have been signs. Warnings. They would have detected it. Something."

Within minutes, the cloud fell over the house. The wind howled and battered the windows. Lightning whipped across the sky, snapping and crackling.

The lights flickered, failed.

The television—still no sign of a weather forecaster—buzzed and faded to silence.

The telephone popped as lightning struck the wires.

"Where did this come from?" Helen asked.

Glass shattered somewhere in the house.

Helen jumped, a hand to her chest, another question forming.

But I already knew the answer, even as I turned to run down the hall, even as my daughters started screaming.

"The girls!"

I threw open the door to their room. It was as if the storm raged within their room as well as outside. Water, blowing in from the shattered window, covered everything, and tendrils of mist clung to everything. Becky, our youngest, cowered in the corner, covering her face.

And at the shattered window—

Jessica, our oldest, clutched bleeding fingers to the frame, broken glass digging into the flesh, cutting her to the bone, as the wind pulled at her, trying to tear her from the room and out into the storm.

"Oh, God!" Behind me, Helen cried out. "Edward!"

I rushed across the room, slipping in the water and twisting my leg. I grabbed for Jessica's hands, but as I reached for her, she cried out and the wind seemed to snatch her away. She called to me as I watched her tumble through the air. She reached out for me, but was swallowed up into the swirling black maelstrom.

And just as quickly as my daughter vanished, the storm broke, and the sun pierced the clouds, leaving me wet, aching, sobbing, as I listened to the hysterical sobs of my wife and looked at my daughter's blood upon the broken window glass.

* * *

We never found Jessica. The sheriff's department scoured the area. Search parties comprised of friends and concerned neighbors roamed the beaches and the forests and the dunes. We spent hour after hour looking for her. I knew that she could not have survived the storm, not the way she was ripped from my hands and hurled into the sky, and I rounded every corner and crested every hill with dread welling in my stomach that I would find her torn and battered body, lying pale and damp and wide-eyed upon the ground.

I heard terms like "tragedy" and "a damn shame" and "freak accident" muttered by the other members of the search party. They could not bring themselves to look me in the eye. Authorities scrambled desperately to brand the event with a "rational explanation".

But I knew better. No natural storm strikes with such precision, shattering only one window, taking only one child, and doing little or no damage to the house or the surrounding area. No, I realized, and the woman's warning came back to me.

"A storm comes. Don't try to hide from it. Don't run."

Helen refused to believe that her daughter was gone. After she was done with her nearly hysterical tears, she joined the search in earnest, and she would not give up, refusing to give in to desperation, refusing to relinquish her fraught grasp of hope. When she realized that I had, on the other hand, stopped looking for Jessica, she asked simply "why?" My only response was a hollow eyed, helpless stare, a shrug, a useless and implausible answer refusing to escape my lips. She looked at me as if I had tossed our daughter into the storm myself. How could I explain to her that no amount of searching would ever find Jessica? Such a realization would have crushed her, and I would have gladly borne the weight of her accusatory glare to save her from that.

There was one person who could tell me what was going on.

Someone who might help.

* * *

She still lived in the tiny shack in the woods. She must have expected me, because she stood in the door as I approached. Walking towards her, I glanced to the window where, as a child, I had watched her seduce my father not long after my sister had vanished.

"I was expecting you sooner," she said, leaning against the door frame. The air was heavy, humid in the aftermath of the storm. Sweat beaded on my forehead. I rubbed my fingers nervously against my palms.

"What is this? What's happening?"

"You already know," she answered, that delicious smile curling the corners of her mouth again.

"Tell me," I said. "Tell me about curses."

"Come inside."

The tiny house was cluttered with bottles and jars, elixirs and powders. Rugs covered the rotten wooden floors. Candles dripped wax upon rickety furniture. The heavy scent of incense coiled sweetly in the air.

She stretched out in a wicker chair, smiling, watching me for several seconds before she spoke.

"You understand the curse that has befallen you?"

"I know what my father told me when I was a boy. He said it was over."

"I know what he told you. I told him the very words he would speak to you, every word, and every word a lie."

"I don't understand."

"Men name the storms that blow in from the ocean. They give them human names. But storms have names far older than man, and hungers and desires just as ancient. When man was young, sacrifices were made to the storms, lest they stretched over all the earth. The storm still requires its due, and it comes seeking its brides."

"How do you know this?"

"This is the story that the storm tells, but it does not speak with a human tongue. I am the voice of the storm."

"But why me? Why my family?"

She only shrugged.

"How do I stop it?"

"You cannot."

"But when they are gone, it's over."

"You think so? Your wife is with child, a man child. The storm will leave you that one, and you will tell him what your father told you."

"I won't"

Even as I denied her, she rose, crossing the room. My head spun, and I thought that perhaps I'd been drugged, drugged by the thick smoke dancing through the room, and then her mouth was upon mine, and I found myself returning her kiss, clutching at her, pulling her close, tight as if I feared she might slip away from me.

But even as I tasted her kisses, even as I felt her rip the buttons away from my shirt and my hands tore at her gauzy blouse, I muttered for answers, solutions to the curse, and I wanted to stop myself as my fingers, my hands, my mouth sought the heat of her flesh, and she did not answer save to draw her across my body and bite at me, drawing blood along my neck and chest, and her touch was searing flame. She dragged me down to the floor, pulling me on top of her, fumbling clumsily with my belt as I kicked off my shoes and pants. I lost my will to ask any more questions, and was only able to cry out at her touch and pant after her.

Only as she drew me into her did I realize her true form, and I thought back on the look of horror etched upon my father's face so long ago. I thrust into her, and her skin withered, grayed, flaked away in places to the bone, and her hair turned white as sea foam, and her cries of passion became rattling rasps as she drew me closer with twisted, curling nails, and I wanted to pull away, dear God, but I could not, could not stop until I found myself spent and sweaty and whimpering upon the floor.

"I-I won't," I stammered.

She laughed then. She had again taken her young, beautiful form, only now I saw it for what it truly was—a disguise pulled taught over old bones, and the knowledge made me want to throw up, especially when I felt a stab of desire when I looked upon her.

I forced my eyes to the floor, sat up.

"Tell me how to stop it."

She wrapped her arms around me. Her lips brushed my earlobe. "I cannot give you the answers you want."

"There has to be a way to stop this, to get my daughter back."

"You cannot."

I turned to her, pushing her back, grabbing her hands in mine. "Then tell me how to stop it."

"The price would be too great."

And I wanted to believe her. I felt her words coaxing trust from me, the way one might coax a frightened child out of hiding. I stepped towards her, pressing her against the wall. Then stopped, shaking the feeling away.

My hands grabbed at her, clenched her throat.

Squeezed.

I felt no anger, no hatred, only the need to break whatever hold she had on my willpower.

She clutched at me, scraped her nails at my eyes, spat at me to release her.

"Tell me," I said.

A dry laughing seeped from her lips. She kicked at me as the last of her strength drained from her legs. She slid down the wall.

"Tell me."

She must have realized that I intended to kill her if she did not answer me. Or perhaps she thought that revealing such secrets could not possibly do harm, as I would never be able to do what needed to be done.

So she told me.

In panting gasps for air she told me how to beat the storm.

Mocking me.

And still I squeezed, squeezed until her face was blue and her tongue protruded from her mouth, squeezed until whatever magic maintained her youthful appearance faded, and her face and arms and body aged before my eyes.

I choked her for several minutes after she stopped struggling, then realized what I had done and staggered back, dropping what looked like a mummified carcass to the floor.

For several seconds, my mind reeled at what I had done, what I had seen, what I had learned. I looked at my hands and told myself that the body lying at my feet had not been human—could not have been human.

Then, regaining my senses, I scrounged through the house for the things that I would need and fled back into the night, back to my family.

* * *

I mixed the ingredients just as the woman had instructed with her dying breath. I stirred the brackish liquid into my wife's tea, my daughter's soda, and watched them over dinner, smiling at their stories, touching my daughter's small hand, looking into my wife's eyes. I sat back, shivering and sweating, as I realized that the storm had finally been beaten, the curse broken, and I wanted to vomit.

The transition was the worst, setting on them like a sudden illness in the middle of the night. I lay awake, watching my wife sleep, seeing her stir fitfully, as if in a dream. My heart hammered in my chest. I could barely breathe. As the hours passed without any reaction, I wondered if the woman had tricked me in the end, gone to the grave with yet another lie on her lips—

Helen opened her eyes and screamed.

Startled, I jumped up in bed, taking her hand and squeezing, trying to comfort her as the drug took effect.

There was pain, yes, but I expected that—a necessary rite of passage. Helen cried out, writhed in the bed, dug her nails into the mattress, and clutched my hand so tightly that I thought she might break my fingers. Her eyes rolled back. She bit her tongue, and bloody spittle speckled her lips and chin. Her bones popped as she flailed about, and still I held her hand, held on tightly as her painful wails submitted to gurgling whimpers and her violent seizures gave way to sharp, quick spasms.

From her room down the hall, Becky screeched in pain.

In the end, as I carried them out into the night air, they were too weak, too wracked by agony, to even question my actions.

The entire process took less than three hours, and I watched it, every second, sitting on the back porch steps, tears rolling down my cheeks. Their skin darkened and grew coarse. Their bones popped and cracked and stretched to strange lengths. Their fingers curled and split, growing out in twisting formations. Their hair turned to sprigs and leaves. Their feet transformed into coiled runners, digging into the earth, taking root.

Where my wife and daughter had once been, rose two trees, each as dark as the night sky. The roots ran deep into the earth and the trunks were thick and strong. No storm, no matter how furious, would ever take them from me.

I laughed. I sobbed. I muttered to myself as I held my face in my hands and wept.

* * *

When next the storm came, only a few days later, it did so more cautiously, a subtle, gradual darkening of the sky, a slight shift in the wind, a few sporadic raindrops, as if it somehow sensed that something was amiss. The clouds hung low over my house, brooding, considering a plan of attack. I stumbled into the back yard, into the shadow of the black trees as the timid patter of the rain increased to a steady downpour and the whisper of the wind changed to a shrieking gale.

Stinging rain struck my face and soaked my clothes.

I cried out in defiance, letting the storm know that I had bested it, and it could rage all it wanted but could never take my family from me.

I heard the storm's anger, heard it in the thunder and the crash of the waves against the shore, and the howl of the wind . . . especially the wind.

Oh, God, the wind.

As the gust swept through the limbs of the black trees, it wailed . . . and, God help me, the wind took on the voice of my family as it passed the trees. I could hear my wife and daughter crying out in torment to me in rhythm with the storm.

I covered my ears, trying to block out the sound, and my own screams mimicked those of the black trees.

In the morning, I found myself cowering in the mud, clutching at my ears to drive the sound away. Even though the storm had passed, I still heard them, my wife and daughter crying out in anguish and fright. I staggered to my feet, rushed inside, and closed the door, but I could not block the sound.

And here I am, more frightened than ever of the storm's return.

Looking out the back door, I see the trees, peaceful in the morning calm. In the texture of the dark wood, I almost see the shape of my wife's face, my daughter's face, staring at me, questioning me. Water drips along the trunk like tears. Even though the air is still, the shrieking never stops, as if the wind continually whips through the branches.

I cannot shake the sound.

I never expected this, and the woman had never warned me.

I promised you the truth when I started this tale, and the truth is this—

I cannot say if it would have been better to let the storm take my family from me or not, for I know that another squall is waiting, just beyond the horizon. I know that I cannot bear the screams that I'll hear when the wind sweeps through the tree branches.

But I cannot leave, either, not after everything I've gone through to keep my family together.

I still have the recipe the woman gave me . . .

And there is time before the storm rushes back to try to take Helen and Becky.

And they are still calling for me . . . calling for me to join them.

"Beneath Black Boughs My Darlings Slumber" was originally published as a chapbook from Naked Snake Press (2007).

Once more, storms and abduction feature into this story. When I was a boy, we lived for a time near the beach, and when the bad storms would blow in, the family would walk down to the end of the street and watch the skies. Years later, I would learn that sometimes when those storms would blow in, other people – people who lived only a few streets away in some cases – would vanish altogether.

- CB

THE CALLER FROM THE VOID

He crossed the lake at midnight, slivers of moonlight dancing upon the black water. The temperature had dropped several degrees since the boat cast off, and he hunched over to shield himself from the spiteful cold. A grotesque mask concealed his features, for no man traveled this path willingly who was foolish enough to allow the sentinel that awaited to gaze upon his true face. His two guides, crouched at the bow of the ship, wore similar disguises, and they communicated with one another in an indecipherable sign language.

The boat sliced through the water without aid of oar or sail, drawn now, ever closer, to shores hidden beyond a shadowy veil of mist. The course was set, and he drew a solemn breath, accepting the finality of his decision to embark on this ...

Pilgrimage.

Questions spun through his mind, begging to be voiced, but he held his tongue. His guides had been mute since boarding the tiny vessel, and no answers could be expected from them. He only hoped that his patience would be rewarded.

Through the fog loomed a craggy mass of blackened earth. The boat, gliding so smoothly and silently across the lake's surface, came ashore with a jolt, the hull rasping across the dark, glittering stones carpeting the beach. Quickly, the guides leapt from the boat, splashing through the shallows as water soaked into their robes. Without word, they dragged the craft to shore and motioned for their passenger to disembark.

The beach stretched for perhaps 100 yards before giving way to a thick forest of ancient, twisted trees. No sign of civilization could be seen, and the beach was silent and still. Even the tide, lapping at the pebbled shore, produced little more than a slight hiss.

He felt as though his legs might buckle.

He had seen all of this before. He had painted every detail of the landscape he now beheld, even though he had never placed foot to soil in this place. He had explored the coastline, delved into the woodlands, and mapped the geography of the island when he brought brush to canvas. Time and time again, waking in the middle of the night, he had struggled to bring the island to life, working feverishly to paint this place—this place that did not exist, could not exist outside of his dreams, except that it did, here, now.

"Where do we go from here?" His voice was unsteady as he turned towards his guides.

But they were gone. He glimpsed them, two shadows dashing like whispers into the darkened wood. Along the beach, their robes lay abandoned in crumpled heaps. "Wait!" he called, and the desperation in his voice shattered the surrounding stillness for a moment and was quickly swallowed by it.

He glanced across the lake towards the mainland, squinted in hopes of making out the lights of the city upon the far shore, but a tapestry of gloom hampered his view. He did not know how far he had come. He could not even be certain the city from which he had sailed existed here, in this place.

As if answering his own cry, a second sound broke the silence. A deep, whining bellow emerged from somewhere deep within the forest. Gooseflesh rose upon his arms. The sound rose to a crescendo, then trailed off, only to return, more insistent.

Trembling, he took a step towards the trees. This, too, was familiar. He crossed the beach and entered the forest, pushing branches aside and snapping twigs in the undergrowth. Darkness swelled around him, and he pressed forward by instinct. No trail cut through the trees, but he knew the way, if not the destination.

From the darkness, he heard the screeching of strange insects, the stirring of unseen vermin. Shadow and mist danced a ballet in the spaces between the misshapen trees. He glanced overhead, and as the blanket of fog parted, he saw unfamiliar stars dotting the night sky.

The bellowing, like whale song, continued from somewhere ahead.

As he pressed forward, he noticed that the trees had taken on the countenance of anguished faces. He knew that many of the trees had once been other explorers who had trod this path and become lost forever. He shuddered, thinking he might lose his way. He wished his guides had not abandoned him. Is this why the masked figures had come to his door, figments of his dream come to life to beckon him to follow? They had promised answers to his questions and wonders unlike any he had ever seen. He had been only too eager to accompany them, to prove that his dreams were more than simple imagination. He had accepted the uncertainty and danger ahead.

He broke through a curtain of hanging vines and stumbled from the brush into a clearing. Before him, a house of ancient weatherworn planks stood. Through the thick glass windows flickered candlelight. The door stood ajar, and from within the bellowing call continued. He crossed the clearing and pushed open the door.

"Hello? Is anyone here?" His voice was muffled beneath his mask.

The call stopped, suddenly, and he sensed that he had reached his destination, but he had not expected this.

The tiny cabin was empty, save for an easel, upon which rested a canvas of pure black. Next to the easel were a pallet, paints, brushes, and jars of clean water.

He stepped towards the canvas. The blackness of the cloth threatened to consume him as he gazed into it, and he knew it was deeper than the waters he had crossed to reach the atoll, and far more treacherous. He felt himself being drawn into the darkness, but he could not avert his eyes. He tried to turn away, but he was snared by the cold emptiness of the canvas. He felt as though his very soul would slip out of his body to fill the void before him.

He reached out and fumbled for one of the brushes. An artist's skill did not guide his hand as he smeared paint across the canvas. He painted with a kind of survival instinct, a frantic desire to fill the canvas before he lost himself entirely.

Sweat stung his eyes. He wanted to wipe it away, but the mask blocked his hand.

The room closed in around him. The walls creaked.

He became distantly aware that the bellowing had begun anew, a constant, ghostly trumpeting, drawing closer.

And still he worked. His mind could not wrap itself around the subject of the painting. He felt as though he worked through some kind of hypnotic trance.

At last, he tossed the brush aside. It clattered against the floor, and the sudden sound, so distinct from the droning call, snapped him from his daze.

Stepping back, he got his first look at the grotesque image he had painted. It resembled nothing of Earth or known space more closely than the barbed, glistening shell of a crustacean, floating in empty space, and surrounded by hundreds of tendrils of pale, luminescent flesh. As he watched, the tendrils seemed to whip about and pulse with a sickly glow. He realized in a moment of gut-wrenching terror that the horrid, piercing cry, now so clear, emanated from the painting.

He staggered away, clutched a hand over his mouth. He felt that he might retch. The sound burrowed into his mind and knitted itself together. The sound started to make sense to him.

He turned and flung himself out of the house. He collapsed into the dirt outside and scrambled into the brush. Limbs whipped at him. Thorns tore his skin. He rushed through the forest and emerged on the beach. He did not stop. He threw himself into the water and waded into the cold depths, until his feet no longer touched the bottom. He dove down, down into the darkness, until the rush of water in his ears drowned out the sound of the painting's call, until the blackness flooded his senses and he could no longer envision the sight that had burned itself into his mind. He surfaced, bobbing in the water, gasping for breath, and saw sheeted phantoms swooping and diving down at him, the beat of their wings blocking out the moonlight.

Then nothing.

He awoke some time later, a rattling gasp escaping his throat as he rose, in his own bed, in his own home.

A dream.

Nothing more than another dream. But it had been so real!

He rubbed his eyes, kicked the bed sheets aside.

He gasped again, and his heartbeat quickened. Across the studio, alongside all of his other recent paintings, was the portrait he had seen in his dream, the massive, writhing crustacean thing. He realized he had spent the night painting again, as he had done so many times before. The fruit of his nightly labors stood before him.

Here, an image of the atoll, quiet and dark in the night, strange stars burning pinpoints into the night sky overhead.

Here, the mysterious guides who had come to his door and offered to show him such bizarre sights. In their gnarled hands, they clutched odd masks.

And there was the house, only in this painting; the building was not empty, but filled with writhing, serpentine things.

A siren wailed in the distance, reminding him of the haunting call of the thing in his latest work of art.

His knees weak, his head heavy, he stumbled towards the bathroom.

As he stepped inside and glanced into the mirror, he froze in shock.

The mask. The mask had been real.

But he had dreamed that his nightly visitors had brought the horrific disguise to him. Had he somehow constructed it during the night?

He tore the façade away....

... And shrieked as his nails dug into flesh.

He fell to the floor. He saw that his shadow was malformed about his head.

He wept then, tears of joy and terror and sadness.

It had all been leading to this.

The dreams.

The paintings. The call. The message.

His masterpiece.

His self portrait.

"The Caller From the Void" was originally published in Dark Legacy (2004).

This was written for a magazine of Lovecraftian horror. I didn't want to write a story that used the names of Cthulhu and Yog-Sothoth as a crutch, though. I wanted to write something that felt like a Lovecraftian nightmare. The title beastie is something I've written about many times. Sometimes I call it "the Stillborn God".

- CB

FOR HER LOVE

Ask almost anyone around the office, and they'd say Kevin Sanders was—
How did Jocelyn in HR put it?

—a dickhead misogynist who couldn't keep his mind off tits and ass for more than a few seconds without going into convulsions.

And if the idea of guilt by association held any water, I was unlucky enough to find him peering over the side of my cubicle like a smug-looking Kilroy.

"Hey, man." He slapped the side of the cube like he was playing the bongos. "We still on for tonight?"

"Guess so." I looked up from the computer screen. After only a few weeks in town, he was the closest thing to a friend I had. That didn't mean, however, that I really trusted him. "But I'd love to know what, exactly, you have planned."

"What? You don't like surprises? Don't sweat the details. Just make sure you've got at least a hundred bucks on you."

"A hundred dollars? That's a pretty big detail."

"A small price to pay." He drummed a farewell on the cube wall. "Don't worry—"

I could have sworn he said, "She'll be worth it," but I figured I heard him wrong.

Kev, as he liked to be called, didn't really give a damn what his co-workers thought of him. You know the guy who has a personality just a little too big for the workplace? That was Kev, opinionated and loud, an off-color joke always on the tip of his tongue. And, yes, he made something of a game of sleeping with every newly-hired woman who joined the company—"fresh meat," he called them—so his rep as a womanizer wasn't too far off the mark.

As he walked off, I smiled to myself and started a mental countdown.

One … two … three—

"Please, tell me I didn't hear that right." Kayliegh rolled in her desk chair across the aisle and into my cube. "Tell me you aren't going on some twisted 'guy's night out' with Kev Sanders."

Kayliegh's workspace was directly across from mine, and she was quick with a friendly hello or a bit of whispered gossip. She had worked for Prescott Marketing for more than eight years, but with her short blonde hair, bright blue eyes, and glowing smile, she could have passed for a kid fresh out of high school. If she didn't have a boyfriend—she mentioned him at least a few times a day—I might have asked her out.

Kayliegh hated Kev.

"So?" she asked. "Are you going to answer me?"

Her sudden closeness took me aback. My cubicle was pretty small, so with her chair pushed in close, I could feel the warmth of her body. Her leg brushed up against mine. Her light perfume managed to smell both fresh and exotic at the same time.

"Sorry," I said at last. "I'm sworn to secrecy."

"Don't be a jerk." She playfully slapped my arm. "You've been here—what?— two months, and you've already started hanging out with the wrong crowd."

"You want to make me a better offer?"

As soon as I said it, I realized I sounded more like Kev than myself.

"You wish." She wrinkled her nose at me, an expression I found painfully cute. "Just promise you won't let him talk you into doing something stupid."

"First of all," I said, "thank you for your unyielding faith in my sound judgment and reasoning. Second of all …"

Just as I was about to string the rest of my witty response together, I lost my train of thought. Jen Hanson, executive assistant to Mr. Prescott himself, strolled by, and I couldn't help but stare. Jen was gorgeous—tall, leggy, and she wore skirts so short they had to violate company dress codes. Not that I'd ever complain.

Kayliegh smacked me again, not playfully this time.

"Jeez, Brandon. You have a little drool on your chin."

My face flushed.

"You really are spending too much time with Sanders," she said.

"Oh, come on." I inched away in case she got the urge to smack me again. "You expect me not to look?"

"I guess that's fine, if that's what you like in a woman." She waited until Jen was out of earshot, then snapped her eyes wide open and chimed in an oversweet voice. "One day, I'll be a real girl."

"Wow," I said. "I never figured you for the catty type."

"Don't confuse cattiness with honesty. Although—" She pursed her lips. "— the two aren't always mutually exclusive."

We laughed at that, but Kayliegh quickly sobered and fixed me with a serious look.

"I mean it," she said. "Be careful around him."

I only wish I'd heeded her warnings.

Within a few weeks, I was out of a job, dead broke, and homeless.

All thanks to Kev …

… And the Doomsday Whores.

* * *

"Wild, huh?" Kev shivered with excitement. "Just … wild."

"That's one way to put it."

I expected maybe a back alley pool hall or a seedy strip joint.

But not a church.

Dozens of cars were parked on either side of the street and in overgrown, unlit lots. Kev found a spot and pulled to a stop. We sat in silence for a few seconds, and I got the feeling Kev was savoring the anticipation. I saw the crooked steeple lancing the night sky. From our parking spot, I saw a line trailing from the church doors, across the yard, and into the street.

"This isn't some sort of religious ambush, is it?"

I was only half-joking. Kev was my friend, but when I boiled it down, I didn't know him all that well. He could have been dragging me to a come-to-Jesus meeting or an Amway pitch or anything in between.

Kev smiled and climbed out of the car. I followed.

The neighborhood gave me the creeps. Condemned building crowded next to condemned building. Old newspapers, crumpled paper bags, and beer bottles littered the gutters. I could feel the eyes of unseen figures watching me from shadow-filled alleys and recessed doorways.

The church itself looked like something that had been demolished decades ago, only to pick itself up from the debris and clamber back together. The roof sagged. The stone walls looked like they might crumble at the slightest touch. The stained glass windows were mostly shattered or boarded over, but here and there a fragment of an angel's face looked down from on high.

Men stood in the long line leading across the weed-choked lot and up the church steps. They were from all walks of life from the looks of it, young and old, white collar and blue collar, but all male. An unkempt, bearded man waited at the top of the steps. He looked like he might have been standing on a street corner with a "Will Work For Food" sign just minutes earlier. Now he wore a black leather apron over his ratty clothes. As he ushered each man through the door, he took their money and stuffed it in the apron's pockets.

I didn't have a good feeling about the church and whatever waited inside. If not for Kev prodding me along, I would have turned around and saved myself a hundred dollars. After standing in line for several minutes, I climbed the steps and reluctantly handed the bearded man my cash. He grinned at me and nodded towards the door.

"G'on. Don't hold up the line."

I looked back and saw that dozens of men had joined the line waiting to enter. The line still stretched into the street.

Kev shoved his money into the doorman's waiting hand. He placed a hand on my shoulder and pushed me inside.

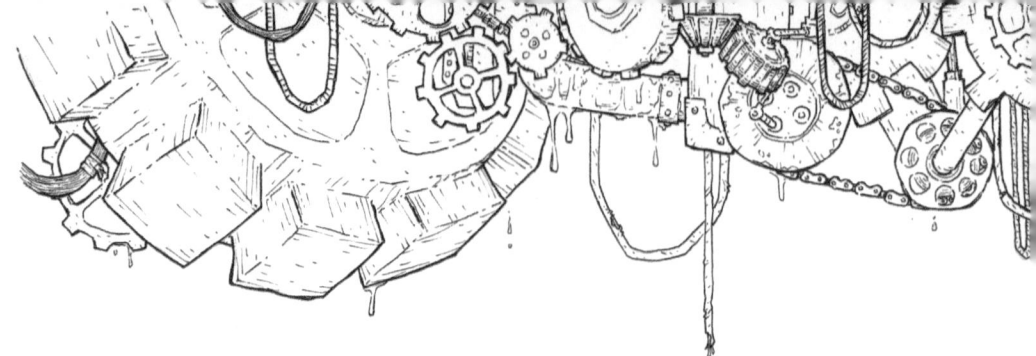

Every stick of furniture had been removed from the church, and the carpets were peeled away, revealing dusty, scratched hardwood. It was dark, the vast chamber lit only by dozens of flickering, mismatched wall sconces. Splotchy oil stains covered the floor. The ceiling—

"W-who did you say put all this together?" I didn't look at Kev. There was too much too see—too much to take in. I raised my voice. "Who?"

"I have no idea." His voice was filled with awe. "Just … wild."

"How does someone even learn how to do … this?"

The ceiling was lost in a bizarre mishmash of enormous gears and pistons and pipes. Belts and metal cables and chains crisscrossed above me. It looked like an M. C. Escher machine shop nightmare brought to life. The metal components glistened wetly and dripped oil onto the crowd below. The men didn't seem to mind.

Kev brushed past me and was swallowed up by the crowd. If the bearded man collected a hundred dollars from every man in the room, then he carried a fortune in his leather apron. They stood shoulder to shoulder, each and every one of them staring at the machine, and there were more eager patrons jostling in from outside.

I shoved my way through the throng of men. I noticed how hot it was in the room, like a sauna. Sweat broke out across my brow, soaked the underarms of my shirt. I looked for Kev, but didn't see him. A couple of the men shot me dirty looks as I forced my way past.

Towards the front of the room, I glimpsed a lone figure standing upon the pulpit. He was dressed in an expensive business suit, but the shoulders were stained with drops of oil. His face was covered by a black, leather hood.

I found Kev just as the hooded figure began to speak.

"All we do, we do for She Who Waits Beyond the Paling." His voice was muffled beneath the hood. "She of the Longing Womb. She Who Births Those Things Seen and Unseen. As she beckons, so we obey! For her love!"

He pulled a lever.

The great, oily gears came to life, metal grinding against metal. Steel cables pulled taught against a system of rattling pulleys.

"For her love!" The cry rose from the crowd, as if they had practiced the chant a hundred times. Even Kev joined in on the second cry. "For her love!"

Kev elbowed me, urging me to join in.

"For her love!"

I kept my mouth shut. The crowd seemed too close. I could smell the pungent sweat of the other men.

In the center of the ceiling, a pair of metal plate doors swung open, revealing a small, pitch black chamber. Cables and wires and rusty chains spilled out of the darkness, and the smell of unwashed skin washed across me. The smell wasn't unpleasant. It was intoxicating, feminine. I breathed it in.

Something moved within the darkened chamber.

As the men continued their chant, a figure descended from the yawning metal doors. She was suspended from dozens of interlaced chains and cables, and she was beautiful. Blonde and shapely. The face of an angel. She was naked, too, and my eyes traced the curves of her body. Woven cables were wrapped around her wrists and ankles, snaking around her legs and hips, under her arms and around her breasts like a lecherous serpent. As the gears turned and chains jangled, a complex system of pulleys caused the cables to constrict—around her neck, across her ample breasts. Wires tugged against her arms and feet. She moved in a herky-jerky dance, like an epileptic puppet stripper shaking her ass for singles.

The crowd cheered.

She opened her eyes. Her lips twitched. Her breasts heaved. Her movements became frantic, and I couldn't tell if it was caused by the clockwork machine or if she was struggling to free herself. The men went wild.

She moaned.

I've never heard anything so unearthly.

Her voice was thunderously deep but feminine at the same time. Even from where I stood, I heard it over the growl of the machinery. The men fell into a stunned silence. I felt the reverberating sound in the marrow of my bones.

A more powerful smell rolled through the room—the smell of sex. I flinched at the strength of it. My heartbeat quickened. I felt a fluttering in the pit of my stomach—something I hadn't felt with such intensity since the very first time I got to third base with a girl. I grew painfully aroused.

The other men in the room suffered from the same effect. Some of them clutched at themselves. Others dropped their pants and began to jerk off.

The woman writhed in the air before us, her moans amplified by unknown means, echoing, burrowing into my every cell.

Kev went down on his knees as he feverishly masturbated. He collapsed, shuddering, upon the already sodden floor.

I looked for the exit. Even as the woman's cries of pleasure pounded in my brain, I wanted nothing more than to get out—

The room plunged into total darkness.

Above me, lost in the shadows, the machines ground to a halt. The woman released a long, pleasurable sigh, and something in her throat rattled. She fell silent, and I heard only the shuffling of the men around me, their labored breathing, the zipping of flies.

A minute ticked by.

The fleshy smell of sex lingered in the air.

The lights flared again. The woman was gone. The chains had been drawn up. The gears were still, waiting like silent beasts to turn again. The men around me looked shocked and ashamed.

I saw the EXIT sign and moved towards the door.

I didn't wait for Kev to emerge from the church. Even though I lived miles away, even though this part of town was dangerous even during broad daylight, I decided to walk. I wanted to be alone. But I felt as though the woman in the chains was still with me. Not walking beside me or stalking behind me. I felt more like I was wearing her as a second skin

* * *

"You must have had a helluva night." Kayliegh made a show of checking her watch. "I don't think I've ever seen you come in late before."

I slumped into my chair. "Bad dreams," I said.

It was the truth. I'd dreamed of the blonde woman, suspended directly above me by a series of bloody cables stretching across the room and vanishing into shadow. Her eyes were missing. Within the gaping sockets, tiny gears spun and clicked. Her every motion accompanied by the whirring of belts and the hiss of steam-driven hydraulics.

God help me, I wanted her.

"You're lucky Mr. Prescott had a breakfast meeting," Kayliegh said. "If he saw you coming in late, he'd show you what bad dreams were all about."

I hit the computer's power button. The hum of the CPU fan, the clunking of the hard drive, sounded like the grind and bellow of the machinery in the church.

A little later, Mr. Prescott staggered into the office. He looked like I felt—like he had lost a fight with a concrete mattress.

An odd thought crossed my mind.

He's one of us.

Followed by:

Where the Hell did that come from?

* * *

A few days later, an e-mail from Kev popped into my inbox, but I deleted the message without reading it. I'd been avoiding him since that night at the church. Friend or not, I had no interest in participating in his weird, ritualistic circle jerks. Not ten minutes after I trashed his e-mail, he showed up at my desk, sporting his very best let-me-sell-you-something-you-don't-want smile.

"Get my message?" he asked.

"I don't think so." I feigned checking my inbox. "Maybe it got caught by a spam filter or something."

"Never mind that. I'm heading out again tonight. Thought I'd invite you along."

"Let me think about it."

"What's to think about?" He looked genuinely hurt. "You had a good time, didn't you?"

"I don't know. I mean, the whole situation … Didn't it seem … bizarre to you?"

"That's the point, man." He clasped my shoulder and squeezed. "It's not everyday you get to see something like that."

My skin crawled.

"I've seen as much as I want."

Kev grabbed a pen and a Post-it from my desk and jotted down an address. He placed the note right in the middle of my computer screen. I could barely make out his scribbling.

"They moved it?" I asked.

"They move around a lot. Raised the price a little, too. Make sure you've got at least two-hundred on you."

"Are you serious?"

"Trust me," he said, "you don't want to miss this."

* * *

The idea nagged at me.

Like rats gnawing at my brain tissue.

Like an addiction.

I tried watching TV, but found myself restlessly flipping through channel after channel. I thought I might finish that novel Kayliegh loaned me, but the words blurred together. In the back of my mind, I heard the distant grinding of gears, the clanking of chains, the sighs of both the machinery and the woman—if they were, in fact, two different entities.

I grew aroused.

It took less than five minutes to get cleaned up, dressed, and out the door.

I suppose it's a little like porn. You look at it once, and it's exciting, but it also feels a little dirty—creepy and wrong. But sooner or later, you get that itch, and not even shame will keep you from scratching.

That's how it was for me. Like the lure of porn.

Only much stronger.

I must have changed my mind a half dozen times between my apartment and the parking lot. And I almost stopped myself again when I swung by the ATM and nearly cleaned out my account. But Kev's warning kept replaying in my mind.

"You don't want to miss this."

I believed him. If I didn't show up, something unforgettable might happen. I'd never forgive myself if I missed out on something … amazing.

I didn't miss out.

Only, it wasn't amazing.

It was awful. Ungodly.

* * *

All around me, the men cheered as the great gears turned and groaned, and the metal doors creaked open.

The abandoned warehouse was stuffy, claustrophobic, despite being much larger than the hollowed out church. A blanket of semi-solid body heat filled the massive room. The crowd was two or three times larger, and I couldn't spot Kev. After only a few minutes, I stopped looking for him and turned my attention to—

The ceiling. Dear lord.

"For her love!"

The call seemed to bounce and echo through the crowd.

My eyes began to water as I looked up.

The ceiling looked like an auto-mechanic's Sistine Chapel—a growling, pumping, clattering nightmare of rods and pistons and trembling chains. I couldn't imagine how anyone could construct such an insane work of interconnecting mechanical components in such a short time.

A hooded figure watched over us from a catwalk. Instead of a suit, he wore baggy jeans and a Cradle of Filth tee shirt. The hood he wore—his vestment— glistened wetly. He waved his arms over us like a preacher in the middle of a hellfire and brimstone sermon, but I couldn't hear a word. His voice was drowned out by the expectant din of the crowd.

Someone nearby cried, "For her love!" and I had to stop myself from answering in kind.

Some of the men were already busily masturbating.

Drops of oil spattered the crowd.

I grew hard. My hand started to stray to my crotch, but I stopped myself. I clenched my hand into a tight fist. My fingernails cut into the palm of my hand.

A woman descended from the darkened opening. Not the same woman, I realized, not the angel from the church, but I recognized her just the same.

Jen.

Mr. Prescott's assistant.

She glided like a spookhouse phantom over us.

The men around me reached for her with grasping fingers.

I looked towards the hooded figure. There was something familiar about him. I couldn't see his face, of course, but from behind the hood's slits, his eyes glittered hungrily in the low light. I knew him.

Kev.

Something wet and warm dripped on my face. I wiped it away and looked at my fingers. Blood.

Jen swept back and forth above us.

I called out for her, but if she heard me—if she recognized her own name—she showed no sign. She continued to writhe. The cable around her throat constricted, and I saw the skin tear at her throat. She moaned.

And bled.

She was ...

Beautiful.

Oh, God. So beautiful. Her muscles pulled taut ... and released ... and constricted again. Her mouth suctioned open, and she sighed and whimpered. The chains and wires shivered, and dainty, gleaming hooks pulled the flaps of her skin open, like the petals of a flower, the tissue within glistening like ripened fruit pulp, until another series of chains and hooks peeled the meaty muscle away from the wet bone beneath ...

And yet another series of intricate barbs.

So lovely.

So sickeningly beautiful.

Somewhere nearby, a man cried out. He clawed and scratched at his eyes, his fingers bloodied, his nails caked with the membranous remains of his eyes. He raised his hands towards the suspended woman—

Jen, I reminded myself. Jen. I knew her.

—like some sort of offering.

The machine droned on in approval, the steam-hiss rushing over us all.

A tremor passed through the crowd.

A silver serving tray was passed from person to person. A couple of the guys nearby started to shuffle anxiously. I heard one of them muttering something about, "the communion." The tray drew closer. It was covered in a quivering mound of what I can only describe as fat curds of overly pink flesh.

And the men around me were eating it.

A skinny kid who stood next to me plucked one of the trembling chunks from the tray like he was grabbing a spring roll from a plate of Hors d'Oeuvres.

He plopped it into his mouth, closed his eyes, and started to chew. A milky oil oozed between his lips and dribbled down his chin.

I thought I might vomit. Not too far away, another man did just that. He went to his knees, puking down the front of his shirt. The whole while he kept his hand down his pants.

Someone passed the tray towards me. The stink of it was overpowering, sharp and acidic. I stepped back, pushed the platter away. The dish clattered to the floor. A gasp rose from the men standing in my immediate area, and I'm certain they were watching me with shock and hate-filled glares. But I couldn't take my eyes off the tiny, pink bits of … God knows what … on the floor.

The fleshy curds twitched.

Crawled.

The crowd surged towards the spilled tray, shoving and pushing, falling upon the—

Communion.

—like starved animals.

I looked up at Jen. She squirmed above me. The wires, I realized, were not just wrapped around her body. They were embedded in her bruised flesh, hooked through her skin, penetrating her orifices.

I wanted to help her, but all I could do was run.

The grinding of the machinery, Jen's inhuman breathing, and the grunting of the men chased after me.

I staggered towards the exit and threw myself into the night.

* * *

I'm not sure why I decided to drive past the abandoned church. Curiosity, maybe, or the unshakable feeling that something was terribly wrong, like the whole world was starting to curdle like spoiled milk.

Cars lined either side of the street near the church, and a group of men milled about outside. It looked like they had just finished with the festivities inside and were calling it a night. A doorman wearing a black leather suit jacket ushered men out the front door.

Some of them were still masturbating as they hobbled out.

It's not moving from place to place, I thought.

It's spreading.

* * *

Kev was sitting at his desk, casually looking at Internet porn, when I grabbed a handful of his hair and slammed his face into the monitor. Mr. Prescott was too cheap to spring for those flimsy flat screens, and Kev's head made a satisfying, meaty clunk as it struck the screen. He flopped onto the floor. A slimy trail of bloody snot oozed down the monitor, while a pixilated vixen gyrated on-screen.

"What the fuck?" Kev grabbed at his busted nose. Blood ran between his fingers. "What was that for?"

"Did you do it?" I swept a desktop full of office supplies to the floor. Pens and paperclips went flying. "Did you put Jen in that machine?"

"You barely knew her. What do you care?"

"I care because this isn't right. None of this. And you can't just kidnap someone—"

"It's not like we're going to get volunteers." He clambered to his feet. "What are we supposed to do?"

I didn't like the way he said "we."

Our co-workers gathered like children watching a schoolyard brawl. Kayliegh stood among the others, an expression of shocked disbelief on her face.

"Did you kill her?" I asked. "Is she dead?"

"She's part of something greater." He wiped blood from his nose with the back of his hand. "She'd thank me if she could."

"You think you've turned her into—what?—some sort of goddess?"

"Only a representation, man." He shivered. "A doorway. She's coming through, piece by piece, but flesh alone isn't strong enough to contain her. That's why they all have to become part of the machine. That's what they were put here to become. It's fucking procreation, man, only we're birthing the only bitch that's ever mattered."

He watched Kayliegh the way a starving man might stare at a steak dinner.

I punched him in the face.

He crashed into his desk and fell to the floor.

"What are you doing?" Kayliegh cried.

My anger swelled. I didn't take my eyes off her as I stomped Kev's balls. He squealed, curled up like a dying spider and squirmed on the floor. Kayliegh flinched and looked away.

On the floor, clutching at his ruptured nuts, Kev choked out a laugh.

"It's no use," he wheezed. "She'll never love you."

I might have killed him if security hadn't shown up to drag me out of the building.

* * *

I wandered a lot after that. At first, I lied to myself, saying I was pounding the pavement in search of another job. By the third day, I stopped bringing my resumes with me altogether. I roamed for hours, sometimes driving, sometimes walking, watching as the world went mad all around me.

I started to notice men gathering outside old movie theaters and condemned meat-packing plants and warehouses.

I noticed trucks loaded with heavy machinery roving the streets.

Sometimes, when it was quiet, I heard women screaming in the distance.

The Doomsday Whores.

The name popped into my head. It sounded a little funny, but I thought it appropriate.

One night, I happened past a fenced lot where a group of men lined up to enter a warehouse. One of the men carried a birdcage, in which four parakeets screeched and fluttered frantically. Another guy held a cardboard box full of mewling puppies. Still another clutched a blood-soaked rag in his hand. He looked around, and I saw tears running down his face … from one of his eyes. Where the other eye should have been, only a pulpy socket remained.

The muscle-bound doorman was dressed in a black leather business suit. As each man passed, they handed over their offerings—the bloody rag, the birds, the puppies—and he ushered them into shadow.

It's the end of the world, I thought, but they've got us too busy fucking off to notice.

As I turned away, I nearly tripped over a filthy beggar. He was on his knees behind me. His pants were bunched around his ankles, and he worked his cock until it was raw and red.

On the ground before him, pink fleshy curds trembled and squirmed.

* * *

Within a week, the flyers started showing up everywhere—stapled to telephone poles, tucked under windshield wipers, plastered to the sides of buildings.

THE TIME HAS COME. SHE AWAKENS. HER LOVE AWAITS.
SHARE IN HER COMMUNION.
THE WOMB OPENS. SEED THE EARTH.

Multiple dates and addresses were listed.
At the bottom, it read:

ADMISSION: ONE FIRST-BORN CHILD

* * *

I spent the last of my money to buy a pistol. Nothing fancy. Just a little added protection. It wasn't unusual to hear about women getting kidnapped or men getting mugged, only the attackers weren't after money. It didn't take much to arrange a viewing of one of the Doomsday Whores. A pinky finger would do.

And it didn't have to be your own.

When I heard the knock at my door, I grabbed the gun and peered through the peephole. I was prepared for anything … almost.

Kayliegh stood in the hall, crying.

As I opened the door, she threw herself into my arms and buried her face against my chest.

"Oh, God, Brandon," she sobbed. "I didn't know where else to go."

"Calm down," I said. "What happened?"

"It's Greg," she said.

Her boyfriend.

"I don't know what happened to him." She said. "I just know that … thing is not my boyfriend. Not any more. He … he tried to sell me to these men … these men in black suits. Leather suits. He was going to sell me to them, but I got away. I got away and I ran."

"It's going to be all right," I said, but I didn't believe it.

"He's not even human. His skin is changing. His … flesh is changing."

I held her at arms length and looked her in the eyes. I knew what had to be done.

"We have to get out of here," I said, "before it's too late."

* * *

The world smells differently now. Like sex and motor oil. It's worse when the polluted air from the city eddies into the country, but the stink is always with us, lingering in the fibers of our clothes, clinging greasily to our skin.

A few nights ago, I woke from a nightmare, babbling about terraforming.

I don't remember the dream at all, but I think it's coming true. The world's being remade in the image of Kev's goddess, his Whore of Babylon. Flesh and metal wasn't enough to hold her, and now she's spilling over into the earth and water and air. I taste her flesh when I eat, her sweat when I drink, her musk when I breathe.

All around me, the word is changing—mutating. And, God help me, nature was never so beautiful before.

Kayliegh and I keep to rural areas mostly, places where the sway of the Doomsday Whores isn't so strong. We barter for food and shelter with the only thing of value we have left …

There are still some of us out here who prefer real sex.

There's no shame in it. Prostitution is one of the world's oldest professions, as they say. As it turns out, it's one of the oldest religions, too.

Last week, Kayliegh asked me, "What's all this mean for the children?" She started weeping, and she hasn't said a word to me since. She shuffles along behind me like a robot, saying nothing, exhibiting no will of her own, and I pimp her out so we can eat. At night, I hold her close. She smells of the sweat of other men.

Kev's words haunt me.

You don't want to miss this.

And, as much as I hate him, I still believe him.

Tonight, like so many nights before, we're bedding down in a barn. Once he was done with Kayliegh, the old farmer warned me to clear out before dawn.

"I don't want you here when Leathercoats come looking," he said.

Darkness closes in around me, but I stay outside for a few minutes longer. I hear her inside the barn, bawling at the misery her life has become. She'll cry herself to sleep soon, and then the nightmares will come.

Somewhere … in the distance … I hear the steady pumping of heavy machinery, working, endlessly. Maybe I'm imagining it.

Sooner or later, the men in black leather will find us.

I'll try to fight them off. But the black-suited pimps travel in packs, and I shiver to think what might happen when they pull the black leather hood over my head. Will I even resist?

I still have my pistol, tucked in my pocket. I've only had to use it a couple of times.

I look towards the barn where Kayliegh weeps.

This isn't the world I would have wanted for her.

I test the pistol's weight.

There's nothing I won't do.

For her love.

The original title of this story was "The Doomsday Whores", but I didn't think that summarized the piece appropriately. It started out as a much shorter story, but it blossomed into something much darker and much more… epic in scale. It's another story in a very loosely knit myth cycle, I guess, but in this one I go ahead and scour the Earth rather than teasing possible Armageddon.

- CB

CRY OF THE MACHINE

The ghost town put the idea for the machine in Cal's head, as fucked up as that sounded, and it drew him—drew all of them—out into the barrens.

Where it tried to kill them.

It had killed before, and its hunger for murder had grown over the years, until at long last it could wait in the dust and silence no longer.

But to bring death, the town needed to live again.

Jen didn't understand any of this, not in the beginning, and even towards the end she had only managed to put a few pieces of the puzzle together. The town didn't speak to her—not like it did to Cal.

But, by God, she'd hear every single ghost in Sessler City scream before it was all said and done.

* * *

The desert stretched out before them, a vast expanse of sand and rocks as far as the eye could see. The highway was empty, save for dust cloud phantoms and the occasional heat oasis. The Sunbird jostled and quaked along the cracked, uneven pavement. The mound of mechanical components and metal odds-and-ends thrown into the back of the station wagon trembled and rattled.

"Pull over." Andi cupped a hand over her mouth. Her muffled voice trembled with a desperate urgency. "Please. Pull over."

The static filled radio was turned up loud. Between fits of hissing white noise, old school Metallica blasted from the speakers. But it wasn't so loud that the driver couldn't hear Andi's pitiful pleas. He heard her, all right. He just didn't give a damn.

Sometimes, Jen wondered how she'd ever managed to hook up with such an asshole. Her mother always said Jen had ghastly taste in men. Cal—another heavy metal wannabe in a long line of heavy metal wannabes—was living proof that mama knew best.

From the back seat, Andi groaned.

"Pull over. I mean it. I'm in trouble."

And there it was.

"I'm in trouble."

Andi always uttered those three words right before the floodgates of her gullet were blown open by a puke tidal wave. It was her little warning that she meant business. She liked to party, and she spoke those words all too frequently, especially when she'd been hitting the wine coolers too hard. Only, she hadn't been drinking.

"I'm in trouble."

No shit.

Cal flexed his knuckles upon the steering wheel. The faux leather cover creaked beneath his fingers.

"Come on, Cal. Stop the car." Jen touched his shoulder, and he flinched away as if she'd jammed her finger in an open wound. His reaction startled her, even though she should have been accustomed to it. Cal didn't like to be touched any more, like he was sporting an awful sunburn, only beneath the skin rather than on the surface. "Listen. I know you're in a goddamned hurry, but you better pull over if you don't want the back seat covered in puke."

Cal kept on keeping on.

"Guys," Andi whined. "I'm in real trouble."

"Seriously, dude." Donny sat in the back seat next to Andi. The edge in his voice, especially when dealing with his lord and master, Cal, was new. Either he was genuinely worried about his girlfriend, or he didn't relish the idea of an upchuck bath, probably a little of both. "Stop the fucking car."

Cal glanced at the rearview, looking past Andi and Donny—looking through them—at the blacktop uncurling into the distance.

He showed no sign of slowing.

"Dude!" Donny fidgeted in his seat. "This ain't cool."

"We're almost there," Cal said.

"Who gives a shit?" Jen growled. "You know, if she gets sick—and she will get sick—she's likely to puke all over your precious machine."

That got Cal's attention.

Instantly, he took his foot off the gas and pulled to the shoulder. Pebbles rasped upon the car's underbelly. A curtain of sand swept beyond the vehicle's hood and dispersed into nothing.

Jen felt a little proud of herself. She smiled sweetly at Cal.

"See? Was that so hard?"

Andi shoved her door open and leaned out. Vomit spattered the hard-packed earth. There couldn't have been much in her stomach, since she hadn't been able to keep anything solid down. But the Gatorade she'd been chugging to keep hydrated came up in retching fits.

Donny's fingers grazed the bare flesh between Andi's babydoll tee and her shorts. Whenever he touched her, he made a point of seeking out skin-on-skin.

"You all right, babe? You think maybe you got food poisoning or something?"

No, you asshole, Jen thought. She's fucking pregnant.

Donny had one thing and one thing only going for him—he was painfully good-looking. Girls like Andi tumbled head over heels into his bed on a regular basis. But Heaven forbid they try to have a conversation about anything other than playing bass guitar or the latest X-Box cheat codes. They'd quickly realize his pretty face was stretched over a skull as empty as the desert.

Jen kept her mouth shut, no matter how much she wanted to tear Donny a new poop shoot. He'd have to figure out his predicament on his own, just like he'd have to figure out that the girl he'd knocked up wasn't actually eighteen. Andi had confided with Jen—from one girl to another—that she was only thirteen years old. Jen guessed the girl would tell Donny soon enough, and if she was lucky, Donny wouldn't skip town and leave jailbait mother and bastard child to fend for themselves.

Jesus, she thought, I'm cranky as hell.

Brushing her damp hair from her face, she leaned out the passenger side window and hoped for the blessed miracle of the slightest breeze.

No such luck.

If anything, the sweltering heat intensified. The Sunbird's A/C was on the fritz. Jen wouldn't have been surprised to learn Cal stripped out the A/C to salvage parts for his whacked-out science project. At least while the car was moving, the air—as hot as it was—circulated a little. Now the heat clung to Jen like a solid thing, a blistering tin foil blanket draped across her body. The merciless sun beat through the windshield. The skin around Jen's eyes felt red and raw and tight.

Andi continued puking her guts out.

Jen smelled vomit cooking on the side of the road. The stench threatened to make her sick, too, and she pinched her nose closed.

At long last, Andi dragged herself into the car. She wiped her mouth with the back of her hand, took a deep breath, and settled back into the seat. Greasy sweat covered her face and neck. Her long, blonde hair was matted to her forehead.

Jen looked back at her. She felt bad for the kid.

"You ok?"

Andi nodded.

"Yeah, I think I'm—"

Cal didn't wait for her to finish. He threw the car in gear and hit the gas.

Jackass.

Jen shifted uncomfortably. Her blouse stuck to her back. Her curly hair clung to her neck in wet strands. She could smell her own sweat, and she hated that feeling. To make matters a little worse, Andi's clothes, hair, breath—all reeked of vomit. The smell filled the car. Jen felt it seeping into her pours.

She looked at Cal, and a sensation of wrongness swelled within her.

He had changed so much in the last couple of months.

Beneath his unkempt bangs, his eyes ticked back and forth as he watched the road. A thin river of sweat trickled down the bridge of his nose. Jen studied his face, seeking a glimpse of the man she had started dating three years ago. A stranger might as well have been sitting in the driver's seat.

A faraway look had settled in Cal's eyes, and he tilted his head, like he was listening to some song playing in the distance.

The ghost town beckoned to him.

Beckoned to them all.

* * *

The plywood sign on the outskirts of town read *How long must God punish Sessler City?* in dripping black paint.

"You gotta be fucking kidding me," Donny said.

Sessler City wasn't much to look at. Here and there, the remains of old buildings sprouted from the dust. A few other structures had been beaten by the wind and time until all that remained was the stone foundations. A few spindly, leafless trees grew alongside the shells of houses, and tumbleweeds crawled across the street.

"All we need are a few vultures," Jen said, "and this place would be real homey."

The rusty bulk of a mobile home was parked not far from the sign. The metal walls were speckled with buckshot.

"I thought you said this place has been deserted since the thirties?"

"Yeah," Cal said. "There used to be a caretaker who lived here, you know, to make sure trespassers didn't come out here and get hurt."

"Get hurt how?" Andi asked.

"You gotta watch your step if you go wandering around. There are dozens of old mine shafts out here, some of them descending hundreds of feet straight down. You fall down one of those, and you're fucked."

"Yeah." Donny laughed. "I saw the Movie of the Week."

"So what happened to the caretaker?" Jen asked.

"He didn't last long," Cal said. "Bad dreams ran him off."

"How do you know that?"

"Just do."

Cal drove towards the center of town. They passed an old cemetery. The gates had fallen in places. The graves were marked by piles of stones.

Quite a stage Cal the Boy Wonder had chosen to unveil his mystery machine.

Maybe "Boy Wonder" was a bit of a stretch. After all, Cal was nearly thirty years old, even though he still sometimes acted half that age.

How about "The Amazing Deadbeat Grease Monkey and his Time-Wasting Erector Set"?

Dance, Grease Monkey, dance, while your mystery machine plays a jaunty tune.

Jesus, Jen thought, when did I become such a bitch?

She knew the answer. She could trace the evolution of her foul disposition to the night Cal first woke her in the middle of the night, rambling about the machine. Since that time, he'd devoted his every waking hour to the construction of the device. He quit his band, which probably wasn't a great loss to the other performers, since Cal sucked. He started skipping classes at the community college where he studied auto shop. He even quit his job at the body shop, and he relied on Jen to keep him supplied with booze and weed. He even lost interest in sex. Nothing mattered except the machine.

And Jen wondered if he even knew what it was supposed to do.

Suddenly, the radio screeched … then went dead. Jen fiddled with the tuner and volume, but couldn't coax a sound from the speakers.

"Aw, man," Donny whined. "We don't got no tunes, man!"

"When are you going to get an IPod?" Andi asked.

"When they start giving them away for free." He scratched his head. "I bet this place is, like, one of those UFO landing sites, you know? Like the whole place is radioactive or something. Sometimes, electronics don't work when there's been a UFO nearby."

"UFOs," Jen said. "You mean like aliens. From outer space."

"Why not? I saw it on Discovery."

Of course, Donny's logic fell apart if he expected Jen to believe he'd ever even bothered to flip past the Discovery Channel, but she decided to play along. It wasn't like she had anything better to do.

"What kind of aliens are we talking about here? E.T. or Predator?"

"Oh, gross!" Andi stuck her tongue out and shook her head. "Predator creeps me out!"

"Predator's badass!" Donny loomed over Andi and conjured up his best Predator impersonation. "Want some … candy?"

Cal pulled to a stop and hopped out of the car without a word.

Jen exchanged glances with Andi and Donny, shrugged, and climbed out of the car herself.

A column of black smoke rose into the sky above the town. It uncurled from a spot beyond the old graveyard.

"What's that?" Andi asked. "Is something burning?"

"Underground fires." Cal wasted no time in opening the back of the station wagon and unloading the pieces of his machine. "The fires have been burning for years."

Andi hugged herself as if suddenly cold.

"Creepy."

Jen watched as Cal spread the assorted mechanical components out on the ground behind the car. Seeing all the pieces together in one place, she could almost see …

Nothing at all, she thought. It looks like a bunch of salvage yard junk.

Cal yanked the keys from the ignition. They rattled as he shoved them in his jeans pocket.

"What?" Jen asked. "Don't trust us?"

"You don't need the keys, do you? The radio doesn't work out here. And it's not like there's an outlet mall in driving distance. The three of you sit tight. I'll be finished soon."

"What do you mean, 'sit tight'?" I thought you wanted our help."

Cal looked over the box of springs and gears he carried, doing a quick mental inventory.

"Nah. I think I got this. Besides, this is something I need to do on my own. I'm gonna find a good place to set up." He nodded towards the decaying steeple of an old church. "Maybe over there somewhere."

"If you wanted to be alone with your precious machine, why'd you invite us along?"

"I didn't invite you, did I? You wanted to come."

"Bullshit! Why would anyone want to come out here?"

Cal lugged another piece of equipment from the back of the car. It looked like the remains of a gas generator.

"Look, I don't feel like arguing about this now. We can talk later. When I'm done."

"Fine."

As Cal shuffled away, Jen kicked a bit of sand in his direction and muttered under her breath.

"Asshole."

It took Cal several trips to haul the pieces of his machine away. By the time he was done, he was covered with sweat and out of breath. Still, when Donny tried to help, Cal waved him away.

"I told you, I can handle this."

He wandered towards the church. He kicked up little clouds of dust with every step.

"Well, what are we supposed to do now?" Donny asked. "Sit out here in the dirt, pulling on our junk?"

"Speak for yourself," Andi said.

"You know what I mean."

"Face it, Donny," Jen said, "you've been ditched for a pile of spare parts, just like the rest of us."

Donny shrugged, and an evil grin played across his lips.

"I got an idea. The two of you can take turns slobbing my knob. Now that's a nice way to spend the afternoon."

"Ew!" Andi whacked him on the back of the head. "Ew! Ew! Ew!"

"I'm just kidding, babe. You know you're the only girl for me."

He was still smiling

"Unless the idea of a threesome starts to appeal to you."

Andi punched him in the arm, but Jen had to wonder how many times that line and that smile had convinced a pair of girls to double-team him. Clutching his bicep, Donny hopped away from his girlfriend. They both laughed, but with her very next breath, Andi looked like she'd just been offered a minced rat milkshake after her hundredth consecutive ride on the Tilt-a-Whirl.

"Oh," she said, "I'm in trouble."

She dropped to her knees and started puking in the dust.

Jen felt a stab of pity for the girl, but not so much for Donny.

"That's all you. Clean up on aisle B.F.E."

* * *

Cal bled.

He had sliced his hand open when a wrench slipped in his fingers.

Now blood dribbled on the floor of the old church.

He wondered if that was sacrilegious somehow.

He had to fight with a few of the components of the machine, had to force them to fit together or beat them with a hammer. But now it seemed to be fitting together nicely. Just as he imagined.

No.

Better.

Jen and the others didn't understand. How could they? They hadn't been chosen. They were still gridlocked in the only world they had ever known, just like the people of Sessler City before Obed Grafton and a group of stubborn miners broke through the rock wall and stumbled into the chamber housing the First Machine.

The True Machine.

Now that would have been something else.

Cal's makeshift contraption was a pale comparison to the ageless device that had been slumbering deep beneath the city.

Jen thought he was losing his mind, but once he finished his work, she would be forced to believe him.

Thousands of ghost towns in the desert, but only one of them dreamed.

Somewhere, deep beneath the ruins, foundry-hot fires still blazed, and if you listened closely enough, you could hear the distant echo of deep bellows and lonely sighs.

Cal didn't understand why he, of all the people in the world, had been selected by Sessler City. Maybe, dreams were like a vast desert, each individual dreamer like a lost and lonely ghost town. Maybe, as the town dreamed, it had reached out, searching for anyone who might hear its call.

And it had found Cal.

Dreaming.

There's a song in there somewhere, Cal thought. Maybe once this is over, I can get back to my music.

But first …

Sessler City was ready to awake.

Cal busied himself with the construction of the alarm clock.

* * *

After being cooped up in the car for several hours, Jen needed some time alone.

A little me time.

She excused herself, saying she needed to use the bathroom.

"Oh, I'll go with you," Andi had said.

You've gotta give the kid props for a positive attitude. She just finished tossing her Technicolor cookies, and she's still all smiles.

But Jen politely declined.

"It's all right. I think I can handle this one on my own. I'll just find a nice rock to squat behind. You two … talk."

So this is Sessler City, she thought, population zero.

She wandered among the skeletal remains of buildings, trying to paint a mental picture of the town that had once been.

Here was—Let me guess, Jen thought—the post office, where ma and pa could send their letters out to the rest of the world. Now it was nothing more than a couple of rotted support beams and the collapsed remains of the roof.

Across the street might have been a general store. Once the men of Sessler City would have sat out on the porch after a hard day in the mines to play checkers and eat pickled pig's feet. Now only a sand-covered foundation remained.

And over here was the vestige of a one-room schoolhouse. The frame rose from the earth like the jutting ribs of a long-dead dinosaur. While the wooden frame was worn bare, Jen imagined it had once been painted bright red.

For some reason, she couldn't help but picture every building as painted red. She remembered some old cowboy movie Cal had made her watch, back when he gave a shit about things such as cowboy movies. In the film, the hero painted an entire town red and renamed the place Hell or something like that. Sessler City reminded her of the town in that movie.

Of Hell.

Here and there, the twisted, rusted bulk of odd machinery erupted from the sand like islands of scrap in a sea of dust. Mining equipment, Jen guessed, although something about the machinery creeped her out.

For some reason, she pictured the machinery as red, too.

But not with rust.

A few of the buildings were still whole. At least, they still had four walls and a ceiling. Jen ducked her head in a couple to look around. Most were empty, except for debris and the occasional ball of sagebrush that had gotten trapped inside. Jen felt an overwhelming sense of emptiness … or loneliness.

Distantly, she heard something that might have been thunder.

Choom!

"Don't tell me," she muttered. "This place has been bone-dry for decades, and now we're gonna get a storm."

Maybe Cal's machine is a rainmaker.

Hell, a little rain might feel good right about now.

She climbed a set of sagging wooden steps and peered into another derelict structure.

"What have we here? A butcher shop, maybe?"

A single piece of furniture stood in the center of the room. Over the years, scavengers had probably made off with anything of value, but they had left a large, wooden chopping block behind. It had most likely been too heavy and bulky to carry. Nicks and slices and gouges from frequent use covered the cutting board surface, scars crisscrossing the wood like an angular roadmap.

Jen approached the chopping block. A vegetarian for the last four years, the room made her flesh crawl. But she knew she was just being silly. She touched the chopping block, tracing a finger along one of the scratches.

Nothing to—

An unseen presence chopped against the board.

Jen felt a rush of air across her face, as if a blade had sliced through the air before her.

She felt vibrations spread through the chopping block, through the rotting floorboards.

She jerked her fingers away.

Something chopped against the board again.

A cleaver.

Somehow Jen knew the sound originated from a heavy meat cleaver, gone dull with years of overuse.

The sound grew louder, more persistent, more frantic, and Jen imagined the metal blade descending again and again, crunching through sinew and bone, thumping into the wood of the chopping block beneath.

A meat cleaver, heavy and dull—rusty.

Caked with dried blood.

Her stomach kicked as she wondered—oh, no, I don't want to know, don't want to know—what might lay beneath the hurried rise and fall of the blade.

A barrage of quick, weighty chops bounced off the board and rattled around the room.

Then silence.

Then blood.

Blood welled up from the nicks and dents, poured out of the long, intersecting scars, as if the chopping block was made up of bleeding flesh. Thick and dark and red, the blood bubbled and oozed in a liquid sheet across the wood. Jen jumped back as a waterfall of crimson cascaded over the sides, dribbling along the broad, round legs, spattering on the floor like rain and pooling on the tile.

The phantom meat cleaver thudded into the wood again. Disembodied hands drove the invisible weapon down again and again into some invisible, squirming prey.

The resonance was horrific—deafening.

Something squealed, and Jen didn't know if she herself had made the sound or if some ghostly victim was crying out for mercy.

The copper pot stink of the blood flooded Jen's nostrils, and she covered her nose and mouth. Snaking in widening streams, the blood seeped across the dusty floor, reaching out with glistening rivulets like narrow, twisting fingers. If she touched the blood, Jen thought, she might fall into it, sinking into the red mire as if plunging into quicksand, drowning, the syrupy fluid gagging her as she breathed it in.

She stepped away, bit back a scream, and the taste filling her mouth was that of her own blood. Real blood. My blood, she thought. Real blood.

The chopping sound, the oozing gore, were only head games.

She closed her eyes.

The chopping timbre faded to a distant echo, and then vanished entirely.

Just my imagination, she told herself. Maybe my brain got a little cooked out in the sun.

But she could smell the blood, taste it in the air, feel the warmth rising from the mess.

Somewhere, in the distance, she heard a steady pounding, different from the meat cleaver's chopping—a loud, mechanical droning. At first she had thought it was thunder, but now it almost reminded her of the ceaseless grind and churn of an oil pump, but not quite.

Choom! Choom! Choom!

She opened her eyes.

Blood still dribbled from the chopping block, spattering the floor.

This was no trick of her imagination.

It was real.

Choom!

Cal had turned on his machine.

* * *

Andi leaned against the Sunbird's bumper. The metal was hot against the back of her legs, but what wasn't? She chewed on her lower lip and watched Donny. Her stomach turned flips, but for once, it wasn't because of the morning sickness.

Morning sickness, she thought. What a joke! It strikes at all hours of the day, morning, noon, and night.

Donny was still fumbling with his radio. Maybe, if she could save up enough money at the grocery store, she could buy him an mp3 player. Maybe not a real Ipod, but one of those knock-off brands. She had already asked her manager if she could start working double-shifts. She knew she'd need to save as much money as possible for the baby, but maybe she could put a little aside.

Maybe.

She steeled her courage and prepared to ruin her boyfriend's life.

"Hey," she said, "while we have a couple of minutes to ourselves, there's something I want to tell you."

"Yeah, babe." Donny turned the radio over in his hands. His brow was furrowed in concentration. "I love you, too."

"No, that's not it."

Donny raised an eyebrow in her direction.

"I mean, I do love you, but there's something else."

"Fire away."

She took a breath. The dry air washed down her throat, filled her lungs.

"There's two things, really."

She was stalling. At least, that's what Jen would have said. But she'd been putting off telling Donny the truth for months now. A few more minutes wouldn't kill anybody.

Choom!

A sound reverberated across the blasted town. The windows of the Sunbird vibrated.

"What the fuck was that?" Donny dropped the radio in the dirt. He looked around. The sound seemed to be coming from all directions at once. "Was that an explosion or something? Maybe underground? Cal said something was burning in the old mineshafts." Choom! Choom!

A strong wind whipped past, sweeping a hissing, stinging cloud of sand into

137

the air. The detritus slapped across Andi's skin like a swarm of angry, stinging insects.

"Ow!" she cried. "Ow!"

She closed her eyes, but not quickly enough, and the sand sizzled across her corneas. Tears flushed the dust down her face, and she kept her eyelids squeezed tightly shut. She turned her head away, fearing the grit might flay the skin from her face.

Choom! Choom!

The steady reverberation wasn't terribly loud, but it was already working its way under Andi's skin, putting her on edge, making the roots of her teeth itch.

"What's happening?"

Choom! Choom!

"I told you!" Donny yelled. "It's the aliens."

Choom!

The wind picked up, swirling more rapidly. Andi tried to cover herself, but the sheet of burning sand lashed against her exposed face, arms, belly, and legs like a scourge. She screamed, even as Donny tried to stand between her and the vicious wind, tried to shield her with his own body.

The roar of the wind made her ears pop, and there was another noise, too.

Popping and creaking.

The snap of cracking wood.

Choom!

"I think the sound's coming from over there!" Donny cried.

He pushed Andi alongside the Sunbird. The sand sizzled against the car, trying to peel the paint away in the same way it was trying to peel the skin from her bones. Donny opened the car driver's side door, helped Andi inside.

"You'll be safe in there. I'm going to find Jen and Cal."

"Don't leave me!"

Andi opened her eyes, but everything was a watery blur.

But she didn't see Donny anywhere.

She sat for a few minutes, letting her vision clear. She knew Donny would be back for her soon, and he'd bring Jen and Cal with him, and they could get out of this place. She felt dirty and tired. There was dirt in her eyes, her ears, her head. She just wanted to go home and take a long shower.

The sand whipped against the car. She could barely see out the windows.

Something moved behind the car. She caught a glimpse of it in the rearview. She turned in the seat and peered into the sandstorm.

For several seconds, she saw nothing.

Then, she saw movement.

Down the street, she saw the dim outlines of several figures standing in the cloud of dust. They shambled towards the car, surrounded it. Leaned down to peer inside.

Andi screamed.

They weren't human. They couldn't have been. Their eyes weren't human. They were the eyes of ghosts.

Of demons.

* * *

In the dream, Cal had descended into a winding, pitch-black tunnel again and again. Each trip, he emerged carrying some misshapen mechanical component. Pieces of heavy pipe. Toothy gears. Tangles of rubber-coated wiring. And each trip, he left more and more of himself in the shadows below. By the final trip—right before he awoke and started drawing crude plans for the Machine—he crawled from the tunnel as nothing more than a blood-soaked skeleton.

Since that night, he'd pieced together an assembly manual of sorts from snippets gathered from obituaries and the backs of packages of rat poison, from treatises on torture and dog-eared pornographic paperbacks. The instructions were hidden in dozens of different places, placed there by other dreamers. The city had told him where to look, and the words just seemed to make sense to him when he saw them. It took several weeks to put everything together.

Everything leading up to this moment.

Here, in the gutted ruins of the Sessler City Community Church.

He couldn't wait to see what this bitch could do.

Tears ran down his face as he gazed up at the metallic monstrosity he had created.

Choom! Choom! Choom!

The machine twisted and whistled and writhed. It expanded and contracted, clattering and clanking, hissing and spitting steam.

It breathed.

Choom! Choom!

And it was getting bigger.

* * *

As Jen turned towards the door of the butcher shop, she was startled to see a little boy. He was maybe seven or eight years old, and he wore a dusty tan shirt and a threadbare pare of brown pants. His blonde hair was a little too long, and it partially covered his eyes. His skin was covered in a fine, pale silt as well, and he looked like a ghost.

"Who are you?"

The boy smiled. His teeth were bright, but crooked.

"This place is dangerous," Jen said. She stood between the boy and the chopping block. She feared the sight of all that blood might frighten him. But if he saw the hideous carnage, he didn't react to it. "You shouldn't be here. Not alone."

"I'm not alone."

"Who?" Jen asked.

The boy was looking past her now, his eyes filling with the sight of all … that … blood.

"Don't be afraid," Jen said. She stepped towards him.

He looked up at her.

"Don't worry. Obed will come for us."

"Obed?"

"He promised me. He's sorry he ever found the machine. He says he's going to destroy it."

"Are you talking about Cal's machine?"

"Can't rightly say that anyone's ever called it that. But Obed's gonna destroy it before it makes anyone else sick."

"Sick? What—"

Outside, the car's horn blared. Were they calling her back? Were they ready to leave? Jen looked away from the boy for only a second, and when she turned towards him again, he looked … different. His eyes were sunken, and his skin was pale and dry and peeling. Bright blood covered his lips and chin.

"Are you all right? You're bleeding."

"It's not my blood."

His fingers glistened with blood. His nails were caked with strips of flaccid skin.

He leaped at her, growling.

Jen kicked him in the throat. She hadn't suffered through six years of self defense and Tae Kwan Do for nothing. The boy squeaked and toppled to the floor. He clutched at his crushed windpipe with bloody fingers and squirmed in the gore covering the floor. His kicking feet left bloody skid marks across the bare boards.

The car horn sounded again, a long, urgent note.

Distracting Jen.

When she looked again, the boy was gone.

Only the blood remained.

* * *

Cal suddenly realized he was surrounded by people. They had not been there seconds before, but now they stood alongside him, watching the pump and grind of the Machine. The men wore filthy overalls, and dirt that would never come clean had settled into the wrinkles around their eyes and mouths. The women wore somber dresses, and their hair was pulled back beneath yellowed bonnets. He didn't know them, but he recognized them just the same.

The townsfolk of Sessler City.

"I did as you asked," he said.

They gazed at him with empty eyes—black eyes, eyes like those of a shark. Something like oil ran as tears down their dusty cheeks. Their faces were weary, pained masks.

Where did they all come from?

Another person materialized out of thin air.

"How many of you are there?" Cal asked.

Dust swirled and congealed, pooling together to shape yet another person, this one a man wearing a miner's helmet.

The machine churned and spun.

Choom!

The wood of the church was reforming right before his eyes. It looked like the time-lapsed work of termites, only in reverse. The church was stitching itself back together as the Machine whirred and droned. The sand was melding to reform the stained glass windows. The pews were unrotting. Even the carpet was stitching itself back together, leading all the way up to the spot where, in a normal church, the preacher's podium should have been.

Only here, the Machine cranked and pumped.

Beneath the Machine—for now it hovered several inches off the floor—a dark chasm yawned, leading down into shadow. The church must have been built atop the mineshaft where the First Machine had been hidden.

And Cal understood.

He had constructed the beating heart of Sessler City. And now that it was in place, the city was waking up, coming back to life.

More townsfolk appeared. Their mouths were covered with blood. Gore ran down their chins, glistening, oozing from their lips.

"What happens now?" Cal asked.

The Machine screeched—a painful sound—metal scraping metal.

The apparitions flinched at the noise.

The Machine loomed over them, growing, drawing closer.

Screaming.

The scream echoed down the mineshaft.

In the dream that spawned the Machine, something down in the darkness had been eating away at Cal, picking the meat from his bones until there was nothing left. As the bloodied phantoms pressed in on him, Cal knew what had been eating him in the dream ... or at least he had narrowed it down to two options.

Either the townsfolk ... or the Machine.

Hands groped at him. He tried to pull away from them, but they were too strong. Their nails dug into his flesh.

The Machine screeched and whined. The clockwork gears smoked. Flakes of stripped metal uncoiled between the grinding components.

A young man leaned in close to Cal. He was big and handsome. And Cal thought he might have known him.

Obed, who discovered the First Machine.

Who fell from grace and tried to destroy the town.

Who, with his dying breath, had realized what an awful mistake he had made. "Obed."

Obed's lips twitched, pulling back. He had no teeth, no tongue.

His throat gaped like a mineshaft.

A spray of sand erupted from his mouth, blasting across Cal's face. Cal shrieked and yanked free of the people who held him. He couldn't see. His nasal cavity and throat were filled with a mixing cement of blood and sand and snot. He brought his hands to his burning face and felt the warm, wet, sticky mess that had once been his eyes, nose, and mouth.

He stepped away from the phantoms …

And into the waiting maw of the machine.

The chewing gears pulped his body within seconds.

His blood spattered across the newly reformed walls of the church.

Oiled the machine.

Not even his bones survived.

* * *

A half dozen figures attacked the car.

Sitting behind the steering wheel, Andi screamed. She pressed down on the horn, praying that someone—anyone would hear her. The ghosts of Sessler City battered at the windshield. They beat at the windows. Their fingernails scrabbled at the glass. They leered at Andi with their black eyes. Any minute and they would break through the window and drag her from the car.

"Hey!"

Donny stood several yards away from the car. He hooted and hollered, jumped and waved.

"Over here, assholes! Come get me!"

The ghastly figures surged towards him.

"Oh, God!" Andi choked out a cry. "Donny, run!"

The townsfolk moved with a feral quickness, but Donny had spent three years in the high school track team, and he could still bring the speed. In the open expanse of the desert, a bunch of dead fucks didn't stand a chance of catching him.

He'd lead them away from Andi, give her a chance to find a better hiding place, then he'd jackrabbit back and come to her rescue.

As he turned, another half dozen other figures materialized from the dust before him. Donny stumbled right into their waiting arms. They carried assorted tools of the miner's trade, such as shovels and sledgehammers and—

One of the men smashed Donny in the head with a pick axe. The point of the weapon ripped through skin and tissue, shattered teeth. Donny's face came apart at the jaw line. The top of his head sailed across the street and landed, rolling awkwardly, in the dirt. Blood fountained into the air, showering the townsfolk.

In the car, Andi screamed.

* * *

Jen rounded the corner.

She didn't remember the building being so ... complete ... earlier.

How could she have missed that?

She couldn't see much through the chaotic storm of wind and sand, but she could see the outline of the Sunbird through the gusting tempest. A shadow moved in the driver's seat, beating frantically at the horn.

Andi.

A group of people stood at the other end of the street. Jen couldn't make out their features, but some of them carried weapons of some sort. Jen knew what they were. They were just like the boy in the butcher shop.

Ghosts.

They stood around something sprawled in the dirt. One of the figures—a man—bent down, wiped something off the prone shape, then rubbed whatever it was all over his own face and neck.

Jen didn't want to know.

For the time being, the figures were ignoring Andi, but it was only a matter of time before the incessant tattoo of the horn caught their attention. Jen figured she had only a couple of minutes before the ghosts turned their attention towards the car.

Or on her.

She broke for the car, moving as fast as she could.

"Open the door!"

Andi kept on screaming. She couldn't take her eyes off the ghostly crowd.

The wind and sand burned Jen's flesh.

She slapped her hand against the window.

"Andi! Open up!"

Jen glanced towards the mob. They were moving towards the car. A couple of them dragged the shape in the dust behind them. They held the shape by the legs.

She knew what—who—that was.

Donny.

She pounded the window with both fists.

"Jesus, Andi! Don't make me leave you here!"

The girl wouldn't open the door.

Sobbing, Jen threw herself away from the car and into the storm. The flying sand sliced her to the bone. All around, Sessler City was piecing itself back together from the dust and rot. Where there had been nothing but crumbling frames and decaying husks, complete buildings now loomed out of the pluming dust. Jen tried to stick close to the newly-formed buildings to protect herself from the storm. Her skin was red and bleeding. The coppery tang of blood seemed to cling to every dust mote spinning in the air, sticking to Jen's sweaty flesh, trying to smother her.

Behind her, she heard the shattering of glass.

Andi's screams.

"Fuck you!" Jen shrieked. "I'm going to kill every one of you motherfuckers!"

She sobbed, almost gave up and fell to her knees, but she forced herself to keep moving. She squeezed her hands into fists. Her fingernails bit into the meat of her palm. The sensation reminded her that she was alive.

And she intended to stay that way.

She left the ghosts behind.

But not the screams.

* * *

The screams stayed with Jen for six months.

She heard them every time she closed her eyes. Andi's screams, yes, but the screams of others, too. Many people had been killed in Sessler City over the years. And, thanks to Cal's machine, the place had the chance to kill again.

Six months.

And that meant Andi was just about due, assuming the city hadn't killed her or she hadn't found a way to kill herself. Jen believed the baby was important. Right now, the town was this kind of half-truth, all spirits and shadow, memories and sorrow, but it couldn't maintain anything of substance for long.

But when a child is born within the town's boundaries, Jen thought, Sessler City will start to solidify, to become real again.

And it might start to spread.

The world had changed a great deal since the town's heyday. The things that lived there wouldn't be satisfied with the taste of ashes for long.

Or maybe you're full of shit, Jen thought, and Andi's just as dead as Donny.

"What are you doing, darling?" Her boss, Stu, slinked in close enough Jen smelled the beer on his breath. "I don't pay you to draw pictures."

She slipped away from him and tucked her ink pen back into her apron. She had been working as a waitress in a highway truck stop for almost as long as she had been hearing the screams. She never bothered to return home after what happened in Sessler City. She assumed her family and friends thought she was dead.

Just as well.

"Sorry." She started to crumple the napkin she'd been drawing upon. "I guess I'm just distracted."

Stu grabbed her wrist before she could completely destroy the illustration.

"Hold on a minute now." He examined the drawing for a second, then tapped it with a thick finger. "What, exactly, is that? Some sort of engine or something?"

"Something like that."

"Hell," he said, "I didn't know you were into cars. I've got a '71 GTO sitting in my garage. Bought it off a buddy of mine and I've been rebuilding it here and there for the past year. You ought to come over and take a look—"

Jen pretty much tuned him out instantly. She knew exactly where he was going. Stu had been trying to get into her panties from the day he met her. The sad thing was, she didn't have any better offers. Once, she had considered herself a pretty girl, but now.

The town had changed her.

Scarred her.

Her face, neck, arms, and legs were pocked from the fury of the sandstorm.

She balled up the napkin and tossed it in the trash. She didn't need the drawings any more. She knew the Machine backwards and forwards. She dreamed about it almost every night.

Just like Cal.

Only, he used the dreams to build the Machine.

Jen planned on destroying it.

And, hopefully, all of Sessler City with it.

* * *

A skinny, unshaven trucker leaned across the seat and held the door for her.

"Where you heading, hon?"

Jen hoisted herself into the cab. Everything she owned—her knife, her gun, and her homemade dynamite—she carried in a canvas satchel.

"Ever heard of Sessler City?"

"Can't say that I have." The trucker's mouth split in an overwide grin. "But I'll take you there if it's on my route."

The truck rumbled onto the open road. The driver started whistling a lonely tune. Every now and again, he stole a glimpse at Jen, looking at her legs or down her top. She didn't bother to stop him.

Take a good long look, she thought, because you'll never see me again.

She didn't plan on making it out of Sessler City alive.

Not this time.

She started trembling. She bit down on her lower lip. She squeezed her hands into fists.

Stop it, she thought. Just stop.

Maybe she could have avoided the place forever.

But she had a promise to keep.

She owed it to Donny, Cal, and Andi.

"I'm going to kill every one of you motherfuckers!"

And she didn't plan on letting something like fear make a liar out of her.

"Cry of the Machine" was originally published in Desolate Souls (2008).

With this story, I intentionally set out to break some rules that I've heard ever since I was in high school. Most notably, I wanted to change points of view throughout the piece and give the story a bigger scope. This is kind of a horror movie in prose format, I suppose, and it was born as I drove through a small Illinois town. The town was run down, on the verge of dying. As I passed through, I saw a sign outside a closed up gas station that read, "What's Wrong With This Town?" I drove straight to the safety of my home and wrote this story.

- CB

THE FEAST OF CROWS

I sketched a picture of him—or tried to at least—the man with the birds.

I had seen him many times before, with his wrinkled and stained olive-green overcoat, buttoned all the way to his throat with the collar turned high as if to ward off a chill, even though the climate was much too warm. He was short and thin, with uncombed and unwashed hair dangling before his eyes, and I couldn't help but think that he had not eaten a decent meal in days. And the birds—let's not forget the birds—crows, I believe, or possibly ravens, large and mean-spirited enough to drive pigeons and even squirrels from their territory as the little man hobbled along, reaching into his coat pockets with filthy hands and tossing dry breadcrumbs to the ground. Screeching, the crows clouded around him like a storm ready to break.

And hadn't I drawn pictures of him before? Paging through my sketches I would have certainly found a dozen or so thumbnails of the man, half-finished images scribbled in haste, hidden among hundreds of similar drawings. But until that day, I couldn't say that I had ever really taken notice of him, and perhaps that's when he first took notice of me. Or perhaps, in paying attention to him, I finally opened my eyes to what every one of us glimpses each day, but are too busy with our lives to notice or remember.

If only I could forget . . .

I often visited the park to pass time between classes. Typically, I sat for an hour or so, my Bristol tablet balanced upon my knees as I quickly sketched picture after picture of the people who passed by, the crisp pencil lines fading to gray shadow as I worked, my fingers stained silvery-black by the lead. The park, being so close to campus as well as a number of businesses, attracted a lot of people—students like myself, businesspeople taking their lunch, joggers working off extra pounds—and the pages of the sketchbook were filled with various drawings.

I often lost track of time as I worked, and my professors had cautioned me more than once for tardiness or for missing classes. Still, few subjects captured my attention and imagination the way the little man with the birds did. If I had paused long enough to dwell on my fascination, I might have been disturbed— and rightfully so! But I found myself drawn to the little man, and I wondered why I hadn't noticed him before.

Shuffling along the sidewalk, he seemed tired, weary, as if each step was more difficult than the last. He paused to lean against a park bench, and the crows beat their wings around him, urging him onward, urging him to throw out another handful of crumbs. His scabbed hand clutched the back of the bench as he lowered himself to the seat. He flexed his fingers and examined his hands, looking at his palms, as if trying to foretell the future in the lines and folds of skin.

From a distance, I put his likeness on the page. The crows, overprotective of the supply of breadcrumbs, often dove at other passersby, and most people gave the man plenty of space. So, he sat by himself, save for the birds flocking around him, and I thought my drawing evoked a feeling of loneliness.

I wasn't certain that I had effectively captured the haunted quality of his eyes, but I realized I had no time, not if I wanted to make my last class of the day, so I quickly applied the finishing touches to the drawing. I frowned in disappointment. The sketch wasn't as good as I'd hoped. But I was honest enough with myself to know that I seldom cared for my own work. Before flipping the tablet closed, I scribbled a phrase across the bottom of the page. I almost wrote "The Man and his Birds," but instead smiled to myself and wrote "The Birds and Their Man." I shoved the tablet and pencils into my bag, took a final bite of a nearly forgotten lunch, and headed back to campus.

A canopy of thick branches shaded the path, and the sun pierced the leaves in shimmering beams. A patchwork of shadow and light covered the ground. I made my way across the park in haste, not wanting another lecture on punctuality. A few people brushed past, returning to their own classes, their own jobs, but for the most part I found myself alone.

The flutter of dark wings caught my eye, and I paused for a moment. One of the crows had separated itself—or had been driven away—from the rest of the flock and now roosted upon a crooked branch. The crow moved in such a fashion as to give the impression that it was pecking at thin air, its head bobbing back and forth upon its neck. I wondered if it was attacking a swarm of tiny insects that I could not see. Within seconds, though, it shook its beak, as if finding purchase with its prey, and tore what might have been a five-inch strip of pale blue from the air itself. The strip dangled from the bird's mouth like a bit of limp cloth. I saw what could have only been the fragment of a cloud crawl through the strip before the bird hastily devoured the morsel. In the air, the tear wavered, like a mirage, and within I saw a yawning, endless blackness, a vast emptiness.

But not empty.

Not empty at all.

I felt myself shaking, felt a sudden cold sweat break out across my forehead, because I knew that if I stared into the void for too long it might draw me in. The sky seemed to spill back into the tear, filling it as water might fill a glass. The hairs on my arms and neck stood on end, and I rubbed my eyes, certain that I had been imagining things.

The crow cocked its head, watching me from its perch—and did I see some hint of almost human intelligence in its eyes?—before squawking, ruffling its feathers, and taking flight.

I looked about to see if anyone else had seen. But I was alone. Within minutes, I had convinced myself that my eyes had indeed been playing tricks on me.

* * *

That night, I dreamed of a flight of crows—crows with beaks and talons of the darkest crimson and large eyes of human quality—soaring by the thousands above a blasted and barren wasteland. The sky tore and ripped at their passing, as if their feathers were like razor blades. Blackness rained to the earth below, and the world seemed to fall in upon itself.

I awoke, covered in sweat, my sheets damp and sticking to my skin.

As I had no air conditioning in my flat, I had left the window open, and the sounds of the city outside roused me to alertness. An oscillating fan purred in one corner of the room, and a neon sign just outside my window flashed to life, then faded, then flared alight seconds later.

Rising, I grumbled softly to myself and rubbed my eyes. It was only a few minutes past midnight, and I knew I probably wouldn't be getting any more sleep that night. I crossed stiffly to my desk and sat down, sliding my tablet before me. My hands trembled and my stomach turned at the memory of the dream. I shook my head, hoping to clear my thoughts and forget the nightmare, but it was no use. I flipped my tablet open and, taking a pen and inkwell, started to draw the man and the crows in more detail . . .

His rumpled coat, buttoned tight, stained by blotches of bird droppings upon the shoulders and sleeves . . .

His shoulders, stooped as if weakened from a terrible weight . . .

His face, wrinkled, creased by deep lines . . .

And the crows, flocking about him in search of food, as much a part of him it seemed as his hands, his mouths, or his eyes.

As I inked the wings of the crows, so close to one another, the lines ran together, and as I drew my shaking hand away, I knocked the inkwell over, spilling its contents onto the tablet. I swore and wiped at the spill without thinking, smearing the page, leaving the image of the man surrounded by a mass of shadow and darkness. The wet ink reflected the pulse of the neon light like a gleaming heartbeat.

I ran my ink-stained fingers across my face, the last of the shakiness from the nightmare finally passing as I stared at the ruined page, my gaze trapped by the cold stare of the man in the drawing.

What did it all mean? The crow in the park had devoured part of the world around it. I knew what I saw. I hadn't imagined it. Understanding it, however, was another matter, placing logic behind it, something I found myself unable to do.

* * *

I resolved to talk to the man the next day.

Not sure what I intended to accomplish, I thought that he, perhaps, could explain what I had seen. More than likely, he would think me mad, and he might not be far from the truth, but if anyone could possibly give me the answers I needed, it was him.

My morning classes would have been wasted—I would never have been able to concentrate—so I went to the park first thing, my pens, pencils, and a brand new tablet stuffed into my backpack.

I made a place for myself on a bench along a trail I had seen the man travel day after day, and tried to occupy myself with my sketches. I achieved nothing more elaborate than doodles, though, until without realizing it, I began drawing a flock of crows circling through an otherwise blank page.

A flapping alerted me to his presence. Three crows flew above me, diving low, inspecting the area, then perching upon a nearby tree. The birds watched the path as the man hobbled into view, tossing breadcrumbs left and right, another dozen crows surrounding him.

Placing my sketchbook aside, I stood and brushed my smudged hands upon my jeans. As he approached, I searched for words of introduction, realizing that I had no idea of what, exactly, I intended to say.

The man stopped short. His eyes were focused upon the walkway, as if he were trying to puzzle out some secret hidden within the cracked concrete, the ants, the crisscrossed twigs and grass. His lips moved nervously as he muttered to himself. He stepped back, and two of the largest crows landed upon his stooped shoulders and screeched a warning at me. I saw a kind of understanding pass between the birds and the man. One of the crows looked towards my sketchbook, which lay open upon the bench, and the man's eyes followed.

Another one of the birds flapped to the bench, surveyed the drawing, and began snatching hungrily at the page. I moved to save the sketchbook from the creature, but it snapped at my fingers, slicing them open and spattering blood across the paper. I jerked my hand away, clutched at my wounded fingers. I had never imagined that a bird's beak could be so sharp.

The crow on the bench stood triumphantly atop the bloodstained sketchbook, eyeing me, its wet beak open, its gray tongue clucking, its talons digging into the paper.

I looked back at the man, the questions now rushing freely to my lips, but he raised his head to look at me and said softly, "Leave me alone."

He continued on, never again looking in my direction, taking his flock of crows with him. The maddening cry of the crows, like laughter, rang in my ears as I gathered up my notebook and rushed home.

* * *

Again, I found myself unable to sleep through the night. Rather, I spent the evening at my drawing table, hoping that with the stroke of the pen I would draw an answer for myself. No longer did I have questions about the man and the crows. I had needs—a need to understand him and his strange connection, a need to understand what I had seen.

You're acting crazy, I told myself. You're obsessed.

I looked upon the crumpled and torn sketch of the birds. Lifting it, the red glow of the neon light streamed through the tears in the page—tears which reminded me of the tear the crow had seemingly torn in the air itself.

Lowering the paper, I nearly staggered from my chair.

One of the crows perched just outside my window upon the fire escape. It titled its head curiously, watching me.

It's eyes . . .

Eyes full of understanding, purpose . . .

The eyes of the man in the park . . .

The crow flexed its talons, and I saw tiny cuts form on the window ledge, cuts that bled black until, rippling, they vanished.

I licked my dry lips, took a step towards the bird, thinking for whatever reason that I might be able to catch it, but it screeched and flapped away, and I only closed the window. I felt strange, as if I might smother on the air itself. I tapped the window ledge. Solid. Real. But I didn't feel safe in assuming that anything was real, and I felt betrayed by my senses.

* * *

Once again forgetting school, I returned to the park, only this time, I kept my distance, hoping to follow the little man, find out where he lived, where the crows roosted at night. He had sent one of them to spy on me, and all I could do was return the favor.

I left my sketchbook at home. It was the first time in years I had been to the park without it. I waited on the other side of the park, waited, waited. Finally, I saw the man, following his regular path, birds swooping around him, gobbling up breadcrumbs as he hobbled along.

I followed him, keeping my distance.

As he left the park, the crows dispersed, and the man was alone, brushing past people on the sidewalk, dodging in and out of the crowd. The birds did not stray far, though. Looking up, I saw them circling overhead.

I couldn't help but wonder if they saw me, if they knew my intentions, and if they had somehow alerted their master.

He ducked into a shabby-looking building. A sign in one of the fingerprint-smudged windows read EFFICIENCY APTS FOR RENT.

I looked up again, and this time saw no sign of the crows.

Stepping into the building, I saw the man open a dented mailbox, find nothing, and continue up the stairs. When he was out of sight, I approached the mailbox. An adhesive label read SIMMS, Apt. 3B. I climbed the creaking stairs to the third floor.

I stood outside his apartment for several minutes, pacing, wondering what to do. From down the hall, I heard a television blaring, someone yelling at the kids. Having followed the man—Mr. Simms—this far, I knew that this might be my only chance to have my questions answered.

I knocked on the door to his apartment, and the door, which had not been closed entirely, slid open. I almost stepped inside, but instead decided to announce myself.

"Hello?"

"Who is it?" the voice called quietly.

"I-I'm sorry to disturb you." I said, deciding now it was safe to step inside. "We spoke in the park yesterday."

From baseboard to ceiling, old newspapers covered the apartment, and bird droppings speckled the floor. A window stood open, and a warm breeze filtered into the room. Several crows perched on the sill. A few others stood upon a nearby table. Still others rested upon the floor and on the back of a ratty chair.

Mr. Simms stood in a tiny kitchen. He still wore his green overcoat. "I know you," he said, stepping towards me. Sweat glistened on his forehead. "You're the one who's been drawing pictures of me."

"I need to talk to you. The other day . . . the other day I saw something. I saw something with one of your crows."

"My crows?" he laughed. "You think they belong to me?"

"I saw—"

"Go home." He waved me away. "Leave me be. I don't like visitors."

"But you're not listening to me."

"I know what you saw. You think I don't know? You think you want to understand, but you don't. Turn around right now and go home."

"I can't."

He hung his head low, shaking it. The crows in the window squawked.

"You don't know what you're asking," he said. "You'd be better off just forgetting what you've seen. But I don't suppose there's much chance of that, is there?"

The crows clucked their tongues.

The heat in the apartment seemed unbearable. How could he wear that coat?

"They lie, you know." He shot a disgusted look at one of the birds. "You'll learn to understand them. But their every breath is a lie, as if the truth might cause them pain. You have to be careful. Never trust them."

"What are you saying?"

Slowly, he unbuttoned the top button of his coat. "I always knew this day would come. One man's not strong enough to guard for all time. The flesh is not enough, and they start to disobey. Start to wander off. You have to watch that. They have to be watched. Always."

"I don't understand."

"You've had the dream, haven't you?" He closed his eyes and whispered, as if quoting scripture. "And lo, I looked upon the earth scoured of life, and knew that dark wings had ushered the way."

He pulled open his jacket, and I staggered back, trying to catch my breath.

No skin covered his chest. Only the bare white bone of his rib cage showed through and inside, what, impossibly, might have been a dozen crows, screeching, beating their wings against his bones.

Sweat stung my eyes. My mouth opened and closed, but I could not speak.

He reached to the center of his chest and pulled open his ribcage as if opening the doors of a cabinet. The crows flew from inside him in a chaotic frenzy, each one ripping at him, tearing at the very fabric of the room, tearing open a hole of total blackness in the center of the apartment. I threw my hands up to protect myself.

Tears streamed down the man's face.

I lowered my hands. The crows had gone. "Where?" I asked.

The room hung in rippling tatters around me. The walls, floor, kitchen, chairs, window—all wavered before me like a mirage, and in the very center of the room, a gaping black fissure, threatening to pull me in. I knew that the crows must have flown into the darkness. I saw the fabric of reality attempting to stitch itself back together, to fill the hole. But the blackness within the fissure writhed, and hundreds or possibly thousands of more crows spilled forth in a black wave, only their beaks and talons were as blood. The sound of their cries was deafening, and as I watched, they tore every shred of flesh from Mr. Simms' body, until only a quivering skeleton remained, clutching feebly at its own ribcage.

The glistening skeleton fell over, shattered upon the floor, as the crows continued their assault.

The wings of the crows buffeted me, and I cried out, but my voice was muffled by a cloud of darkness that settled upon me.

* * *

I emerged from the room sometime later—I could not be sure how long—and walked downstairs, through the hallway, and into the light.

A crowd of people passed by, and I thought I heard one whisper at the sight of me. For the most part, though, no one noticed me. No one paid attention to the filthy olive green overcoat that I wore, even though the sun beat down upon the sidewalk.

Above, several crows circled the sky, a sky which I knew was no less fragile than one of my painted canvases.

One of the crows started to stray, and I tossed out a handful of breadcrumbs to lure it back.

The crows squawked, and I understood their trickery as they cried for release.

I walked along, keeping my head down, muttering soft prayers to myself that no one would pay me or the birds too much attention. In the end, Mr. Simms hadn't been strong enough to face his task alone. Now, as I felt the stirring inside my chest and saw the birds circling above me, I only hoped that I was stronger.

"Feast of Crows" was originally published in Black Petals (2002).

Hell if I know where this one came from. A nightmare, most likely. Regardless, it's part of a myth cycle of sorts that I return to time and again. The world in which this story is a place where a thin coat of paint has been splashed over the true horrors waiting just beyond the veil. One day, those horrors are going to rip their way through, and then all Hell is going to break loose.

- CB

REMAINS

The dead rats danced the day the hired man came round.

My father, rest his soul, might have scolded me for saying such a foolish thing. He didn't care much for dreams and fancies—nightmares, either. But that's how it started, way back during those last warm weeks of September, more than thirty years ago.

With dead rats.

Dancing.

My little sister spotted the stranger before I did. I was shelling peas, like Mama had asked the both of us. Sitting on the warped front steps, I snapped pods, scraped peas into a large bowl, and tossed the husks into the yard for the chickens to squabble over. Abbie, on the other hand, did everything in her power to avoid anything remotely akin to a chore. I could hear her crawling around the crawlspace beneath the front porch.

"What are you doing?" I asked.

"I'm busy."

"Sure you are." I glanced at the bucket of unsnapped peas. The supply didn't appear to be diminished, despite my efforts. "You know, you're supposed to be helping."

"I'm busy," Abbie said again.

"Mama doesn't want you playing under there anyhow. You're gonna ruin your clothes, and there's spiders down there big enough to bite your fingers off."

I grabbed another snap from the bucket and cracked it open for emphasis. Abbie hated spiders, and I hoped to startle her out from under the porch. Considering how hard-headed my little sister could be, though, I should've known better.

"Ain't no spiders down here, Seth, not that I ever saw."

"You sure about that?"

"Yes, I am, thank you very much."

I sighed in defeat. Since scaring her didn't work, I decided to give guilt a try.

"Maybe not, but you should come on out of there anyhow. I wouldn't ever stick you with doing the chores all by yourself."

That was a lie, but as I hollowed out yet another shell, it felt like the truth.

Abbie started humming a lighthearted tune, partly to let me know our discussion was at an end. I halfway considered tattling on her, just to watch Mama drag her out from under the porch and take a switch to her backside. But Abbie and me, we had an understanding—we didn't snitch, no matter what. Sometimes, the agreement bit me in the behind, but a deal's a deal. I kept on snapping peas, and before I knew it, I was humming right along with my sister.

I didn't notice the lone figure approaching our house, but eagle-eyed Abbie spotted him right away.

"Who's that?" It took me a second to realize she'd stopped humming. Her voice was hushed and muffled. "Somebody's coming this way."

I shaded my eyes from the sun and looked down the tree-lined path.

The stranger was tall and lean, dressed in dirty jeans and a button-up work shirt. He carried a bulky duffle bag slung over his shoulder. For some reason, he reminded me of a scarecrow that had crawled down from its perch in the corn field. I couldn't really see his face, because the shadows from the trees seemed to cling to his features. He didn't so much walk as lope, like an animal, and every few steps he paused to glance over his shoulder, as if expecting to see someone following him.

"What's he doing?" Abbie's small fingers jutted out through the lattice work lining the porch. Through the holes in the trim, I saw her big blue eyes peering out from the shadows. "He looking for someone?"

He's on the run, I thought, from the law ...

Or something worse.

The idea just popped into my head. Unexpected thoughts like that often exploded through my noggin, and I'd been accused of letting my imagination get the better of me more than once. To hear my folks tell the tale, I read too many of those crime and horror comics Mr. Oswald stocked at the drug store. Maybe I did, maybe I didn't. Either way, I'd learned to keep my lips sealed when it came to my wild notions.

But I didn't like the stranger from the moment I spotted him.

Something about him put me on edge.

He gave me the creeps.

"You just stay put." I rapped my knuckles against the porch, and Abbie pulled her fingers back into the shadows. "Stay quiet. Stay out of sight."

For once, Abbie didn't backtalk me. I figured the stranger spooked her as much as he did me. In its time, the filthy crawlspace beneath the porch had served as a fairytale castle and the Lone Ranger's base of operations, an army bunker and a mud pie bakery. But today, Abbie used it as a hiding place.

I continued shelling peas, but I didn't take my eyes off the man as he tramped my way. I couldn't guess his age with any accuracy. He might have been in his late thirties or early forties. His face was weathered from countless hours wiled away in the sun, and his longish hair was more gray than black.

"Afternoon," he said. His voice was deep and gravelly, like road grit coated his throat.

I nodded and scowled at him.

He shrugged his bag from his shoulder. The duffel thunked into the dirt. Placing one of his steel-toed work boots on the lowest porch step, the stranger leaned close and draped his arms over his knee. His sleeves were rolled up to his elbows, and I saw dozens of scars crisscrossing the flesh of his forearms—some of them still pink and only recently healed by the looks of it. Dirt had settled into the wrinkles of his face and hands, and his fingernails were crescents of pure black.

"Your daddy home?" he asked.

Underneath the porch, Abbie shuffled in the dirt, crawling back into the darkest of the shadows. The stranger tilted his head. His eyes strayed towards the latticework, and one corner of his mouth rose.

"I'll fetch him," I said.

I put the bowl of shelled peas aside and stood up.

His eyes ticked away from Abbie's hiding place and met mine. His grin came across like a bestial thing. His teeth were yellowed and looked sharp. I backed towards the screen door. I called for my father, and I felt a rush of relief when I heard the heavy tread of his approaching footsteps.

The stranger looked over his shoulder again.

I narrowed my eyes. What are you running from?

He stood up straight when Daddy stepped onto the porch. My father was a big man, tall and broad-shouldered, and he'd worked hard almost every day of his life. He wore his favorite pair of blue coveralls. His greasy cap was folded up and shoved in his pocket, because he never—never—wore a hat indoors. I could tell his hands were bothering him. His knuckles were red and swollen as thick as tubers, and his fingers curled like the legs of a dying spider. Sometimes, his rheumatism flared up so bad he could hardly pick up his fork to eat breakfast. Today was one of those days, and Daddy's voice was laced with a painful weariness.

"Help you?"

"I sure hope so." The stranger kept on smiling. "Word is you're looking to hire a man to pitch in around your place. Figured I'd come by and see about the job, unless you've already brought somebody else on."

Daddy eyed the man for a second or two, sizing him up.

"You ain't from around here, are you?"

"No, sir. I was just passing through when I heard about the job. Thought I could stay around for a while, though, maybe earn some extra traveling money."

"Where is it you're headed?"

The stranger nodded and sucked at his teeth. "No place in particular."

"You ever work a farm before?"

"Worked tobacco since I was a boy, and I spent a couple summers as a farmhand outside of Knoxville."

"I can't offer much of a wage," Daddy said, "barely enough to get by, really. There's a backroom in the tool shed that's got a cot and a washbasin. You can bed down there. We'll feed you three times a day, but you'll have to take your meals either in the shed or outside."

The rule about eating outside didn't sit particularly well with Daddy. As far as he was concerned, anyone who worked the land deserved a seat at our supper table. But he knew my mother would never stand for a stranger sitting alongside her family.

In this case, I was glad for my Mama's ways.

"All that sounds fine," the stranger said. "I don't need much, and it'll be nice to sleep with a roof over my head and get three squares for a change."

Three squares, I thought. Sounds like something an escaped convict might say.

Nah. That's just your comic books talking.

"All right then," Daddy said. "Sounds like you've got yourself a job."

The stranger thanked my father and introduced himself as Cole Jensen. He stuck out his hand. Daddy hesitated for a second, then reluctantly reached out to shake the hired man's hand. He winced painfully as Cole's fingers closed around his own. I could have sworn I saw that disdainful smirk wriggle across Cole's face.

"Why don't you go put your bag away?" Daddy pointed to the tool shed. "I'll be over directly to show you around."

As Cole trudged to the shed, I whispered to my father, "You don't need to pay somebody to help. I can handle anything needs doing."

"I know you can. But there's too much for any three people to do, let alone two. You're mama's about to pop with the new baby, and you and your sister have your schooling to attend to."

"I could stay home and help instead."

It wasn't a completely selfish gesture. Matter of fact, I liked school, especially reading and writing. But I didn't like the idea of Cole Jensen lurking around the farm when I wasn't around to keep an eye on him.

"You can help in the mornings and the afternoons. Don't fret. We won't do it all without you."

He rubbed his hands together, trying to work the ache from his bones, and he tapped his foot against the porch steps.

"Abbie, get out from under there before your mama catches you and tans your hide. I don't want to listen to your wailing when your rear end's stinging."

My sister scurried out into the light.

Daddy smiled and said, "Why don't you two take Jerry Lee out to the barn for a while?"

"Yes, sir," I said, all too glad to take a break from field snaps.

"Do we have to?" Abbie whined. "We were gonna go out to the pond this afternoon."

"Don't give me any duff," Daddy said. "You know you aren't supposed to hang around at that old mud hole. But if you hurry up you can finish your chores and still have some time to play a little before suppertime. The more bellyaching you do now, the less time you'll have for fun later."

Pouting, Abbie made a spectacle of dragging herself away.

Daddy only shook his head. Like the rest of the family, he was accustomed to Abbie's overdramatic antics.

"One day," he said—more to himself to anyone, "that girl will break all the hearts in Hollywood."

I fought back the urge to warn him about the hired man. Daddy was a hard-working man, though, and he toiled in the real world, not in a world where boys spied boogiemen in the shadows.

But he might be an escaped criminal ...or maybe even a killer.

Daddy wouldn't see it that way.

From around the other side of the house, Abbie called impatiently. "Hurry up, Seth!"

I watched my father greet Cole Jensen by the tool shed. I looked long and hard at the road that bordered our farm. I didn't see anyone coming to haul the hired man away. But I sure wished I did. After a few minutes, I went to join my sister.

Something told me nothing would ever be the same again.

I had never known any home other than the farm. Our house, tall and white and surrounded by Mama's rose bushes ... The old shed, with its sagging roof and rotting walls, and its replacement, with its fresh coat of paint and that eyesore of a tractor parked beneath ... The cement birdbath, where cardinals sometimes gathered in the mornings ...

I loved that old farm.

But the hired man ruined it all.

Spoiled it.

After it was all said and done, I hated the farm.

And I hated Cole Jensen and what he had brought with him.

This is how it happened.

* * *

We kept Jerry Lee chained to a post in the backyard. The little rat terrier would get to running and never stop if he got a wild hair. I'd spent more than a few afternoons chasing him from darn near one side of the county to the other. He wasn't good for much, except for one thing, but Abbie loved him anyhow. As I rounded the corner, I saw my sister kneeling down beside the black and white dog. She scratched behind his ears, and he wagged his stubby tail. His tongue lolled out of his mouth.

"Come on, Jerry Lee!" I clapped my hands together. "We're going to the barn!"

As soon as he heard the word "barn," the dog jumped to attention, his muscles tense, his eyes darting and alert.

"Why'd you go and do that?" Abby stood up and put her hands on her hips defiantly. "We were having us a relaxing time."

"We don't keep him around to be your pet."

"You're just jealous because he's my best friend."

"A dog like this, he ain't nobody's friend." I unhooked Jerry Lee's chain from the post in the ground. I held one end of the chain like a leash. "You're a dyed-in-the-wool killer, ain't ya, boy?"

Jerry Lee tugged at the chain.

Abbie wrinkled her nose and shot me a raspberry.

"I wish a green fly would land on your tongue," I said.

Jerry Lee pulled in the direction of the barn. He might have been small, but he was strong. I kept a firm grip on the chain. For Jerry Lee, the barn meant one thing.

Rats.

He jumped and yipped as Abbie and I opened the barn doors. Light spilled across the dirt floor, chasing shadows into the corners. The barn was old and dark and smelled of dust. Along the wall leaned a couple of thick, three foot long sticks. Abbie grabbed them and handed me one as I undid the chain around Jerry Lee's neck. He might have been a runner, but I didn't worry about him charging off while he was on the job. Sniffing the ground, he walked into the center of the barn, like he had done a hundred times before. A low growl rattled in his throat. He stood at attention, waiting.

Rats infested the barn. Big ones. Some almost as big as Jerry Lee. Nothing we did deterred them. Daddy had tried poisoning them with d-CON, and for a while we discovered a bunch of mummified rat corpses in the corners. But eventually, they stopped taking the bait. We brought in barn cats, but some of them vanished altogether or—as I believed—were devoured by the rats, and the remaining felines decided to avoid the barn altogether. We lined the feed barrels with metal, but it wasn't long before the rodents gnawed right through. If a rat could gnaw through metal, I didn't want to think what it could do to flesh and bone.

163

I wasn't worried, though, because my sister and I were armed with the most lethal rat-killing weapon known to man.

Jerry Lee.

Abbie and I used the sticks to jab at the shadowy corners of the barn and behind feed barrels, flushing rats from hiding. As soon as the squealing vermin scurried across the room, Jerry Lee pounced. He clamped the rat in his jaws, gave it a quick shake, and tossed the creature—shattered spine and all—into the dust. On a good day, Jerry Lee could kill three dozen rats in an hour, and he never grew tired of the carnage. The whole time, Abbie wore a look of pure disgust as her favorite pet vented his bloodlust. I hate to admit it, but I almost enjoyed myself, and I made a little game out of scaring the rats into Jerry Lee's waiting teeth.

Once we were done, I chained the exhausted terrier to the yard post again. Panting, he flopped on his side to rest. Abbie and me carried out the gruesome task of scooping up the crushed, slobber-matted rat carcasses, tossing them in burlap sacks, and dumping them in the burn barrels around back. I got the feeling the surviving rats watched us with hate-filled eyes from the darkness, but they didn't dare creep out of hiding. We tossed the last of the dead rats in the barrels, and Abbie mopped sweat and dust from her forehead with the back of her arm.

"Think we can go to the pond now?" she asked.

"You heard what Daddy said."

"He don't really care. Besides, he's too busy showing Cole around."

My stomach knotted up at the mention of his name. Maybe getting away from the farm, even for a couple of minutes, wasn't such a bad idea.

"All right." I shrugged. "Let's go."

She grinned at me and dashed off.

Jerry Lee hopped up, growled, and chuffed a quiet warning. He stood defiantly in the circle of dirt he'd worn in the grass from his prowling, but he stared towards the front of the house. I followed his gaze, and saw Daddy talking to the hired man. Cole didn't seem to be paying much attention to whatever Daddy was saying. Instead, he looked back at me.

I jumped when Abbie called out to me.

"You coming, Seth?"

She stood at the edge of the corn field, shifting from one foot to the other, almost like she had to pee. I moved towards her, but glanced over my shoulder.

I realized something that chilled my blood.

The hired man wasn't looking at me.

He was staring at my sister.

Giggling, Abbie raced through the corn field. Tall stalks loomed around us. Soon, it would be harvest time. Not long after that, the field would be beaten flat in preparation for next season's crops. For now, though, a thick sea of cornstalks enveloped us. I followed Abbie as she weaved back and forth between the rows, kicking up dirt clods, making the stalks shake and sway. By the time we reached the pond, I was covered in sweat and gulping down mouthfuls of hot, dusty air. My shirt and jeans clung wetly to my skin.

Situated right in the middle of the field, the pond was ringed by a high mound of dirt. Climbing to the crest of the earthen hill, I could see row after row of corn stretching off in every direction. Looking back the way we'd come, I saw the roofs of our house and the barn. In the distance ahead of us, I saw the grain silo of the McKinley place. The pond itself was a milky brown color, and was probably more mud than water.

My friends and I had played many a game of King of the Mountain on the hill, and I myself had been soaked in the pond's muddy shallows more than once upon being dethroned. We didn't play there much anymore, though, not after what happened to Delroy McKinley last summer.

To me, the pond seemed lonely and bleak these days.

"I wish we could go swimming." Abbie still loved the spot. She liked throwing stones into the depths or launching paper sailing ships across the surface or watching tadpoles along the shoreline. She scooted down the hill and stood on the pond's bank. "It's hot enough, that's for sure."

"I wouldn't want to swim in that mudhole."

"You would too."

"Go ahead and take a dip if you want." I knew good and well she wouldn't. Abbie never swam in the pond, even before what happened to Delroy. "I'll stay right where I am, thank you very much. You enjoy yourself."

"Maybe I will."

She kicked off her shoes and dipped her toes in the water.

"Have fun," I said. "It'll just be you and Delroy."

"Shut up!" Abbie hopped back from the water as if she'd spotted a shark's fin slicing across the surface. "You ought not say that!"

"Well, it's true." I smiled wickedly. "They never did find his body."

"That's because he didn't drown. He ran away from home."

"If that's what you want to believe, that's fine. But I think he's down in the deep, dark water, sunk in the mud at the bottom so he don't float to the surface. But I bet if you go swimming he'll come up to give you a hug!"

I rolled my eyes back in my head and did my best stiff-legged, stiff-armed voodoo zombie impersonation, reaching out for my sister with spastic fingers.

Abbie shrieked.

Spiders might not have scared her, but ghosts were another story.

She scurried up the hill and pushed past me. She didn't even bother to pick up her shoes.

"You're a jerk, Seth!"

She crashed through the corn stalks and vanished. I had a good laugh at her expense, but it only lasted a few seconds. If Abbie broke our agreement and told on me, Mama and Daddy would be none too pleased with me for frightening my sister. I scrambled down the hill to grab her shoes, then climbed back up and hurried after her.

The leaves of the corn stalks slapped me in the face as I called for my sister. Somewhere up ahead, I heard Jerry Lee's high-pitched barking. It might have been easy for someone who didn't know any better to get lost among the cornstalks, but I would have known the way home with my eyes closed. When I emerged on the other side of the field, I found Abbie, standing in the backyard. My heart jumped in my chest.

The hired man was on his knees in front of her, and he held her hands in his own.

I rushed to her side.

"What's wrong?"

Abbie pulled her hands away from the hired man. "N-nothing," she said. Her face was flushed.

Cole stood up. He towered over the two of us.

"Something spooked her pretty bad." He fished a pack of cigarettes from his breast pocket. "I'd hate to think her big brother was trying to scare the poor little thing to death."

Ain't none of your business, I thought, but I didn't say a word.

"There's plenty of things to be scared of out in the world," Cole said. "Hell, I bet some of them would even scare the spit out of a big, strapping boy such as yourself. How about that, you ever been real scared, Seth?"

I ignored him and took Abbie's hand.

"Come on. We need to get cleaned up for supper."

"I bet you have." Cole sneered. "I bet you've been so scared you nearly wet your pants from time to time."

I pulled my sister along as I walked away from the hired man. I trembled like I'd been out in the cold. His words chased after me, nipped at my heels.

I felt his eyes watching me.

Watching Abbie.

* * *

We should have burned the rats.

Daddy didn't like us manning the burn barrel without him around, but we'd done it before, more than once.

Maybe if we had burned the dead rats right away, everything would have turned out differently.

That's a silly thing to think, of course. The rats didn't cause the troubles that beset our farm. They were just the first of the symptoms.

Symptoms, like with a disease.

A disease Cole Jensen brought down upon us.

We went to bed pretty early that night, because Daddy's hands were worrying him something fierce, and Mama, who was due to give birth to my baby brother or sister any day, wasn't feeling good at all. I shared a bedroom with Abbie. It might have been a nice place to rest my head. It was plenty big, and the second story window overlooked a good portion of the farm, including the barn and the new tool shed. But an imaginary line split the room in two. On one side was my stuff—my Matchbox cars and comic books and Indian arrowhead collection. The other side was done up in pinks and flowers and paint-by-number portraits of ponies. The room could have been the size of a castle and it still wouldn't be big enough for my little sister and me. Abbie's side of the room seemed to grow larger with each passing day, while mine became more and more claustrophobic.

In a few months, I thought, I'll be thirteen. That's too old to be sharing a room with my sister.

I had hoped that when the baby was born, my folks might let me move out to the guest quarters in the tool shed. Mama didn't like the idea, but Daddy thought I was plenty old enough. It had been a long time since I'd had any real privacy, and I had big plans for fixing up the room. Now that Cole was living out in the shed, my dreams had been dashed. With my luck, I'd soon be sharing a crowded room with Abbie and the new baby's crib.

The hired man had been there for just one day, and I was already anxious for his departure.

I sat in bed, reading an issue of *Famous Monsters of Filmland*. Abbie lay on her belly on her own bed and played with a set of paper dolls. We both liked to stay up as late as we could, regardless of how tired we'd be the next day at school. Sleeping was for babies and old folks.

Outside, Jerry Lee barked. I didn't really pay attention at first, but the dog kept on yapping, like something was driving his poor little doggie brain into a frenzy.

"What's that mutt going on about?" I put my magazine aside. "Daddy's gonna wring his neck if he don't shut up."

"Maybe there's somebody out there," Abbie said. "Somebody who shouldn't be."

Yeah, I thought, like Cole.

Maybe Jerry Lee was barking at the hired man. After all, the dog didn't know him at all, and it was likely he sensed something strange about him. Dogs had a keen nose for such things.

Something crashed outside—a metallic thud and rattle.

I knew right away what it was.

The burn barrel.

I hopped out of bed. Every now and again, raccoons or possums got into the trash, and it was usually my job to run them off. If I didn't haul my behind out there and scare them away tonight, there'd be trash and dead rats strewn from one end of the farm to the other come morning. And I knew who'd get stuck with the chore of cleaning up the mess. Better to take care of it now rather than later.

Abbie started getting dressed, too, and she dragged the flashlight out from the top dresser drawer. One thing about my sister—she was plenty curious, even about the smallest things. There was no way she was going to let me get out there by myself.

The farm was dark and quiet, except for Jerry Lee's incessant barking. I was a little surprised Daddy hadn't heard the racket. Sometimes at night he took pain medicine for his hands, and the stuff near about knocked him out. That might be the only thing saving Jerry Lee's life.

Abbie carried the flashlight, and the glow bounced across the ground ahead of us. The barn rose out of the shadows like a great fortress.

A fortress full of rats.

The blinds were drawn over the window to the tool shed's guest room. The room was dark. Obviously, Cole could sleep like the dead, too.

Abbie flashed the light around the corner of the barn. Sure enough, the burn barrel lay on its side. It rocked gently back and forth. Trash spilled out of the mouth. My sister turned the light towards Jerry Lee. His eyes gleamed in the dark. He pulled at his chain as he barked at the overturned barrel.

"Hush!" I hissed at him. "Be quiet now!"

I approached the barrel and lifted it back upright, spilling a little more garbage onto the ground. Something twitched at my feet. Dozens of smallish forms crawled all around me. At first, I thought an entire family of possums had gotten into the trash and were now scurrying all around the barrel. But I saw the burlap sack spread out across the ground.

Saw the hole ripped in the cloth.

Abbie pressed up behind me. She aimed the flashlight's beam at the ground. "Look, Seth! Look!"

Those rats had been dead as doornails when he threw them in the barrel. I would have put my hand on the Bible and sworn it. But they were alive now ... and squirming and squealing and hissing in the dirt.

I backed away.

Slowly.

"What's wrong with them?" Abbie asked.

Some of the rats writhed and wriggled towards us, but they moved in herky-jerky spasms. Others just squirmed around in circles. Still others simply trembled and spasmed violently where they lay.

"They almost look like they're dancing," Abbie said.

But they weren't dancing, not really, and they weren't alive, either. The rats we'd tossed into the burn barrel had been ripped and torn and broken by Jerry Lee's attack. Blood still covered their fur. The hair and skin peeled away from the glistening flesh of a few of the rodents. At least one trailed a fleshy strand of its own guts. There was no way the rats should have been convulsing and scrabbling and shimmying before us.

They were dead.

And they were dancing.

Behind me, Jerry Lee barked.

"Abbie," I said, "quiet Jerry Lee down before he wakes up the entire county. I've got to get something from the barn."

"What are you gonna do?"

"Just keep the dog quiet, ok?"

Abbie nodded and rushed to Jerry Lee's side. She calmed him as best she could, but he still woofed and growled.

From the barn, I gathered a shovel and another cloth sack. I saw the red eyes of the other rats—the living rats—staring at me from the shapeless dark.

I hurried back to the burn barrel and laid the sack open on the ground. Using the shovel, I scooped up the shuddering rat carcasses and tossed them into the bag. As I bent down to shovel up one of the rats, the creature twisted and lurched at me. I dropped the shovel and staggered away, but the rat sank its fangs into the meat of my palm.

"Ahh!"

The dead rat clamped its teeth into my flesh. I flung my arm about wildly, trying to shake the rat free. My hand stung where the rat bit me …

But it was also cold.

Like ice.

Only colder.

For a second, I felt like I was sinking into icy water.

Finally, I flung the rat to the ground. Clutching my hand, I drew my foot back and kicked the rat. It squeaked and rolled across the ground.

My hand bled from several small puncture marks. The skin around the wound looked dry and gray. Several black veins ran across my skin, leading away from the bite. I felt like I'd stuck my hand against a piece of frozen pipe. As I watched, the dark markings faded and the color returned to my skin. All that remained was the bite marks.

What in the world …

Thankfully, I didn't think the bite was serious enough to need stitches. It was going to hurt like hell over the next few days, though. I flexed my fingers. The memory of the sudden, strange coldness lingered in my nerves.

I snatched up the shovel and used the flat end to bash each and every one of

169

the rats. Some of them stopped moving as soon as I smashed them. A few others needed three or four good whacks before they lay still. The one that bit me, I must have hit a dozen times or more, and when I was done there wasn't much left of it but a puddle. Then I went back and finished off the rats I'd already tossed in the bag before they got a chance to gnaw through the burlap. When I finished, a greasy stain covered the sack-cloth.

My hand throbbed. Blood dribble down my fingers.

I tied the bag's opening into a knot.

Jerry Lee had stopped his barking altogether now that the rats were dead. Really dead.

I looked at my sister.

"Why don't you go back inside. I'll be along directly."

"Where are you going?"

"I'm gonna bury this bag out in the field." I tested the weight of the sack. "I'm not sure how far just yet, but out somewhere we won't find it again, I hope."

"And then what are we gonna do?"

I looked out into the darkness of the field. The stalks hissed at me in the wind. The sound reminded me of whispered secrets.

"Then we'll try to forget what we saw."

I only wish we could have put the night behind us.

But, like I said, the rats were only the beginning.

* * *

On the bus ride to school, I asked Abbie to keep what she'd seen secret. She'd managed to get through breakfast without mentioning the rats, mainly because Mama was still in bed feeling poorly and Daddy was already working the farm. We had made ourselves cereal and toast, and we'd eaten in silence. I didn't know if she'd be able to make it through the entire day without telling her friends. I'll admit, I wanted to tell my buddies about the rats, too. I was sure I could spin one helluva yarn.

But something about the rats ...

Something told me this was one of those secrets that needed to stay buried.

"It might be best if we keep our mouths shut about last night," I whispered. Abbie had her forehead pressed against the window, and she sighed as she watched the world pass by. For her, the ride to school every morning might as well have been a trip down death row. "We should keep this between us, I think, at least for a little while. Abbie? Are you listening to me?"

"I hear you." She scrunched up her face the way she did when she saw or smelled something disgusting. "I don't even like thinking about those rats. Why would I want to tell anyone?"

"Swear?"

I held out my hand, and Abbie wrapped her pinky around mine.

"Swear," she said.

For Abbie and me, a pinky swear was as good as a blood oath. She could always go back on her word—either of us could—but to do so was unheard of when it came to me and my sister. She'd let the story die. In time, she might even forget about it altogether.

My hand ached like you wouldn't believe. I'd bandaged it up as best I could. Blood had already seeped through the gauze. If somebody asked me how I'd hurt myself, I'd just tell them I slipped and cut my hand on my pocket knife.

Eventually, the bite would heal, and I doubted it would scar.

As long as the rats stayed dead, we'd be all right.

* * *

Some time after sunset, Jerry Lee started barking again. The memory of those rats, shuddering and jumping on the ground, biting me with their icy teeth, sent a shiver up my spine. Daddy was having a devil of a time with his rheumatism, and even though Mama had cooked up some oats to soothe his swollen knuckles, he was in a foul temperament.

"Seth," he said, "go out there and do something about that dog. His barking's getting on my last nerve."

I didn't often hear such an edge in my father's voice. Daddy wasn't a cruel man by any stretch of the imagination, but he wasn't one to trifle with, either, especially when the dreadful pain in his hands flared. I put my homework aside and stood.

"Come on, Abbie."

My little sister, who had finished her own homework and was busy coloring, put aside her crayons.

"Leave her be," Daddy said. "Can't you do this on your own?"

I looked down. "Yes, sir."

Abbie pouted, but returned to her coloring book. I didn't need her help, but I would have certainly felt more comfortable with her by my side. That's something I would have never admitted back then, but these days, I don't see any reason to deny it.

Daddy winced at the dog's yipping.

"Just hush him up. I don't care if you have to bring him inside with you."

That last drew a stern look out of my mother, who hated the idea of having animals in the house. Daddy didn't notice the look, though, and Mama decided not to argue.

The night air was still, and the only sound was that of Jerry Lee barking up a storm. I stomped down the steps and around the house to where we kept him leashed, but the dog wasn't there. His chain lay in a silvery pile on the ground.

The clip on the business end of the leash was snapped open. That happened sometimes, usually when Jerry Lee tugged and pulled too hard. I still heard him barking, though, so I figured he hadn't gone far. I hollered and clapped for him. For a second, he stopped barking, and I halfway thought he might be heeding my call. But only a few seconds passed before he started yapping again—this time louder than before. Sighing, I followed the sound.

Jerry Lee stood guard outside the old shed—the one with the sagging roof and crumbling old walls. The door to the shed stood ajar, and the little dog vented his fury in the direction of the opening. The pitch of his snarling sounded different up close—less menacing and more frightened—and he didn't dare take another step towards the building. I walked right up and hooked my fingers around his collar. I gave him a quick jerk to quiet him. He yelped and looked up at me.

"What's gotten into you? You keep making such a ruckus and Daddy will haul your sorry hide to the pound."

Jerry Lee cocked his head to the side and regarded me with large eyes that seemed to say, "What's the matter with you? Can't you tell something's wrong here?" Then, he caught wind of something in the shed again, and despite the fact that I had ahold of him, he started barking again. He thrashed and jumped so violently, he almost pulled free of my hand, and nothing I did seemed to calm him.

More than likely, one of the lazy barn cats had managed to nudge the door to the old shed open and had crept inside. If not cats, then maybe—

Rats.

I thought of those dead rats … dancing … and I started to drag Jerry Lee away from the shed. As I looked up, I saw a shadow move beyond the open door. Whatever it was, it didn't look much like one of the cats to me.

"Who's there?" I asked. No one answered. I asked again—"Who's there?"—this time raising my voice to be heard over the dog's frenzied barking.

I knew I should just hurry back inside and tell Daddy what I'd seen. If there was a prowler about, Daddy would see to running him off. But I also knew that if I was just jumping at shadows—and shadows were, after all, the only thing I'd seen—my father would be none-too-pleased, considering his mood.

I stepped closer to the shed. Just a peek, I told myself, before I jump to conclusions. Bolstered by my company, Jerry Lee cautiously followed. A low growl settled in his throat.

I looked inside. Daddy threatened on a regular basis to tear the old shed down. We didn't use it any more, but my father must have had a soft spot for the old shed, like he believed it added a kind of weed-overgrown charm to the farm. Inside, deep pools of shadow gathered in the corners, spreading along the walls. Here and there, weak beams of moonlight shone through small holes in the rusty ceiling and rotting walls. Dust spun lazily in the damp light.

I didn't see any skulking prowler, though, so I stepped inside for a better look. "Ugh!"

A veil of sticky webs swept across my face. I spat and frantically slapped the sticky strands away. Even after the webs were gone, I continued to brush at my face, and I imagined spiders crawling all over me.

Jerry Lee growled at the darkness.

"Come on, boy."

Suddenly, the shadows didn't look so empty. It seemed as though the shed had grown in the darkness, swelled inside to hold all the haints and goblins of the world. I wished I had brought the flashlight with me.

I heard a faint humming somewhere above. I looked up. The pale moonlight shimmered through a delicate canopy of webbing overhead. Here and there, small, dark objects were entangled in the web—almost like stars dotting the night sky, only if the sky was white and the stars were black as pitch. Flies, I realized, and wasps and horseflies and snake doctors, all caught in the webs and long dead.

Only, they weren't dead at all.

Each and every one of the insects twitched and buzzed in the web, wings vibrating, legs quivering as they tried to free themselves. The entire blanket of webs trembled overhead, and I worried that the frantic spasms of the trapped insects might bring the whole thing down on top of me like a net.

One of the insects—a large horsefly—shook free and plummeted to the dirt floor. It lay on its back, wings buzzing, legs kicking frantically. Jerry Lee took a step towards the bug, lowering his head to take a sniff. I grabbed his collar again and pulled him back.

The horsefly was nothing more than a shell, an exoskeleton hollowed out of all the meat within by the spiders living in the webs. It was a dead thing—had probably been dead for weeks or longer—but it still moved as if alive. The horsefly managed to right itself, and it began crawling in crazy patterns upon the floor.

Something … foul … was happening on our farm, something bringing the dead back to life.

For the first time, I noticed all the buzzing and chirps and clicks, not just coming from the death's web above, but from all around. From the shadows along the left wall, a trio of desiccated crickets scurried. They, like the horsefly, were but empty shells. One of them was missing a leg. Another looked as if it had been crushed at some point. Across the room, I spotted a large, dead spider scurrying crab-like in the dirt, only half of its legs working like they should.

More insects fell from above.

Something buzzed past my ear.

Jerry Lee snapped his jaws at empty air as a dead fly swooped by.

I took a step back, pulling the dog along.

Another.

And I backed into the man who stood behind me.

Cole placed a firm hand on my shoulder to hold me still as he looked around the shed. His cold gaze lingered on the crawling insects, then he looked up at the web.

"They're dead!" I blurted. "They're dead but they're still alive."

Cole took a half-step, and crushed the twitching horsefly under his boot. The crunch! seemed as loud as a gunshot. Still, he held onto me, even as I held onto Jerry Lee. The dog snarled and growled, this time at Cole himself, and struggled against my grasp. The hired man paid the dog no mind. He squatted down in front of me, so he could look me in the eye.

"Don't let them touch you," he said.

I wanted to get out of the barn and away from the dead things, but Cole held me fast, his fingernails digging through my shirt and into my shoulder.

"Ow," I whined. "Let go!"

"Listen to me." Cole's gravelly voice was low. A halo of dead flies seemed to circle around him. "Some secrets are meant only for the dead. I'd hate for your mama or daddy to learn a hard lesson because you've been seeing spooks."

He gave me a quick shake.

"Some secrets are meant only for the dead," he said again. "Get me?"

I didn't answer. At least, I don't think I did. For all I know, I might have agreed with him, then recited the Gettysburg Address and the Pledge of Allegiance. The world around me seemed to be a chaotic, chittering mess, and my mind couldn't seem to get a lock on anything tangible.

Cole released me, and I stumbled from the shed. I didn't remember doing so, but I had scooped Jerry Lee up in my arms. I clutched him close, hugging him. He fidgeted and whined but I didn't let him go.

Cole didn't follow me, and I didn't dare look back to see what he was doing. I pictured him stomping and crushing all the dead insects in the barn, dancing a grim jig on their empty, fragile shells. And I imagined him smiling as he went about his work.

"Some secrets are meant only for the dead. Get me?"

His words and his sneer and the foulness of his breath haunted me.

My mother saw me carrying the dog into the house, and she pursed her lips in disapproval.

"I couldn't keep him quiet any other way."

I forgot all about my homework and carried the dog upstairs to my room. Abbie, excited to have Jerry Lee's company for the night, bounded upstairs after me, giggling all the way.

Her happiness left me cold.

I lay in my small bed and stared at the ceiling. On the other side of the room, Abbie laughed as she used a corner of her bed sheet to play tug-of-war with

Jerry Lee. The dog growled playfully as he tried to pull the covers from her grip. Jerry Lee lived only in the here and now, and he had already forgotten what had happened in the old shed. I envied him.

Something tapped lightly against the window pane. A moth fluttered just outside, flying into the glass again and again in a futile attempt to reach the light within. After several attempts, the moth gave up and flew away.

I wondered if it had been alive or dead.

* * *

The next day, I couldn't pay attention in class, and Mrs. Sutton jumped on me for daydreaming more than once. She even threatened to send a letter home to my parents if I didn't shape up. It didn't help that I hadn't finished my homework the night before. When the final bell rang, I stepped out of school with the usual amount of homework … and orders to finish what I'd skipped the night before … and an assignment to write an essay about why paying attention in class is important.

None of that mattered, of course, not as long as I worried over the evil stirring back home.

Now more than ever, I was convinced that Cole had brought it with him.

"Some secrets are meant only for the dead."

Even if not for Cole's threat, I couldn't tell my father what I was thinking. I guess there comes a time in every boy's life when their father's stop believing them, at least for a little while. Maybe he thought I always had my head in the clouds, that I spent too much time playing and making up stories, that I read too many comic books. It might have bothered me on the best of days, but now—when something awful was unfolding all around me—it ate away at my insides as if I had swallowed a belly-full of those dead insects.

"Why're you so quiet?" Abbie asked as we walked along the road. Our house was only a couple of miles from school, and while we could have ridden the bus, walking got us home more directly. "What's wrong with you?"

"Nothing."

She didn't argue, but she didn't believe me, either.

Daddy and Cole were working on the old tractor when we got home. Unlike the rats and the bugs, the tractor didn't show any signs of coming back to life. Daddy's hands were still hurting. I could tell by the way he held them close, protecting them, not wanting to so much as brush them against anything. He watched over Cole's shoulder as the hired man took a wrench to the tractor's guts.

I didn't like my father working so closely with Cole. What's more, I hated the nagging idea that if it came down to believing me or Cole, Daddy would take the hired man's side in an instant.

I silently wished the tractor's engine would suddenly spring to life, clamp down on Cole's hands, and yank him into the engine and mulch him among the gears.

Cole stretched his back, wiped his brow, and stared at me. His mouth was set in a tight, toothless smirk. He stared me right in the eye, trying to cow me, daring me to look away. I forced myself to meet his gaze for as long as I could, but I only made it a few steps before turning my eyes towards my feet. I could feel his smile grow.

A rush of heat washed over my neck and face.

In that moment, I hated myself almost as much as I hated the hired man.

* * *

At supper that evening, I decided I could no longer keep my mouth shut. I don't rightly know what got into me. The questions just sort of slipped out.

"How much longer are we gonna need him working here?"

"What's that?" Daddy asked.

"Cole." I put my fork on the edge of my plate. I wasn't hungry anyway. "How long is he going to be here?"

Mama glanced at Daddy, then looked at me. "Why?" she asked. "Don't you like him?"

I shrugged.

"There's nothing wrong with that man," Daddy said. "He's just trying to make a living same as the next. And he's already been a damn big help around here, especially considering the wage I pay. He's only been here a couple of days. Let's not run him off just yet."

"He's—"

My words fell short.

"The dead. Get me?"

What would I have said anyway? "He's bringing the dead back to life just by being here." I could envision Daddy's reaction to something like that, and it wasn't pretty.

"Seth thinks he's creepy," Abbie said, almost cheerfully. "Cole gives him the wiggins."

"Does not," I said.

But everyone around the table knew she was right.

"Well—" Mama clumsily rose from her seat. She kept one hand on her round belly, the other braced upon the edge of the table as she pushed herself up. "—it never hurts to help someone who's down on his luck. And like your father said, he's been very helpful."

"That's right." Daddy sat back. His chair creaked like straining bones. "But if it makes you feel any better, son, I don't imagine he'll stay with us more than a few more weeks. I'll be sorry to see him go, truth be told, but I can see it in his eyes.

176

A man like that, he don't stay in one place for too long."

"Sounds like you envy him a bit." A smile played at Mama's lips.

"Maybe I do." Daddy smiled back at her. It was a forced effort, because he was still in dreadful pain. He started to reach out and take her hand, almost like he'd forgotten the gnarled claws his hands had become. He stopped himself and let his hands fall to his lap. He winked at her. "Almost every man longs to be free every now and again."

"Well—" Mama's words were light and playful. "—you think about how cold it's going to be come winter before you go a-wandering." She rose from her chair and whispered something in Daddy's ear. Daddy smiled and laughed. Mama laughed, too, and pretty soon Abbie was giggling right along with them, even though she hadn't been let in on the joke.

I didn't laugh, though. I didn't think anything was funny. Cole couldn't leave our farm fast enough for my tastes.

And Daddy might have seen a restless soul in Cole's eyes, but I knew the truth. I'd known the truth since the moment I first laid eyes on the hired man.

He was running from something.

Daddy stood up from the table. "Seth, why don't you go ahead and bring the dog in for the night?"

"Why's that?" Mama asked. "I haven't heard a peep out of him."

"And I'd like to keep it that way, too." Daddy looked at me, almost pleadingly. "Please, son, just bring him in."

"Yes, sir."

I staggered to a stop as I stepped outside. My breath caught in my tightening throat. Cole sat on the front steps, finishing his supper. He glanced back at me, nodded, then returned to sopping up gravy with a bit of cornbread. He didn't make way as I descended the steps, and my leg brushed his shoulder.

"Is it true what they said?" he asked.

"Huh?"

"Is it true? Do I scare you?"

We usually only keep the screen door closed in the early evening. From the front porch, Cole must have heard every word coming from inside. He fixed me with those cold, dead eyes of his.

"You scared of me?"

"No."

"Don't lie to me." He dropped his plate to the steps. The silverware clattered against the plate. "Because I ain't going to lie to you."

"What do you mean?"

He looked back at the front door to make sure no one else was listening. "What your daddy said, about me moving on soon? He's wrong. I ain't going nowhere, not for a long while."

He used his fingers to wipe grease from his lips, and nodded to himself as if entertaining a cruel notion.

"No," he said, "I like it here."

* * *

"There's somebody outside," Abbie said.

"Probably just Cole having a smoke."

"I don't think so."

She stood at the bedroom window, staring out into the yard. The curtains draped over her head and shoulders, and she looked like a sheet ghost, the way she just stood there, real still, staring.

I sat on the floor, my back propped against the side of the bed. Jerry Lee lay next to me, his head across my legs. I leafed through a big stack of horror comic books I'd bought for ten cents at the flea market. I usually enjoyed the eeriness of the stories. *House of Mystery* was my favorite, but I liked *Witching Hour* and *Dr. Graves* and *Screamfest*, too. But tonight I didn't take pleasure in the tales of murder or monsters or ghosts.

Or curses.

One of the stories was about a man who'd been cursed by an old gypsy woman. Everywhere he looked, the man saw awful, twisted monsters. His boss, his best friend, even the pretty girl he met at the park—they all looked like hideous monsters. The ghastly sights drove him mad until, while crossing a bridge, he looked over the edge and saw a tentacle-covered, many-eyed thing staring back at him from the waters below. He hurled himself over the side of the bridge and to his death below.

The idea nagged at me.

Maybe Cole was cursed, too; only his curse was that wherever he went, the dead grew restless. Maybe not all the dead; otherwise, every place he visited would be crawling with the zombies, like in *Night of the Living Dead*. Maybe only the unburied dead came to life when Cole was nearby. Maybe—

"What's he doing out there?" Abbie said.

I shivered like someone had just traipsed across my grave. I tossed the comics aside and went to the window. Jerry Lee growled softly. There have been times in my life when I knew deep down in my bones that I didn't want to see whatever it was I was about to look upon. This was probably the first of those times, but I went to the window just the same.

A boy—just a little older than me by the looks of him—wandered around our yard. He was skinny and pale—so pale that his skin seemed to glow in the moonlight, so skinny I could count his ribs. He was blonde-headed, and his hair was matted wetly to his scalp. He wore only a pair of cut-off jeans, and they were soaked, too, the denim dark and sodden, the long strings dangling from the hem and stuck to the boy's bare legs. He staggered across the yard like he'd been hitting a secret stash of home-brewed whiskey pretty hard.

"What's he looking for?" Abbie asked. "Who is he? Do we go to school with him?"

"I don't know. I can't see his face."

I had no sooner uttered the words then the boy shrugged around, and I got a good look at him.

Abbie moaned and turned her head. She still gripped the window sill. The blood drained from her fingertips she held on so tight.

For a second or two, I didn't quite understand what ... who ... I was looking at.

Then it hit me like a speedball to the gut.

Delroy McKinley.

He had drowned in the swimming hole last summer, but there he was, plain as day, shambling around behind my house. His wet hair hung in tendrils in front of his face, but I could tell—

"He's got no eyes," Abbie whispered.

Where his eyes should have been were only gaping, pulpy sockets. I imagined fish and water bugs nibbling away at Delroy's down in the cold, muddy depths. I got the notion that he could somehow still see, at least well enough to know he wasn't where he was supposed to be.

"Where's he going?"

He's lost, I thought.

The boy shambled past the barn ... past the new tool shed ...

A flare of red caught my eye.

A figure stood in the shadows between the barn and the shed.

His face lost in the shadows except when he took a deep drag on his smoke. The cigarette cherry painted his face in stark crimsons and deep blacks. He looked, I thought, like the Devil might look if he were spying a lost soul that had wandered into his stomping ground. Only, in this case, he stood guard over the farm, not Hell.

Cole. Abbie hadn't noticed the hired man, but I saw him. I couldn't tell if he was watching the dead boy or gazing up at me.

"Abbie, get back to bed," I whispered.

"But what about—"

"Don't argue. Get back in bed."

For a split second, Abbie looked like she might pitch a fit. Her face reddened, and a veil of tears glistened in her eyes. But she must have realized I meant business, and instead of crying, she crawled into the bed and threw the covers over her head. Jerry Lee hopped onto the bed and burrowed under the covers with her.

"We should wake Daddy," Abbie muttered. "Daddy would know what to do."

She might have been right. Part of me wanted to wake Daddy, too.

"Some secrets are meant only for the dead," he had said.

And I knew the hired man would kill me, Abbie, Mama, Daddy, and anyone else who threatened to expose his vile secret. I had seen it in his eyes. He was no stranger to death.

More importantly, he was no stranger to killing.

"Only for the dead." And he had smiled as he said it. "Get me?"

Cole pulled himself away from the shadows. He dragged a rusty shovel behind him—the same shovel I'd used to kill the rats the second time. The point of the spade scratched a trail through the earth and spit up a tiny dust cloud. The hired man stalked up behind Delroy, and I couldn't help but watch, my eyes growing large, a scream catching in my throat. The dead boy didn't see or hear Cole's approach. As the hired man raised the shovel, his face twisted into a grimace of disgust and rage.

He brought the shovel down, and Delroy's head came open like a pumpkin dashed against the pavement on the day after Halloween. The dead boy fell, and Cole stepped after him, raising the shovel again and bringing it down sharply. Delroy didn't scream, but he squirmed and kicked on the ground as Cole bashed at him with the shovel. He grasped blindly for his attacker, and Cole was careful not to let Delroy touch him. Flesh and bone gave way beneath the assault. Bits of pale skin and chunks of meaty tissue caked the shovel's head, but there was no blood left in the corpse. Only cold water spilled across the ground. Black-shelled insects that had been nesting in the boy's body scurried for safety. As Cole continued to strike the dead boy, he turned his gaze towards my window.

Get me? His eyes seemed to say.

At last, Delroy lay still.

Cole tossed the shovel aside and grabbed the dead boy by the ankles. He dragged the corpse across the yard and around the side of the barn. I figured Cole was dragging the body off into the fields somewhere.

Just like I had done with the rats.

"What is it?" Abbie asked. "What's happening?"

"Nothing," I lied. "It's over."

"The boy …"

"He's dead."

I should have said the boy was gone—not dead—but the truth sort of slipped out.

"What's going to happen to us?" Abbie asked.

This time, I found the wherewithal to lie.

"We're going to be fine. Just fine."

* * *

I dreamed about dead rats, only they weren't dancing.

They were eating me.

The rotting, broken creatures scurried and scrabbled and spasmed across my body, tunneling under my clothes, gnashing at me with needle-like teeth. Their filthy nails scraped at my flesh as they climbed up my legs, across my privates, over my belly—moving towards my face. They squealed and chattered …

And whispered.

The rats hissed through blood-soaked sneers, and their voices sounded like the hired man.

"We're gonna eat you up, and there's nothing you can do about it. Get me?"

Their touch was as cold as ice. I felt black veins spreading through my body like icy worms crawling beneath my skin.

I frantically brushed the rats away, but they clawed at my arms, snapped at my fingers. I tried to scream for help, but one of the dead rats leaped into my mouth, and I tasted the musk of its fur, the rush of my blood down my throat as the creature sank its fangs into my tongue.

I jumped up in bed, gasping.

And they were gone.

I could still taste the blood in the back of my throat, but the rats were nowhere to be seen.

Abbie slept quietly in the other bed. Beside her, Jerry Lee raised his head and looked at me.

I pulled my pillow close to my face so they couldn't hear me crying.

I knew I was going to have to stop Cole before something awful happened, and I got my chance the very next day.

I failed.

* * *

When we got home from school, I noticed right away that Daddy's pickup was gone.

"Something's wrong," I said.

"Maybe he just went to town for something," Abbie suggested.

"No. Something's wrong. I just know it."

I felt it deep in my gut, like a nest of ice cold eels wriggling in my belly.

I crossed the yard with my sister in tow. I don't even remember my feet touching the porch steps I climbed them so fast. As I pulled the screeching screen door open, I looked around the farm. I didn't see any sign of Cole, but I thought I detected a trace of cigarette smoke hanging in the air. The hired man was around somewhere—I just knew it, just like I knew that if something bad had happened, he was responsible.

"Mama?" I called.

The house was too quiet. Too warm. Sweat tickled my collar.

I yelled for my mother again as I roamed from room to room.

No response.

My heart slammed in my chest. A terrible image flashed through my mind—Cole Jensen tossing the mutilated bodies of my parents into the bed of the pickup, driving out to the middle of nowhere and dumping them in the weeds to rot. I squeezed my eyes shut, wished the idea out of my head.

It wasn't so unusual for my parents to be gone when we got home, but it wasn't an everyday occurrence, either. But nothing seemed out of place. I saw no sign of a struggle. If it hadn't been for Cole lurking around the farm, I might not have thought twice about it.

Abbie yelled, "Mama?" but no one answered.

I almost missed the slip of paper on the kitchen counter, but I breathed a little easier as soon as I saw the hastily written message.

"Gone to town." The handwriting belonged to Daddy. "Be back soon."

Almost an afterthought:

"Make yourselves supper."

I was shaking and sweating and out of breath. I steadied myself and read the note to Abbie. She smiled.

"See? Told you there was nothing to worry about."

"I guess. I wonder where they went."

"Maybe they're at the hospital!" Abbie beamed. "Maybe Mama's having the baby! Maybe when they get back I'll be a big sister!"

That might have been a possibility. Mama was due just about any day. But the note didn't say anything about the baby.

We grabbed our book bags and headed up to our rooms. It was a strange and exciting feeling, having the house to ourselves, even if just for a little while. Like we were growing up. When Mama and Daddy got home, everything would be different. We'd have a new member of our family. I couldn't even begin to imagine all the adjustments we'd need to make. Still, for a brief moment, I felt excited and happy.

Hopeful.

I smelled the cigarette smoke just as I opened the bedroom door.

I'm pretty sure my heart skipped a beat.

"Come on in," the hired man said.

He sat on the edge of my bed. One of Abbie's stuffed toys lay in his lap. He paged casually through one of my comics. His big, meaty fingers crinkled the cover.

"What are you doing in here?" I asked.

"Thought I'd make sure you two children were all right, seeing how your folks aren't around."

"We're fine." The eels swam frantically through my bowels again. I tried not to let my voice shake, for all the good it did me. "Now, get out."

Cole looked past me. Abbie stood in the hallway, her eyes wide.

"It's her room, too," Cole said. "How 'bout it, little darling? You want me to leave?"

Abbie looked at me, then Cole.

I took a half-step closer to the hired man, positioned myself between him and my sister. "Doesn't matter what she wants. I'm the man of the house right now, and I told you to get out of my room."

"That right?"

Cole stood. The bedsprings creaked as he rose. He crumpled the comic book and tossed it to the floor.

I'd be a liar if I said I wasn't about to wet my pants.

Cole moved towards me.

"So, you're the man of the house, huh?"

He threw his head back and laughed like a villain from one of my comic books.

"Ain't but one man here," he said. "You're just a little boy can't keep his mouth shut."

"What do you want?"

"What I wanted was a few weeks of peace, but I ain't gonna get that I figure, thanks to you. And I thought we had an understanding."

"What are you talking about?"

"I saw you, last night, watching me. I know it's just a matter of time before you go sniveling to your Daddy about the boogieman. You probably said something already."

"I didn't—"

I wanted to tell him that it wouldn't have mattered even if I had said something. Daddy wouldn't have believed me.

Cole drew his hand back and slapped me. I don't think a mule could have kicked any more forcefully. I spun on my heels, slammed into the wall. My head spun. Everything went fuzzy for a second or two.

"Seth!" Abbie cried.

"Oh, he's all right, little darling." Cole's voice was a growl. "I just needed to teach the little bastard a lesson is all."

The floor creaked as he lunged across the room and grabbed my sister. He buried his fingers in her hair, yanked her close.

Abbie squeaked.

I moved towards them, but Cole swung Abbie out of my reach, like he was playing a game of keep-away. Abbie clutched at his arm, scratched at him, but he refused to let her go. His knuckles cracked as he clenched his other hand into a fist. He punched me in the stomach so hard my feet came off the ground.

"Oof!"

I went to my knees. I couldn't breathe. Couldn't think straight.

"I warned you not to say anything." Cole's voice seemed even deeper than before. "Didn't I?"

"I … I didn't." My stomach turned. My lunch threatened to come up. "I swear."

Cole pitched his cigarette butt to the floor, stomped it out. He threw Abbie towards her bed. She tumbled across the mattress, and her skull struck the wall. She cried out, grabbed the back of her head, and curled up into a little ball.

I could barely string words together as I struggled to catch my breath.

"My Daddy …"

"Your daddy ain't here to help you. He's too worried about your mama. Seems like some d-CON somehow got into her lunch. I wonder how something awful like that might happen …"

"You …"

"You should have heard her moaning and wailing as your daddy dragged her out to the truck. Hope he made it to the hospital in time. Hope the baby's all right, too."

I've never felt so angry in all my days. My every muscle trembled. I screamed like a wild animal as I threw myself at the hired man.

Cole smashed my face with his elbow. Blood leapt from my nose. I staggered away and fell. The side of my head struck the hardwood floor.

Cole raised his foot.

I flinched and threw my arms up to protect my face.

He planted his boot across my throat. He pressed down, near about crushing my Adam's apple. I wheezed and clawed at his leg, tried to push him away.

"You should have just let me be, boy. You should have let me be and you should have kept your mouth shut.. I bet your sister can keep secrets even better than you. How about it, girl?" He looked at Abbie. "Can you keep a secret?"

He barked out another laugh when she didn't answer.

"Don't you touch her." I forced out the words. "Don't"

"You just don't know when to quit, do you?"

God help me, I wanted to give up.

It would have been so much easier to just let darkness drag me down. But I couldn't leave my sister to Cole's whim.

Tears and bloody snot ran down my face.

"Leave … her … alone."

"God damn, but you are a stupid little bastard." Cole pulled his foot away, and he bent down. His fingers clamped down on my neck like a vice. He pulled me to my feet. My legs felt like rubber. My arms flopped uselessly at my sides. "All you had to do was lay there and play possum and I'd be gone by the time you woke up. But all of a sudden you want to act like some kind of tough guy."

I flailed weakly.

"Well, tough guys don't scare me none. I've known a whole bunch of them, and you'll never guess how every one of them ended up."

He grabbed hold of the front of my shirt, yanked me close.

I spat in his face.

His lips peeled from his teeth.

Cole shoved me as hard as he could. I felt my legs pedaling beneath me, my arms pinwheeling, my back smashing into the bedroom window.

Glass shattered.

I pitched backwards over the window sill.

The world spun out of control. The sky filled with glittering shards of broken glass. For a second, I felt weightless.

And then I landed.

My brain bounced in my skull. My teeth sank into my tongue, and my mouth filled with blood. My bones popped and snapped.

I couldn't move.

I wanted to, but couldn't.

I knew I was hurt pretty bad, but didn't feel much. I thought that was probably a bad thing.

Time seemed to slow.

I'm not sure how long I lay there.

All around me, the world dimmed.

I heard only the rush of my blood in my ears, like ocean waves breaking upon the shore.

The rush of blood.

And Abbie's screams.

* * *

Somewhere in the darkness, Mama called to me.

I heard the roar of the truck's engine …

… The front door slamming …

… Daddy's voice—or was that Cole?—yelling …

… Something crashing over … shattering …

… Cole, cursing …

… Mama, calling to me …

Her voice roused me.

"Seth, baby, are you all right? Oh, sweet Jesus, Seth."

Pain rushed in now, like water filling an empty glass.

I coughed. Blood speckled my lips, ran down my chin. I opened my eyes.

Mama looked down at me. Her face was blurry. She was pale, sweaty.

I still lay on the ground, but my mother knelt in the dirt next to me. She squeezed my hand. I just barely felt my fingers in her own. Every nerve in my body cried out in pain. My bones felt as though they were scraping against one another in all the wrong places. Dozens of tiny cuts covered my body.

"Seth, baby."

"Mama." My voice was little more than a rattling breath.

"Try not to move, baby, not until we know how bad you're hurt."

"Mama …"

"Shh. Just be still."

"Cole … Abbie …"

I was surprised I could move at all, but I managed to lift my head. From where I lay, I could see the shattered window of my bedroom. I could see the front porch, too, and Daddy's truck, parked crookedly, in front of the house. A cloud of dust still drifted in the air, settling upon the truck.

Suddenly, the front door whipped open and cracked on its hinges. The frame splintered as Cole Jensen toppled out of the house, smashing through the screen door. The wire mesh covered him like a funeral shroud. The hired man spun like a drunken ballerina, tripped on the ruins of the screen door, crashed through the porch railing and Mama's rose bushes. He fell on his ass … hard … and started kicking in the dirt, pushing himself away from the house.

I struggled to push myself up on my elbows.

Cole was bleeding from a split lip. His right eye was swollen shut. The flesh of his cheek was puffy and purple.

Daddy plowed out of the house like a rampaging bull. The cry that erupted from his lips was the most unearthly, inhuman thing I have ever heard.

I hated the sound of it.

Cole scrabbled to his feet, just as Daddy tackled him, knocking the air out of him. Both the hired man and my father slammed into the ground.

I tried to get up. Pain lanced up my legs.

Mama staggered to her feet. Her stomach was still large and round. The rat poison Cole had slipped her hadn't hurt the baby.

"Stay here," she told me.

Like I had much choice.

Daddy and Cole rolled around in a billowing cloud of dust. Daddy kept right on screaming as he pounded his fists into Cole's face over and over again. Cole flailed and tried to wriggle away, but Daddy dragged him back into the fight. The hired man didn't look so big and bad any more; he looked weak and afraid.

Cole's hand slipped into his pocket and reappeared holding a switchblade. The knife flicked open.

"Daddy!" I yelled.

The blade darted towards Daddy's face. My father jerked away, and the point of the knife nicked his cheek. Cole clambered to his feet, and he waved the blade back and forth before him, warding Daddy off.

My father couldn't even rise to his full height. He stood more like some sort of half-beast than a man. He hunched over, holding his trembling hands close. His fingers looked like raw, red hamburger. Tears and blood ran in mixing rivulets down his reddened face.

Cole flashed the knife from left to right. He kicked sand in my Daddy's direction.

"My children!" Mama shrieked.

She came at Cole with her fingernails bared. He turned towards her, and she clawed at his face. Her nails tore gashes across his forehead, and if he hadn't flinched away, Cole might have lost an eye.

He brought his knee up into her stomach.

Hard.

Mama wheezed and crumpled.

Daddy lunged at the hired man, but Cole's blade lashed out, slashing through my father's arm. Daddy staggered away. Blood flowed between his fingers as he clutched at the cut.

Mama bled, too.

Between her legs, her dress was a crimson ruin. She grabbed feebly at her stomach, trying to protect her unborn child.

Cole spat blood and teeth to the ground.

"You stupid fucks." He wiped the knife upon his pants leg, leaving a crimson arc on the denim. "You think I'll just let this pass? I'll fucking kill every one of—"

His words caught in his throat.

He looked past me, and his mouth opened and closed in silence, like a fish out of water.

A shadow passed over me.

Several shadows.

A half dozen figures walked past me.

Little girls, every one of them, some younger than Abbie, a couple older than me. Their skin was pale, their eyes the color of spoiled milk. They didn't so much walk as shamble. Some of them wore tattered dresses, and the fabric hissed softly. Others were dressed in soiled jeans and ripped blouses. Others wore nothing at all. I noticed purple bruises around the necks of a couple of the girls.

Dead, each and every one of them.

The knife slipped from Cole's fingers and embedded point-first in the earth.

Fear flashed through his eyes.

I knew what he'd been running from.

Cole had a hunger—a hunger that left the dead bodies of girls in his wake.

But he also had a curse that brought the unburied dead to life. The girls he'd killed, they'd been searching for him. And they'd finally caught up with—

Their prey.

Cole turned to run, but Daddy threw out his bloodied arm and caught him across the throat. Cole's feet went out from under him, and he slammed to the ground.

The dead girls fell upon him.

Cole screamed.

The girls clawed at him, their fingernails shredding his clothing and peeling away strips of flesh. They scratched at his throat, his face, his chest, and stomach … and lower still.

"Get them off!" Cole's voice was shrill. "Get them off!"

Like I said, there are plenty of awful things I've seen that I never wanted to witness. This, however, I watched with joy.

He kicked and spasmed and trembled.

The dead rat danced.

Wherever the girls touched him, black veins spiderwebbed through his flesh. His skin turned grey as the rivers of black crawled beneath his skin, intersecting, forming pools of darkness. His flesh dried, began to flake. The girls were sharing bits of their death with him, pulling him down into the cold depths of nothingness.

His screams became gurgles, then whimpers, then a long, rasping breath, dying on his withered lips.

When the girls were done with him, only the desiccated corpse of Cole Jensen remained. It was already beginning to flake in the breeze and blow apart like ash. Within minutes, nothing remained.

The hired man was gone.

The girls stepped back to observe their work. Their arms were covered in splashes of gore up to their elbows. Their fingers dripped blood. As the droplets fell, even they turned to dust.

Daddy moved past the girls to Mama's side. He fell next to her, lifted her head into his lap. Mama whimpered and moaned.

The dead girls looked us over.

I wanted to thank them, but I didn't have the strength.

Mama opened her eyes, looked back at the girls, and muttered something about angels.

A flash of movement on the porch caught my eye.

My little sister, wearing her tattered school clothes, staggered outside.

"Oh, Abbie," Mama whispered.

"Jesus." Daddy gaped at his daughter. His lower lip trembled. "Oh, Jesus, no."

One by one, the dead girls turned their backs on us and started walking away. They formed a neat, single file line. I figured the girl in the front was the first Cole had killed, the next his second. The last girl …

Was my sister.

Abbie didn't speak a word to any of us. She descended the steps and quietly took her place with the other little dead girls. Her legs were wobbly, like those of a newborn calf. Her skin was ashen, her eyes pale white.

A necklace of purple bruises surrounded her throat.

Mama called out for her. Daddy held my mother close and shushed her.

Tears obscured my vision. I blubbered and trembled.

I like to think I saw Abbie look back at us, just for a moment, before she vanished from sight. But I couldn't be sure.

Mama buried her face in Daddy's chest and sobbed. He hugged her tightly. His own tears were silent.

I painfully dragged myself towards them. The ground around Mama was soaked in blood so dark it was almost black.

"You need a doctor," I said.

I reckoned we all needed one.

She gazed up at my father.

"I think the baby's all right," she said. "It's still kicking."

* * *

"Take it out to the pond," Daddy said. "Take it out to the pond, Seth, and throw it in. I don't think it can drown, but if you weigh it down, we'll never see it again. You can do that, can't you?"

I said I could.

But I lied.

* * *

All those years, gone in the blink of an eye, and the only thing that remains are the memories.

I guess you can pretty much figure out we didn't live happily ever after.

Cole Jensen, dead as he was, saw to that.

Mama never recovered from what happened to Abbie and Becca. Becca. That's the name we gave my little sister. Mama lived the last two years of her life in the nervous hospital in Raleigh.

Daddy died another year after that. Cancer took him from me.

I was almost a man grown by that time, and I was alone. Even good old Jerry Lee was gone. I never saw the dog again after the day the hired man died. My guess is that Cole untied him from his post and the dog dashed off on one of his runs, never to return. Or maybe Cole killed him. I preferred to imagine Jerry Lee survived, though, and maybe he found his way to Abbie's side. I like the idea that he spent the rest of his days alongside my sister, keeping her and the other dead girls company.

The old house is gone now, burned to the ground not long after my eighteenth birthday. The fire took the barn and the sheds, too. I live in a decent apartment in the city. I work in marketing and make a good living. I still walk with a cane, even to this day, but I get around just fine.

I don't have any other family left, really. Cole took them from me. All that remains of my mama and daddy and sister are the memories.

But it's odd.

Family's fall apart and die. Childhood homes crumble to rot and dust. That's just the way of things, the cruelty of time. Even memories fade. But Cole managed to give me something to always hold onto—something that would last forever, I supposed.

I keep Becca in a shoe box in the closet.

And she's still kicking.

"Remains" was originally published in LIKE A CHINESE TATTOO (2008).

This one started with one sentence that sprung into my head.
"The dead rats danced the day the hired man came round."

I think I wrote and re-wrote the first scene at least a dozen times. I knew there was a story in there somewhere, but I couldn't quite get it started.

Around the time I decided that Seth's father suffered from a crippling arthritis, the story seemed to come together. I'm not sure how that one element became the glue for the story, but that's how it works sometimes.

This tale has been adapted into a graphic novel titled DEATH FOLLOWS from Dark Horse.

This is one of my favorite stories, and I hope you like it, too.
The lake (a different lake than the one mentioned in "Still Waters"), by the way, is real. A boy drowned there when I was a child. At least, that's what all the older kids said... and I believed them.

- CB

SCHOOL FOR THE DEAD

Headlights peeled the darkness away from a roadside sign, and Abe read it aloud as the car rocketed past.

"School for the Dead."

"Come again?" Eyes glassy from too many miles behind the wheel, Tom glanced at his passenger.

"That sign back there." Abe jerked a thumb towards the stretch of highway vanishing into the night behind them. "It said 'Midway County School for the Dead.'"

"Probably said 'School for the Deaf' or something." Tom craned his neck and looked in the rearview. "You know, one of them places where they teach retards who can't hear so good. You must have read it wrong"

"I can read just fine," Abe slouched down in the seat, arms crossed, jaw set in stubborn determination. "I'm just telling you what it said."

"School for the Dead." Tom coughed out a laugh. "Maybe we should get your brain enrolled."

The radio picked up nothing but static along this stretch of blacktop, and they rode in silence for a couple of minutes. The '76 Impala jostled and rattled, and every dimple in the pavement felt like a gaping pothole. Dashboard gauges illuminated the cab in an eerie blue-green wash.

Tom knew if he pushed the issue about the sign, he'd be asking for a fight. Many miles had passed since either of them had slept in a decent bed, and the spoils of their last several meals—Moon Pie wrappers and Chili-Cheese Fritos bags—littered the floorboard. They were both cranky as a limp-dick badger. Better to let the matter drop than risk an argument.

No such luck.

"That's what it said," Abe said at long last. "I didn't put the sign there."

Tom's blood rushed to his head like whitewater rapids. "Why in the world would there be a school for the dead? The dead? That don't make a lick of sense."

Tires screeched as Tom hit the brakes. Abe, not wearing his seatbelt, lurched forward and braced himself with one hand on the dash. Tom spun the steering wheel and pulled a u-turn.

"We're gonna see for ourselves what that sign says, and if you don't apologize when you see I'm right, I'm gonna leave your sorry ass on the side of the road, and you can catch a ride with one of those deaf kids."

"Dead," Abe said.

Tom bit his tongue and pressed the gas.

Tom wanted nothing more than to find a Motel Six and bed down for the night. Maybe catch a movie. There always seemed to be one of them horror pictures on the tube at this hour. But he knew he'd never be able to sleep peacefully letting Abe think he was in the right about something so obviously wrong.

I'll teach the pig-headed sonovabitch a lesson, he thought.

Abe was a failed Old Order Mennonite—failed because of his love for Jack Daniels, Lynyrd Skynyrd, and Big Macs—and Tom was failed at just about everything worthwhile he ever put his mind to. They'd been best friends ever since meeting during a barroom brawl that put two mouthy frat boys in the hospital and a third into an early grave. Now they lived wherever the road took them. They answered to no-one, and sought adventure around every bend.

And they got on each other's last nerve every chance they got.

Pig-headed sonovabitch, Tom thought again.

Trees flanked the road. This time of night, a deer might bound across the lanes at any moment, and a driver either drove carefully or risked a totaled car. Tom wasn't in the mood for caution, though, and he urged the trembling MPH needle towards the triple digits. Fallen leaves spun in whirlwinds in the glowing red wake of the car. Mile markers slipped into the headlights' beams and back into shadow as the car drew closer to the object of contention.

"You're gonna miss it," Abe warned.

"I wouldn't miss the chance to see you eat crow for all the rib-tips in Parker's Barbeque."

Up ahead, a dirt road punched a hole in the trees on the left-hand side. A metal sign painted brown and decorated with white reflective letters stood next to the track. The car heaved again as Tom braked and pulled off the main stretch. Gravel clicked and clattered along the car's underbelly.

The stark words MIDWAY COUNTY SCHOOL FOR THE DEAD glowed in the high beams.

"Must be some kind of misprint or something," Tom grumbled.

"Probably so," Abe said, "but that doesn't change the fact that I was right and you, you cantankerous so-and-so, were wrong."

Tom flexed his fingers on the steering wheel, then set the car to idling down the shadowy path.

"What are you doing?" Abe asked.

"I want to see this place for myself."

Gravel rasped beneath the tires.

"It's after midnight." Abe pointed to the clock. "What if it's some kind of boarding school? You're gonna wake up a bunch of kids."

Tom snorted. "Hell, whether they're deaf or dead, it ain't like they can hear us."

"They'll see the headlights."

Tom sneered at him and flipped the lights off, and the car rolled on, the path lit only by the pall of the moon.

"You are one contrary bastard," Abe said.

A quarter mile or so down the path, the remains of an ornate metal gateway partially blocked further passage. One of the gates leaned catawampus from the hinges. The other was overgrown with climbing vines, now dry and gray and brittle. Beyond, a massive building loomed from the darkness.

"Don't look like no school I've ever seen," Abe said. "Looks more like a nuthouse. Quiet as a ghost town, though, like it's been closed for a long time."

"Wait a minute—" Tom leaned forward and squinted at the house.

A light flickered through one of the building's lower windows.

"Maybe it ain't empty after all," Abe said.

Cutting the engine, Tom yanked the jangling set of keys from the ignition and stepped out of the car.

"Tell me you ain't going up there," Abe said. "Let's get back on the road and find some place to crash."

Slipping between the gates, Tom continued on foot towards the school.

Abe unrolled the passenger side window and stuck his head out. "You're trespassing. You know that, right? Somebody's gonna blow your nuts off with a shotgun, and they're gonna be in their rights to do it, too."

"Hush up. You're loud enough to wake the deaf. Just wait in the car for a minute if you're getting cold panties. I'll be right back."

Abe's head disappeared into the car again. Tom couldn't see his friend through the dark windshield, but he could feel his glare boring into his skull like a two-inch drill bit. He considered returning to the car, but this was, after all, why the two of them had set off together in the first place—to seek adventure, just like the A-Team or BJ McKay and his best friend Bear. Now, Tom thought, after all the bar fights, the odd jobs, and the sleazy truck stop bimbos, he wasn't going to let a gothic building and some ghostly light scare him off.

Once, the grounds might have been covered with lush gardens and hedges, but now tangled messes of arid weeds crawled across the lawn. A few wooden benches, painted white but flaking and peeling from years of neglect and weather, surrounded a cement fountain brimming with stagnant muck. Run-off from overfull rain gutters streaked down the sides of the building in mottled patches.

Tom glimpsed a tiny red light winking at him from the shadows. A security camera, he realized, tucked away in the bushes, oscillating from left to right, recording his every move. He saw another tell-tale red light a little closer to the house. And another on the other side of the yard. Now that he was looking for them, he spotted cameras all over the place.

He might have high-tailed it back to the car … if not for the scream.

Coming from the building.

Distant, quiet, but a scream for sure.

The light beyond the window brightened, then faded, and brightened again in an almost strobing effect. Creeping closer, Tom crouched beneath the sill. He heard muffled voices coming from within, a groaning sound, and a woman's cry. His heartbeat quickened, gooseflesh blazed across the back of his arms, and he rose to peek inside.

A hand grabbed his shoulder, and Tom whirled around, slapping both hands over his mouth to suppress a scream.

"Little jumpy?" Abe asked.

Tom toughened up right quick. "What the hell are you doing sneaking up on me? You're lucky I didn't slug you. You near about gave me a heart attack."

"Lay off the cheeseburgers and onion rings," Abe said, "and you wouldn't worry about your heart so much."

"That right? You earn your doctor's papers on that Mennonite farm?"

"Don't need papers to know those rings make you fart something awful."

"My farts smell like petunias," Tom said. "Thought you wanted to wait in the car, anyway."

"Reckon the idea of you getting into trouble without me just didn't sit right."

"Well, we may have found a whole mess of trouble, old son. Listen."

Abe's face blanched now that he heard a gurgling cry of pain coming from within. A chainsaw roared. Tom's eyes grew wide and his mouth dropped open. Abe's expression mirrored his own. A thought passed between them. Whatever awful things awaited, they would face them together. They looked through the window.

Peering down into a sunken room, they realized the flickering light and the horrific sounds came from a big screen TV standing along the far wall of the room. On screen, a screaming woman cowered behind a blood-covered madman who brandished a chainsaw like a broadsword as he ripped through scores of desiccated, undead creatures. Bright red fake blood gouted across the camera lens and dripped down in an oozing sheet, obscuring the scene for only a couple of seconds before the saw-wielding hero once again appeared, wading through a sea of zombies.

Abe breathed a sigh of relief. "Break out the popcorn, huh?"

A dozen or so figures, all seated in cramped schoolhouse-style desks, faced the television, but from the window Tom only saw them from behind, the television's glow silhouetting them in the darkened chamber. The group didn't move, didn't fidget in the uncomfortable seats. They only watched the movie intently.

The scene ended, and the lights went up. Still, none of the figures moved from their seats. A whip of a man walked across the room. He wore a long white doctor's jacket over jeans and a black *Evil Dead* tee shirt. As he ejected one tape from a VCR atop the television and put the new one in, he talked either to himself or to the seated figures. If he was addressing the audience, though, they didn't react.

Another horror movie started up, this one featuring a S.W.A.T. officer sharp-shooting zombies in the brain pan.

Now Tom saw that the seated figures were dressed in filthy rags, and that their skin was so pallid it was almost gray, and that their hair was limp and dry—

"Oh shit!" said Abe, dropping away from the window.

Tom saw the young doctor—if he was a doctor—striding out of the room, the tail of his white lab coat flapping behind him.

"He saw us!" Abe said. "Let's get out of here!"

They nearly tripped all over each other trying to make a getaway. But before they scrambled more than a few yards away, the front doors swung open. A sliver of weak light spilled across the yard. The man in the lab coat stepped onto the front stoop.

"May I help you, gentlemen?"

Tom stopped in his tracks, Abe bumping into him from behind. No sense in running, he thought, because their faces were already on camera. He faced the man and blurted the first excuse that popped into his head.

"Our car broke down, and we saw your sign along the highway. Wondered if we might use your phone."

"My phone." The young man pursed his lips and looked off towards the road … in the direction of the gates, where the car waited in darkness. His expression didn't betray whether or not he believed the story. "Of course. Of course. Come in."

Tom and Abe looked at each other, shrugged, and followed their host inside.

Inside, the sound of the horror movie playing in the other room was even louder—machine gun fire, zombie groaning, and synthesizer soundtracks. The ghastly noise reminded Tom of a carnival spookhouse, and the foyer and hallway were lined with framed horror movie posters. *Evil Dead. Night of the Living Dead.* Several versions of *Dawn of the Dead. Overdark.* Near about every zombie flick imaginable held a place of honor upon the wall.

"Welcome to my school" the young doctor said. He hadn't shaved in a few days, and his eyes were bloodshot, staring out from dark circles. "My name's

Regis."

"Like the guy on TV?" Abe asked, perking up. Abe did love his morning talk shows.

But the doctor cocked his head curiously, as if he had no idea what Abe was talking about.

Tom made some quick introductions, shaking Doc Regis' hand. His skin was cold and clammy, his handshake weak.

"You must really like horror movies, huh?" Tom asked, eyeing the macabre memorabilia.

Regis nodded. "All part of my work."

"Just what kind of school is this?" Abe asked. The big Mennonite looked ready to bolt.

"Ah. The sign has you curious, doesn't it?" He waved his hand before him, as if tossing the words into the air. "School for the Dead. I can't begin to tell you how many people come here just to see what that sign means. No doubt you thought it was a misprint."

"It's not?" Tom asked.

"Not at all." Regis suppressed an excited giggle. He fidgeted, unable in his excitement to stand still. "Would you gentlemen like a tour?"

"It's getting awful late," Abe said. He didn't want any part of the creepy doctor's antics, whether he was named after his favorite television personality or not. "We should probably just call a tow truck."

Regis clucked his tongue. "Gentlemen, let's do away with the charade, why don't we? There's no shame in being curious. And the sign is nothing if not curious."

Abe stepped back towards the door. "We don't want to keep you up or disturb those people in the other room. We saw some people watching movies."

"Oh, you won't disturb them. They're quite docile."

Docile, Tom thought. Helluva thing to say.

Abe started to offer another excuse, but Tom interrupted him.

"You know what? I'd love a tour."

Tom had to admit, he was damn curious about what was going on at the "School for the Dead," and he kind of got a kick out of all the horror movie souvenirs.

Doc Regis smoothed out his white lab coat and stood tall and proud. He guided them through the house as he told his tale with the flair of a White House tour guide.

"Not too long ago, I was earning my living creating special effects for the movies—mostly low budget gore pictures, but a few high profile films as well. I had a talent with makeup, and it was a nice way to earn a buck."

"You used to work in Hollywood?" Tom asked, impressed. He'd never known anyone who worked with honest-to-God celebrities.

"I worked on many of the movies you see here." He waved towards the posters. "Mostly zombie movies, I suppose, and it was zombie movies that brought about the revelation that I was meant for something more. Something important. I quit my job, moved here, and started my school in pursuit of my destiny."

Every wall was decorated with a poster. Here and there, latex zombie props in glass cases leered at them. The young doctor stopped before a pair of double doors. He raised his voice to be heard over the movie sounds coming from the other side.

"I started to think these zombie apocalypse films could be something more than mere entertainment. They could be educational. Help to make the world better. What if these movies were used as a kind of ... preventative measure?"

"So, what? You use horror movies to teach people about zombie invasions?" Tom snickered and nudged Abe with his elbow. "Any money in that?"

"This isn't about capital gain." Doc Regis grinned back at him, but his smile glowed with a kind of humorless malice. "Nor did I say my students were even alive."

"I don't get your meaning. We saw—"

"Perhaps it would be best if I showed you." With a flourish, he threw open the doors. "I'll introduce you to the class."

Regis descended a short flight of stairs. Tom and Abe followed him into the viewing room—the very room they had spied into earlier ...

A room full of dead bodies.

More movie posters lined the walls. A glass cabinet in one corner was filled with what looked like tribal artifacts—voodoo masks and drums and blowguns. Numerous schoolhouse desks were lined up facing the big screen.

And in almost every chair, a corpse had been propped. Some were recently dead, still looking vaguely human, except for the doll-like, staring eyes, the slack jaws, the pasty flesh, but others were as dry as tree branches, lips and eyelids gone, faces skeletal. Some wore the filthy rags of vagrants. Others, rumpled and stained hospital gowns. Still others seemed to be wearing the formalwear in which they had been buried. The earthy, rotting stink was awful.

On the TV, a group of zombies were being doused in gasoline and set ablaze.

"I like to think of it as aversion therapy," Regis said.

The scene on the TV changed, and now a man was driving a screwdriver up a zombie's nose, bright red blood and snot spilling down the shaft, the handle, the man's fingers.

"Wait a minute." Tom's every muscle was tense. He was ready to flee or beat Doc Regis to death, whichever needed to be done, without hesitation. "You better explain what's going on here."

"Remember those old driver's ed films that showed horrible car wrecks as a result of driving recklessly? It encouraged kids to drive more safely. This is the same theory, just applied to the undead. I show them the dangers of attacking humans. Massive head trauma. Being crushed beneath a muscle car. Electrocution. Chainsaws. They see the drawbacks associated with the hunger for human flesh. It's my way of keeping them calm. Notice how none of them—" He motioned towards the seated corpses. "—are reacting to your presence. They have no interest in feeding upon your flesh!"

"But they're dead," Abe said.

"Yes," Regis piped, "and completely passive! Isn't it wonderful?"

This guy is off his nut, Tom thought, and in a dangerous way.

He looked around the room for an easy exit. Besides the doors they had just come through, he saw another closed door, but it might have led to a closet for all Tom knew.

"These ain't zombies," Abe said. "They're just dead."

"And I intend to keep them that way," Regis explained. His voice dropped a little. "Of course, I only show them the movie clips in which zombies are destroyed."

The scene on the TV changed again, and this time to a very low budget movie, filmed on a lurching video camera, of a zombie getting its head bashed by a shovel.

"Would you gentlemen excuse me for a moment? This tapes almost over, and I need to get a new one. Then we'll call a tow truck to get your Impala."

He stepped through the door on the other side of the room.

"Let's get out of here," Abe said.

Tom readily agreed. Here he was surrounded by dead bodies, monster movies, and a display of devil's masks, totem dolls, and blow guns.

How did he know we drove an Impala? The thought sprung into Tom's head, quickly followed by another:

One of the blow guns is missing from the case.

"Ow!"

Tom felt a stinging sensation at the back of his neck, like a hornet on steroids had just planted its stinger ass-deep in his flesh. He reached back and pulled a feathered dart free.

He heard a soft puffing.

His vision was already watery, his legs rubbery, by the time he turned towards Abe. A similar dart jutted from his friend's arm.

"Oh, shit."

Tom blacked out and fell over.

He came to some time later, and realized right away he was strapped to a chair. He tried to look around, but his head lolled as if too heavy for his neck, and he only got a quick, spinning view of the room. He was in a garage, he thought, spacious with unfinished walls and a concrete floor. He glimpsed a pegboard on one wall, tools tidily hanging in place above a workbench. On a small folding table next to his chair, he saw cotton swabs, a little bottle of brownish liquid, and several messy plastic canisters of theatrical makeup.

"My apologies, gentlemen, for the harsh treatment." Regis was busy loading a tape into a video camera pointed in Tom's direction. "I wouldn't resort to this kind of drastic measure, but my work is far too important."

"Untie me," Tom slurred.

"I'm afraid not." Regis pressed a button on the camera. The tape inside clicked and whirred. The red light started flashing. The young man turned towards them, rubbing his hands together eagerly. "Let's get started, shall we?"

"Started with what?"

"Why, furthering my work, of course." Regis removed his lab coat. "You see, I worry my students might be growing bored with the current batch of movies, too accustomed to them, if you will. It's almost as if they're building an immunity to seeing the same old movies over and over, and the current crop of zombie movies is simply too sparse. They can't be expected to continue learning unless I introduce something fresh into the mix. So I thought I'd make a few movies of my own."

Someone groaned.

Tom swung his head around and saw Abe tied to a chair next to him. Only, Abe had been covered in makeup, his skin painted blue grey in flaking cornmeal thick patches. His eyes were rolled up, and drool oozed down his chin. On the table next to Abe's chair, an empty hypodermic needle lay.

Tom also noticed his own hands were painted in gray makeup, made to look weathered and decayed. He felt the itchiness of makeup on his face.

Regis approached Abe, tilted his head back, looked into his eyes.

Abe growled at him.

"What did you do to him?" Tom asked.

But Regis didn't answer. With expert efficiency, he untied Abe, then turned and casually walked across the room to the workbench.

Abe staggered to his feet, knocking the chair over with a clatter.

"Get him, Abe!" Tom said. "Wring his neck!"

His back turned, the doctor fidgeted with something at the workbench. On unsteady legs, Abe lurched towards him. Whatever drugs Regis had pumped into him kept him off balance, but if he got his hands on the doctor, that would be all she wrote. He'd break the little bastard like a twig and they'd be back on the road again in no time.

Abe didn't move like a person at all, though. He moved more like one of those zombies he'd seen getting killed over and over again on Regis' classroom television—

Tom choked. "Oh, Jesus."

Regis turned. He held a cordless power drill. He pulled the trigger a couple of times, revving it up.

Abe reached for the doctor with twitching fingers. He tried to say something, but it came out as, "Hrrgh grrrr hurgh urgh."

Zombie speak profanity.

The camera rolled.

Regis ducked under Abe's outstretched arms, used some sort of judo move to sweep the big Mennonite's legs out from under him.

"Abe!" Tom struggled to tear free of his ropes, but he was held tight.

Regis crouched down on top of Abe, and his back blocked Tom's view, but he saw Regis raise the drill and drive it towards his friend's face, and he heard the spinning bit grind down as if mired in thick wood as Abe's arms spasmed and fingers twitched and legs kicked in a pool of spreading blood and piss oozing across the floor.

"All...flesh eaters...must...die!" cried Regis, hamming it up for the camera as he pushed the drill down. He threw his head back in a kind of rapture. Blood speckled his face. The drill ground to a halt.

Abe's legs twitched for a couple of seconds, then lay still.

Regis stood, wiping his bloody hands off on his black shirt, leaving the drill embedded in Abe's face. He let the camera roll for a little longer, then walked over and shut it off.

"Wrap," he said.

"Why?" Tom asked. "Why'd you kill him? You could have faked it. You didn't have to kill anybody, especially not Abe. Not for real."

Regis walked up to him and patted his cheek.

"Where was all that smart thinking when you decided to trespass on my property?"

Tom bucked and kicked, trying to break free and get ahold of Regis. The doctor danced away with ease, and Tom's bindings held.

"You let me go!" Tom shouted. "You let me go, you little bastard!"

But his voice had lost its deep, mean rumble, and instead sounded high-pitched and scared.

Regis was breathing hard from his scene with Abe, and he grabbed his lab coat and walked towards the door.

"I'm going to get cleaned up, have a little dinner, and do a quick wardrobe change." He waved his finger, as if just remembering an important point. "I need to think up a new scene, too, something innovative. See if you can come up with anything while you wait. Then, lights ... camera ... action."

He closed the door behind him.

Tom wasn't about to sit idly by waiting for his moment in the spotlight.

The chair to which he was tied was a creaking wooden number, the kind you might find in an elementary school cafeteria. The floor beneath him was cold and hard. Even though his ankles were bound to the chair legs, he could move his feet a little. He pushed up onto his tiptoes, and the chair leaned back. He let himself drop down and immediately kicked back off his tiptoes again, this time with all his might. The back legs of the chair scooted on the floor, and Tom toppled backwards.

The weight of his body—bolstered by cheeseburgers and onion rings—shattered the wooden chair into kindling. A fart escaped his bowels, a quick one-gun salute to his fallen friend.

He shrugged the remaining ropes off.

He forced himself to look at Abe. The sight of his best friend sprawled on the floor in a pool of blood, a Black and Decker jutting out of his face, filled Tom with a bitter rage. He was going to kill Doc Regis, he decided. But first he needed to get out of here. He still felt groggy and weak, and he needed time to prepare himself. He'd split for now, but come back bringing hell with him.

On the wall, he saw an automatic garage door opener. He pushed the button and let the door rattle open. A cool fresh breeze flooded into the room. Tom didn't care if Regis heard the door opening. With any luck at all, he'd be long gone before the scrawny doctor caught him.

Still wobbly, he rushed outside. He didn't recognize this part of the yard, and he guessed he was around the back of the house. Still, if he stuck to the woods and shadows, he'd be able to make it to the car pretty easily. As he rushed through the woods, he felt some of his strength flooding back into his muscles. He dug the car keys from his pocket, clenched them in a tight, makeup-covered fist.

I'll pay him back, Abe, he thought, *pay him back good.*

The Impala was where they had left it, and as he opened the door, he saw his reflection in the window, a ghastly undead version of himself. He jumped into the car, cranked the engine, and threw the transmission into reverse. The rear of the car crashed into the brush. He threw it into drive and hit the gas, tearing down the path at full speed.

He looked in the rearview, saw the ruined metal gates vanish in a cloud of red. He wiped his sweaty forehead with the back of his arm, smearing some of the makeup into his eyes. He grunted, blinked—

Just as a deer leapt into the road.

Tom hit the brakes.

The deer struck the grill, rolled over the hood, and smashed into the windshield.

The car careened off the path, wrapping itself around a tree.

Tom's jaw smacked against the dash, breaking teeth.

A blast of steam sprayed from beneath the hood, and the deer bleated and kicked against the blood-smeared windshield. Tom pulled himself out of the car and sprawled onto the path.

He couldn't catch his breath, and the taste of blood in his mouth almost made him puke. He blacked out, came to, blacked out again and somehow forced himself awake because he had to get moving.

But he didn't have the strength to stand.

He heard the crunch of approaching footsteps.

Doc Regis stepped out of the darkness.

On quivering arms, Tom pushed himself up.

If this is where we're gonna fight, then by God I'll give him the fight of his—

Regis planted a boot on Tom's chest and pushed him down. For such a little fella, Regis was strong, probably from lugging all those bodies around. Sweat-diluted pancake makeup seeped into Tom's eyes, blurring his vision, but he noticed the winking red light of a security camera flickering at him from a nearby copse of trees, recording everything. Looking up again, he gazed into the yawning barrel of a pistol pointed right between his eyes.

Regis pressed the cold metal against Tom's forehead, hard enough to bruise flesh. His finger tensed on the trigger.

"You better hope I don't come back, asshole," Tom spat.

"Don't worry," Regis chimed. "We have an open enrollment policy."

He pulled the trigger.

"School for the Dead" appears here for the first time.

This is a weird little zombie story without any "real" zombies in it. It's also one of my favorite pieces. While driving home from a meeting of my horror writers' group, I glimpsed a roadside sign that read (I thought) "School for the Dead." What can I say? It was late and I was tired. Of course, the sign read "School for the Deaf" but this mean little yarn was born from the idea that I did read it correctly.

This story has been accepted by three different publications. In the case of the anthology, it never happened. In the cases of the magazines, they folded before this story saw print.

- CB

DANCE, DANCE UPON THE NIGHT OF THE BALL

There was much of the beautiful, mush of the wanton, much of the bizarre, something of the terrible, and not a little of that which might have excited disgust. To and fro in the seven chambers there stalked, in fact, a multitude of dreams.

The Mask of the Red Death
Edgar Allen Poe

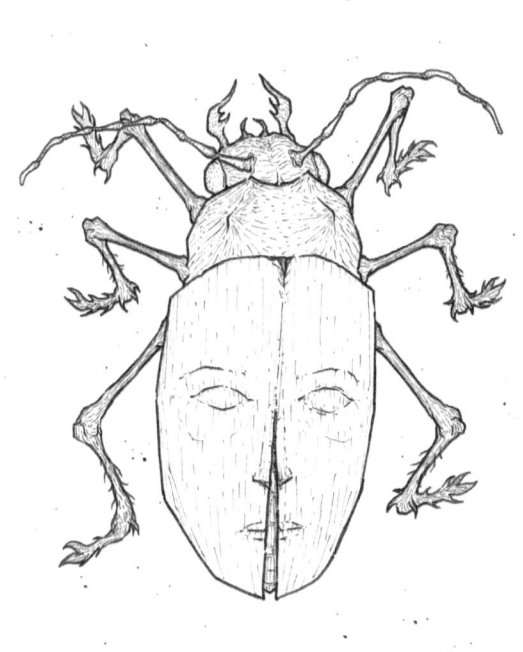

"Isn't this just amazing?" Judith beamed from behind the feathered mask she wore. She gazed across the ballroom and struggled to find the right word to describe how she felt. "It's simply ... grand."

Pushing his way through a crowd of ghouls and specters, vampires and hobgoblins, Nicholas felt awkward, rude, and somewhat out of place. "Excuse me," he muttered, forcing his eyes to follow the intricate tiled pattern on the floor, not wanting to look any of the strange characters in the eye. He didn't know these people – at least, he didn't believe he did. He couldn't be sure, not with all of them wearing elaborate costumes and masks.

He emerged from the assembly and approached a gracefully appointed buffet table adorned with finger sandwiches, decorative cakes, assorted fruits, and a brass bowl filled with dark red punch. He grabbed a cocktail napkin from the table and discreetly dabbed the seat from his forehead. A pirate captain – looking as if he had stepped off the label on a bottle of rum – stood nearby, speaking quietly with a dour-faced harlequin. He glanced in Nicholas' direction, twirled the end of his fake mustache, and sneered.

Of course, Nicholas knew that he looked the perfect fool. Rather than a complex guise, he wore a gray business suit that hadn't fit properly in more than three years and a blue felt bandit-style mask he had purchased for $1.50 at a five-and-dime – a costume that demonstrated a total lack of effort and creativity.

Why had he bothered to come? At the last Halloween party he remembered attending he had bobbed for apples, played pin the tail on the donkey. How old had he been? Ten? Eleven? A child, for certain, for the holiday was, in his opinion, set aside for children. It held little charm for him now.

A chandelier of brass and crystal hung above the immense chamber, twisting arms supporting candles, the glow of which, when reflected through the crystal ornamentation, sent flittering beams of illumination dancing across the ceiling, walls, and floor. Candelabras stood in each of the six shadowy alcoves lining either side of the chamber, and vague silhouettes crawled across the walls as the other guests moved through the light. Numerous supports and rafters crisscrossed in the shadows of the vaulted ceiling in a puzzle-like configuration, and statues, seemingly chiseled from the very stone of the walls, loomed overhead. Angels? Nicholas wondered. Or devils? He could not be sure if the hulking winged shapes, partially concealed in the darkness, were semblance of hope or despair.

All about him, costumed guests mingled, a sea of colorful faces and bodies crowding close to one another, laughing, joking, flirting, debating. Clowns gossiped with knights, musketeers made advances upon princesses. In one corner of the ballroom, a small ensemble of musicians played, and several outlandish characters waltzed in the center of the room. Nicholas stood beside the buffet table, his napkin clutched tightly in his hands, nursing a cup of punch and speaking to no one. He hated the idea of being surrounded by strangers, hated the idea of making small talk with people who, for all practical purposes, couldn't care less about him. He feared that with the slightest utterance he might misrepresent himself, and therefore, it was best to keep quiet. Do not speak unless spoken to. And he saw no sign of interest upon the grinning and grimacing facades filling the room. Hidden by their masks, everyone was a stranger, and no one offered Nicholas a word of greeting or welcome.

Reaching into his pocket, he fished out the crumpled, handwritten invitation he had received by post only a few days earlier.

> Attend! Attend!
> A Masquerade Ball
> In Celebration of
> All Hallow's Eve.
> Reveal Your Identity
> To No One
> Not the Closest of Friends
> Till the Toll of Midnight
> And the Grand Unmasking.
> Attend!

He saw no indication of who, exactly, had invited him. He wondered if he had received the invitation by mistake. Wouldn't that be just his luck? Here he was, making an idiot of himself at a party at which he wasn't welcome! More than likely, though, he had been invited by someone from the office, a co-worker who felt sorry enough for him to ask him to come, never thinking, not in a million years, that he would actually show up.

He should have known better. Historically, he didn't function well at social gatherings. Why did he think that this would be any different? He decided that he would only stay for a few minutes longer, put in an appearance so to speak, then make a quiet exit. He wouldn't be missed.

On one end of the room stood a massive grandfather clock of dark oak. The pendulum swung back and forth in a hypnotic monotony. On the other end of the room, a staircase spiraled up towards chambers above. Something about the stairs piqued Nicholas' curiosity.

As he stepped towards the staircase, though, a hand clasped him on the shoulder. Almost spilling his punch, he spun around, nearly tripping over his own feet.

Behind him stood a man dressed as a servant. He wore a mask of solid black, a mask molded in such a way as to resemble a human face, but in a ghastly manner, for the black material – Plastic? Ceramic? – the staring eyes, the expressionless lips, lacked any detail or hint of emotion.

"I-I'm sorry," Nicholas said. "You startled me."

"I hope you are enjoying yourself," the servant said, his voice garbled underneath the mask.

"I . . . Yes, I am." Nicholas could not see the man's eyes. Indeed, the mask had no openings at all for the eyes, nose, or mouth. How could he see? How could he breathe? "I guess I feel a little out of sorts, perhaps. I don't really see anyone I know."

"Oh, you will, come midnight and the Grand Unmasking."

"Yes I suppose. That's an interesting mask you're wearing."

The servant said nothing more, however, but instead turned, stiffly, and strode away, vanishing into the ever-growing gathering of costumed partygoers.

A werewolf and a man in a straightjacket brushed past, neither of them paying attention or offering apology, as they stepped onto the dance floor. As the first of the musical numbers wound to a halt, the dancers applauded the musicians for only a moment, before the music started, and the dance began anew, Indian chiefs pirouetting with ballerinas.

Looking across the dance floor, Nicholas saw a figure dressed in a plain white sheet into which circular holes had been cut for eyes – a ghost. A simple costume, at best, but in a room full of colorful, gaudy, and extravagant garb, the ghost stood out perhaps more than anyone else, yet he or she stood alongside a wall, alone, watching the crowd.

Another lost soul, Nicholas thought. He thought of approaching the ghost, starting a conversation, but thought better of it. He wouldn't have known what to say.

As he sipped his punch, he noticed someone else -- a woman in an Elizabethan gown – wearing a mask almost identical to the servant's. The featureless visage covered her entire face, from beneath her chin to the hairline of her powdered wig.

Suddenly, the music stopped, replaced by regal trumpeting. All of the guests turned their attention to the staircase, where two servants, masked in solid black masks, announced the arrival of the host.

"All heed," cried the first in a muffled voice.

"He comes," cried the second. "He comes."

"Your host, our master," they intoned together, "the Hierophant of the Ball."

Next to Nicholas a girl dressed as a sailor in a short skirt giggled at the melodrama, but quickly fell into awed silence as a figure appeared upon the stairs behind the servants.

The Hierophant – and who else could it be to suggest such grim majesty? – wore a flowing cloak of the finest garments, the colors of which changed in the flickering light and with the slightest movement or suggestion of a breeze. Shimmering shades of blue and green and gold roiled over the cloth like watercolor, mixing with each other, swallowing each other, a unique trick of the light. He stood much taller than anyone in the room. One might have imagined that he stood upon short stilts beneath the robes, but his every movement as he descended the stairs to a landing overlooking the crowd was so smooth, so natural, that walking upon stilts was an improbability. The masqueraders gasped in amazement as a half dozen large crows swept through the room, diving low over their heads, then rising and perching in the rafters above. With one pale hand, the Hierophant clutched a bejeweled scepter, and in the other he held a black mask without detail before his face.

"Welcome, welcome to my home," said the Hierophant, his voice hissing, rasping. How he could be heard was a wonder. "Enjoy my hospitality. Enjoy my food. Enjoy my drink. Enjoy, for the time draws near to tear way your facades and find out who you know and who you do not."

Nicholas thought he caught a glimpse behind the Hierophant's mask and that something . . . cancerous . . . grew beneath, writhed beneath.

"Do you feel it, my friends? Can you taste the magic upon your lips? A sort of sorcery lingers in the air, a sorcery which we can breathe into our bodies but once a year, on this night when the veils are weakened and the doors between worlds are thrown open. In but one hour, the clock --"

He pointed the scepter towards the grandfather clock.

"—strikes the hour of midnight, when the spirits scatter back into shadow, into darkness, into nothingness, and our celebration of masks ends. At the tolling of midnight is the Grand Unmasking, when the spirits return to their corners of space and time, and we are safe once again to reveal ourselves."

Softly, the music began again, a lurid waltz.

"Until then," said the Heirophant, "Dance, dance."

As if on command, the guests flooded back to the dance floor, the music swelling, guiding their steps.

"Dance," commanded the Heirophant, and with that, he turned, striding up the staircase, his robes swishing across the steps, as he returned to the chambers above.

Nicholas felt dizzy as he watched the spinning colors of the tall man's robes.

The pirate who had sneered at him earlier bumped into him and then staggered away, and Nicholas saw that he, too, wore one of the black masks. What might have been blood ran down the pirate's neck, staining his ruffled collar.

"Pardon me," Nicholas said, trying to catch the man's attention, but the pirate shuffled away from him to join in the dance.

Now Nicholas saw that many of the guests wore the masks -- there, across the room, a shapely witch wore one, and there, in the corner, a man in a black and white striped convict's outfit wore one, too.

His eyes were playing tricks on him, he decided. It was too hot in the room, too loud, too crowded. His head spun and he thought that perhaps there was something more to the punch than fruit juices. He sniffed the punch, set his cup aside.

A fair skinned angel stumbled out from amid a coterie of dancers. A black mask covered her face. Her fingernails were cracked and broken and bleeding, as if she had been clawing at something. She held her arms close to her chest, her hands curled in pain. Blood ran down her wrists, smeared her white dress, speckled the pristine feathers of her wings.

Nicholas held a hand to his mouth. The aftertaste of the punch burned in the back of his throat, sour, tainted. He need some fresh air. He stepped towards the massive archway and the hallway beyond and stopped, because he did not remember how, exactly, he had gotten to the party. For that matter he couldn't remember where, exactly, the ball was being held. No matter. He needed to get out.

As he shoved his way through the dancers, he noticed that what had once been a sea of colorful faces now resembled a storm cloud of blackness, for so many of the guests wore the featureless masks, their other masks covering the floor like leering cast-off skins.

He walked quickly down the hallway, the echo of his footsteps chasing after him, the darkness closing in after him. His hands shook. His heart raced. Beads of greasy sweat formed on his forehead. He was going to be sick.

What had been in that punch?

The hallways seemed to wind in upon each other, meander through the darkness like a coiling serpent. Even though he walked along only one hall, taking none of the side tunnels and opening none of the doors, he felt as if he walked in circles. He wondered if the hallway would ever end. Looking over his shoulder, he saw what might have been miles of twisting mazeworks, curving doors, sickly torches burning along the walls. And somewhere, far away, he heard the music form the masquerade ball.

He continued, almost at a run, and finally, finally came upon a massive door, stretching from floor to ceiling. Standing before the door was a familiar figure. The bed sheet ghost. She stared at him silently. Nicholas wondered if she – he was suddenly certain that it was, indeed, a woman underneath the sheet – was lost, just like him, trying to find a way out.

"Uh, hello," he said, stepping towards her. "I seem to be a bit turned around."

The ghost did not respond.

"I wondered if you might be able to point me towards the exit."

The phantom said nothing. The white cloth rustled as a draft swept through the hall.

"Are you all right?"

Nicholas reached out and lifted the sheet away.

And saw that the shape beneath the fabric was not a woman at all, not even a person, but rather a mound of massive, beetle-like creatures, each with a smooth, glistening black shell, the curvature of which resembled nothing more than an expressionless human face.

He reeled away, tossing the sheet aside, as the insects skittered across the floor, climbing onto his feet, scurrying up his legs. He kicked them away, stomped one. A high-pitched screech echoed along the hall as the insect's long, barbed legs twitched under Nicholas' shoe. One leapt at his face. He threw his arms before his face, blocking the creature. Before he tossed it away he saw what might have been a dozen smaller, twitching appendages on the soft underbelly beneath the shell.

He threw all of his weight into the door and forced it open as a mass of chitonous horror scrabbled across the marble floor after him. As the door slid open, he staggered into the cool air beyond, slamming his back into the door and pushing it closed once more. He nearly fell down a short flight of stairs to the walkway, tearing his five-and-dime mask away, sweat stinging his eyes, and he heard the chirping of the insects as they scratched at the heavy wooden door. Gasping for air, he ran, ran as far as he could without looking back, ran until his lungs felt as if they might burst and his legs would carry him no farther.

He paused, leaning against a lamppost, clutching at his chest, thinking, please God, don't let me have a heart attack. Let me live through this and I swear I'll lay off the fried food. And perhaps his prayers were answered, for after a few minutes, the pain subsided, and he breathed more easily.

How far had he run? He felt dizzy and disoriented, the effects, he supposed, of whatever hallucinatory drug had been slipped into his punch. And the culprit who had drugged him would be waiting, he suspected, for him at work in the morning. Wouldn't he be the laughing stock of the office, poor frightened little Nicholas, afraid of the boogie man.

Calm down, he told himself. Calm down.

A group of giggling children rushed along the sidewalk across the street, their small bodies shrouded in reflective capes, their faces masked with grinning skulls and pumpkins. In their hands, they clutched bags full of candy. Perhaps they were returning home after the evening's festivities. It was awfully late.

Nicholas looked along the street, hoping to spy a cab, but he saw none. He saw no cars at all, in fact. Had he driven to the party? He couldn't recall. Not that it mattered. He only wanted to get home and go to bed.

It must have rained while he was at the masquerade, for water glistened upon the street, pooled in potholes. Several sheets of damp paper danced across the street, brushing against street lamps, clinging against the poles for a few seconds before being snatched away by the wind. Wet ink spread across the pages in winding black rivulets.

Nicholas didn't recognize this part of town.. All of the windows were dark, save for the glow of numerous jack-o'-lanterns. None of the shops looked familiar. One displayed all manner of dolls in the window, porcelain faces peering out into the night, glassy eyes opening and closing, tiny mouths clacking open and shut. Another displayed meat – and such meat – spread out in the window and running blood, which pooled against the glass.

A sheet of wet paper slapped against his leg. He grabbed it and read.

Attend! Attend!
A Masquerade Ball
In Celebration of
All Hallow's Eve.
Reveal Your Identity
To No One
Not the Closest of Friends
Till the Toll of Midnight
And the Grand Unmasking.
Attend!

He tossed the page away in horror and disgust. The paper fluttered off to join the others, dozens of similar announcement that seemed to crawl along the street.

Somewhere, a clock tolled, a deafening sound echoing though the city.

Nicholas saw tall spires and slanted roofs, crooked buildings and hundreds, possibly thousands of slowly spinning weathervanes, silhouetted in the night by an orange glow somewhere in the city.

Nearby, a spidery figure loped across a rooftop.

A clanking resounded from beneath the streets, as if somewhere, down in the dark, strange denizens sent messages back and forth by tapping against sewer pipes.

Shadows played across the alley walls – tall figures stalking along the cobblestone streets.

Cobblestones?

Where the hell was he?

"Trick or treat!" a voice cried.

Nicholas turned and saw a group of masked children standing before him, gleeful goblins and witches and skeletons. They held their bags towards him.

"Trick or treat!"

The clock chimed in the distance.

A nervous laugh escaped Nicholas' throat.

"I'm sorry," he told the children. "I don't have any –"

But he stopped and stepped back, the hairs prickling on the backs of his hands and neck . . .

. . . the spirits return to their corners of space and time . . .

. . . for the masks the children wore were much too real.

"No," he muttered, shaking his head slowly as he peered into the bags they clutched in their taloned hands.

The clock chimed.

. . . the doors between worlds are thrown open . . .

Something inside the trick or treat bags crawled.

Nicholas screamed as the black insects jumped out of the bags, one of them leaping onto his face, digging long legs into his flesh, piercing bone and sinking into the soft meat of his brain. Under the shell, tiny feelers and pincers worked, scratching at his skin, slicing paper thin sections away from his eyes and lips, nose and cheeks, tearing flesh apart and stitching it back together in alien configurations.

In the distance, the clock chimed.

The children, laughing, danced in the street.

And as the clock struck twelve, Nicholas removed his mask, revealing his new face to the world.

"Dance, Dance Upon the Night of the Ball" was originally published in Whispers from the Shattered Forum (1999)

I'm a believer that editors shouldn't publish their own stories, but when I was editing the horror zine Whispers from the Shattered Forum, I broke my own rules. We didn't have enough stories to fill our first issue, so I threw this one (published under the pseudonym Roman Franklin) into the mix. It's a story that draws inspiration from various sources — my love of Halloween, various nightmares, and the works of Robert W. Chambers.

- CB

THE LAST NIGHT OF THE FAIR

Twisted, leering monsters surrounded them—dozens of shambling, malformed creatures, closing in, lurching after them down the winding hallway.

Robert and Cheryl, huddled close together, turned a corner, shuffled across the scuffed floor.

The monsters followed.

Cheryl clutched Robert's arm.

The monsters, looming only a few feet away, imitated their actions, mocked them, silently.

"We're never going to find our way out of here," Cheryl giggled.

"You might be right." Robert paused, searching for a new passage. "This way's a dead end."

The rippling mirrors lining the black plywood walls spawned a mob of misshapen images, warped reflections of warped reflections, each progressively more horrific than the last. Here lurked short and squat things with faces squeezed into wrinkled messes. There loomed tall and whip-thin goblins with crooked limbs and stretched, sorrowful features. Some of the wavering mirrors had been cracked either during rough transit or by rowdy patrons, and the lost and wandering misrepresentations presented therein were splintered and angular.

"Well," Cheryl said, pulling closer, "I guess I could be in worse company."

Robert blushed. Thankfully, the hallway was cast in shadow, and his companion could not see his embarrassment.

As they proceeded down another corridor, neither one of them in any real hurry to find the exit, a dozen warped reflections slinked across their path. Their likenesses meandered and flowed, colors dancing through silver. The mirrors were no longer cold and still, but were like living things, expanding as they drew breath, expelling warm, stuffy air smelling of sweat and cotton candy and spilled soda pop. From within, the maze seemed much larger than it actually was. Impossible reflections tricked the eye and wavering doors opened and paths coiled in all directions.

Robert heard approaching footsteps, and his heart sank. He had thought—hoped—he and Cheryl would have the mirror maze to themselves for a while longer.

The shuffling footsteps drew closer.

He looked over his shoulder, expecting to see another couple, knotted together and laughing nervously, round the corner.

But no one appeared.

No shadows played across the walls.

No reflections.

His imagination?

This was, after all, a place of dreams and—he looked at a hideous, perverted likeness of himself—nightmares.

* * *

Twilight rocketed like a rollercoaster from the peak of daylight to the valley of darkness and wonder. The midway came alive, townsfolk who had avoided the unseasonably warm afternoon now paying their five dollars at the gate to visit the fair on this, the final night of the event. Families milled through the crowd, parents digging into their pockets to pay for rides and snow cones, children racing this way and that with balloons on strings bobbing behind them. An excited gasp rose as the Zipper whipped passengers into the sky. The air was ripe with the smell of vinegar fries, funnel cakes, and sizzling sausages.

Shaking his head, Tom approached a bank of blinking, ringing games. A half-dozen people tested their luck against the money hungry amusement. The gimmick was this: at each station, a metal bar swung back and forth before an alluring mound of quarters. By dropping additional quarters into the machine at just the right time, players chanced pushing dozens of coins into their waiting hands. Shawn had been playing for nearly an hour. He sidled up to check on his friend's good—or ill—fortune, letting out a low whistle as he craned his neck to peer at the loot teetering on the brink.

"Aren't you bored with this thing yet?" he asked.

"This is almost the only thing that holds my interest any more." Shawn absently slipped another quarter into the slot. "There are no more worlds to conquer."

"That's funny for you to say," Tom jibed. He had been hitting the thrill rides steadily, and his face was flushed with excitement. "You wouldn't even ride the Gravitron."

Shawn shrugged, concentrating on the potential cascade of change. "Not really my style."

"Yeah, but feeding quarters to this thing suits you just fine."

Grinning, Shawn grabbed a large plastic cup from atop the machine. He shook the container like a metallic rattle.

"You're kidding!" Tom peered inside. Scores of George Washingtons, packed almost to the brim, stared back at him. "I've played this stupid game dozens of times and never won anything!"

"Skill and finesse," Shawn said. "Skill and finesse."

"Yeah, bite me."

Shawn noticed that one of their trio was missing. "I thought Robert was with you," he said.

"Nope. He ditched me pretty quick. He's bound to be around, though." Tom eyed Shawn's winnings. "Maybe we should check over by the video game tent."

"Guess I've done enough damage for one night." Shawn fired one more quarter into the machine and was rewarded with the clinking of several falling coins. "Skill and finesse," he said again, but Tom was already walking away.

"Hey, wait up!"

They pushed through the midway crowd—lanky, dusky Shawn, dressed in his trademark tee shirt, black jeans, and canvas Converse; Tom, jovial and ever smiling, wearing his UNC Tarheels shirt and cap, even though he had no real interest in sports.

They passed a dozen or so games of chance—children pulling numbered rubber ducks from a churning whirlpool, guys trying to impress their girls by throwing darts at balloons to win a framed heavy metal poster, high school jocks trying to best each other's records pitching radar-monitored fastballs. Hucksters called to them. "Step right up! Give it a shot! Win and walk away a hero!" They continued without stopping.

"Don't make eye contact," Tom said under his breath. "We'll never make it out of here if you do."

Shawn laughed at the joke, but avoided looking directly at any of the men or women working the booths.

A symphony of computerized bells and whistles from the arcade could be heard from several yards away. Inside, video games lined the canvas walls. Most of them were out of date and, despite being shielded beneath the tent, the monitors were sun-faded. Robert was not to be found, but the boys decided to wait for him. And why not? The games, ancient though they may be, were appealing, the flashing lights and scores alluring. Shawn was generous with his winnings, and they played for a while, setting new high scores. Eventually, though, the quarters ran out, and there was still no sign of Robert.

"It's getting late," Tom said as they exited the tent in search of their missing friend. "You don't think he's in some kind of trouble, do you?"

Beyond a collection of hotdog and gyro vendors, the double Ferris wheel careened into the air, the passengers screaming in delight, the lights spinning and flaring in multi-colored brilliance. Later, the sky would be filled with wooshing and popping fireworks, rockets blasting high above the fairgrounds, sparkling showers of green and red and blue sparks sizzling as they fell. When the last of the fireworks faded into ash and darkness, the monstrous rides would grind noisily down, the tents would be rolled up, and the carnies would pile into cars and trucks and mobile homes to head for the next stop. By morning, only trampled grass and litter would mark that the fair had ever been here.

Shawn felt a stab of sadness. He would miss the fair—miss the tents and barkers, the rides and animal smells.

A ridiculously morbid thought raced through his mind:

If they didn't find Robert before the fair moved on, they may never find him.

A chuckle caught in his throat. A familiar, although not necessarily friendly, face broke through a line of people waiting to buy candy apples. He quickly turned, trying to act as if he didn't see the approaching figure.

"What?" Tom asked, then groaned when he saw who was heading their way.

Mark Casey wore his letter jacket, even though it was much too warm, like a uniform of office. His hair was black and curly, his eyes dark as storm clouds. His brow was furrowed, and his lips peeled away from his teeth.

"Hey, you little pubes!" he growled. "I want to talk to you."

Shawn's flight or fight instinct kicked in, only he didn't know which impulse to obey. He knew that if it came to a fight, Mark would kill him, but he hated the idea of backing down from this bully.

Before Shawn could react, Tom stepped out to face Mark. He puffed up his chest, stood straight, but was still dwarfed by the older boy. "What do you want, Casey?"

"Where's that punk friend of yours?"

Great, Shawn thought. Mark was looking for Robert, too, and with blood in his eyes, which could only mean one thing.

Cheryl.

"Could you be a little more specific?" Tom feigned a polite smile. "I have so many punk friends it's hard to narrow them down."

"You know who I mean."

"Yeah, I guess I do. I haven't seen him though." Tom paused, drumming his fingers against his chin, contemplating whether or not to finish his sentence.

Don't, Shawn thought. Let it drop.

No such luck.

"And I haven't seen Cheryl, either," Tom said.

A wash of mottled red spread across Mark's face. He looked ready to lunge. Shawn spoke up, hoping to prevent his friend from getting pounded. "We're looking for him, too, Mark. Last we heard, he was going to the exhibit hall for the car show. He's been obsessed with getting a Mustang ever since he got his license, you know?"

Mark glared at Shawn, nodding his head slightly and chewing at the inside of his lip. "All right. You find him, let him know I'm looking for him." He turned and stomped off.

In the distance, a muscle car engine roared.

"Why'd you lie like that?" Tom asked.

"In case you hadn't noticed, he was getting ready to kill you." Shawn shot Tom a dirty look. "I wanted to get rid of him."

"Great idea." Tom shrugged. "But what if Robert really is at the car show?"

They exchanged worried glances.

"We better hurry up and find him," Shawn said.

* * *

As much as Robert enjoyed Cheryl's company, a needling sensation of claustrophobia chewed at his nerves. He tried not to let it show, but the unventilated mirror maze grew more narrow, more stifling, and more frustrating as he searched for an exit.

A crowd of ghoulish reflections around them.

Up ahead, the glass walls and mirrors parted, revealing a dark portal.

"Guess we should try this door."

"Not that we have much choice," Cheryl joked, "but my fate is in your hands."

"I'll find the way." His voice was shaky, unsure, betraying his cavalier facade. "I'm the Columbus of mirror maze explorers, you know."

Through the gloomy passage, they found a single straight hallway—a relief after the winding corridors of glass. The walls, rather than mirrored panels, were painted the deepest black. Only four mirrors stood along the right side, the glass in each rolling like ocean waves in the lacquered frames. A light was set into the ceiling above each mirror, feebly beating back the darkness.

After so many reflective surfaces, this corridor seemed bare.

Abandoned.

They walked slowly past the four mirrors. Each twisted their image in the most awful way, stretching their arms and legs into spindly, spidery lengths or warping their faces to goggle-eyed, large-mouthed masks.

A moment of unease slipped away, and they laughed and posed before the mirrors.

Odd symbols were carved into the frames.

"What language is that?" Robert ran his fingers over the carved lettering. He wondered why these mirrors had been set aside from the others. "Egyptian?"

"Probably just gobbledygook."

Up ahead, another door presented itself, leading perhaps to an exit.

Robert glimpsed movement out of the corner of his eye. A light flickered from between the sections of the black wall. Shadows moved behind the panel. There must have been a walkway back there, probably used by fair employees.

He heard growling, angry and frantic, then a muffled grunting.

"Hold on a second," he said.

Dry wood creaked underfoot. He peered between two of the panels.

In the narrow, dimly lit walkway, he saw two men—one he did not recognize but the other might have been the gangly mirror maze attendant who had taken their tickets. They grunted and cursed and carried a squirming burden shrouded in burlap.

"What is it?" Cheryl asked, her voice dropping to a whisper.

Robert was about to answer when he was startled by a painful cry.

"Christ! It bit me!"

The second man—definitely the attendant—cried out and dropped his end of the bundled shape. He clutched at the meat of his palm. Blood glistened upon his fingers, dribbled to the floor.

"Come on, come on," the other man, a short mean-looking fellow chewing on smoldering cigar, said in a gruff voice. "We need to get this thing out to the truck. There's another one in here somewhere."

Cheryl touched Robert's shoulder. He jumped, almost screamed.

"What is it?" she asked again.

"I'm not sure."

He looked again, but the men were gone. Shadows crept along the walls of the back hall. He heard the shuffle of footsteps, the scrape of nails upon the wood. A trickle of sweat rolled down his back.

Pulling away from the makeshift spy hole, he took Cheryl by the hand and raced through the rest of the maze, not pausing to look at the final mirrors.

"What's the matter?" Cheryl asked.

Something moved behind the walls, matching their steps with a staggering gate, like an abnormal reflection of their movement.

Cool air washed over them when they rounded a turn and spotted the exit. It was darker outside than Robert had imagined. How long had they been lost in the maze? They descended the metal steps to the sawdust-covered ground.

At the entrance, the attendant was gone. A sign tacked to the front of the podium read "Back in 15 Minutes".

"You're acting strange," Cheryl said, annoyance rather than concern edging into her voice.

"Sorry." He struggled to catch his breath. "Listen, I just want to check on something real quick. Then, we'll do whatever you want. My treat."

Cheryl nodded. Robert casually walked past the front of the mirror maze and past the next attraction—The Amazing! Amazing! Amazing! Nine Foot Mystery

Mummy—and turned down an alley between the tents.

In the lot behind the attractions, numerous tractor-trailers were parked upon the dried grass. Some of the trailers were colorfully decorated with the logo of the Eldritch Brothers Fairworks. Others were unpainted hulks of metal squatting in the shadows.

"We probably aren't supposed to be here," Cheryl said.

As Robert watched, two figures re-emerged from the back of the mirror maze. In the shadows. He could not see their faces, but he recognized their shapes as those of the attendant and the short, plump man. They were dragging a third, smaller figure.

From one of the trailers—the one directly behind the mirror maze—arose an awful racket, as if someone had been locked inside by accident and was yelling and beating upon the metal doors.

A chill raced down Robert's spine.

This was no accident.

The small captive kicked and grunted and thrashed about.

"Hold him," said the short, mean-looking man. "Hold him."

In one hand he held the flaring stub of a cigar. With the other, he grabbed a stick from beside the trailer. Two wicked prongs, like those of an oversized barbeque fork, gleamed in the moonlight. He bit down on the cigar and flung open the screeching trailer doors. Several dark forms moved inside, hopping and crawling over each other. He jabbed at them with the fork, driving them back.

The mirror maze attendant drug the prisoner to the trailer and threw him inside.

A tortured, terrible clamoring rose from the trailer as the doors slammed shut.

"What's going on?" Cheryl asked. "What are they doing?"

Robert shushed her. He ducked down behind a fold of the tent as the two men started back, climbing metal steps and disappearing into the mirror maze. A trail of cigar smoke lingered in the air behind them.

"Can we go now?" Cheryl asked.

"Yeah," Robert said, "but I want to find Shawn and Tom. I need to tell them about this."

The cries from the trailer went unheard by all but Robert and Cheryl, drowned out by the sounds of the fair.

* * *

Shawn couldn't really explain what Robert saw in Cheryl, besides the obvious. She toyed with him and played him against other guys. She pushed him away, kicked him when he was down, and waited for him to come crawling back for more. Robert, of course, was blind to this. But if they didn't find him soon, he might very well be pining after her from a hospital bed.

It was getting ever later. The sounds of the fair built to a frenzy in the final, last-gasp hours. The plinking tune of the carousel ascended, then descended, quickly replaced by blasting Aerosmith tunes from the whirling Himalya.

"There he is!" Tom cried.

Robert ran towards them, kicking plumes of sawdust and sand. Cheryl pouted and stomped after him.

"You're not going to believe what I've found."

Robert told them what he had seen in the mirror maze, about the mysterious figures, about the unmarked trailer and the screams from within.

"You're kidding, right?" Tom said.

"Come see for yourself."

"I'm not going back there." Cheryl wrapped her arms around her body as if cold. "I think I should just go home."

"Oh." Robert's shoulders slumped. "All right. I'll talk to you tomorrow?"

"Sure." She was already backing away from the group. She turned and walked quickly away, vanishing into the crowd.

"You know she's heading straight to Mark, don't you?" Tom smirked.

"Yeah," Shawn said. "He's looking for you. He knows you were with Cheryl."

"This is a lot more important than worrying about Mark Casey." He tried to hide his concern for his bodily health. "You guys have any idea what I've stumbled on to?"

"Just like when you thought your neighbor murdered his wife and hid her in the carport?"

Robert grumbled. "Come on. You'll see."

They followed him back to the mirror maze. Barkers called to them, hoping to get one last rube before the night was out. A happy couple paraded past, the girl clutching a stuffed pink and blue puppy almost as big as she was.

Nearby, compressors snapped and hissed.

"Let's assume Robert's right." Tom's voice reeked of sarcasm. "Let's say they're kidnapping kids from the mirror maze, maybe from all over the fair, and tossing them in a trailer. Why?"

"I don't know," Robert said. "Could be anything. Slave labor. Black market."

"This better not be another wild goose chase," Tom said. "All we need is a repeat of what happened last Halloween. I was grounded for a month."

Robert winced.

"We're just going to take a look," Shawn said. "We'll be out of there before anyone catches us."

They passed a freak show tent, painted gaudily with monstrous images, "Human Oddities, Children of Forgotten Fathers," in stenciled lettering across the front. Flapping banners dangled on either side of the ticket booth. The Giant, the Four-Legged Girl, the Seal Boy, the Dwarf, the World's Ugliest Woman—all were depicted, cartoon-like, upon the banners. A short, gruff-looking man stood upon the stage out front. "Step up, my friends. You've never seen a show more terrifying, more mystifying, more mesmerizing than what you'll see right through this doorway." He motioned flamboyantly towards the door. A blackened cigar was clenched between his yellowed teeth, the smoke wreathing his head.

"That's him," Robert said.

"What?" Tom asked.

"That's him." A wave of panic elevated Robert's voice. "That's him. The guy from the mirror maze."

"Quiet," Shawn said. "He'll hear you."

The man watched them pass.

"Calm down, man." Tom patted Robert on the shoulder. "What would he be doing lurking around the Mirror Maze?"

Robert looked back at the man and muttered, "I don't know."

As they drew closer to the Mirror Maze, Robert regained his composure. He held a finger to his lips and motioned for Shawn and Tom to follow as he ducked down an alleyway and crept around the tent.

All was quiet.

Darkness enshrouded the hulking tractor trailer.

"Seems normal to me," Shawn said.

"I'm telling you," Robert said, "they were screaming."

"Let's go see," Tom said. He scanned the lot and dashed towards the trailer.

"Wait!" Shawn hissed.

They followed Tom out, not wanting him to risk danger on his own.

He reached for the trailer door, fingers twitching. Tom grabbed the cold steel bar.

From the fair, a cry rose, one last gasp as the Tilt-a-Whirl or Pirates Galleon thrilled passengers.

Robert spotted the oversized barbeque fork leaning against the side of the trailer. The tips of the fork were speckled brownish-red.

"Be careful," he said.

Tom grinned, started to turn the bar.

Suddenly, the door rattled as something slammed against it from the inside. A dozen voices, maybe more, rose in a scream.

"Yaah!" Tom jerked away, stumbled over his feet, and crashed to the ground.

Robert's feet shuffled, ready to bolt.

Only Shawn stood his ground. His heart pounded in his chest. He pressed close to the door, listened. "Who's there?"

"Shawn, come on man." Robert grabbed his arm. "They're going to catch us for sure. We know someone's trapped inside. Let's just call the police."

The cries subsided, replaced by a few, mewling voices. "Hhhalp. Haalllp usss."

Tom scrambled to his feet and rushed to Shawn's side. "We've got to get them out of there."

"Come on!" Robert said. He edged a little farther away.

"Keep lookout," Tom said.

The latch was harder to throw than they expected, and Tom and Shawn strained to lift the bar. The metal groaned as it turned and slid free. The doors swung open, revealing a yawning black expanse.

The smell of sweat and unwashed flesh wafted out.

On the far end, in the darkness, several shapes moved, clustered together for protection, hunched over, crawling, curled into fetal positions. Eyes glittered from the shadow.

"Hurry," Tom said. "We need to get out of here. We need to call the police."

They started to inch forward—slowly, slowly.

"Tthhannnnnk you," came the answer.

"Guys!" Robert's voice was shrill. "Someone's coming!"

The figures shuffled back into the gloomy recesses of the trailer.

"Come on, come on," Shawn whispered.

"Let's go!" Robert cried.

A rough voice called out. "You pubes are in for it!" Mark Casey strode towards them, along with two of his grinning buddies, Scott and Clint. Trailing behind them, sheepishly, was Cheryl.

"You think I'm playing games?" Mark towered over Robert, who backed away.

Scott and Clint chuckled. They were both easily as big and mean as Mark himself.

"We don't want a fight," Shawn said.

"You should pick better friends then."

"Damn," Clint said, holding his nose. "What's that smell? Stinks like the Ag exhibits."

"Did one of you babies shit your pants?" Scott hooted. "You did, didn't you?"

Mark reached out, quick as a striking snake, and grabbed Robert, twisting his arm hard, forcing him to his knees.

Before Tom had a chance to react, Scott jumped him, driving fist after fist into his stomach. Tom wheezed and sprawled to the ground.

Mark shoved Robert to the ground, kicked him in the gut.

"That's enough!" Shawn threw himself at Mark. Clint plowed into Shawn's mid-section, lifting him from the ground and letting him drop to the hard-packed earth.

"Don't hurt them…" Cheryl said, quietly.

"Just keep your mouth shut. I'll—"

He fell silent. He stood over Robert, but gazed up into the back of the trailer. His mouth hung open, his lips trembling.

Scott and Clint followed their leader's gaze.

Cheryl shrieked.

Something pounced from within, crashing into Mark with bare feet. He toppled backward. It was a twisted thing, dressed in rumpled rags. It sank its teeth into Mark's throat and tore away a ragged strip of flesh. A spray of blood speckled the open trailer door.

More of the creatures rushed out, ripping at Mark, Scott, and Clint with their teeth and nails.

They were unnatural things, each one misshapen, some tall and stick-thin, some squat and knobby. Some flopped about on flipper-like appendages while others scurried like spiders on multiple sets of human-like hands and feet.

Talons gouged dark red holes into Mark's letter jacket. His cries were wet and gurgling.

Clint tried to stumble away, three of the creatures bared down on him like hyenas taking down a wounded gazelle. He squealed as he vanished beneath the tangled dog pile.

Scott was grabbed by a thing with arms that were much too large—much too muscular—for its smallish frame. The monster flung Scott like a rag doll into the trailer, picked the boy up and hurled him again.

Robert recognized the features of one of the creatures—it was like looking into a funhouse mirror.

The creatures, covered in blood, feasted. The smacking, slurping, cracking sounds, like those of starving children, were awful.

"Let's go," Tom said, pulling himself to his feet.

For a moment, Shawn thought the creatures might try to stop them, but one of the creatures—one that looked like Robert's deformed twin brother—hissed, "Go."

They fled.

Before them, fireworks blasted into the sky, flooding the alleyway with color, washing their skin in green and blue and red light. Cries of delight erupted from the fairgrounds.

In the lead, Robert faltered. He looked back to make sure his friends had made it.

"Cheryl," he cried. "Where's Cheryl?"

Shawn looked back.

The creatures grabbed Cheryl, dragging her back. One of the hideous creatures clapped a hand over her mouth to muffle her screams. It looked like her, only her body parts were mismatched and knotted.

"Cheryl!" Robert called.

Shawn stutter-stepped, almost went after her.

"Where is she?" Robert asked.

Shawn shook his head. "She's gone. She must have went another way."

Tom caught Robert before he could charge back to find her. "She's gone already," he said. "You go back there and you're as good as dead."

They ran without stopping to the fairgrounds gate, piled into Shawn's car, and sped away. Shawn was too shaken to drive safely. He almost ran down a few fairgoers on their way to their cars. They yelled, but he pressed down on the gas and swung onto the road.

In the passenger seat, Tom, bruised and battered, rocked back and forth. In the back, Robert looked out the rear window, hoping to catch a glimpse of Cheryl as she made it to safety.

Shawn wondered if they had done the right thing, freeing those things.

Those creatures—what were they? He thought he might have known, but he didn't want the thoughts to linger in his mind for long.

The fair would be gone by morning, taking the Mirror Maze and the freak show with it.

And Shawn wouldn't miss it as much as he thought he would.

"The Last Night of the Fair" was originally published in the anthology CARNIVAL OF HORROR (2004)

When I was a kid, I got trapped (along with my pal Vardell) in a county fair mirror maze. We found a narrow passage that I thought was the exit, but the carnie running the attraction wouldn't let us out. He went so far as to yell at us to "Go another way!" when we tried to slip out. We were in there for... I dunno... what seemed like forever. We finally slipped out the narrow exit while the carnie was looking elsewhere. The whole experience scared the hell out of me.

- CB

PIASA DREAMS

"While skirting some rocks, which by their height and length inspired awe, we saw upon them two painted monsters which at first made us afraid, and upon which the boldest savages dare not long rest their eyes."

--The Journal of Father Jacques Marquette, 1673

Shielding my eyes from the afternoon sun, I squinted at the cliffside painting. "That has got to be one of the most grotesque things I've ever seen."

"Don't be like that." Kate waved a colorful visitor center brochure at me. "It's historic."

"It's horrible."

Jim sidled up next to me and clasped me roughly on the shoulder. He smiled, his eyes hidden behind prescription shades. His fingers gripped my muscles tightly. "Never let it be said that good old Rodge has any interest in folklore."

Rodge. I hated when people called me that … and I had told Jim I preferred "Roger" at least a half dozen times. Funny how that sort of thing flew right over his head.

"Folklore is fine, but this—" I shrugged his hand away and jabbed a finger towards the painting. "—is a tourist trap, not folklore."

"According to legend, this area was once the Piasa Bird's hunting ground." Kate read from the brochure. "It devoured entire Illini villages before it was finally killed. It took twenty Illini warriors with poison arrows to kill the beast."

"And now you can buy your very own Piasa Bird Beanie Baby." I rolled my eyes.

Jim chuckled.

Kate swatted the brochure against her thigh and faked an injured pout—the kind that always managed to play a heavy metal riff on my heartstrings.

"All right," I said. "All right. Sorry."

"So what do you think it was?" Jim's wife, Valerie, snapped a picture of the painting with her digital camera. "A dinosaur or something?"

Kate shrugged. "No one really knows."

High upon the bluff, the painting of the Piasa Bird was fifty feet wide and nearly twenty feet tall. The creature's body was that of a winged lion, covered in colorful scales. It had the head of a bearded devil, fangs and tusks jutting from fat lips, and deer-like antlers of the deepest crimson sprouted from its forehead. A long, segmented tail curled around its body.

The mouth of a massive cave yawned beneath the painting. A weed-choked garden of gravel and large stones littered the ground leading to the craggy opening. It looked as if the monster had burst from the earth and slithered out only to become a two-dimensional, painted horror upon the side of the bluff.

"Anyone want a closer look?" Jim called as he hopped the wooden fence enclosing the parking area. He traipsed across knee-high weeds towards the cave. Loose stones crunched beneath his Birkinstock sandals.

"What do you think you're doing?" Weariness edged Valerie's voice, as if she called after a misbehaving child and not a grown man. "Come back here!"

"Oh, come on. Where's your spirit of adventure?"

A chaotic flock of birds erupted from the cave, a cloud of screeching, fluttering blackness. Jim yelped, nearly fell on his ass, and covered his head as if he feared an attack. The birds cackled their protest at his intrusion as the rose past the Piasa Bird painting and vanished around the side of the craggy precipice.

Jim picked himself up, brushing the seat of his khaki shorts.

"The fearless explorer," I said. "Nice sense of adventure, buddy."

Kate and Valerie laughed.

Jim shook his head, grumbling to himself, and flipped us off. He approached the cave—more cautiously—and peered inside. He took a step, then another. Shadows closed around him.

"Careful," Valerie called.

With another step, he vanished into the fissure.

For a few seconds, Jim's footsteps echoed from the cave.

Then silence.

"I wish he wouldn't go in there by himself," Valerie whined. "What if he hurts himself?"

I fought off the urge to smile.

"Honey," Kate said, "why not go with him?"

I started to protest, but Kate shot me a stern look, and I saw that Valerie was genuinely worried. Sighing, I trudged across the parking lot and jumped the fence. I imagined the weeds crawled with ticks and chiggers. I'd probably be itching for the rest of the weekend.

The face of the Piasa Bird leered down at me.

Like a morsel of meat, ripe for the taking, I thought.

I would have preferred a relaxing weekend catching up on my reading and vegging in front of the TV. I didn't mind taking a weekend trip with Kate—"mini vacations," she called them—but this time she had insisted on inviting Jim and Valerie along. Valerie was nice enough, smart and sweet if somewhat nervous— and she was certainly pleasing to the eye. But Jim was a jackass who delighted in cracking unfunny jokes and telling off-color stories of his glory days playing amateur hockey. I didn't know how Kate could stand working with the guy, let alone tolerate socializing with him.

The tunnel curved sharply to the right, descending away from the opening, away from the light. The air was cool and damp. Small islands of rocks rose out of puddles of water. Rivulets of run-off snaked down the rough, wet walls.

A shadow—Jim—moved up ahead.

"Decided to show a little backbone, eh, Rodge?" Jim called.

"Just trying to keep you out of trouble."

"I was thinking," Jim said. "Maybe the Piasa Bird nested in these caves. The painting was probably put up as a warning."

"I don't think so. This isn't even the original site of the painting. That was farther downriver, but wind and rain eroded it. Locals painted the new one only a few years back." I almost laughed. Kate would have been proud of me for paying attention at the visitor's center. I stepped over a patch of crushed beer cans, cigarette butts, and used condoms. "Looks like this cave is just a party spot for horny teenagers."

Didn't I sound like an old man? Wasn't too many years ago that I might have joined those horny teenagers in their partying. Now I held down a steady job, stayed in on Friday nights as often as I could help it, and was seriously considering asking Kate, my girlfriend of eight months, to tie the knot.

All grown up and playing around in caves.

Jim fished his cigarette lighter out of his pocket. He flicked the lighter and held it out in front of him as he walked beyond the pall of the ambient light from the cave opening. "Lots of graffiti back here," he said.

The tunnel grew a little narrower, the gradation more steep. Spray-painted phrases, some faded beyond legibility, decorated the walls. The messages lead deeper into the cave. Weird shadows crawled across Jim's face as he held the flickering lighter close to the walls. With his glasses off, his eyes looked like black marbles in the darkness.

Mark Loves Cheryl, the graffiti read.

I Feel Like Dancing.

What's For Dinner Mama?

And, a little deeper in the cave:

Beware the Piasa Dreams.

"Creepy, huh?" Jim said.

I touched the wall and ran my finger along the lettering. The paint was rust-colored and thick. I rubbed my fingers together, then shrugged and wiped my hand dry on my shorts. The tunnel continued into an almost solid darkness, but I didn't go any farther. "I think I've seen just about everything this cave has to offer," I said.

Outside, the girls called for us. Their voices seemed too distant.

As I walked back towards the cave entrance, Jim followed, calling "Wait up," like an annoying little brother.

Sunlight stung my eyes as I stepped from the cave. The warmth felt good, soaking into my bones. I hadn't realized just how cold the interior of the cave had been.

"You boys done spelunking?" Valerie asked.

"Honey, I haven't even started." Jim's voice was lewd.

I wondered if he even knew what "spelunking" meant.

Valerie took a picture of us as we emerged from the cave. If nothing else, I couldn't fault Jim's taste in women. She was dark-skinned, curvaceous, and exotic, wearing a skimpy outfit most women her age would have packed away ten year's ago. I couldn't imagine how Jim had won her over. Such an oddity almost made me believe a creature such as the Piasa Bird might have once existed.

"So … did you find anything interesting?" Kate asked. She pursed her lips. She had probably noticed the way my gaze lingered on Valerie's backside.

"Not really," I said as I crawled over the fence. "We didn't go too far."

She smiled knowingly and winked.

"This has been fun and all, but isn't there a winery up the road a ways?" Jim looked at his bare wrist as if checking a watch. "I don't know about you guys, but I'm beginning to get a bit thirsty."

After Valerie snapped a few final photos, we piled into the car and continued down the Great River Road. I drove. Kate reclined in the passenger's seat while the other couple sat in back. Jim crouched in the middle, leaning between the seats and blocking the rearview mirror.

On our right, a jagged limestone bluff rose, covered in thickets and vines. Numerous bicyclists pedaled along a bike trail running between the road and the cliff. A roadside sign warned of FALLING ROCKS. On our left, the Mississippi River wound through the valley. According to the legend, when the Illini warriors fired their poisoned arrows into the Piasa, it fell from the skies with a terrible shriek, plunging into the deep, dark waters of the river never to be seen again. Now, a pair of jet skis rounded the river bend, tearing frothing trails through the monster's grave.

A few miles down the scenic route, we arrived in the town of Grandview. Tourist attraction fare lined the streets. T-shirt shops. Ice cream parlors. "Starving artist's" markets. Antique stores. Signposts advertised bicycle, jet ski, and paddleboat rentals. The girls beamed as we drove past the shops. Both Kate and Valerie were dedicated bargain antique hunters. I wondered how we would fit all their purchases in the car for the trip home.

"Shopping comes later, ladies," Jim said. "First, we eat, drink, and make merry."

Up ahead, I spotted a rustic looking building of mismatched river stone. Decorative wine barrels-turned-flower pots stood on either side of the door. To the left, picnic tables and chairs had been arranged on a covered deck with a river view. A sign out front read PIASA WINES. Beneath the words, an etched Piasa Bird growled and clutched a wine bottle in its talons.

I swung the car alongside the curb.

"Pop the trunk for me," Kate said.

I flipped the trunk release and climbed out of the car.

Jim was already crossing the sidewalk and climbing the three steps to the winery's front door. Kate rummaged in the trunk for the cooler full of sandwiches and bottled water. Valerie braced her arms against the roof of the car, closed her eyes, and breathed deeply. As she leaned over, the neck of her top fell open, and I could see the soft mound of her breasts.

"Smell that fresh air," she said.

"Yeah," I replied. "It's great ... unless the river starts to stink, of course."

Valerie opened her eyes and smiled at me. "Always the cynic."

I shrugged.

"It works for you, though."

The trunk slammed shut, and I went to the back of the car to take the cooler from Kate. Valerie joined us. Jim was already inside, and the three of us climbed the steps to join him.

The winery offered vintages from dozens of local vineyards, from merlots to chardonnays to numerous sweet and semi-sweet fruit wines with names like Riverside Red and Spring Creek Blush. Wine racks, decorative bottle stoppers, soup mixes, salsas, and homemade jellies and candy were also available.

"Who's up for some wine tasting?" Jim asked as we stepped inside. He already had a small Dixie cup in his hand, and a chubby, smiling woman was lining several bottles up along the counter.

"Well," Kate said, "I wouldn't want to miss out on the entire experience." She approached the counter and set the picnic basket at her feet.

"You coming?" Valerie asked as she brushed past.

"No. You guys have fun. One of us has to be the responsible one."

The three of them booed and hissed at me.

"Besides," I said, "I've never been much of a wine drinker, myself. I'll just browse around while the three of you get trashed."

As I explored the shop, the floor beneath me creaked and groaned, as if it were ready to buckle. An old building like this, I thought, was likely to fall in on itself at any moment. The winery had quite obviously been a house years ago, but the bedrooms and living rooms had been gutted and lined with shelving, and re-carpeted in a matching deep maroon, all the better to conceal the occasional spill, I assumed.

I rounded a corner, leaving the dry wines behind and entering a chamber filled almost to the ceiling with dessert wines. Even for a guy who preferred beer to wine, the selection was impressive. I wasn't paying attention to where I was going, and I walked right into a stock clerk.

"Excuse me," he said, almost dropping the armload of bottles he carried.

"My fault," I said.

The young man tried to kick the door from which he had emerged closed, but was having a bit of trouble without spilling the bottles.

"Let me help you with that." The door opened into a rough stone staircase leading down into a dimly lit chamber. A stock room, I assumed, but I felt the same cool air wafting up from below that I had felt in the caves beneath the Piasa painting. I pushed the door, marked Employees Only, closed. "I bet this old place has a heck of a history."

The clerk offered a polite, if insincere, smile. "I wouldn't really know to be honest. Just started a few days ago." He thanked me and carried his burden towards the front.

This time, he almost ran right into Jim, who didn't even pardon himself when he almost knocked the kid over. "There you are, Rodge. Take a look at this."

He thrust a bottle of red wine towards me. The label depicted the same fearsome half man, half bird creature painted upon the river bluff. Piasa Dreams, the label read.

"Beware! Beware!" Jim laughed. "Come on, buddy. I think we're about ready to check out."

I smiled to myself again. Jim had a bright red wine mustache, but I wasn't about to tell him.

To complement our sandwiches, we purchased a couple of bottles of wine— the deep red Piasa Dreams Jim had shown me—along with some crackers and a garlic-heavy cheese spread. I picked a six pack of cold beer from the cooler. Nothing fancy for me, just something to quench my thirst. The cashier, a pretty young girl, had trouble with the cash register and asked the manager, the smiling woman who had served the wine samples, for help.

"Sorry for the inconvenience, folks," she said. "New employee."

"You must have a couple of new hires here today," I said.

"Yes. Start of the new season means employees-in-training, you know."

"Bet you get really busy this time of year, don't you?"

"Pretty soon now, sure." The manager worked the cash register while the trainee bagged the bottles.

We spent a couple of hours on the covered deck, eating the sandwiches we had brought, sipping our wine and beer, and enjoying the view as the sun crept below the horizon, painting the river in golds and reds.

Kate, Valerie, and Jim drained the first two bottles of Piasa Dreams and purchased two more.

"One for here," Jim said, refilling glasses with a freshly opened bottle. "And one for the road."

No one else had pointed out his wine mustache, either.

"This is a local wine, right?" Kate asked, swishing the piteous remainder of her wine in the glass. "So where do they get the grapes? I didn't see any vineyards."

"I imagine they have the grapes trucked in," I said.

Kate finished her glass and Jim poured a little more. I had finished four of my beers and felt the hint of a buzz. I noticed several large vultures soaring overhead. They were huge, their wings arcing out around them as they rode updrafts like feathered kites. I didn't know much about vultures, really, only that they were carrion birds, feeding on the dead. I figured with all the tourist traffic, the road provided them with a smorgasbord of roadkill.

After dinner, we milled around town for a while. Kate, Valerie, and Jim stumbled around, but the shopkeepers seemed accustomed to such behavior and took their antics in stride. Kate bought a couple of pieces of furniture from an antique shop—and asked to have them shipped home. Valerie picked up a large oil painting from the artist's market. Jim didn't care for the selection. "I like my art to feature naked women," he said. "Know what I'm talking about, Rodge?" Soon, the lights along the main street started to dim, and the signs hanging in windows were turned from "Come In, We're Open" to "Sorry, We're Closed. Come Back Soon." I confirmed the directions to the cottage with the owner of the artist's market and led the group back to the car.

"So where's this cottage we've rented, Roger?" Valerie asked.

"Actually, I think I'll be fine driving." I looked over my shoulder. A side road branched off the main street, winding up the hill towards several small buildings nestled in the trees. "If I understand the directions correctly, the cottage isn't far."

As we drove away from town, I noted how dark it looked, all of the lights extinguished along the trail, with only a few streetlights guiding the way.

The cottage, as Jim put it, was quaint. Again, nothing fancy, just a den, a bathroom, and a couple of bedrooms, overlooking the town and the river beyond. It was certainly nicer than most hotel rooms we might have rented … and more private too. If not for Jim and Valerie, it might have been the perfect getaway spot.

Actually, I would have been much happier if Jim hadn't been along, just the ladies and me. The possibilities boggled the mind.

Looking downhill as I unloaded our luggage, I noticed that the winery was still brightly lit, but it only made sense that their hours might run a bit late.

We sat on the patio as the night cooled. My companions opened the final bottle of Piasa Dreams and drank from paper cups.

"You sure you don't want to try some of this, honey?" Kate asked.

I took a sip. It tasted like honey and had the thick consistency of port. "It's tasty, I guess, but I think I'll stick with beer. It's a little too sweet for me, and wine gives me a hell of a headache."

"I'm sure Kate has the cure for that," Valerie said. She grinned devilishly in my direction.

My face flushed. I hoped that no one noticed in the darkness.

"Too much information," Jim said. "No offense, but I don't want to know about your sordid sexual escapades."

"Well, maybe I want to know," Valerie said. Her speech was slightly slurred.

We all laughed.

Once the wine was finished and we all started yawning more than talking, we retired for the evening. As tired as I was, I had trouble getting to sleep. I tossed and turned, listening to Valerie and Jim in the next room, giggling through the too-thin walls. Kate had no problems sleeping. Drunk and exhausted, she slept peacefully, curled close and snoring softly. Her breath smelled faintly of the honey-scent of Piasa Dreams.

Finally, after the lovebirds next door settled down, I closed my eyes and drifted off.

I dreamed of Valerie, of course. Somehow I had known I would.

She sauntered into the room, dressed in a skimpy negligee that showed off her figure—attractive in reality but improved, perfected, here in the dream. She smiled but didn't say a word as she tiptoed towards the bed.

I eased myself up. I was naked. I never slept in the nude, but I felt the sheets—satin—sliding against my skin and I knew I wasn't wearing a stitch.

Valerie crawled onto the bed. Her nails scratched at my bare chest lightly, hooked the satin sheets and started to pull them down. She raised herself and straddled me. I felt her warmth. She growled hungrily.

Suddenly, I wondered where Kate had gone. She was not in the bed with us. If she caught us—

"Valerie—"

She put a finger to my mouth. A smile slipped across her face. She leaned close, her lips parting ever so slightly.

And she shrieked.

Valerie sat bolt upright, cocked her head, and cried out. Every muscle in her body clenched. She gripped at me. No human sound escaped her throat. It was the sound of train wheels squealing against the tracks.

I awakened.

I ran a hand over my face and caught my breath.

I looked over, afraid I might have awakened Kate. Her side of the bed was empty. I was alone.

Must have gone to the bathroom.

I lay still, listening to the hum of the A/C unit for several minutes. I was shivering; the memory of the dream was so fresh, the image of Valerie's face contorting into something inhuman as she rode me.

As she screamed.

Maybe Kate was sick. After all the wine she drank—

I heard the shrieking again, this time distantly. I was awake and, yet, I heard the shrill sound as clearly—or maybe more clearly—than I had in the dream.

Gooseflesh rose upon my arms.

I threw aside the sheets. Moonlight trickled in from the windows, a pale luminescence filling the room.

A cold light.

I padded across the bedroom and opened the door. The cottage was dark. Across the hall, the bathroom door stood open, the room beyond dark save for a nightlight.

No Kate.

The terrible cry rose again from somewhere outside, somewhere in the distance, but not too far away, not far enough to make me feel safe.

The village.

I walked back to the bedroom window and pulled the curtains aside. Moonlight bathed the hillside in patches of light and shadow. Down below, in the village, lights glowed from the winery.

Awful late to be open, I thought.

I heard the shriek again. My teeth ached at the sound of it.

Somehow, I knew it originated from the winery.

I slipped into my jeans, shirt, and tennis shoes. The clothing smelled faintly of my sweat. I stepped into the hall, walked past Jim and Valerie's room. The door stood ajar. The room was empty.

Had they all gone out to investigate the sound? Why hadn't they waked me?

The front door was also open, a cool night breeze filtering into the foyer. Something felt wrong. I wondered if I was still dreaming.

Following quickly on the heels of that thought, I wondered if Jim had convinced the girls to play a prank. He seemed the sort to try, but surely they wouldn't go along with it.

I stepped outside, closing the door behind me.

I left the car where it was parked and followed the downhill road on foot. Trees loomed along either side of the street. The houses—quaint, like the cabin, Jim might have pointed out—lining the street were dark, but I could have sworn I saw a pallid face peering at me as I walked by, the curtains falling quickly back into place when I looked that way.

I reached the main street and approached the winery. The patio was empty, even though the lights glowed, attracting mosquitoes by the dozen. I saw no movement through the windows.

Maybe a few folks working late, performing an inventory or something.

Jim, Kate, and Valerie must have been watching from hiding places, barely able to contain their laughter.

All right, I thought. Play along.

I climbed the steps and peered through the window. I saw no one. I grabbed the doorknob and carefully turned, expecting to find it locked. The door swung open. "Hello?" I called, quietly, almost a whisper, unwilling to break the silence, almost afraid someone might answer.

The place seemed abandoned.

Just as I decided to leave, I heard the shrieking again, louder now.

Closer.

Bottles of wine rattled on the shelves, threatened to fall to the floor. I almost clapped my hands over my ears. The sound was that of metal screeching against metal … only it sounded too … organic.

It was the sound of a living creature.

The creaking floorboards beneath my feet seemed to shiver.

The sound came from below.

The bottles stopped shaking. I looked at the shelves and found the perverse face of the Piasa Bird staring back at me from a wine label.

I needed to leave, but I caught myself as I stepped towards the door.

What if Kate, Valerie, and Jim had come here for some reason? What if they had followed the sound? What if they had snuck in, just as I had, and encountered—

The face on the label silently snarled.

The door to the basement storage room stood open. Somewhere down below was the source of the shrieking. It couldn't hurt to take a look, just make sure the others were not down there. I crept down the stairs. The descent was dark, but a flickering light glowed from the cellar. Patches of shadow crawled, spider like, along the rough-hewn walls.

I covered my nose. What was that smell? For a moment, I thought I might vomit. It was the musky stink of a serpent, only overpowering, as if thousands of snakes slithered in the darkness below.

Now I heard voices.

The stairs ended in a spacious chamber with walls of natural stone. Oil lanterns lined the room. From above, dust trickled down from the wooden underside of the floor. I stopped before reaching the bottom, afraid someone might see me. I saw shadows moving in the light.

I took a step, carefully, then another, proceeding just far enough to see—

In the center of the room lay a massive, bloated creature, the body like that of a great cat, only scaled, the face vaguely human and feminine with eyes as black as a shark's and tusk-like teeth protruding from plump, cracked lips. Once it might have had wings, but the remaining appendages were tattered and withered as from years of disuse. It lay on its side, like a nursing bitch, and distended, dimpled gray teats sagged against the cold, stone floor.

Horribly, I saw my three companions sprawling on their hands and knees, their naked bodies glistening with greasy sweat. They suckled at the creature's teats, making satisfied slurping noises and grunting. Red fluid with the consistency of spoiled buttermilk smeared their faces, slicked their lips, and dribbled down their chins.

I recognized the manager and the clerks from the winery. They surrounded the monstrous creature, watched my friends as they slurped up the monster's crimson milk. The manager talked to the trainees as if instructing children on a common chore. They approached the flaccid teats from which Kate, Valerie, and Jim did not feast. They held bowls, gathering the oozing, dark fluid as it dribbled from puckering nipples.

My stomach churned. I wanted the liquid. Wanted to taste it. I shivered with desire.

Piasa Dreams.

I had only sipped a little, but now, seeing it, I wanted more.

"The milk of the Piasa is a great gift," the manager said. "We must always remember to treat it as a precious treasure. We care for the Piasa, nurture it as our ancestors did ..."

The creature looked back, almost casually, at the three people nursing.

I noticed that Jim still wore his wine mustache.

"Feed it," the manager said.

A scream formed in my throat. I clutched a sweaty hand over my mouth.

The Piasa stretched its neck and snatched Kate by the head. Its tusks punched through her skull with a crunch. Kate kicked and grunted, then lay twitching as the bird tugged her body before it and, holding her down with its massive paws, tore bits of her flesh away, shaking its head to tear away the gristle.

Jim and Valerie continued slurping up the Piasa's milk, unaware as Kate's blood spread in a pool around their hands and knees.

Fighting back a wave of nausea and biting back a scream, I turned and half-crawled, half ran up the stairs. I staggered, nearly falling, banging my knees, but I didn't stop running. I could not be sure if anyone saw me. I didn't care.

As I flew from the winery, the cry of the Piasa pursued me.

I fled back to the cabin, jumped into the car, and sped away. I thought of Kate, and the memory of her suckling at the Piasa Bird like an animal almost shattered my senses. I slammed down on the gas and tore past the antique shops and ice cream parlor at close to one hundred miles an hour.

I drove for a ways without even looking in the rearview mirror. When I did chance a look back, I gasped. The Piasa Bird flew through the air in pursuit. I slammed on the brakes instinctively. But it wasn't the actual creature, just the cliffside painting reflected in the mirror. The red glow of the brake lights washed like blood across its face.

Kate's blood.

A knot of anger uncoiled in my stomach.

The winery manager had said they were getting ready for tourist season, and there was no way of knowing how many people would be buying bottle after bottle of Piasa Dreams. There was no way of knowing how many people had already consumed the stuff over the years.

I turned the car around.

My hands were slick upon the steering wheel as I guided the car back into town. The shops, all except the winery, were still dark. When I saw the glow of the winery's lights, I punched the gas again.

The car rocketed towards the building.

Twenty poisoned arrows had failed to kill the monster so many years ago.

Not tonight.

My car was my arrow.

The winery loomed ahead of me. I pointed the hood of the car right for it.

At the last minute, I threw open the door and leapt free of the car. I struck the pavement hard, my face skidding across the asphalt, snapping several of my teeth off at the roots. I heard the crash of the car striking the building, punching through the walls and crashing through the weak wooden floor.

The Piasa Bird screamed.

The cry was interrupted by a thumping explosion.

The winery went up in flames.

I staggered to my feet. Tears and blood ran down my face.

The vultures, I hoped, would eat well tomorrow.

I watched the building burn.

"Piasa Dreams" appears here for the first time.

On the road between Alton and Grafton, Illinois, you'll find a hideous painting above a cave mouth. The Piasa Bird is something of a local legend, the kind of thing that's always captured my imagination. Keep driving, and you'll reach an artsy little river community with restaurants, galleries, and more than a few wineries. Drive past that painting and take part in a few wine tastings, and this is the kind of story that results.
This tale, like "School for the Dead" was accepted for publication in a magazine that folded before it saw print.

- CB

GREAT BALLS OF IRE

When your last name is Blue ... and when you run the annual Midway County Testicle Festival, you come to expect a certain amount of ball-busting.

No pun intended.

Seemed like man, woman, and child became a regular stand-up funnyman whenever the festival rolled round, a regular bunch of Richard Pryors and Jeff Foxworthies armed with ball-centric one-liner after one-liner. I like to think all the years of friendly ribbing helped me develop a pretty well-rounded sense of humor. But I didn't find Tom's joke—the one about the corpse—funny at all.

First of all, it was the wrong day to start playing pranks.

Second of all, dead bodies, as a general rule, ain't funny.

"I'm telling you, Mr. Blue—" Tom planted his hands on his knees as he panted for air. "—there's a dead man in the field over yonder."

The festival had been open for business less than a half hour, and a healthy curtain of greasy smoke and the heady aroma of frying bull balls lingered in the air. Looking across the grounds, I counted a good three dozen patrons wandering through the maze of sno-cone stands, carnival-style rides, and game booths. By noon, the place would be swarming with people. Happy people. Carefree people. People who forked over five bucks at the gate to have a little fun and taste some authentic home-cooked barnyard jewels.

Word of a dead body got out, the thirteenth annual Testicle Festival would spoil faster than a bucket of goat milk left in the sun.

"I ain't in the mood for jokes, Tom."

"I'm serious as a heart attack." He looked like he might keel over and have a coronary, just to prove his point. Mottled red splotches spread across his throat and pudgy cheeks, and sweat matted his thinning, unkempt blonde hair to his forehead. "There's a dead body in the field behind the Knights of Columbus beer garden ... and that ain't the worst of it, neither."

It can't possibly get any worse, I thought.

Of course, Tom proved me wrong.

"The body—" He gasped for breath. "—it looks like it's been skinned."

Tom was about as dense as one of Martha Mueller's prize-winning six layer double chocolate fudge cakes, but dumb as he was, he knew better than to pull my leg on the most stressful day of the year. And if he wasn't kidding—if there really was a dead man sprawled in the weeds somewhere nearabouts—my day was about to go from bad to crawl-up-your-ass-with-a-rusty-chainsaw awful! I reached into my pants pocket and fished out a little plastic bottle full of aspirin and Pepto tablets. I poured an assortment into my hand, popped them in my mouth, and dry swallowed, hoping to dull the headache building behind my eyes and plug some of the holes in my stomach lining.

"You better show me," I said in a hushed tone, "but be discreet about it. No need to panic anyone until we figure out exactly what's going on."

Tom dashed off in the direction of the beer garden. Despite his ape-like stride, I had to hustle to keep up. Passing near the front gate, I saw a small line of people shuffling past one of the admissions booths. In another couple of hours, all three booths would have lines backed up to the parking lot. With billboard ads placed on all the major highways and human-interest pieces appearing in several papers and on the evening news, we were expecting our biggest turn-out ever.

The walkie talkie on my hip squawked. I stopped and called for Tom to wait up. He stumbled to a halt and leaned against a trash barrel, puffing for air and clutching a painful stitch in his side.

The voice crackling over the static-filled airwaves belonged to my assistant Spence.

"We got a bit of a problem, Mr. Blue"

You think you have problems, I thought, wait and see if I find a skinned corpse in the thickets.

"Joe Phelps took a spill while roofing his house," Spence said. "He's busted up pretty bad from what I hear, and he won't be able to judge the hollering contest this year."

I grumbled under my breath, then spoke back into the transmitter. The curse of the number thirteen had struck again. For a dozen years, the festival had gone off without a hitch, but this year had been fraught with headache and heartache.

"I'll step in for him if I have to," I said, "but ask around and see if anyone else is available."

"Ten-four."

Spence loved using radio lingo.

Honestly, I didn't know why a third judge in the hollering contest was so all-fired important anyway. Clayton Spears had won the contest ten years in a row, and he was a crowd favorite this time around, too. Hands down, Clayton was the best communicative hollerer in six counties. He could move his tongue and lips in ways bordering on the unnatural. Not only was he a shoe-in for our annual contest but, as I understood it, his talent made him quite popular with the ladies as well.

All of which made not one whit of difference at that very moment.

Lord, I thought, give me the strength to make it through the next twelve hours.

"One more thing," Spence's voice squawked. "Looks like we got another pack of stray dogs roaming around again. Four or five of them."

Dogs, attracted to the smell of cooking meat, posed a problem just about every year.

"See if you can borrow a couple of spare BB guns from the shooting gallery," I said. "Pass them out to some of the crew and let them know to chase any dog they see with extreme prejudice. But, Spence, try not to let any patrons see you shooting dogs. Last thing we need is some animal cruelty nut breathing down our necks."

"Ten-four. Over and out."

I clipped the walkie talkie to my belt and waved for Tom to lead on. He darted off again, slipping between two tents and ducking under a line of triangular pendants, each one decorated with this year's logo—a wide-eyed cartoon bull standing on his back hooves, front hooves covering his privates.

I followed, a feeling a dread knotting my intestines every step of the way.

* * *

We found the body, just as Tom said, amidst the overgrown weeds not far from the plywood and canvas façade of the KoC tavern. The lot wasn't part of the festival grounds proper, but it was close enough. We sometimes used the piece of land for overflow parking. I looked over my shoulder to make sure no one was watching, then knelt down to examine the grisly scene.

The corpse was naked and skinned like a deer ready to be butchered. Muscle and sinew, exposed to the elements, glistened in the morning sun, attracting fat green flies. Blood soaked the ground surrounding the body, creating a quagmire of crimson muck. Because he was laying face down, I couldn't be sure, but I guessed the victim was a man, and a pretty hefty one at that.

"Who is it?" Tom asked. "Do we know him?"

"Can't rightly tell. Any identifying marks were removed with the skin. Big fella, though."

"Who could have done something like this?"

I shook my head. Not that I had any way of knowing for sure, but I would have placed my money on an out-of-towner, maybe one of them hitchhiking drifters sometimes seen slinking along the highway. A lot of strangers passed through town around festival time. I didn't like to think any of my friends and neighbors capable of such an act.

Tom wasn't done with his questions, though. He kept shaking his head. He couldn't take his eyes off the body.

"Why would anyone do something like this?"

Now that was a little tougher to figure out.

"What I want to know," I said, "is what did they do with the skin?"

"You ever seen that movie, Mr. Blue?" Tom was trying to latch onto anything that might ground him in the world he was accustomed to, and he spent a damn good portion of his time renting movies from the video store. "You know the one I'm talking about, where the man skins those girls so he can wear their skin?"

"Don't be stupid, Tom. You think there's somebody walking around the festival wearing a bloody skin suit?"

Tom shrugged.

Flies buzzed in my ears. I dug my handkerchief from my pocket and mopped sweat from my brow and the back of my neck. It was going to be a hot one, and sales of pop and lemonade and beer would be high. The festival always made more profits from refreshment sales than admissions costs. Over the years, the testicle recipe called for more and more salt, and beverage sales had skyrocketed accordingly. The dead body didn't stink yet, so I surmised he'd been dead for only a short period of time. But the afternoon heat would cook a terrible stench from the dead flesh before the day was done.

"What do we do?" Tom asked.

A few hundred yards away, a line of trees stretched across the other side of the vacant lot. As a kid, I'd always believed those woods to be haunted, crawling with ghosts ... and more terrible things. The forest stretched for miles into the hills beyond.

"What do we do?" Tom asked again.

Instead of answering him, I got on the horn to Spence.

"Drop whatever you're doing and get over to the south lot," I told him.

"Ten four," Spence said.

I thought for a second and wrinkled my nose at the corpse at my feet.

"And, Spence," I added, "bring a couple of pairs of rubber gloves.

* * *

Didn't take long before I spotted Spence hustling our way. He carried a flapping tangle of yellow dish gloves in one hand, his trusty walkie talkie in the other.

When he saw the body, he came to a screeching halt and lost his footing. He stumbled to his hands and knees, his face mere inches from the dead body's flayed ass. Like the red-fleshed maw of a pulpy Venus flytrap, the crack of the dead man's behind crawled with flies. The insects scattered to the air, buffeting Spence's face. He near about puked up his biscuits and gravy. He flopped back and kicked away, pressing the back of his hand to his mouth. He coughed and heaved, but he didn't vomit.

"Hold it together, Spence." I grabbed him by the arm and helped him to his feet. "I'm gonna need you to keep your cool if we're gonna get through this."

"What do we do?" Tom asked for what seemed like the hundredth time.

I wasn't the superstitious type, but damned if I wasn't starting to feel like the number thirteen was cutting a steaming, countrified fart right in my face.

"I'll tell you what you're gonna do." I clapped my hands together. "Each of you put on a pair of those gloves."

They shot curious looks in my direction.

"You don't want to touch him with your bare hands, do you?"

"What do you mean, 'touch him'?" Tom asked.

Spence sucked his teeth and shook his head. "I reckon we should keep our hands off until the sheriff gets here." He raised the walkie talkie to his lips, started to press the button, but I slapped the radio from his hand. It thumped to the ground, cracking open, and spilling double A batteries into the soggy, bloody mud.

"We can't tell the sheriff about this," I said. "Anyone finds out about this and we can flush the festival straight down the shitter. They'll shut us down, boys, and we can't afford to let that happen. We've worked too damn hard these past couple of months."

Like a kid with his feelings hurt, Spence squatted and picked up the radio and batteries.

"Look, Spence. I'm real sorry about that. I lost my temper is all. But I need your help here. I really do. We drop the ball this year, you can bet your asses none of us will be on-staff next summer. Hell, we might not even get paid for this year, and you fellas need the extra money as much as me."

"He's right about that," Tom said, "especially since our hours got cut at the plant."

"Besides," I said, "the body isn't even on the festival property. Technically, it's somebody else's problem. We're better off dragging this poor fella over to the woods for now, and we'll tell the sheriff once the last patron goes home."

Spence considered his options for a good five minutes, scratching the back of his head and squinting at the mutilated thing before him. At long last, he looked me in the eye and nodded.

"Good choice," I said. "Now you and Tom put them gloves on and haul this carcass over to the woods."

Tom snapped the gloves onto his hands, but Spence eyed me and asked, "And just what are you doing while I'm lugging a dead body into the woods?"

"Somebody's got to keep lookout, don't they? Now hurry it up. Time's a wasting."

Together, Tom and Spence rolled the body over. Dirt and blades of dry grass stuck to the glistening meat. It was a man's body for sure, and I looked away from the shriveled, skinned pecker between the fatty thighs. A gruesome thought tickled my brain, and I looked again, just to make sure the fella's balls were still intact. I didn't like the idea of some psycho tossing his latest kill's nuts into the festival's supplies. Thankfully, everything seemed to be in order. The man had been murdered and skinned, but not castrated.

Tom grimaced as he grabbed the dead man's ankles. The skinless flesh squished under his fingers. Spence lifted the body by the underarms.

"Aw, damn!" Spence coughed. "He stinks!"

"Stash him over there." I pointed in the direction of the trees. "Go in a little ways. Ought to be far enough that no one will see … or notice the smell."

They shuffled towards the forest, Tom looking over his shoulder, away from the corpse and walking backwards as he led the way.

Catching Spence by the shoulder, I said, "We'll do what's right, Spence, but only at the proper time."

He offered a quick nod, shrugged free of my hand, and continued on his way.

My walkie-talkie screeched again.

I snapped the radio from my belt. "What now?"

"Don't take that tone with me, Blue." The gruff voice belonged to Clara Belle Hinkey, who managed the ticket booths. She also happened to be my best friend in all the world, and she never took any crap from me. "You might want to get over to the front gate if you can."

"I'm a little busy at the moment. What is it?"

"Satan's Lapdogs just arrived."

"Who?" I asked.

"Satan's Lapdogs. The motorcycle gang."

* * *

Soon as Spence and Tom dumped the body and re-emerged from the woods, I hightailed it to the front gate. As I made my way over, I heard the thunderous roar of two dozen or more motorcycle engines, so loud it drowned out nearly every other sound. A few patrons wandered in the direction of the racket. Sometimes a classic car show had been part of the festival, and a couple of years ago, we even brought in the General Lee from *The Dukes of Hazzard*. No doubt they believed we had once again put some muscle car on display.

Beyond the front gate, a line of cycles, mostly Harleys from the looks of it, circled the gravel parking lot. Machines of black and red and silver rumbled past, chrome wheels glimmering, painted flames blazing. Lines of round headlights flashed in the sun. Riders in denim and leather and bandanas, riding high and proud—some two to a bike, some in sidecars—whooped and hooted and cheered.

The patches on the backs of their jackets depicted a growling bulldog resting on the Devil's lap.

A few of the kids we paid to collect money at the admissions booths watched the procession with wide, fearful eyes.

I dabbed my forehead with my handkerchief again.

"You all right, Blue?" Clara Belle sidled up beside me. "You look a might peaked."

I nodded, watched the bikes cruise by, and chewed my inner lip.

"Helluva sight, isn't it?" Clara said.

Clara Belle Hinkey and me went to high school together many years ago. Back in the day, she was considered the loveliest girl in school, slim and buxum and blonde, a real prize catch. She captained the cheerleading squad and wore the queen's crown at homecoming. I never worked up the nerve to ask her out, her being out of my league and all, but came to find out she might have said yes if I had. In the days since graduation, though, she gained close to a hundred and fifty pounds, lost most of her hair due to an Estrogen deficiency, and sprouted a colony of hairy wart-like growths along her chin. She was a living testimony to the cruelty of fate. But she had stood by me through good times and bad, through a bad marriage and an even worse divorce. Her personality was still that of the sweetest, prettiest girl to ever grace the halls of Southern Midway High … unless she got riled, in which case she was as dangerous as a silverback gorilla.

I trusted Clara Belle with my life.

The lead biker—a big man sporting a thick red beard and silver aviators—raised his hand and clenched his fingers into a gloved fist. At his signal, the serpent of revving hogs pulled to a stop. My initial count was a little low, I decided, because there must have been close to fifty motorcycles parked out front.

I hoped they hadn't come looking for trouble.

Maybe it was a little unfair, thinking the bikers were gonna run roughshod through the festival. After all, I knew that a good many bike clubs were involved in charitable and community events. There was no reason to think this gang was anything more than your average group of free spirits who loved the feel of the wind in their hair and the Devil splashed across their backs.

Except that that old bastard, the unlucky number thirteen, was still looming over the festival.

I wasn't afraid of a fight. Back in the day, before my ex-wife bled all the spit and vinegar from my veins, then ran off with it, along with my car and mobile home, I'd been known to get in a row or two. But the Satan's Lapdogs had us hopelessly outnumbered. If they started a ruckus, wouldn't be anyone but Clara and me to stand in their way. I figured I could take on a couple myself, and Clara could probably handle a good dozen or so all by her lonesome, but they'd eventually bring us down.

"Where did they come from?" I asked.

"Got me. No bike clubs around here that I know of." Clara shrugged her slightly hunched shoulders, then grinned mischievously. "Maybe they rode straight outta Hell."

"That ain't funny."

"Oh, come on, Blue. You used to have a sense of humor. Besides, it looks like you'll get your chance to ask."

The gang leader swung his massive leg over his bike and strode towards me. When I say he was a big man, I mean he looked like a leather-clad brick wall lumbering across the parking lot. His red hair was parted down the middle and pulled back into a pony tail hanging down to the small of his back. His faded tee shirt read, "My other bike waits for me in Hell." He removed his sunglasses, and a grin split his face as he drew close. Strangely, the smile didn't comfort me.

Clara elbowed me in the side. I stepped forward and greeted the biker, putting on all the charm I could muster.

"Good afternoon, sir." I extended my hand for a shake, hoping he wouldn't crush my finger bones to jelly. "Welcome to the Midway County Testicle Festival!"

The big man stopped short. He left my hand hanging in the air, and he looked over my head at the tents and banners and attractions awaiting him and his crew. When he turned his bright blue eyes towards me, he only said:

"Group discount?"

My fake smile faltered a bit. "Pardon?"

"Group discount." Not a question this time. "Figured you might offer some kind of discount on admission for such a large group."

Leaning to the side, I looked around the massive biker and did a quick mental count of his buddies. The motley crew glared back at me with a sort of shared menace. Arms crossed. Lips curled into sneers.

"Well, I'd say you brought quite a few of your friends with you." I reached into my shirt pocket and pulled out a handful of brightly colored coupons. "What would you say to some vouchers for free samples of our famous barbequed bull's testicles?"

The red-headed biker glanced back at his gang and smiled. When he looked at me again, he straightened and hooked his thumbs through the belt loops of his faded jeans.

"I reckon I'd say that sounds real nice. But not as nice as a discount on admission."

Before I could offer a counter-proposal, a bleach-blonde strode up behind the biker and swatted him on the bicep hard enough to leave a mark. I'd seen her riding on the back of the gang leader's bike.

"Why do you always got to be such a cheap bastard?" she asked him. "Take the coupons and quit your haggling."

A growl swelled from the biker's throat, like he had eaten one of the motorcycles for breakfast with the engine still running. The woman pursed her lips and stuck her hands on her hips. She might have been a pretty woman if her hair hadn't been teased and piled so high and the makeup wasn't slathered over her face an inch thick. She had the massive breasts of an overweight woman and the stomach, waist, and hips of a swimsuit model. I'm not sure how she managed to keep from tipping over. She wore a tank top that looked like an American flag stretched over a pair of mammoth knockers.

The stare-down between the biker and the bleach blonde lasted about half a minute. In the end, the biker backed down from her and turned away. He smiled at me and politely took the coupons from my hand.

"That's mighty fine," he said. "Thank you kindly."

His gang—including the fearsome, patriotic woman—marched past and started paying their admission at the gate. The biker shook his head, grimaced, and muttered under his breath.

"I'm guessing that's your wife," I said, watching the busty woman.

"That obvious, huh?"

"I was married for ten long years. I could recognize that look of yours anywhere."

"You mean the look of eating shit and learning to like the taste of it?"

"That very one."

"Ain't it the truth!" The biker laughed and slugged me in the shoulder, almost knocking me over. Now he reached out to shake my hand. "Name's Stick."

"Friends call me Blue," I said.

"Blue," Stick laughed. "As in 'blue balls'?"

Like I said, everyone's a damned comedian. I didn't much feel like laughing, especially with a bruise swelling on my arm where the biker punched me, but I chuckled politely. "That's me, I guess."

"Me too!" Stick slugged me in the arm again, and I almost cried out in pain. "You met my old lady. She don't put out like she used to."

And that's how Satan's Lapdogs arrived for the show.

Nearly a hundred of them, all big or mean or a combination of the two, even the women.

Not even a tenth of them made it out of the festival alive.

* * *

"So what's got you so worried, Blue?" Clara asked.

"Oh, nothing. Just the same old worries as every year."

"That's horseshit, and you know it."

"Maybe I'm just worn out from all the trouble we've had this year."

"I don't think so." She shook her balding head, the top of which already looked bright red from the beating sun. "I've known you for a long while, and something ain't right. Something you ain't telling me."

We strolled along the midway. Since the disposal of the body and the arrival of the motorcycle gang, the day had proceeded without a hitch. The air smelled of sizzling beef, cotton candy, and funnel cakes, except when we walked too close to one of the port-a-johns, in which case the odor of urine and antimicrobial sanitizer clouded the air like a swarm of gnats. Visitors delighted in games like the bull chip flinging contest and cow patty bingo. The souvenir booth—selling tee shirts bearing such phrases as "Have a Ball at the Testicle Festival" and "I Went Nuts in Midway County"—did a brisk trade. The first round of pasture golf was about to get underway, the golfers already laughing and kicking back Budweisers. And, of course, everywhere I looked, people were helping themselves to heaping, steaming plates of swinging beef.

In years past, as many as 2,000 visitors dined on more than one and a half tons of bull balls. I hoped to beat the record this year, and it looked like we were well on our way.

"They're chewy!" I heard someone exclaim, obviously their first time trying fried testicles, and I realized I hadn't even had a chance to sample this year's batch.

"Why don't we head over to Bud Lewis' tent," I suggested, "maybe get ourselves a bite to eat."

Over the years, a number of creative chefs have added their own personal flare to the festival's offerings. What started as a simple one-recipe event had blossomed into a culinary extravaganza. In addition to the old standbys, we had a variety of sauces and flavors, ranging from orange glaze to Mexican spice to sour cream and chives. We also had turkey and goat testicles, but I'd never tried either, being more of a traditionalist. We even had one joker who thought he could get away with cooking up a batch of faux tofu testicles for the vegetarian crowd. Guess it never dawned on him that a testicle festival wasn't high on any vegetarian's must-see list. He didn't last long at the festival.

Still, while there was a testicle vendor on just about every corner, only one held a true place of honor. Bud Lewis had won Best of Show every year of the festival, and if there was a reason to drive hundreds of miles to sample bull's balls, he was it. Bud took extra special care with the farm oysters under his watch. "I handle them like they were my very own," was his motto. Only Bud's award-winning recipe provided that little something extra that made a world of difference between a plate full of balls and genuine cowboy caviar. If you wanted the very best flavor a mouthful of testicles could provide, Bud Lewis was the man to see.

Not that all was right with the world—a dead body ditched in the woods pretty much trumped feelings of total elation—but seeing the festival running relatively smoothly, I could almost relax a bit … but I had to keep my wits about me.

I kept waiting for the other ball to drop.

And to make matters a little worse, Clara wouldn't give me a moment's peace.

"So are you going to tell me what's going on?" she asked. "Or do I have to start snooping around?"

"All right. All right." I knew if she put her mind to it, she'd figure things out for herself anyway. She's as tenacious as a bulldog and nosier than that old bitty who lived across the street from Samantha on Bewitched. "But let's talk somewhere else, some place with some privacy."

"Ooh." She giggled in a way that might have been girlish if not for her husky voice. "Sounds lurid."

We ducked behind a set of bleachers. Funny, when you think about it. In high school, I would have traded my right nut to steal a few moments under the bleachers with the lovely Clara Belle, but these days only the discovery of a skinless cadaver could lure me into such a situation. The benches faced a raised wooden stage. In a couple of hours, the testicle eating competition would be held upon the stage, followed by the hollering contest and, after most of the little ones had been taken home, the wet t-shirt contest. Every seat in the place would be taken. For now, though, no one else was around, so I told Clara about the dead man and what we had done with him. At first, she thought I was pulling her leg, but as my story unfolded, she realized I was telling the truth.

"You just dumped him in the woods?"

"Wasn't sure what else to do."

"For pity's sake, Blue! You tampered with a crime scene!"

"I didn't really consider that," I admitted. "Not much I can do about it now."

"Well …" Clara scratched her wart whiskers. "That was a damn fool thing to do."

"You think I don't realize that? But what am I supposed to do? As soon as we close down tonight, I'll take the sheriff straight to the body."

"I ain't gonna lie to you." Clara scrunched up her face. She kinda looked like one of them little faces carved into a dried apple. "But I guess I'll stick by you whatever you decide to do."

I sighed with relief.

"Besides—" Clara winked. "—this way I'll be able to blackmail you for sexual favors."

I got the sinking suspicion she was only half joking.

She tugged my arm. "Now, let's get over to Bud's tent before the lines get too long."

As we continued on our way, I noticed a crowd of people gathering around the porta-potties. Not all that unusual. The dumper was always one of the festival's most popular attractions, especially when Bud added a few habanera peppers to his recipe. Among the crowd, several bikers milled about with a few folks from a local church group. I smiled to myself. Nothing brings people together like eating and shitting bull's nuts. An undulating cloud of flies and gnats hovered above the line of blue plastic outhouses like buzzards in search of roadkill. Smelled like someone had given three kinds of hell to one of the poopers, and I noticed most of the crowd shied away from the last stall on the left.

"Peppers!" Clara scrunched up her nose and waved her hand in front of her face. "Definitely peppers!"

We were almost past the crowd—and the smell—when I heard a wet, retching sound. I turned my head and spotted a young man leaning over and clutching at his stomach. Unable to make it into a stall in time, he puked up mouthfuls of half-chewed testicles and barbeque sauce. The vomit spewed from his lips and splattered the dirt without any sign of stopping. The other patrons waiting to use the facilities gave him a wide berth. The sick man looked green around the gills—literally. His flesh had taken on a pasty, yellow-green color. He coughed up three more partially-eaten testicles, and as the vomit sputtered to the ground I noticed what might have been a little dark blood mixed in with the sauce.

Clara and I pushed our way through the crowd and rushed to the young man's side. He barely acknowledged our presence, he was so busy upchucking.

Oh, please don't let this be some kind of food poisoning, I thought.

He groaned and heaved up a oozing mass of dark, fibrous bits of tissue.

Clara and I looked at each other. Her mouth flopped open slowly. I quickly kicked dirt over the glistening mess before anyone else got a good look at it.

This is no mere case of undercooked beef.

A smell assaulted my nose, and I realized the young man had shit his drawers, too.

There was no easy way to get the fella to the first aid tent without cutting through the crowds, so I tried to handle it like ripping off a Band-Aid—it wasn't gonna be painless, but at least it could be quick. "Coming through, folks," I called as we guided the young man through the crowd. "Give us a little room, please. We've got a sick man, here."

Already I could hear the whispers dancing through the spectators.

"Think we got a case of the flu here," I said loudly, hoping to squash any rumors before they got a running start. "Nothing to be concerned about."

Clara shot me a look, and I shrugged.

"Better get on the horn to the paramedics," Clara said. "Tell them to drop whatever they're doing, cause we're bringing someone to the first aid tent who needs immediate attention."

As I grabbed the walkie talkie, a panicked voice cut me off and buzzed over the airwaves.

"It's coming your way, Tom!" Spence's voice. "It's coming fast!"

Tom answered: "I don't see it! Where is it?"

"It slipped right by me. Catch it! Catch it!"

What in the world?

But then I saw.

Coming through the crowd full speed ahead.

A filthy dog bounded right past me, leaving tiny clouds of dust in its wake as it tore down the thoroughfare.

And it carried a skinned human arm in its mouth.

* * *

Clara's eyes grew as wide as mile-high pie plates.

The dog slipped almost unnoticed through the throngs of people as it darted this way and that, weaving through the crowd like a NASCAR racer with mange. The severed arm in its mouth bounced. The hand flopped up and down as if waving goodbye.

Clara gaped at me, but didn't know what to say.

"Where did it go?" Tom's voice crackled over the radio.

"Should be coming right for you!" Spence sounded out of breath. "Don't lose him!"

Cursing under my breath, I pushed the sick man towards Clara, letting her carry his entire weight—not that the burden caused her any trouble. I took a step, then another, not wanting to draw any more undo attention as I set off after the dog. I glanced back at Clara and the young man, who had stopped puking but looked like he was only taking a short breather before starting up again.

"Take care of him," I said.

I didn't wait for her response. Another couple of steps and I was running full speed, ducking and dodging past people. I didn't think anyone else noticed the dog. At least, no one seemed to notice what the mutt was carrying.

Hopefully.

I ran track back in high school, and I still kept in pretty good shape, even though Doc Witters always bitched that I could do a little more.

With every long stride I closed in on the dog. Sweat beaded upon my brow, soaked my underarms, and tickled at my collar. The dog paused to gnaw on the arm a little, and my heart plummeted into my stomach. All someone had to do was look down, and they'd see the grisly, dog-chewed limb. I picked up the pace, planning on tackling the mutt and its prize, but when I got within a few feet the stray shot off again, leaving me choking on dust.

The dog's tail whipped back and forth.

Bastard's having fun with this, I thought, like he's playing a game of keep-away.

I didn't like dogs all that much. My ex had one of those little yapping poodles.

Damn thing pissed all over anything and everything, including me. Kind of soured me on canines altogether.

A terrible thought entered my head.

What if this is a different arm? What if there's more than one dead body around?

Up ahead, Tom stumbled into the dog's path. He was drenched in sweat, too, and his face was beet red. He blocked the dog's path and dropped into a goalie's stance.

The dog skidded to a stop and dashed off between a couple of tents.

"Go that way!" I yelled at Tom, jabbing my finger in the direction the dog had darted. "I'll try to head him off."

The dog was running in a direction that would take it out of the festival grounds proper. Maybe I'd squeak by without anyone noticing the severed arm. I still had to catch the damn thing, though. Didn't want it doubling back and chowing down on its pulpy prize right in the middle of a gathering of more observant patrons. I slipped down another alley and hoped to God we could corner the mutt.

When I emerged on the other side of the tents, my heart sank so low I'm surprised it didn't plop out of my asshole and drag on the ground behind me.

Tom stood frozen in surprise, his mouth opening and closing in his fish-like manner. He looked at me, as if to ask, what the hell do we do now?

The arm lay on the ground before us. The dog sat next to the body part. His tail swished gleefully in the dirt.

Stick, the leader of Satan's Lapdogs, squatted beside the dog, petting its head.

He regarded the arm, took a drag on the cigarette hanging out of his mouth, then looked at Tom and me.

"Someone want to explain this?"

* * *

The simple answer, of course, was "no," but I didn't think Stick would settle for that.

The biker rose to his full height, his leather jacket creaking with his slow, deliberate movement. He looked like he might have grown a few inches taller since he'd arrived. With his cigarette clenched between his teeth, he sneered and expelled a cloud of smoke. Whining, the dog slinked off behind him. It left the mauled, disembodied arm where it lay.

"Did you know my old lady don't like me to smoke?" He plucked his smoke from his mouth and regarded the smoldering butt disdainfully. "Here I am, a grown man who's been smoking Millennium Reds since he was a teenager, and out of nowhere she decides I need to quit. Cold Turkey. Man, it ain't like she didn't know I like a cigarette every now and then. Hell, I was smoking at the alter on the day we got hitched. She watches one episode of *Mystery Diagnosis*, and now all of sudden she's worried about clean living."

I had to struggle to pay attention to the big biker's words. I couldn't tear my eyes away from the skinned arm, and my mind raced trying to concoct an explanation.

"So, I figured I'd duck back here for a quick smoke," Stick said. "You know, get my nicotine fix without the ass-chewing that normally goes along with it. Was having a nice, relaxing time of it, too. Imagine my surprise when some mutt carrying a severed human arm comes running around the tent and almost barrels right into me."

My mind latched onto an idea. Not a good one—downright flimsy, in fact—but the only one I had.

"Well, that's not a real arm, of course." I said.

Stick's face drooped. "Huh?"

I forced a laugh. Sweat dripped from my underarms. "They hold the fall carnival on this same spot of land every year. So, you see, that arm there is from the spookhouse storeroom."

"Spookhouse?" Stick asked

"Spookhouse?" Tom echoed.

"Yeah, you know." I shot Tom a dirty look. "The spookhouse. From the fall carnival. You remember, with the creepy music and the papier-mâché skeletons. Pretty scary. Little kids near about pee their britches in there every year. Wonder how that mutt found it's way in the storeroom, though. Guess we ought to keep the doors locked up a little better."

But Stick wasn't having any of what we were serving.

"I may not be the smartest fella in the world," he said, "but I ain't the dumbest either. I've seen plenty of severed limbs in my time, and that—" He pointed to the arm. "—is the real thing."

I couldn't help but wonder when and where Stick had seen severed body parts before, but I didn't dare ask. For all I knew, his gang might have been responsible for the dead body.

About that time, Spence stumbled around the corner and lurched to a stop beside me. He was drenched from head to toe and his breath came in furnace-hot gasps. He clutched his walkie-talkie tightly, but it almost slipped from his sweaty fingers when he saw the arm. His face blanched, and I could tell he was flashing back to the sight of the dead man's fleshy ass crack staring him in the eye.

"It's all right, Spence," I said. "Everything's all right."

"Man, ain't nothing all right," Stick growled. "Not until somebody tells me what the hell is going on. Or maybe I should go find a pig to sort things out for us."

A pig? I thought. It took me a second to realize the biker was talking about the police.

"So what do you say, Mr. Blue? You gonna give me some other bullshit story? Cause, if you are, I'll just save you the time and find the au-thor-i-tees right now. Hell, I'll take the arm right to them, if that's what you want."

I regarded Stick through narrowed eyes. All day long, I'd been scrambling around, trying to put out fire after fire. Dead bodies. Unexpected motorcycle gangs. Wild dogs. Deathly ill patrons. I'd just about had my fill of problems, and I was in no mood to be pushed around by some biker, no matter how big and mean he looked. I puffed up a little and looked the biker right square in the eye.

"Tell you what," I said, "why don't you do just that? Why don't you find the sheriff and fill him in on whatever you think might be going on? Course, since you and your friends are strangers in these parts, you'll probably be subjected to a little questioning. So we better round up the rest of your gang ... starting with your 'old lady'. I'm sure she'll be real interested in what you were doing back here. What was it you said you were doing? Oh, yeah, getting you nicotine fix ... without the usual ass-chewing."

Stick snatched the smoldering Millennium Red from his lips, flicked it to the ground, and crushed it out beneath his heel. Red sparks flared up beneath his boot.

The stray sniffed the remains of the cigarette and flinched away from it.

"I've got an idea." I snapped my fingers and smiled. "While you go get your friends, I'll put in a call to the sheriff for you. That'll save us both some time."

I snatched my radio from my belt.

I pressed the talk button.

"Now wait a minute." Stick raised a steadying hand. "No reason to get hasty, now is there?"

I didn't know if Stick was more afraid of the scrutiny that might befall his gang if the sheriff became involved or of his wife if she found out he'd been smoking. More than likely, he didn't want the headache that came with either prospect.

Didn't much matter to me, as long as he didn't call my bluff.

"You got a better idea now?" I asked.

"I guess I don't see why we can't just put this matter behind us. You say that arm comes from a carnival spookhouse, who am I to argue?" He glanced at the arm. "We might as well just carry on with our business, the both of us."

"Sounds like a sensible plan to me."

I reached into my pocket and pulled out another couple of coupons for complimentary plates of fried testicles.

"No thanks," Stick shook his head. "I just can't bring myself to eat those things, you know? Let's just call us even."

"Fair enough. Enjoy the rest of the festival."

The biker took one last look at the arm, then nodded at me and slinked away.

The dog watched him go, then tilted its head in our direction.

"Get outta here!" I threw my hands in the air and hollered. The dog jumped and darted off for high country as quick as he could.

I turned to Tom and Spence.

"Do me a favor and clean this mess up, will you? Tom, I want you to stand guard with the body. Don't let any more dogs get at it."

"But I'll miss most of the festival," Tom whined.

"Spence will relieve you in a little while, won't you, Spence?"

Spence swallowed back his vomit and nodded. He didn't look happy with the idea of spending any extra time with the body, but he was a hard worker and dedicated employee.

"Good," I said. "You two can take turns."

The pair of them argued over who was going to pick up the severed arm as I left them to their work. I rubbed the back of my neck, trying to work the kinks out of my muscles. My body was becoming a breeding ground for assorted aches and pains and acid reflux and irritable bowels—all the product of the stress I'd been under lately. At this point, if I managed to get through the festival without a nervous breakdown, I'd consider it a huge success.

I spotted Clara not far from where I left her with the human upchuck machine. She didn't appear phased by the day's events. At least, not her appetite. She leaned against a plywood counter at one of the testicle stands. As I walked over, she dabbed daintily at her lips with a little napkin.

"These are really good this year," she said. Some sauce dribbled down her chin. "Spicy."

"That's terrific," I grumbled. "I thought you were gonna wait to try Bud's batch with me."

"Got too hungry to wait. How was I supposed to know how long you'd be?"

"All right. All right. How's the sick fella?"

"The paramedics picked him up and hauled him back to the first aid tent. Said it looked like he was having some kind of allergic reaction, but they thought he'd be all right."

"I just hope he doesn't decide to blame us and sue."

"Who's Sue?" Clara asked.

"Real funny."

"Just trying to bring a little levity into your otherwise stress-filled day." She licked a little extra sauce from her stubby, sausage-like fingers. "You catch that dog?"

"Yeah, but that biker fella—"

"Stick?"

"That's the one," I said.

Clara experienced a quick shiver, and she smacked her barbeque-laced lips.

"He is one fine-looking man."

"Yeah, well he saw the skinned arm the dog was gnawing on. Had to think fast to keep him from calling the sheriff. I hope he keeps his mouth shut about it."

"Maybe I should follow him around." Clara grinned and winked. "You know, to keep an eye on him."

"If that'll make you happy." I shrugged. "But don't forget he's married."

"So?" She placed one hand on the back of her stubbly head and the other on her hip, posing like an over-inflated swimsuit model with two mustaches—one of barbeque sauce and the other of wiry hair. "Think his wife can compete with this?"

"Not on her best day."

She punched me on the arm—hard enough to leave a bruise—because she knew I was full of beans.

"I need a drink," I muttered, even though I hadn't touched the stuff in more than six years.

"Cheer up," Clara said. "What else can go wrong?"

I flinched as if she'd walloped me in the arm again. In my experience, whenever someone asks that question, that's about the time fate kicks you in the ass, and my ass was already more black and blue than my ex-wife's ass the night after our divorce was finalized.

In this case, the ass-kicking struck with the sound of an explosive whump! Followed by panic-stricken screams.

A wave of heat rolled over me, and a blast of roaring flame shot into the sky like a geyser of fire.

"Spoke too soon," Clara said.

* * *

Clara and I rounded a corner to see flames dancing across the canvas roof of a concession stand specializing in deep-fried Snickers bars. A frightened group of patrons scattered away from the fiery rain of peanuts and napalm-like nougat. The stand's wooden frame nearly buckled under the onslaught of the roaring flame.

"What the hell?" I asked, more to myself than anyone else. I'm not sure anyone else could hear me over the screams.

The flames jumped from one tent to another. Bits of ash and flaming canvas rained from the sky around me.

"What the hell?" I asked again.

I got my answer soon enough.

A young woman stepped into my line of sight. She wasn't a local. Anyone with at least one good eye could tell that straight away. She was so pale, she might not have seen the sun in months, and her hair was coal black and tied into slender, snaking braids. Her lipstick was black, too, as was her blouse and ankle-length skirt. Her boots looked sort of like combat boots, only the kind you pay a hundred dollars or more for at some shopping mall instead of 24.99 at the army surplus. She wore a pair of round, wire-rimmed eyeglasses, and a bulky leather satchel hung from her hip.

She clutched a lighter in one hand and what looked like a short, fat stick of dynamite in the other.

A homemade firebomb, I figured.

"All of you—" She cried to the crowd, but they could barely hear her over their own screams. "—you have to get out of here! You have to leave this place! Before it's too late!"

She flicked the lighter, moved the flame towards the bomb's wick. The guttering flame licked the short fuse hungrily.

"Now, just wait a minute." I stepped towards her. "There's no need for any more fireworks. You're endangering these people. Can't we talk about this?"

"There's nothing left to talk about. If you don't leave right now, it will be too late! You all have to leave! Now!"

Clara nearly shoved me aside trying to get to the girl. She jabbed a finger at her.

"Listen here, you morbid-looking little shit, you don't put that cherry-bomb away, I'm gonna shove it right up your ass."

"Clara," I said, "please. Let's try to hear the young lady out."

If I could talk the girl down from whatever mental ledge she was tiptoeing, I figured I might be able to resolve this crisis without anyone else getting hurt.

"Please, Miss. Somebody's gonna get hurt."

The flame grazed the fuse, and a tiny curl of smoke slithered into the air.

"I don't want to hurt anyone." For a second, she didn't sound like a crazed bomber. She sounded like a scared little girl. "Don't you understand—"

A figure jumped out of the crowd at her. One of the bikers, I realized, a burly man with a pockmarked face and a thick, bushy beard. Several of his buddies, including Stick, stood in the crowd, cheering him on. He reached out to catch the girl in a massive bear hug. She ducked out of his grasp and used some sort of kung fu move to punch him in the chest and sweep his legs out from under him. He crashed to the ground with a thud. The bandana he wore fell off his head, revealing a bald spot beneath.

The bomb's fuse caught fire.

The crowd gasped. Several people scattered for cover. An old woman got knocked off her feet by a group of teenagers, and they didn't even look back as they trampled her.

"Everyone stay calm," Clara cried, for all the good it did.

The girl in black didn't have much of a choice. She either tossed the bomb away or she lost her fingers. She hurled the bomb. It sailed over my head, hissing and leaving a trail of drifting smoke behind it. The stick landed on the roof of another booth and immediately exploded into a ball of blue, sizzling flame.

I threw my arms over my head and ducked.

The pockmarked biker hadn't learned his lesson yet. He clambered to his feet, dusting the sleeves of his jacket. He charged the girl again. She was reaching into her bag—probably for another firebomb—and didn't see him coming.

"Get her, Rex!" The call came from Stick, who shoved his way through the frantic crowd to stand next to me. "Don't let her sucker punch you again—"

The cheer stuck in his throat.

Rex might have gotten the drop on the girl … if she hadn't been alerted by Stick. She looked up, braced herself for Rex's assault, and unleashed a flurry of lightning-quick punches that dropped the pockmarked biker on his butt. Rex sat on the ground, dazed, for a couple of seconds, then flopped onto his back, out cold. I swear, you could almost see little birds tweeting around his head.

Stick hooted and slapped his thigh as his friend fell over.

"I'm trying to help you!" the girl cried. She pulled yet another firebomb from her satchel. She waved it at us menacingly. "Get out of here before—"

BONG!

Bud Lewis, master chef of the testicle festival, had crept up behind the girl and struck her on the back of the head with one of his heavy, cast iron frying pans. He put all his great weight behind the swing, and the girl's glasses flew from her face and hit the ground. She went stiff as a board for a second or two, and she wore a dazed expression for a second or two. The unlit bomb fell from her hand. Her eyes crossed, then rolled back in her head. Her knees folded, and she fell face first into the dirt.

"Man, I gotta admit," Stick said, "you throw a helluva party!"

"Yeah," I told him, "thanks."

And under my breath I added a quick "fuck you."

Clara Belle immediately set about playing crowd control. I wondered where the sheriff might be. I knew he was around the festival somewhere, and he couldn't have helped but see and hear the explosions.

Bud stood over the unconscious girl. His fingers flexed on the frying pan's handle, as if he expected the girl to get back up, and he was waiting to smack her again. The pan dripped cooking oil.

"Good job, Bud," I said. "Glad you happened this way when you did."

He said nothing. His greasy white tee shirt hung loose on his frame.

"You losing weight, Bud?"

He took his eyes off the unconscious girl, and looked at me. His eyes had a kind of dead-tired quality, and I figured he'd been slaving away cooking for too long today.

"Why not take a break?" I said.

Without a word, he nodded, then turned and shuffled off.

I shrugged and knelt down beside the girl. I rolled her over. She almost looked like she was sleeping peacefully. I picked up her eyeglasses and put them in my shirt pocket. I grabbed her satchel and opened it up. I found almost a dozen more of those firebombs—one of them as big as a coffee can—and a moldering old book.

A shiver raced along my spine. Something about the looks of that book gave me the creeps. I didn't even want to touch it.

I found a wallet, too, and I rifled through it. The girl's driver's license showed her name to be Alison Meyers. The photo on the license was a couple of years old. The girl in the picture looked more like a sorority girl than Elvira, Mistress of the Night. She had a college ID, too, so I knew she went to school in Chicago.

"Guess your day's just going from bad to worse, huh?" Stick stood next to me. He nodded his head as if agreeing with his own statement. "What are we gonna do with her, man?"

"What do you mean, 'we?'"

"Hey, the way I see it, you're little ball-fest here seems to be falling apart. Dead bodies. Mad bombers. You need all the help you can get."

Couldn't argue with his logic.

"All right. We'll take her to the first aid tent. Soon as she wakes up, we'll ask her what all this was about. Maybe we can at least make sense of something today."

Stick took her arms, and I took her feet. I was reminded of Spence and Tom carrying the skinned body off to the woods. Of course, she was a much prettier burden. I noticed her legs, beneath the black lacy skirt, were wrapped in black and white candy striped stockings.

Alison moaned something that sounded like, "Must stop it," but I couldn't be sure.

"Man, this is one crazy bitch," Stick said.

We lugged the girl across the fairgrounds. A couple of the Devil's Lapdogs followed along behind us. Rex walked between them, his arms thrown over their shoulders. From the looks of him, you might have thought he had gone a few rounds with a prizefighter instead of a girl who couldn't have weighed more than a buck-ten soaking wet.

Inside the medical tent, I found Spence hovering over the man who we had found sick earlier. The young man lay on his side, a bucket on the ground next to the cot, a line of drool oozing from his lips. The bucket was just about full of some of the nastiest stuff I had seen in a long time. Spence looked plenty worried.

"Who's she?" he asked, nodding towards Alison as we hauled her in and put her on one of the cots.

"Mad bomber," Stick said, matter-of-factly.

"Jesus!"

I grabbed him by the arm and pulled him aside.

"I thought I asked you to help Tom."

"He didn't need much help carrying an arm into the woods." He tugged free. "Besides, on the way back, I found this woman over here, sick as she could be."

He waved to the other side of the tent. A pudgy woman in white shorts and a pink tank top lay on a cot. Her mouth and chin were sticky with barbeque-colored upchuck. Her shirt needed a few cycles in a washing machine, too.

"Looks like we got a pretty big problem on our hands," I said.

In all my years managing the festival, this was as crowded as the medical tent had ever been. Sure, we got our share of cuts and bruises. Once, a few years back, two of the contestants in the eating contest got in a brawl and knocked each other around a bit. And last year a kid had been bitten on the ass by a brown recluse in one of the porta-potties. But this seemed more serious.

"What's going on here?" I asked.

"Well," Spence said, "it might not be the end of the world, but you can damn sure bet it's the end of the festival."

I nodded solemnly. This would, without a doubt, go down as the worst Testicle Festival in years.

And I was the man responsible.

I looked around the tent. We had three patients, but I didn't see a soul tending to them.

"Where the hell are the paramedics?"

"They rushed out of here a few minutes ago," Spence said, "right after the explosions. I guess some people might have gotten hurt in the blast."

Alison—our mad bomber—mumbled in her sleep, starting to come around.

"She's still going on about stopping something," Stick said.

"Seems to me she succeeded," I said.

I imagined patrons leaving by the dozens. I got on the horn right quick to Clara.

"What's the verdict?" I asked.

"Not good." The signal was filled with screeching static. "Lots of people are packing it in. I've got a few staffers handing out some coupons to get them to stay, but it might take an act of God to keep them from leaving at this point."

On cue, the sick man started puking again.

Alison sat up, gasping for breath.

"Oh—" Clara gasped into the walkie talkie. "—gross!"

Just outside, someone cried for help.

266

* * *

I threw open the tent's flap.

On a day that had shoved me into the path of skinned corpses and biker gangs and pretty, kung fu fighting mad bombers, you might have thought I'd be prepared for just about anything. That's what I thought, too, but as I looked outside, I froze like a deer in high beams.

A whole mess of people gathered outside. When I say "mess," that's a pretty accurate description.

"Oh ... Jesus!"

I might have thought I'd stumbled onto the World Bulimia Championship. Several people leaned over, puking up dark, bubbling puddles of their lunches. One man leaned against a tree, retching and spitting. Another—the one gasping for help—lay clutching his stomach as if in the throes of the worst bellyache ever. As he cried out, vomit sprayed from his mouth like he was auditioning for a part in *The Exorcist*. A woman staggered past. She held both hands over her mouth, but that didn't stop the upchuck from seeping between her fingers. It ran in brownish rivulets down her hands and forearms. Everywhere I looked, somebody was tossing their cookies.

The stench hit me like a tidal wave.

Food poisoning. Had to be.

One more nail for the Testicle Festival coffin.

Fuck you very much, lucky number thirteen.

I grabbed my radio. "Tom! Tom! Get to the medical tent!"

Tom's voice crackled back at me. "You told me—"

"Forget what I told you and get over here. Right now!"

The dead body was the least of my worries.

A trio of children ran past, shrieking. A fourth child chased after them. "Wait up!" he cried. "Wait up!" His clothes were covered in puke, and another mouthful spewed up between every word he spoke.

"Clara!" I held the walkie talkie as if I feared it might leap from my sweaty fingers. "I'm gonna need your help, too!"

"I can't get there right now," she barked back at me. In the background, I heard people crying out around her. "People are getting sick all over the place. Almost everyone! Oh, Lord! This is bad, Blue. Bad!"

I ducked back into the tent. My hands were shaking. Sweat covered my face.

"Spence! Help me get some of these people inside! I think we may be dealing with—" I hated to say it aloud. "—food poisoning!"

"No." Alison was sitting up on her cot now. She rubbed the back of her head and winced when she felt the knot. "It's not food poisoning. At least, not really."

Spence rushed past me to drag people inside, but he was damned interested in what the girl had to say. He could barely take his eyes off her.

Alison clutched the sides of the cot with white knuckles. For a second, she looked like she might throw up, too. She swallowed hard. Stick towered over her, his arms crossed menacingly.

"What the hell is going on?" I asked her. "What do you know? This isn't something you did, is it? You didn't poison these people, did you?"

She looked at me, her mouth agape. "You're kidding, right?"

"Not one bit. You show up waving homemade bombs, trying to burn the whole festival to the ground. Why wouldn't I suspect you of trying something else. Maybe you're some kind of terrorist."

Stick chuckled. "Osama Bin-Gothy."

"I'm not a terrorist," Alison said. "I was trying to save these people."

Spence dragged one of the men into the tent. A constant stream of lumpy puke dribbled down the poor bastard's chin. One of the bikers helped Spence dump him on another cot.

Stick pointed at his pals, then at Spence. "Give him a hand, why don't ya? No sense in you standing in here with your thumbs up each other's butts."

The bikers hurried out to help Spence.

Stick raised his eyebrows at me. "We're gonna run out of cot space real quick."

"All right." I sat on the cot across from Alison. "You seem to know a little bit about what's happening here. Why don't you enlighten me?"

"I know this isn't something that will be fixed with a few sips of 7-Up." She tried to wobble to her feet, but I put a hand on her shoulder and kept her sitting. She shrugged my paw away. "I tried to warn everyone."

"You tried to blow us up."

"I didn't know any other way to get people to safety."

"You could have told someone."

"Would you have listened? If I showed up telling you to shut down your festival, would you have given me the time of day? Or would you have chased me off as quick as you could."

"Guess that depends," I said, but I knew she was right. Hell, I didn't let a murder scene stop the festival, I certainly wouldn't have listened to some stranger. "What in the name of God is happening here?"

Alison let out a rattling sigh that bordered on a sob.

"I just didn't see the signs soon enough or maybe this could have been prevented."

"No offense, but you're starting to give me the creeps," I said. "Maybe you should just take a breath and start at the beginning."

She started to stand again. She looked as though she'd caught her second wind.

"We can still stop this, but we have to act fast. Otherwise, we may be facing the end of everything."

Stick guffawed.

"Wooo-eee-ooo-weeee-ooo!" He bugged his eyes out and made a face that would have put a late-night horror movie host to shame. "We're talking about end-of-the-world kind of stuff here. I told you she was crazy!"

Alison bristled.

"You won't think I'm crazy once—"

The man on the cot—the one covered in a blanket of his own puke—let out one of the most terrible sounds I've ever heard. "Aughrrghhh!" or something like that. His throat swelled as something pushed its way out of his gullet. Whatever it was, it was the size of a tennis ball, and it stretched his skin to the point of near bursting. His cheeks puffed out as something wriggled into his mouth—from the inside—and his lips parted in a spray of blood.

"Too late," Alison said.

"Oh, shit!" Stick said.

A brownish, meaty mass squeezed itself out of his mouth. It rolled off his chin, leaving a trail of oily slime, struck the cot, then thumped to the ground. It squirmed and trembled.

Spence hobbled back in. He and one of the Devil's Lapdogs were helping a woman inside. When they saw the horror before them, they staggered back in unison. They let the woman fall, and she crashed to the ground.

"Tell me that ain't what I think it is," Spence said.

He shook his head, like he couldn't believe what he was looking at.

The thing looked like a big, bloated, cancerous testicle, deep brown and coated in glistening barbeque sauce. But it began to palpitate and split open, revealing what looked like a tiny maw lined with fangs, but also an eye, red and white and veiny, staring out at us. The orb rolled around in its socket. It looked like it suffered from a nasty case of pink eye, and it was filled with a malice that struck me like a slap across the face.

I realized I was looking on something not of this earth.

And then Alison said something that chilled my blood.

"It's only the first."

* * *

On the floor, the woman tried to push herself up on her hands and knees. She convulsed, and her neck nearly burst open. She spewed forth a pair of the ball-like, squealing creatures. Across the room, the young man Clara and I had found by the porta-potties puked up one of the creatures, too … and another … and another.

I did a quick mental count. A half dozen of the round, snapping eye-creatures squirmed in pools of the slimy glop that dribbled from their bodies. And there were more disgorging themselves from the mouths of the sickly patrons even as

I watched.

The creatures opened and closed their mouths, revealing the eye within, staring out at us.

The walkie talkie crackled. "Are you seeing this?" Clara Belle asked. She was almost screaming.

I didn't answer. I couldn't think straight, couldn't form words.

"Blue? Blue? Are you all right?"

The testicle terrors—that name just popped into my head—started to move. They quivered and undulated, their spherical bodies contracting and expanding. They slid towards us, leaving slimy barbeque trails on the dirt floor behind them.

"Don't let them bite you!" Alison said.

"Bite us?" I asked. "These fuckers bite?"

Stick stepped forward and planted his boot on two of the creatures. They squealed as he crushed them. Stinking, jiz-like goo spurted out from beneath his boot.

The pair of bikers who'd been helping Spence decided they'd seen enough. They couldn't get out of the tent fast enough, and they near about knocked each other over in their bid to escape.

"Where the hell do you think you're going?" Stick bellowed. "You cowards!"

"Maybe they had the right idea," I said.

Alison looked from the testicle terrors to me, then back at the terrors.

"You're right." Her legs were shaky. "We need to get out of here. Now."

Outside, someone screamed. I hustled to the tent flap and peeked outside. Several people writhed on the ground. Their throats were discolored and bruised. Dozens of the ball creatures slithered in the dirt. Several patrons clutched at their necks as more of the testicle terrors forced themselves up through their throats. I saw a few other people, not sick, but shrieking as the creatures launched themselves into the air. The tiny monsters hit their victims with the force of softballs, and when they struck, they sank their teeth into meaty tissue. More than a couple of people had barbeque-slathered ball-beasts attached to their bodies, gnawing at their bloodied flesh.

"What's happening?" Spence cried.

He pressed up behind me to get a look.

"They're … they're attacking people … eating people!"

"No shit!" Stick cried.

I turned and saw the big biker kick a testicle terror across the room. The creature smacked against the tent wall, oozed to the floor, and started slithering hungrily towards him.

More testicle terrors converged on us. Their numbers had multiplied since the last time I looked, and the awful birthing still continued. As I watched, a meatball-like creature pushed itself out of the greasy lips of each of the victims within the tent. The young man from the porta-potties moaned, but from the looks of it, the other victims were dead.

"This is the second part of the feast!" Alison cried. "Before the Black Goat appears!"

"The Black Goat?" My head was spinning. "What are you talking a—"

Something thumped against my back.

"Don't move," Stick said. "It's on you."

I felt a tugging at my shirt as one of the testicles inched up my back, seeking out my neck. My muscles felt tight. A cold sweat broke out across my back.

"Get it off me!" I said. I didn't want to raise my voice above a whisper.

"Don't let it bite you!" Alison said. "If it bites you, you'll be infected!"

My bowels rumbled.

Infected?

I didn't want to be part of anything's feast, but I most certainly didn't want to be infected.

"Hold still!" Stick said. He swiped a blanket off one of the cots, rolled it up like he was rolling a towel to snap someone on the backside. With a flick of his wrist, he snapped the cloth against me. The tiny creature flew across the room. It didn't waste any time before it started worming its way towards me again.

Alison stomped it with her high-dollar combat boots.

The stink must have been like that of an overused peepshow booth.

"You better tell me what this is all about," I said.

"It's all here in this book." Alison hefted the large, wormy book from her bag. The spine creaked as she flipped through the yellowed, flaking pages. "The original manuscript was destroyed long ago, but this is a translation of the original text. It details the end of the apocalypse."

"The end of the world."

"That's right. See—" She pointed to a passage in the book.

I scanned the text. Some of the words were a little hard to make out.

"The Great Feast ... The thirteenth year of the Great Festival ... the calling of the Black Goat of the Woods with One Thousand Tentacles ..."

Alison looked at me as though she expected me to make some brilliant connection.

"Don't you see?" she asked. "It's a mis-translation. The author wrote 'tentacles,' but what he meant was ..."

Testicles.

"You gotta be kidding. This is all just a little too much to take."

I heard a familiar voice coming from outside.

Tom.

And he was screaming.

I looked out and saw him striding straight towards the opening of the tent.

A dozen or more testicle terrors clung to him from puckering, bleeding wounds. They covered his hands, burrowed into his chest and neck and cheeks, chewed at his eyes. I jumped back as he crashed through the tent opening. He threw himself to the ground, kicking and screeching and swatting at himself. A couple of the creatures were crushed beneath him, but the others detached themselves and moved for us.

"Tom!" Spence cried, rushing to his buddy's side.

"Leave him!" Alison said. "He's gone!"

Stick was stomping at the testicle terrors, swatting them with his bed sheet whip. They burst open in squealing messes, exploding gelatinous gunk across the tent walls. Clots of the stuff dribbled down the canvas walls, congealed on the ground.

Spence shook Tom's shoulders, trying to wake him up.

Tom's back arched. He started puking up testicles by the dozens. From the tears in his flesh, more of the creatures squirmed, like his body was full of them.

I suddenly knew what Alison meant about infection.

"We've gotta get out of here!"

Sensing a meal within, testicle terrors slipped through the flap of the tent. A few at first, then a dozen, then more. They squeezed under the canvas walls. They threw themselves against the tent from the outside. I heard the thump-thump-thump of their fat bodies colliding with the tent. I saw the shadows of the creatures rolling down the walls outside. Soon they would overrun us.

One leaped at my face, but I swatted it away.

Stick pulled a switchblade from his pocket and flipped the blade out. With a deft move, he sliced a new opening in the tent. He pulled it open for us.

"Come on!"

"Get the book!" Alison cried.

"The book?" I asked.

"The book!" She pointed towards the wormy old book. "We'll need it!"

I grabbed the tome. As I did so, four of the testicle terrors nipped at my fingers. I lifted the book and brought it down on top of them, crushing them in a sticky mess. I grabbed Alison's explosive-filled satchel, too, and I followed the others out of the tent.

I emerged from our impromptu escape hatch into an alley between rows of tents. I saw no sign of the creatures. But even as I breathed a sigh of relief, I heard a chittering squeal. Looking up, I saw several of the testicle terrors crawling on top of the tent. They peered down at us with their red, alien eyes. They quivered and gibbered to each other.

The balls dropped.

They jumped down at us. I ducked aside, but Spence was not so lucky. One immediately attached to his face, ripping into the cartilage of his nose with a gristly, tearing sound. Another sunk its teeth into Spence's Adam's apple. He fell to the ground, gurgling and grabbing at his wounds.

Stick didn't wait around to see what happened. He sprinted down the alley.

"Spence!" I yelled.

"Leave him!" Alison grabbed my arm. "There's nothing you can do for him now."

"My ass."

I muttered a silent prayer for my fallen friend. Spence reached out for me with trembling fingers. I raised my boot and brought it down as hard as I could on the bridge of his nose. He kicked out, every muscle going tense, then lay still. His face felt too soft beneath my foot.

Alison yanked the book from my hand, used it as a shield from two small monsters that leaped at her.

"We have to go!"

There must have been two dozen of the testicle terrors sliding through the dirt towards us.

Stick was several yards ahead of us, running fast, swatting ball-creatures with his towel or stabbing them with his knife.

Grabbing Alison's hand, I took off after him.

I was a little surprised to see him stop and wait for us. He motioned for us as if waving us home.

My walkie talkie buzzed.

"Blue!" Clara asked. "Blue! Are you still alive?"

Now I had the wherewithal to respond to her. As I ran, I held the radio close and pushed the talk button.

"Where are you?" I asked.

"I'm heading towards you!" she said. "There are … are …"

"I know," I said. "Meet us at the south gate if you can make it! We're getting out of here!"

"No!" Alison stopped in her tracks. Another testicle terror jumped at her, and she battered it away with the old book. The tome's cover dripped slime. "We can't leave. We leave now—without stopping this—and it will keep spreading."

"What the hell are we going to do?" Stick asked. He was out of breath and panting. "We need the state police, national guard, the army."

"They can't do anything! Now that the ritual has begun, only the incantations in this book can stop the Black Goat from being summoned."

"Summoning?" I asked. "Does that mean someone's doing this? Like a Satanist or something?"

"Yeah," Stick said. "I'd like to kick his ass."

"I don't know who it is," Alison said, "but it all started with the testicles. Whoever's eaten them is infected."

"Are you saying they're all going to die?" I asked.

"I'm afraid so. Someone changed the recipe. Corrupted it, if that makes sense. One of the cooks, maybe."

"There's two dozen different cooks here every year."

"Anything else unusual happen today?"

"Where do you want me to start?"

"I'm serious. Has anyone been acting strange?"

I thought of Bud Lewis, our prize-winning cook, and his dead-tired eyes, his unexplained weight loss.

"I think I know who started this," I said, even though I could hardly believe it.

"Point me at him," Stick growled.

"I don't think it will do any good," Alison said. "The feast has already begun."

"Bullshit! More than half my crew has eaten some of those balls. No telling how many others might have been bitten. Maybe there's a way to reverse all of this."

"The only way to stop this is to use the spells in this book," she said.

They both looked at me as if seeking guidance.

I put the radio to my mouth. "Clara, meet me at Bud's tent."

Stick wore an expression of smug victory. Alison looked down and shook her head.

"It won't do any good," she said.

"Maybe not," I told her, "but I don't know if your magic will do any good, either. If Bud Lewis poisoned everyone, maybe he knows some sort of antidote. One way or the other, we need to know."

"And what if there is no antidote?"

"Then get your spell book ready."

Up until that day, I never believed in magic.

Now I prayed we wouldn't need it to save our lives.

To save the whole world.

* * *

Stick took the lead. At every corner, he swished the blanket whip around a few times to ward off any testicle terrors that might have been lurking in wait for us. I couldn't help but wonder just how smart the little monsters might be. Could they be stalking us? Waiting for us to drop our guard before pouncing?

Alison walked along behind Stick. She wasn't really watching where she was going. Instead, she flipped through the musty old book. She held the book close, squinting at the words written upon the pages. I tapped her on the shoulder and offered her the glasses I'd picked up off the ground when she'd been knocked flat.

"I think you dropped these."

"Thanks."

I think I saw a flush of red pass through her pale cheeks. She put the glasses on. She was one of those pretty girls who actually managed to look even better when she wore her spectacles … like a hot librarian.

Cut it out, you old pervert. She's young enough to be your daughter.

Of course, that made me think about my daughter. She hadn't talked to me in a good many years. Her mama had her wrapped around her little finger, and she'd been selling her a pack of lies for years. Still, I loved her dearly, and I wondered if I'd ever see her again.

My ex—well the testicle terrors could have her. It's not like she hadn't had plenty of gonads thrown in her face over the years. I couldn't help but smile at that. But I didn't want anything bad to happen to my baby girl. If I had to make a stand against the balls of Satan right here and now, then that's what I'd do.

Up ahead, Stick let out an almost girlish scream.

He jumped back, snapping the blanket wildly.

"Watch where you're swinging that damn thing!" someone cried. "You big, dumb sumbitch!"

I knew the voice. It belonged to Charlie St. Claire. The bastard's tone set my teeth on edge.

Stick composed himself right quick. As far as he was concerned, that feminine yelp hadn't belonged to him. I didn't see any reason to argue.

A small group of survivors rounded the corner before us.

Survivors.

Already I was thinking of ourselves in terms of having survived some terrible catastrophe, something that would, for all time, change our lives. But we hadn't lived through anything yet. We might not survive at all, if it got to be as bad as Alison claimed it would.

Charlie St. Claire; his wife, Missy; and Clayton Spears, reigning hollering contest champion, quickly scampered around the corner and huddled behind the tent. They were all sweating and panting for breath. Their clothes were covered in dirt. Blood soaked the sleeve of Missy's blouse.

"Are you bit?" Alison asked.

She reached for Missy, but Charlie slapped her hand away.

"Don't you touch her," he said.

"Listen, Mister, if she's been bit, she's most likely infected—"

"Well, she ain't been bit." Charlie's face was as red as a beet. "She scraped her arm on a nail."

"Either way," I said, "she looks like she's about to pass out. Let us help her."

Charlie's face contorted in an angry grimace.

"I figure you've done just about enough, haven't you, Blue? It's your job to make this place safe, isn't it?"

It was only a matter of time before the old bastard threatened a lawsuit.

Charlie St. Claire was the only lawyer who lived for miles around. There used to be a couple of others in the area, but Charlie's pure meanness drove them off. Take a wild guess who he represented in my divorce.

"I'm doing the best I can," I said. That wasn't exactly the truth. I could have done a lot better, starting with reporting that dead body as soon as I found it. If I hadn't been so concerned with the success of the festival, things might have turned out a whole lot different. "Now if we all just try to work together—"

"From where I'm standing, you have screwed the pooch on this one." Spit flew from Charlie's lips. "There are … monsters … attacking people out here."

"Those ain't monsters," Stick said. "They're just props from the spookhouse."

The red-headed biker winked at me.

I stifled a laugh.

"You think something's funny here, Blue? I'll be the one laughing as they run your sorry ass out of the county once and for all."

I tried to keep my cool. "I had no idea something like this would happen, Charlie. How could anyone have known? Maybe you didn't know this, but safety plans don't usually include anything about demonic testicles."

"You asshole! Don't get smart with me!"

Stick pushed past me and kicked Charlie right in the groin. Charlie wheezed, pressed his knees together, and toppled forward.

Behind him, Clayton drew his lips into a little bitty "o". He cringed in sympathy pain.

Alison pulled Missy aside and tried to tend to her arm. She tore a bit of her own skirt loose and wrapped it around Missy's wounds like a black bandage.

Charlie curled into a fetal position on the ground.

"Your nuts hurt?" Stick asked Charlie. "Well that's nothing compared to the hurt those demon nuts will put on you. You have a bone to pick, you save it until we're all out of here alive, got it?"

Tears rolled down Charlie's face and he chewed on his lower lip, but he nodded.

"We think someone's tampered with the testicle recipe," I said, "and whatever was done is making folks awful sick. We're going to see if there's a cure or something—some way to reverse this. If we can't, we may have another way to stop it."

"What do you need from us?" Clayton asked. He was a good man. I'd played poker with him on more than one occasion, and I knew he was straight up and decent. I didn't hesitate to trust him with my life.

"Just stick together. There's safety in numbers. Help Charlie to his feet and follow us."

We moved as quick as we could, but we had to stop every now and again. We almost stumbled right into a horde of squealing testicle creatures. There must have been over a hundred of them. They gathered near a group of people, each one lying in a vomit-covered, blood-soaked heap in the dirt.

"Are they dead?" Missy asked, her voice low and shaky.

"I don't know," I said. "I hope not."

But I knew better—

"They're dead," Alison said, "and nothing we do is going to change that."

So much for subtlety, I thought.

The smell of bull balls was heavy in the air, but now they smelled like overcooked spoiled meat. The stench seemed to cling to us, to seep into the pours of our skin.

"We're almost there," I said. "Keep moving."

We rounded the corner, and saw Bud's tent. Bud stood just outside.

And he was choking the life out of Clara.

* * *

The fat man's pudgy fingers squeezed my best friend's throat. His fingers pressed into her flesh, nearly crushing her larynx. I thought for sure he'd kill her before we reached them. She grabbed his wrist, digging her nails into his skin. Her legs kicked in the dirt.

All around them were the bodies of festival patrons. They were covered in bile and blood.

Bud squeezed Clara's throat more tightly. Her eyes rolled back in her skull.

"He's killing her!" Stick shouted.

But Clara had other ideas.

She reached out and jammed her fingernails into Bud's eyes, like she was grabbing a bowling ball on league night. She sank her Lee's Press-Ons deep into his eye sockets and he screamed, letting her go and pulling away.

But Clara didn't let go. She held on tight.

Bud's face tore free.

I think we all gasped.

Well, Charlie didn't gasp. He wheezed. That's just about all he could manage.

It looked like Clara Belle had torn a latex mask off the face of a cartoon villain. The flesh pulled away into a sagging, empty-eyed, empty-mouthed parody of a human face. It dangled from her fingers and she flicked her hand to shake it free. Bud's face fell in a crumpled wad on the ground.

The thing that had worn Bud's face was a glistening, grisly monster. It's real face was an oozing, bloody sore. Oily blood dribbled down onto the white of the apron it wore. Its teeth chattered. Its eyes were the same reddish, infected coloration as those of the testicle terrors. You might wonder how I could even tell, seeing as how Clara had driven her nails into its eyes. Yes, a couple of gaping holes remained where Clara had inflicted her grievous attack ... but the horrible thing had plenty of other eyes to spare. Another three pair stared out from its awful mug. The eyes blinked out of sync, and they leaked milky tears. What appeared to be a ring of razor-sharp fangs surrounded each eye.

I got the weird idea that it was made up of hundreds of the testicle terrors, all mashed together like some kind of tripe casserole in the shape of a man.

The creature grabbed at its injured face and screeched.

"Rawhead and Bloody Bones," Alison breathed.

And I realized who lay in the woods not so far away. This monster had skinned Bud alive and wore his flesh like a Halloween costume in order to contaminate the bull's testicles we served.

Damn if Tom hadn't been right all along.

"What is it?" Clayton asked.

"It's one of the servitors of the Black Goat," Alison said, as if that made a bit of sense to me. "It's the harbinger of the Feast."

Old Rawhead lashed out with one of its meaty paws. Clara ducked beneath the attack. She held her hands in front of her face like a bare knuckle brawler. I stepped up to give her a hand, but she barked for me to stop.

"I got this one," she growled.

In my time, I have seen a number of things that I found both beautiful and appalling at the same time. The birth of my daughter springs to mind. I will always remember the sight of Clara Belle Hinkey tearing into the demonic creature before her. She moved with a grace usually reserved for jungle cats, almost dancing around the monster, dodging its attacks. She tackled the monster, and together they crashed backwards, into Bud's tent. The wooden counter, the canvas tarp, the cast iron skillets and pots of boiling hot oil—all folded in upon the brawling duo in a splintering crash.

Some of the oil spattered across Clara's face, and it sizzled and smoked upon her flesh. She cried out as her skin blistered and bubbled.

That really pissed her off.

Clara squatted down on top of the Bud-thing, walloping it with her big fists again and again. Then she set about ripping the monster apart. She tore the demon limb from limb with all the torque and power of one of Stick's motorcycles. I heard Missy choke behind me. Charlie breathed, "Oh Lord, oh Lord!" and Stick let out a low whistle of respect.

When Clara was done, she walked towards us, covered in blood, panting for air, and smiling.

A quivering pile of still-moving body parts lay upon the ground. The earth was a bloody swamp. Bud's skin was in tatters.

Clara brushed her gore-covered hands together.

Charlie had pretty much lost it. He whimpered "Oh, Lord! Oh, Lord!" over and over, and we couldn't shake him out of it.

"Well, I guess that's that," Stick said.

"No." Alison shook her head. "Not hardly."

From every direction came a hideous, sickly chittering. Our little group stood back-to-back-back as a massive swarm of what looked like a thousand testicle terrors hopped towards us, forming a tightening circle.

But that wasn't the worst of it.

At first I thought some of the people who had been sprawled on the ground weren't dead after all. Then I realized they were dead, they just weren't resting peacefully.

The bodies started twitching. Then they stood up.

And started walking.

* * *

"Zombies!" Stick said.

I didn't have time to stop and smell the dead folks. I grabbed the blanket from his hand and started swatting at the approaching testicle terrors. Alison and Clara and Clayton all set to kicking and stomping. We almost looked like were dancing to the music of Missy's screaming. We mashed out a path through the monsters and hauled ass. The squished bodies of the testicle terrors sucked at our feet like mud.

"Stick," I yelled. "Let's go!"

He hustled to catch up with us.

The zombies didn't chase after him.

"How come they ain't trying to eat us?" Stick almost sounded a little disappointed. "Ain't they supposed to want to eat our brains or something?"

"This isn't like a movie." Alison flipped through her book. I don't know how she managed to read a thing as we ran. "They're making the final sacrifice to the Black Goat. If we don't stop this now, we never will. The earth will be overrun by her progeny."

"What do we do?"

Alison paged frantically though the book. She wasn't looking where she was going, and I had to guide her along.

The testicle terrors bounced and squirmed after us. Their prattling almost sounded like laughter.

"Alison!" I said. "What do we do?"

She looked up.

"I … I …"

"You said there was something in the book—some sort of spell or something—that could save us."

"Look alive!" Clayton dashed ahead of us. "I've found our Alamo!"

Up ahead was the plywood façade of one of the game booths. Above the booth was a painted sign that read, "A Day at the Races". The back wall was designed to look like a race track. Upon the front counter, six high-pressure water guns were mounted. Patrons could use the guns to spray targets that caused the miniature figures of horse and rider to move along the track. The more accurate you were with the water gun, the faster your horse moved along the track. If you were the first to cross the finish line, you could win one of the goofy-looking stuffed dogs that hung upon the side walls.

Clayton vaulted over the counter. I did the same, and Alison followed. Clara had a little more trouble crawling over the counter, but she flopped over the side. Stick helped Missy over, and he hoisted Charlie over his head and nearly body-slammed him into the booth. The big biker jumped the counter just as the testicle terrors nipped at his heels.

I shook Alison by the shoulders.

"Find the spell!" I said.

Clayton and me spun the water guns around towards the hordes of testicle terrors. We let loose with a barrage of water blasts, washing the ball creatures back. They rolled over one another in the mud.

"This water ain't gonna last forever," Clayton said. He was using two guns at the same time to flush the testicle terrors away from our safe haven.

Even Missy manned one of the guns. She screamed the entire time she blasted the monsters.

"Looks like somebody was enjoying a little nip on the job!" Stick pulled a couple of half-full bottles of Jack Daniels from under the counter.

"Now's not the time for drinking!" I snapped.

But, man, I wanted to take a hit of that J.D.

Nothing like the end of the world to ruin all those years of sobriety.

"Fire in the hole!" Stick yelled.

He snatched one of the stuffed puppies from the wall and drenched it in some of the whiskey. Sensing what he planned on doing, Clara fished a lighter from her pants pocket and lit the dog on fire. Stick tossed the blazing toy into the sea of testicle terrors. The tiny creatures caught alight and squealed. Stick and Clara readied another dog.

"I found it!" Alison cried. She pointed to a passage in her book. "We've got to perform this ceremony, but it's complicated. The text is in English, but the words are not easily pronounceable. One misspoken word, and we can make matters worse."

"But you know the ritual?" I asked.

Yes, I suppose so, but you must understand, these words weren't written to be spoken by human tongues. It will be difficult, but it's the only chance we have now."

"Not meant for human tongues?" I asked, and I looked at Clara.

Together we turned towards Clayton.

He knew what we were thinking.

"I guess there might be some hollering today after all," he said.

For a half second, I actually felt hopeful.

"But there's one problem," Alison said.

Aw, shit.

"We've got to wait until the Black Goat manifests. The ceremony has to be performed in the presence of the god itself."

"You mean we have to wait until this thing—an honest to goodness Old World god—appears?"

"I don't think that'll be an issue," Alison said.

A deafening trumpeting sound echoed through the fairgrounds.

The cry of the Black Goat.

* * *

Missy clapped her hands over her ears to block the sound.

"Where's that coming from?" Stick asked.

"Just follow the zombies!" Alison said.

Several of the walking dead shambled past us. They didn't pay us a bit of mind. Instead, they shuffled towards the cry of their lord and master, the Black Goat.

"They'll feed themselves to the Black Goat," Alison said. "Once it has eaten its fill, it will vomit forth a horde of those testicle creatures."

"What do you mean when you say 'horde'?" I asked.

"I'm talking about a Biblical plague. It will sweep across the world. That'll be it. All she wrote."

"How much time do we have?"

"Not much."

"Let's get moving then," I said.

We had blasted a pretty good hole in the swarm of testicle terrors. There were still plenty of them around, but we had at least a little breathing room. I hopped over the counter first. One of the little monsters slithered across the muddy ground and jumped at me. Missy was more of a deadeye than I would have imagined. She used the squirt gun to pick the little bugger right out of the sky.

"Not bad," I said. I offered her my hand and helped her over the counter.

"Charlie always wanted me to know how to defend myself," she said. "I've been going to the shooting range every week for two years."

People are full of surprises, I thought.

Clara had an even harder time crawling out of the Day at the Races booth.

She was breathing hard. Her face was waxen and sweaty.

"You all right, Clara?"

"Don't worry about me. I'll be just fine."

The Black Goat cried out again. Its voice sounded like a cross between a freight train and an elephant. I heard a terrible crash, and I felt a tremor beneath my feet.

"Just how big is this thing?" Stick asked.

Alison and I exchanged looks.

"Big," she said.

We followed a pack of zombies. It was a bit unsettling, because I recognized some of the walking dead. Dale Friedkin from the hardware store. Becca Davis from the grocery. Nanny Graves, the sweet old woman who'd been teaching second grade for as long as any of us could remember. All dead and shambling towards—

Something massive moved beyond the festival grounds. I only caught a glimpse of it as it undulated and roiled beyond the tents. It was a fleshy thing, gray-skinned with tufts of wiry hair sprouting upon its body here and there. It moved on what might have been two dozen cloven feet. Dozens of writhing appendages rose from the monstrosity's body and whipped in every direction. The musky smell of the creature wafted over us.

"You sure that books going to work?"

"It has to."

Suddenly, Charlie jumped forward and snatched the book from Alison's hands.

"My lord!" he cried. "My lord!"

He held the book above his head and danced around.

"My lord!"

"Charlie!" Missy snapped. "You put that book down right this instant!"

She sounded like she was scolding a rambunctious child.

Her husband paid her no mind. Holding the book above his head, he scrambled in the direction of the Black Goat.

"Stop him!" Alison cried. "Without the book we're done for!"

Stick leaped after the insane attorney, closing the distance between them in three long strides. He tackled Charlie around the legs. Charlie sprawled forward, dropping the book. He scrabbled across the ground, trying to retrieve his prize.

"My lord ..."

Several zombies shambled right past without so much as looking at them.

One of the undead women wore a red, white, and blue top.

Stick picked himself up off the ground. His face went slack. "Baby?" he said, looking at a zombified woman stumbling past him.

His old lady.

"Stick!" I cried. "Don't!"

Before we could stop him, he rushed to her side. The bleach blonde zombie showed no emotion as he approached. Blood ran down from either side of her mouth. It made her look like one of those ventriloquist's dummies. I reckoned that's what all the zombies were—puppets. She didn't even acknowledge her husband as he threw his arms around her and embraced her.

"Oh, baby! Not you!"

Clayton and Alison wrestled the book from Charlie. He clawed and spat at them like a wild animal.

I went to Stick's side, put a hand on his shoulder.

I heard a strange ripping sound.

Stick jumped back from his wife. Her patriotic top ripped open across the chest as several testicle terrors chewed their way out from within one of her ponderous breasts. They spilled from the ground-up flesh of the orifice and thumped to the ground. The newly-born things mewled and squealed.

The woman's shirt fell open, and I could see that something squirmed beneath the skin of her other breast.

I pulled Stick away. I stomped at the testicle terrors, popping them beneath my boot.

"Come on, man! She's gone! There's nothing you can do!"

He just kept shaking his head.

His old lady started shambling away again.

I looked at Alison and Clayton. They were paging through the book.

"Where's Charlie?"

Alison shrugged.

Clara staggered up behind me. She leaned on Missy for support. Missy sobbed.

"He's gone," Clara Belle said. "We saw him run off towards whatever the hell that thing over yonder is."

"He's just like them." Missy pointed at the zombies. "He's not even human anymore."

"I'm real sorry," I told her.

I heard the boom of massive footsteps. The Black Goat shrieked. Beyond a row of porta-potties, its numerous tentacles lashed in the air. I saw now that numerous hairy, gigantic ball sacks descended from each of the tentacles. Each massive scrotum was swollen to the point of popping.

My stomach turned.

From where I stood, I saw hundreds of walking corpses approaching the Black Goat. I wondered if almost every visitor to the Testicle Festival had been turned, if we were the only ones left alive. I wondered if I had done something more when we discovered the body, if all of this might have somehow been prevented. Maybe

I had sent all these people to the grave through my act of neglect.

Alison handed Clayton the book, turned the pages for him to find the right passage.

"Once you start," she said, "don't stop, no matter what."

"Don't you worry, Miss. I'm here to take care of business."

A blast of hot, rank air swept through the fairgrounds.

"It's coming," Alison said. "Start reciting the passage. Don't get distracted. It will try to stop you."

"Hell…" Clayton laughed nervously. "Nobody said anything about that."

"We're here to protect you," I said.

Clayton's eyes played across us. Me, exhausted to the point of near collapse. Alison, a tiny, frail-looking goth. Stick and Missy, both of whom were nearly catatonic after the loss of their spouses. Clara Belle, who looked like she was suffering from the worst case of flu ever.

"Damn." Clayton sucked at his teeth. "Ain't I the lucky one?"

As soon as he started reading from the book, the Black Goat shrieked as if in pain.

Clayton continued reading, his tongue moving in ways unbelievable.

The loathsome god raged and flailed. It whipped its tentacles. It threw several of the porta-potties into the air. One crashed down nearby, raining urine and bits of shit. The door flopped open, and the putrid body of the sheriff flopped out. He still wore his hat, but his pants were pulled down around his ankles. No wonder we hadn't seen hide nor hair of him. The poor bastard had died on the can.

"Don't stop!" Alison cried.

Something slithered through the midway corridors—long, wriggling tentacles, grasping blindly for us.

I barely managed to jump past one. I ducked another. The ball sacks hanging from each tentacle trembled hideously upon the ground as the appendage whipped past.

One of the tentacles snaked around Clayton's leg.

It yanked him off his feet.

But he held onto the book as tightly as he could and he kept on hollering.

Now there's a true professional, I thought.

The Black Goat started fishing him in.

Clayton's voice grew louder. It echoed through the festival grounds. He put all his faith in us that we'd save him before the Black Goat gobbled him down.

The awful behemoth rose up before us and bellowed its terrible bleating cry. A single, ooze-encrusted red eye gleamed down upon us.

"We've got to save him," Alison said. "If it kills him, we've lost."

Clayton was still chanting, but his voice sounded a little more frantic.

"Give me those bombs of yours," Clara said.

I turned towards her.

"Give them over," she said. She grasped at the satchel. I had nearly forgotten about the homemade bombs Alison hadn't had the chance to use.

"What are you going to do?"

"I'm going to try to stop that big bastard," she said. "I'm a goner anyway. I ate some of those testicles. I'm already starting to hurt, right down in the pit of my stomach. This way I'll be gone before I start puking up any of those little fuckers."

"Clara …" The words caught in my throat.

"Shut up, Blue, and let me save the day."

She smiled at me. She had tears in her eyes. In that moment, she was every bit as beautiful as she was back in high school.

I handed her the remaining bombs.

She slung the satchel over her shoulder and made sure the fuses were hanging out. I used her lighter to ignite the fuses. She kissed me on the cheek.

Clayton was still reading from the book, but the Black Goat lifted him into the air. He flailed about like a rag doll, but he held the book tightly.

"He's so close," Alison whispered.

Clara ran towards the Black Goat, the firebombs trailing smoke behind her.

A second tentacle wrapped around Clayton's waist. The monstrosity was going to rip him in two.

The explosion shook the hill.

The Black Goat cried out in misery. It trembled and quaked, lashed out wildly. Flaming bits of flesh showered down around us.

It dropped Clayton. He must have fallen thirty feet to the ground.

He kept right on chanting on the way down.

The last of the words were louder than the first.

A geyser of black and green and red smoke rocketed into the air around the Black Goat's awful form. It cried out, mournfully, and started to fade and vanish from our world.

The remaining zombies stopped moving and toppled over, dead once and for all.

"It's over," I said. "We did it."

Alison nodded.

"For now."

* * *

It's been almost two years since the Thirteenth Annual Midway County Testicle Festival.

Now we travel the world—Alison, Clayton, Missy, Stick, and me—seeking out signs of the return of the Black Goat, trying to prevent his summoning when we can. In the time since I was thrown into the world of occult testicles, I've attended three dozen testicle festivals, almost all of them completely innocent.

I've almost been assassinated by members of the Black Goat's cult at least twice. I've got the scars to prove it. But you should see the other guys.

Stick taught us how to ride. Missy taught us how to shoot straight. Alison taught us a little about the occult and a little more about Tae Kwan Do. Clayton taught us how to holler.

Me, I don't reckon I taught the others much of anything.

Alison and Clayton ended up together. I should have known that would happen. It gets awful lonely out here on the road, and they're close to the same age. Me and Missy have been growing close, but I've kept her at arm's length. I'm not sure it's such a good idea to get attached to anyone.

I don't expect to live forever.

And when I die, it'll be my penance for neglecting the body on that fateful day. I've never told the others about that. I doubt they'd ever forgive me. That's a secret me and Stick keep, and we talk about it sometimes over shots of whiskey in honor of Tom and Spence and Clara Belle and the Satan's Lapdogs.

Just yesterday, outside of Nashville, I found a flier for an upcoming Testicle Jamboree. "New Recipe," the flier claimed. "Thirteenth Year of the Festival."

I rev the motorcycle and tear down the highway in search of redemption.

As Clayton says, it's time to take care of business.

"Great Balls of Ire" was originally published in the collection
CULLEN BUNN's HEAVEWORLD (2010).

I'm not sure what kind of explanation I have for this messy novella. I've never been to a testicle festival… but I have been to a few hollering contests and CB jamborees. I also got the flu right after eating a ton of barbeque meatballs at a party. Not pretty. I wrote this tale to complement a group of stories I wrote for the World Horror Convention gross-out contest. Believe it or not, this tale is a lot classier than those gross-out pieces.

- CB

KILLER FROG BLUES

No matter what you might read in the papers, first and foremost, Joe was a musician. He played the kind of music that was so good that it was painful—the kind of music that struck you right in the center of your heart and demanded an emotional reaction. He was too good, too talented to ever be recognized by a major recording studio, but he carried a suitcase full of homemade cassettes whenever he played a gig. He sold them for two dollars each in smoke-filled bars that smelled of sweat and cheap beer and Marlboro Reds. Joe lived for his music, played all the time. Some folks used to say that if you cut Joe open, he would bleed blues rhythm.

Joe traveled with a frog. Not just any frog, mind you. This frog was big—at least as big as Joe himself—and had a mean temper when he'd been hitting the booze a little too hard. Whenever Joe walked into a joint for the first time with that massive frog following behind him, he got the strangest looks. But soon enough he'd start playing that guitar of his, and folks would forget all about the six foot tall, pale, warty creature sitting in the shadows, chain smoking and knocking back shots of Jack Daniels.

Every now and again, that frog would join Joe on stage, croaking and playing the spoons along with the sounds of Joe's guitar and sweet gravelly voice. It was an unusual combination, to be sure, but it never failed to bring the audience to their feet with cheers and applause. Word traveled fast on the blues circuit, and soon every bar owner for miles around wanted Joe and his frog, both of which were killers when it came to the blues, to play at their establishments.

When it came to people, only the frog was the killer, although the media would get that wrong.

No one ever forgot the first time they saw the two of them on stage together: Joe sitting on a stool, his gray pinstriped pants riding high over his white socks and patent leather shoes, his hat pushed back on his forehead, his eyeglasses glittering under the stage lights. His fingers worked magic upon the guitar as he sang. The frog crouched next to him, his bulbous eyes scanning the crowd as he slapped a pair of spoons against his knees and joined Joe's song in a startling and heart-wrenching duet.

Woman, you done me wrong.
I can't believe you done and gone.
Woman, you done me bad.
And there you were, the best woman I ever had
Now I've got to hit the road—oh oh!
Traveling with my best friend—and he's a toad!

CRRROOOOOAAAAKKKK!!

That sure was a sweet melody.

One night, after a particularly fine gig, somebody asked Joe how he and the frog had met. Joe just smiled, and wrinkles formed around his eyes. He finished off the rest of the beer that was in his bottle, ordered another, and told his story.

* * *

The road, as Joe describes it, is a dreary companion, and he spent a lot of time out there by himself. He would often leave one gig and drive to the next, sometimes stopping at a roadside motor inn to catch some z's, but more often than not just pulling into a rest area and sleeping for a couple of hours. Sometimes, driving alone could get to you, Joe said, and you can become just as stir crazy as you could cooped up in a windowless room.

So, when Joe passed by the frog, standing in the rain alongside the road with one webbed thumb out, he pulled over. A hitchhiker could make good company on a dark and stormy night, and Joe figured that a giant frog might have some mighty fine stories to tell.

As he pulled onto the shoulder, Joe leaned across the seat and opened the door. The frog, dripping water from his wart-covered hide, slipped inside.

"You picked a bad night for hitchhiking," Joe said.

"I guess I did," the frog said. "I really appreciate you stopping."

The two of them got to talking, and they found that they had a lot in common. They both liked to smoke unfiltered cigarettes (Joe offered one to his passenger). They both liked to drink straight from the bottle. And they both shared a love of music, especially the blues.

They rode for some time, talking and laughing, sharing stories of their lives on the road. Joe noticed that every now and then the frog looked over his shoulder nervously, like he expected to find someone following them, but he decided not to mention it, at least not right away. Instead, he posed a question he'd been dying to ask.

"If you don't mind me asking, friend, how did you get so big?"

"Well," the passenger said, "as you may have guessed, I'm no ordinary frog. There are a lot of reasons for that, I suppose, but the simple fact of the matter is that I was never born to be ordinary."

"What do you mean?"

"You ever heard of Frog-in-a-Box?"

Joe shook his head. "Can't say that I have."

"Well, about fifteen years ago, a toy company called Malco released a new product that they were sure would knock the socks off every kid in America. Working with a bunch of scientists, they came up with what they called "powdered life". Basically, they used DNA splicing and genetic engineering to create a whole bunch of powder which, when mixed with water and a special activation solution, grew into a tiny tadpole."

Joe whistled long and slow. "Let me guess. You were one of those tadpoles."

"That's right. Only all of the Frogs-in-a-Box were engineered to grow faster than normal. They sold us along with a tiny plastic aquarium full of purified water and a miniature replica of a tropical island. We were a big hit with the kids."

The dark road uncoiled behind them, fading in the red glow of the taillights and the mist of the rain.

"Still," Joe said, "that doesn't explain how you got to be so big."

The frog nodded. "Basically, tampering with nature is not an exact science by any means, and when we were created, there were a couple of side effects that the scientists never really anticipated. The first was that we were a lot smarter than a normal frog. The second was that we possessed certain dormant DNA which could make us grow at incredible speeds and to enormous size under the right conditions."

"And just what kind of conditions are those?"

"You see, I was sold to a little boy who lived in Decatur, Illinois, and from the very first day that I sprung to life, I could tell he was nothing but trouble. He was mean all right, the kind of kid who tortures puppies. At first, I have to admit, I didn't really care that much. Yeah, he pulled the wings off flies before he fed them to me, and sometimes he dripped food coloring into my water, but he never did anything to really hurt me.

"Eventually, though, he turned his attention towards me, and I ain't even going to start to tell you some of the things he did. Let's just say that he put me through living hell."

Joe shuddered, his imagination running wild as the frog continued his story.

"Then, one day, the sadistic little brat picks up my entire aquarium and carries it into the kitchen. He looked in at me, grinning evilly, and put the aquarium right into the microwave. I got to tell you, when he closed the door and the lights came on, I figured I was done for—that the only thing I'd be good for was frog's legs.

"But a funny thing happened. Instead of boiling me alive, the microwave must have activated my dormant DNA. I started to grow—and fast. I broke right out of the microwave, broke out of my aquarium, knocked the microwave door right off the hinges, and continued to grow until I reached this size."

"Man," Joe said, shaking his head. "I bet that scared the pants off that little boy."

"Yes, sir, it did. I'll never forget the wide-eyed look of fright on his face." The frog chuckled to himself. "Then I ate him."

The car swerved a little. Joe looked over. "You what?"

Suddenly, the car seemed too small for both Joe and the monstrous green thing in the passenger seat.

"I ate him. Ate his parents, too."

Joe couldn't look away from his passenger. He was certain that the creature was going to swallow him up, too.

"Eyes on the road," said the frog. "Don't worry. I'm not going to eat you. Although I must admit I never planned on eating anyone. Sometimes, when I'm especially hungry, it just happens. My tongue comes snapping out of my mouth and I gulp somebody down whole."

"Well," Joe said. "I guess I'll just have to make sure you're well fed when you're around me."

The frog looked somewhat shocked. "You mean you're not afraid of me?"

"Guess not." Joe shrugged. "I figure as long as you don't get a hungry look in your eye when you're around me, I don't have anything to be afraid of. If you don't mind me saying so, though, you have the look of someone who's on the run."

"I guess that's the truth. You see, ever since the day I escaped, there has been this covert government agency tracking me down. As far as I can tell, they want to use me as some sort of prototype weapon, but I'm just not a violent frog, except for the eating people thing. So, I keep moving, trying to stay two steps ahead of them. I guess if you really think about it, I'm a pretty dangerous fella to be around."

"Well, it gets lonely out here on the road." Joe smiled. "Somebody like me can't be too picky when it comes to his friends."

* * *

They were fast friends after that. Joe's nomadic lifestyle was perfect for a frog on the run, and the frog helped ease Joe's loneliness on those long drives between gigs. Every once in a while, someone would disappear from a rest stop or roadside diner along the way, and sometimes a drunk sleeping it off in an alley behind one of the bars went missing, but other than that the two of them lived what they considered the high life.

Their friendship even worked its way into Joe's songs.

> Met me a genetically engineered frog
> The coolest cat that ever hopped out of the bog
> His skin is of a green and motley hue
> But, man oh man, can he ever sing the blues
> The government's got him on the run
> Cause he don't want to be an amphibious weapon!

The way word got around about the two of them, though, it was only a matter of time before the government tracked them down.

It happened one night at a watering hole called the Silver Bullet. The frog was packing up their gear and Joe was counting money from selling tapes when these six men in black suits and sunglasses stepped inside.

"Sorry," the manager said. "We're closed."

The men said nothing, but one of them held up a government ID.

The manager looked over to Joe and the frog, then back to the suited men. "Anything I can do for you gentlemen?"

"It took us a while to find you," one of them said, talking to the frog, "but now the game is over. It's time for you to come with us."

The frog looked up and he knew that he was caught.

The men reached into their suit jackets and withdrew pistols from shoulder holsters. "Come along peacefully now," one of them said. "We don't want to hurt you."

Joe stood up, clutching his suitcase of cassettes to his chest. "Now, wait a minute here," he said. "Maybe you've got the wrong guy. Maybe you've made a mistake."

"Step aside, sir," the agent said. "There's been no mistake."

Joe looked over at the back door, above which an EXIT sign gleamed red. He nodded towards the door and hissed to the frog. "Go. Get out of here."

The frog looked at his friend, a grim understanding flashing in his goggle-like eyes. "I can't let you do this, Joe," the frog said. "This is my—"

But Joe yelled "Go!" and tossed his suitcase at one of the agents. The luggage struck the man square in the face, knocking him off his feet. Joe grabbed a microphone stand, launched himself off the stage, and charged, ready to bludgeon the first agent who made a move towards his friend. Before he took four steps, though, the agents unloaded their guns. Bullets riddled Joe's body. He dropped the microphone stand, staggered, and fell back.

The frog caught him in his webbed hands. Joe looked up at his amphibious friend and smiled, a bit of blood staining his lips.

"Why'd you do it, Joe?" the frog asked.

Joe only coughed once, then closed his eyes and lay still.

Later, the manager of the Silver Bullet would swear that he saw a tear roll down the frog's warty cheek.

"It didn't have to happen this way," the agent said. "Now, come with us."

The frog gently placed Joe's head on the dusty floor, then rose. A snarl crossed his lips, and a look of worry passed between several of the agents.

Before they knew what hit them, the frog's tongue shot out, ensnaring one of the agents by the neck and snapping him forward. The frog's mouth distended, and he swallowed the man whole. The other agents panicked, turning their weapons towards the frog while their leader called out, "No, we need him ali—"

With a flick of his tongue, the frog gobbled the lead agent up.

Gunfire erupted in the bar, but the frog was quick and hopped out of the way. Before it was over, two more agents had been swallowed, and the frog's belly was swollen with its contents. The remaining agents dropped their weapons and bolted for the door.

Joe lay in a pool of blood. The frog waddled over to his friend's body.

"You better get out of here, son," the manager said. "It won't be long before they come back with reinforcements. You might be able to take out a few of them, but this is a fight you can't win."

The frog sighed heavily, grabbed up the suitcase of cassette tapes, and waddled out of the Silver Bullet and out of our lives forever.

* * *

Of course, the newspapers and television reports got it all wrong. They made no mention of a giant frog at all, but instead reported that Joe had gone crazy at an out-of-the-way drinking establishment and law enforcement agents on the scene had to kill him to put an end to his murderous rampage—a rampage which cost three men their lives. Folks who knew Joe and the frog knew the truth, but they all knew better than to talk about it. Instead, they kept the truth about what happened to old Joe to themselves, and they silently mourned the loss of his music.

The frog disappeared after that, fled into the night and vanished into the swamps. None of the folks on the blues circuit ever saw him play the spoons again. Still, there were a few people who, when very drunk, claimed that they sometimes heard a sad blues song being croaked out from somewhere deep in the swamp, a song that made them think back on Joe, the King of Blues, and the killer frog.

Ain't got no home
Nowhere to roam
No place to prop up my feet
No steady supply of flies to eat
Ain't got nooooo lilly pad
You know that makes me sad
Oh, you know it's true-hoo
I got me some killer frog blues . . . .

"Killer Frog Blues" was originally published in the anthology
KILLER FROG 101 (2000)

Once upon a time, there was an annual competition to write the "worst horror story possible." The contest, called The Killer Frog, often featured entries with murderous amphibians. I entered this tale in the contest. It was one of the runners-up.

-CB

A PASSAGE IN BLACK

Half truths.

Most of the lessons I learned in my formative years were a mixture of truth and deception. Looking back after all this time, I could almost see humor in it, if I were capable of feeling mirth any more. Old Ezra, whom I charged with tending my youthful inquisitiveness, would have told me that he never once lied to me.

He was not providing the wrong answer.

I was asking the wrong questions.

How I loathed him—I see it now—and if he were not already dead, I would kill him all over again.

A thousand times.

I am eight years old, and my father is dead.

My earliest memories of my father are of his cruelty.

He did not vent his malice upon me. Indeed, he had little to do with me, good or ill, and I saw him only rarely, a seldom-glimpsed phantom, roaming from room to room on some cryptic errand. The servants who tended our family's needs, however, were subject to frequent beatings and—judging from the way they regarded my father with such a tempestuous mixture of fear and loathing—worse. Yet, they looked upon with a kind of reverence as well.

I worried that one day he would turn his hateful gaze towards me, but he avoided me as much as possible, and I grew up with a stranger for a father.

I did not remember my mother, either. She did not stay with my father after my birth, and in later years I would come to believe that she was brought to the estate for the singular purpose of breeding with him to begat my mewling nativity.

I was eight years old when he passed away. I don't remember tears. As I said, I hardly knew him, and the servants who had raised me now recognized me as the lord of the manor. In this, I suppose, I was lucky, for they could have just as easily swept me away and drowned me in some remote river or lake. I looked so much like my father, they might have wanted to do away with me once and for all and put his memory behind them.

But even Old Ezra, who constantly chewed his ragged, bloody lips and stared at me hatefully through milky cataracts, accepted me as the new master. Ezra saw too much of my father in me, and I doubted, even as a child, there would ever be peace between the two of us. Dreams of his prunish old face haunted me, and I sometimes woke at night thinking he was chasing me through the dark. I would lie in my bed, shivering, praying as I fell back to sleep that Ezra would die and I would never have to worry about him again.

The library, and the thing in the basement.

I learned my letters from a whispering black woman who swatted my hands with a cypress switch when I made a mistake. By my eleventh birthday, my knuckles were swollen and cracked and inflamed, but I could read even the thick, forbidden tomes in my father's library, scribed in such alien languages and heavy on the tongue as I sounded out each word.

Did I understand the passages, the incantations, and the formulae? Not always, at least not on a conscious level. I comprehended the meanings in the same way one comprehends a dream in the moments following awakening. Many of my days were passed in a dream state, from one strange lesson to the next. Often, while sitting in the still of the library with my instructor silently watching, I felt as if another presence lingered in the room, for my father had spent countless hours studying the works of criminals and madmen in those very chambers.

I read of gigantic, wormy creatures digging tunnels through the innards of the world ... of faceless, black-winged nightgaunts who could be tamed by a human master, but only after a ceremonial hunt was held ... of great charnel feasts in honor of nameless, hungry spirits older than man, older even than the spoken word ... and of the terrible wasteland of chewed bones left behind after countless, orgiastic celebrations.

What practical information I was meant to gain from the lessons, I could not guess.

The library was possessed of a singular and fascinating feature. The numerous bookcases divided along one wall to give access to a door. This door was always locked, but I could feel a cool breeze slipping through the edges, and the air carried a moldy scent.

When I asked about the door, my crooked old instructor bade me not to worry upon it.

"Leads to the basement," she hissed, "but you don't want to be going down there. That part of the house hasn't been used since before I was born, and that was some time ago."

She cackled, then caught herself, and her expression turned serious once again.

"There's a mold growing down there, young master," she said, "and it's such a thing as you wouldn't want to be breathing in."

We spoke no more of the basement, and I returned to my studies, but for several nights afterwards I was beset by horrid nightmares of the living, growing thing lurking beneath the floor, and I could not take a breath within the house without thinking that the entire structure stank of a damp and budding yeast.

The village in the shadows.

The manse stood at the top of a great hill, surrounded by the primitive dwellings of the servants. Farther down the slope, an ancient cemetery sprawled, teetering headstones and decaying crypts forming an embracing crescent around the abandoned village over which my ancestors once watched.

As a child I sometimes crept from the house at night, sneaking past the shanty shacks of the servants, tiptoeing through the winding alleys formed by the graveyard's tombs and plots, to wander the desolate streets of the ghost town.

I knew many stories about the sudden disappearance of the townsfolk who once called the place home. While I was not allowed to play with the children of the servants, I sometimes watched them and listened to their fanciful chatter. They knew many legends of the area, and spoke of them in hushed tones. Some said the villagers packed their belongings one night and fled of their own free will, escaping their master's vile ways. Others believed they had somehow angered the overseer, and the headstones of the cemetery came to life and chased the villagers away. Still others claimed all of the villagers—down to the very last infant—were offered to some ageless thing dwelling within the woods.

This last story is what I believed, thinking of the bizarre feast-rites I had studied in my father's wormy books.

I heard other things from the children as well. They spoke of "devourer spirits" and "the corrupters" and Mayombe—and when they whispered this last phrase they always cast wary glances in my direction.

Old Ezra.

My father's death was a mystery to me. I knew only that he had been alive and well one night and was gone the next morning. Surely, I had noticed his weakening condition, a deep set weariness in his features, a stooped walk as if he was burdened with a dreadful encumbrance. As to the malady that brought on these symptoms and eventually ended his life, I was unfamiliar.

I asked milky-eyed Ezra what he knew of my father's decline, and the twisted old man sucked at his ragged lips as if tasting something foul.

"I'll tell you what done him in," Ezra said, "but only if I have your word you'll not punish me if the truth sets your blood a-boiling."

I assured him I would not rebuke him for speaking the truth. I had never treated the servants with unkindness before and I did not intend to begin anytime soon. He snorted, spat, and told his tale.

"The master ought to have known better, but he was blinded. He would have told anyone who asked that love had affected him so, but love drained from the holes in his black heart the way water runs from a sieve. It was lust and desire what tormented him, though I doubt he knew the difference.

"He took a fancy to one of his serving girls. This was after your mother had birthed you and went back to live with her people."

I felt a stab of sorrow, thinking of my mother, whom I had never known.

"The girl would not return his advances, though, and he had her brought into the house, had her act as your wet-nurse so she would be close to him."

I dimly remembered the girl. She was a pretty, dark-skinned wonder with almost elfin features, and even as a young boy I wanted to be near her and steal glimpses of her. I remembered her dancing around when she thought no one else was looking to the plinking tune of a music box.

A gift, perhaps, from my father?

"Still," Ezra said, "she spurned him, said she could never love a man like him. And his rage grew, and even though he dared not touch her, he punished her kinfolk, whipped and beat them, gave them the most difficult labors. At night, his heartbroken, sorrowful cries echoed from his chambers."

"What happened to her?" I asked. "I don't recall—"

"Gone," Ezra snapped. "Your father condemned her to hell when he couldn't have her."

The old man fell silent, shifting uncomfortably.

"What does any of this have to do with how he died?" I asked. Frustration edged into my voice, and I had to force myself to remember my promise to Ezra.

Ezra showed me the crooked stubs of his rotted teeth in a smile. He was trying to provoke my anger.

"Some say the girl's family poisoned his meals over time," the old man said. "But I know he made himself ill. He felt empty after so long, hollow, because he couldn't feel anything but remorse because she would not love him. He learned to see love and physical pain as the same thing. He had several of his servants work day and night to construct a device to bring him to the heights of pain he had felt in the girl's presence."

"What sort of device?" I asked.

Ezra shuddered. "It was something the likes of which I'd never seen. Belts and hooks and pulleys. At night, instead of cries of sorrow, we heard cries of pain. His use of that machine weakened him, and eventually cost him his life."

I thanked him for the story, although I did not believe a word.

A few nights later, Ezra died.

Even though the old man had hated me, I felt a stab of regret. He had been such a part of my upbringing—the frightening boogieman—that I hated to see him pass on.

And it took days for me to wash the blood from my hands.

Burying the past.

When I was old enough to move away, I left the estate. I attended a university in the West, and I forgot about the mysteries of the family estate. Experiencing the world with fresh eyes, I grew to curse the home in which I grew up, and I laughed, thinking of an entire village full of people who had escaped to greener pastures, and how I could not blame them. I envied my university classmates their childhood spent playing in the sun and attending normal schools full of pretty girls and wallflowers and bullies—normal, happy children who smelled of crayons and finger-paints and sun-kissed flesh.

I met a girl during my senior year, and we quickly made plans to marry after graduation. Before we could become man and wife, though, I had affairs to attend, so while she went to the west coast to make ready for our new life, I booked passage to my ancestral home on the east coast to make final arrangements for the past.

I returned with the intent of selling the place, only to find it had changed little in my absence. The house looked just as I remembered, and the servants greeted me as if I had been gone for only a few hours and not four years. My quarters, while spotlessly clean, were unchanged, and the library was much as I left it— even the book I'd been reading just before I left lay open upon the reading table.

"I'd like to have all these books catalogued," I told the servant who guided me through the house, "then I'll decide what to keep and what to sell."

"What to sell, sir?"

"Yes. I plan on getting rid of the old place, along with most of its contents. But don't fret. I'm sure it won't be for at least a couple of months, and perhaps the new owners will take a few of you into their employ."

That night, I was awakened by a distant cry. I rose from my bed and padded to the window. Moonlight washed over the grounds, and the trees surrounding the house were dark as pitch. The cemetery grounds were likewise dark, and the tombstones looked like hunched figures in the shadow. I thought I saw someone move through the darkness, but it might have been a trick of my weary eyes.

The cry from outside rose from the darkness again, this time taking on a steady cadence, an almost tribal sound.

I returned to my bed, and slept.

It was not until much later that I realized I had forgotten to call Caitlin, my bride-to-be, to let her know how my trip was proceeding.

Leonora.

News came the next morning of a tragedy in the night.

A child, playing carelessly in the cemetery, had fallen through a kind of sinkhole into subterranean chambers below, breaking his neck in the fall. While his parents, with the help of others, recovered the body, they were horrified to find that his small, broken form had been chewed upon.

Rats, I told myself.

And in this way lied to myself again.

I attended the graveside services for the child, despite the winnowing gazes of several of the servants. Strange, I thought, how similar their expressions to the uneasy faces they wore in my father's presence. At the graveside services, I noticed a beautiful, fine boned girl among the mourners. She was dark and sweet, her eyes bright against her dark skin, and slender. I asked after her, and learned she was Ezra's own grandchild, Leonora. It was strange that the old man had never brought her near the manor, and it was likely her mind was poisoned against my bloodline, but I arranged for her to be brought before me.

We chatted over dinner, and after a few glasses of wine had loosened her conservative tongue, I found her to be delightful company. Leonora was learned beyond her years and upbringing, and her gentle beauty by the candlelight fueled a hunger in me no amount of food or drink would ever satisfy.

But even under the effects of the alcohol, she spurned me. Upon the stairwell I groped at her firm body and kissed the clover-scented hollow of her throat. Her hands and lips responded to my caresses, and a whimpering moan escaped her throat as I suckled at her neck. But as I tried to guide her by the hand up the stairs to my bedchambers, she pulled away.

"No," she gasped, "I cannot."

Before I could protest, she fled from the house.

I wanted to chase after her, wanted to bear her down in the front yard and beat her to death. How I would savor her cries of pain. How I would relish the sensation of my fists pounding into her yielding flesh.

Sorrow.

Once my anger subsided, my heart felt as though it might break. I spent days locked in my room, refusing food and drink, refusing to bathe, refusing to rise from bed. I wept until my eyes felt like dry, withering husks, until my throat was raw from my tormented cries.

I would have rotted there, had it not been for an answering whimper.

I heard the sound late one evening, and it startled me from my wallowing. As if mimicking my sobs, either through some act of mockery or through a profound expression of empathy, someone wept from an undetermined place nearby. The sound was a desperate mirror of my grief.

I raised my head from my tear-soaked sheets only to see a fleeting shadow move away from the sliver of light beneath my door. The floor beyond creaked. I rose. The muscles in my legs felt atrophied, and I trembled with the simple exertion of walking across the room. I opened the door to see who lurked on the other side, but the hall was quiet and empty. The dry stink of freshly turned soil clung to the air, and I noted small patches of dirt upon the carpet, trailing down the hall. I followed the trail to the library, but found the room unoccupied. Still, I heard the distant echo of retreating footsteps and ghost-like mournful sobs, emanating from beyond the ever-locked cellar door.

I resigned myself to demanding the key to the door from the servants the following day.

This house would hold secrets no longer.

Prayer to the Mayombe.

That night, I heard the tribal chanting once again. From my window, I saw the servants circling a bonfire of greenish flame. They tossed items into the greedy fire. Kindling, I thought at first, but quickly realized the offerings looked more like moldering bones than branches.

My eyes strayed to the cemetery, and again I thought I saw figures moving among the headstones.

My heartbeat quickened. I gripped the window sill so tightly the color bled from my fingers. I recognized a word chanted over and over during the servant's mantra.

Mayombe … Mayombe … Mayombe …

Their rite continued well into the night. As I drifted to sleep at the sound of the primal cries, I turned my thoughts towards my mission of breaching the forbidden door and delving into the basement's depths.

But I was quickly swayed from my task. Descending the stairs, I found Leonora waiting for me. She looked down at her delicate bare feet and wrung her hands together, as if trying to squeeze water from an invisible cloth.

"What is this?" I asked.

"I—" She started, but faltered.

I reached the ground floor and stepped close to her. I felt almost as if I couldn't breathe. Being close to her again, breathing in her intoxicating clover scent, caused my head to spin.

She looked into my eyes.

"I was wrong," she said.

And we fell into each other's arms. This time, she did not deny me.

The fairy realm.

By this time, I had all but completely forgotten my fiancé, forgotten my intent to rid myself of the estate. I spent day and night in Leonora's company. We enchanted each other by dining on the most rich desserts and drinking the finest liqueurs. We played child-like games. She told me stories as we lie in bed, fairy tales so different from the ones my wet nurses had told me. She spoke of the fairy realm, a kingdom of endless delight not far from our own mundane lands. She told me that the fairies of that realm sometimes stole into houses at night to kidnap infants, taking them to live forever in bliss, and leaving in the crib a changeling to prank and pester unsuspecting parents.

"Is that what you are?" I asked. "A lovely fairy from another land?"

"Silly," she said, "these are only stories."

She was a delight, challenging my college learning in every way, and educating me in the arts of love far beyond anything I might have learned during my collegiate carousing. For weeks, the house was filled not with sorrowful tears, but with laughter and cries of passion.

One bright afternoon, while I lounged on the terrace, she came to me. I reached for her, but she stepped away from my embrace. Her eyes were red, her cheeks swollen, and I knew she had been crying.

"What is it?" I asked.

She spoke only four words in a cold, dead tone so different from her usual, joyous demeanor, then she turned and strode from my presence.

I did not follow, and I did not see her for some time after.

"I'm with your child," she said.

A passage in black.

While Leonora was away, my thoughts drifted first to despair, then to the weeping I had heard on that night weeks earlier, then to the locked door in the library.

Despite the warnings of the servants, I had them unlock the door with a large, rusted key they kept in a secure place. As the creaking portal opened, I was greeted with the overwhelming stink of decay and mold, and a darkness so thick my lantern barely pierced its gloom. The servants would not follow me as I descended the sagging staircase, and before I reached the bottom, the library door was sealed once again. The shadow folded around me like a smothering blanket, and in a brief moment of fright I wondered if they had sealed me away forever.

The stone floor was damp, and covered in fuzzy black patches. I avoided stepping on the spots as I walked through the massive chamber. The flickering ring of lantern light did not even reach the walls around me, and the stairs quickly vanished from sight. For all I knew, I walked in circles through an endless void.

Even though it was cold within the vastness of the basement, sweat beaded on my forehead and rolled into my eyes. My breath came in labored gasps. I was lost and …

Alone.

Just then, I detected a shuffling sound ahead of me, and I held the lantern out as far as I could. Something moved just outside the radiance of the lantern, and when I stepped forward, the moving figure also moved to stay away from the light.

"Who's there?" I asked sharply.

The answer came as a soft weeping. A woman's sob.

"Hello?" I said. "Who are you? Are you all right?"

But she did not answer.

I heard rapid footsteps—bare feet against the cold stone—leading away from me.

I followed. The sound vanished, but still I pressed forward, until at last I reached the far wall. A massive, thick patch of black, fibrous mold spread across the wall before me. Instinctively, I recoiled from the growth, and the spores seemed to react to the light and my movement. Just then, I heard the sound of footsteps and the weeping cry again, echoing in the darkness, moving away from me, beyond the patch of mold!

With shivering fingers, I touched the mold. The growth puckered around my fingers. I pressed forward, and my hand passed through and felt cool air beyond.

I stepped through, and felt the spores break against my flesh and cover me in a fine dusting of black.

The light of my lantern was extinguished as I moved through the barrier, and I found myself in a void of darkness. I tried for several minutes to re-light the torch, but achieved no success. Just as I contemplated returning through the mold barrier and feeling my way back to the staircase, I discovered that my eyes, without aid of light, were adjusting to the darkness, and I could see a narrow earthen tunnel stretching out before me. I heard movement up ahead, and the woman's weeping called to me. I took one step, then another, and at last found myself near running towards the beckoning source of the tormented cries.

I stumbled into a vast chamber. The walls were decorated with roots ... and bones. Ribcages protruded from the walls. Skulls descended from the ropey tendrils of runners dangling from the darkness. Skeletal arms crisscrossed like support beams in the earth.

Several figures moved around me, hunched over and shambling. I gasped. They were misshapen, hideous things. Their faces were animal-like and snarling. Their hands were curled talons. Some walked on human-feet, but others were hooved like a storybook devil.

"Do not fear," one of them said. It did not speak English, but I somehow understood the strange, meeping tongue.

"What is this place?" I asked.

"Do you not know?" the creature said again. It stepped closer. It was obviously female. "Have you not been here in your dreams?"

Wet streaks ran down the creature's cheeks.

"It was you," I said, "that I heard crying."

"Yes," she answered. "Does it surprise you that a ... thing such as myself might feel sadness?"

"Who are you?" I asked.

Her tears started anew, and her dog-like snout quivered. An uneasy tremor passed through the group around us.

"Do you not recognize me?" she said. "Do you not remember? You have come to us too soon, it would seem, but no matter."

She grasped one of her sagging teats and held it toward me as if offering food. As horrified as I was, I felt an overpowering sensation of hunger well up inside of me. My legs went weak, and I fell to my knees before her. She offered her nipple to me, and I pressed my lips to her withered flesh and suckled her mildewed milk.

An approving barking rose from the crowd.

"My son," the creature said, and we both wept together.

Another of the creatures emerged from the throng of others. I did not stop drinking of the mother's milk, but my eyes widened in fear at the thing's visage. It's canine face was somewhat familiar. It wore a strange device of wood and steel around its waste. A handle like that of a wine press jutted from the center of the device, and numerous hooks and chains spread from the center and burrowed into the creature's stomach. A gaping wound opened in his grey flesh, and a dry loop of intestine dangled down to the floor.

"Welcome," he rasped. "Welcome home."

I am ageless—

My beloved Leonora was denied to me, for while she carried my child, she was of the other world, and I only ever returned to the surface to scavenge delights for the celebrations we held in forgotten places only seen by my kind and the eyeless nightgaunts. The servants from above still pay us homage, and tend to my son as he grows to adulthood and learns—slowly, slowly—our secret, the secrets of what the servants call the hungry spirits. He knows his mother, as I did not, but his father is unknown to him for the time being, and occasionally he might hear phantom sobs on dark nights outside his room.

I have had several mates during my time below, but none of them have helped to ease the pain I've felt at the loss of Leonora. From time to time, I run my clawed hands over the scarred flesh of my stomach, where my father's device has brought me a brief escape from my sadness.

Even when my mother entered my warrens with the freshly dead body of Leonora—an old woman who had lived a full life and passed away of natural causes—I did not feel my torment lesson, even though I dragged the corpse to my nest and cuddled it as I slept for years following, until it fell to dust in my arms.

One day soon, my son will be led to the basement and sent forth on his passage in black. I've heard that he has learned his lessons well—better than I did—but I will have to judge for myself, when he arrives. But he cannot be sent on his way until he has planted his seed and fathered a child of his own.

Soon.

Mother goes to tend him, as she could never tend me.

—I wait.

"A Passage in Black" appears here for the first time.

Mold. Lovecraftian ghouls. Voodoo. These things came together in this piece. It's a strange story, but I've always had a soft spot (in my head) for it.

As with a few other stories in this collection, this story was accepted for publication in an anthology that (to my knowledge) never saw publication.

-CB

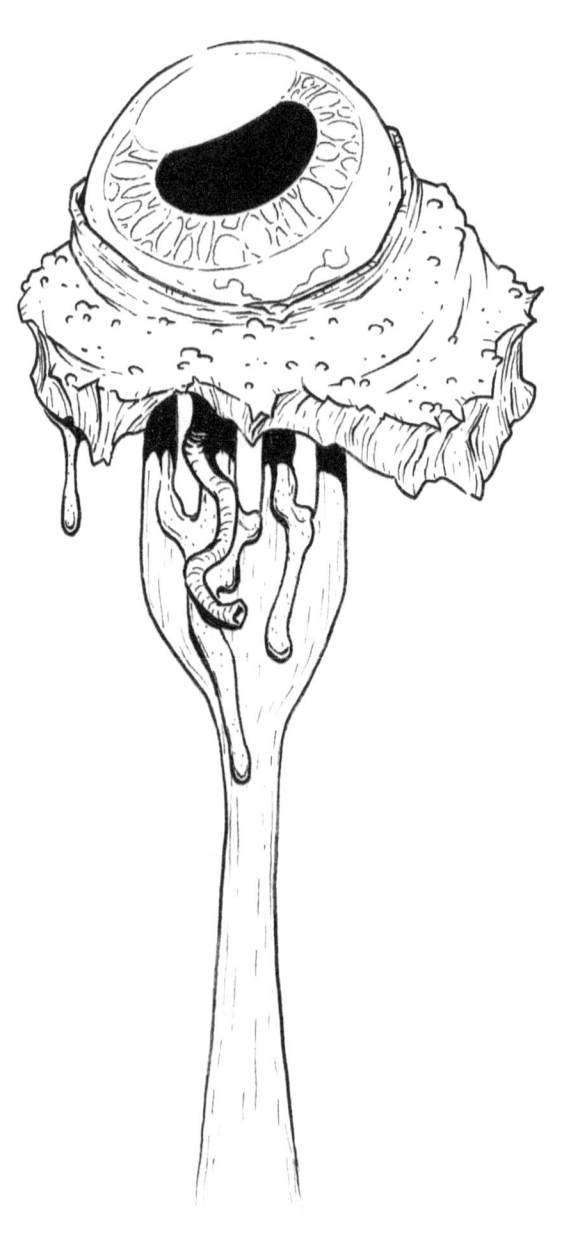

PAPPY'S DEEP FRIED DEEP ONES

This is a recipe passed on to me by my granddaddy, who was known lovingly by his friends and relatives as Pappy. Now Pappy considered himself to be something of a master chef, especially when it came to dishes that no one else had even heard of. This recipe, found in his personal cookbook, which he called his "Book o' Secrets," was his specialty. Alas, Pappy vanished one day while gathering the ingredients for this very dish. Members of the search party that combed the salt marshes looking for him claimed that they found only his clothes, neatly-folded, laying alongside the bank, and a trail of strange footprints, both human and otherwise, leading through the muck of the bayou, headed towards the sea.

Fixins ---

1 tub of cooking oil
2 bags of salt
3 sacks full of dried breadcrumbs
4 dozen eggs, slightly beaten
1 Deep One, thoroughly beaten until dead
1 baseball bat or similar implement, just in case the beating was not thorough enough, for the Deep One, not the eggs

First things first, you've got to find yourself a Deep One. Now, those critters are most often found in the depths of the ocean, performing foul rites to their scaly gods. Don't you let that worry you none, though. If you're lucky enough to live in or around certain coastal towns, you may be able to find yourself a Deep One just by looking real close at your friends and relatives. Now, you need to be real careful before passing judgement on someone as a fish-headed beastie. You don't want to find yourself frying up a mess of Deep-Fried Deep Ones only to find out what you're cooking isn't a Deep One at all, but just some gal with a bad case of the bug-eyed, flat-lipped uglies. Usually, you can spot an honest-to-god Deep One by whether they got gills or not. Once you've found a Deep One, you need to figure out how to catch it. I find that day-old raw fish makes as good a lure as any, but keep your baseball bat handy. There's a few things to keep in mind as you prepare your Deep One for frying. Most importantly, don't even think of scaling it. They got hides so tough you'll waste every piece of cutlery you own. Besides, cooking them with their scales softens them up a bit and gives the dish a satisfying crunchiness. Coat the Deep One from head to toe with the eggs, then roll its carcass around in the breadcrumbs. Then, all you got to do is plop the Deep One in the fryer. At this point, you may want to have your bat close at hand, because quite often the boiling oil will revive the critter and, as you can guess, it will be awful mad. Fry for five to ten minutes, bashing the thing in the head or holding it under the oil as necessary, until the critter does the dead man's float and its black eyes have turned white. Daub-drain over paper towels and serve immediately. Please note, some people have experienced fierce stomach pains and bad cases of the back-door-trots after eating Deep-Fried Deep Ones.

"Pappy's Deep Fried Deep Ones" was originally published in the "cookbook" CONJURING DARK DELICACIES (1999)

This "recipe" was written as part of a charitable horror-themed cookbook. I think I missed the point of the submission guidelines, because almost all of the other recipes were real. Actually, if you substitute "catfish" for "deep ones" and adjust the measurements, this recipe would probably work. But I'd just recommend hitting Captain D's instead.

-CB

WITCHING EYES

"You think we might see her?" Toby leaned on his knees, looking out over the lake. His eyes were vacant and distant, as if he stared beyond the quiet, shimmering water, beyond the reeds upon the far shore, beyond the surrounding pine forest. "The sun's setting, so we might see her."

"I sure hope we do." Cozy was younger and easily excited. He craned his neck and looked into the darkening woods surrounding our little patch of shore. "Doug Herron said that him and Jimmy Mervin saw her not far from this very spot."

I shook my head. "Would the two of you shut up? Better be careful what you go hoping for. Way I see it, don't none of us really want to see her."

"I do too," said Cozy.

"Yeah, you say that now, but I want you to really think about it." I looped another length of tobacco twine around a couple of logs and tied them tightly together. My fingers were sore from splinters and hard work. "We see her, none of us might not be going home."

"Don't scare him, Tate," Toby said.

"I ain't trying to scare anybody, but I didn't come out here to get killed by no ghost."

Toby and his younger brother Cozy were my best friends, but when they weren't fussing with each other, they were arguing with me. Funny how when you're a boy, things like that don't bother you. I didn't care that they often annoyed me more than all three of my sisters rolled into one. All that really mattered was that I had someone to join me in exploring the hollows and the swamps, the crumbling old cabins and tobacco barns. The world was a lot bigger back then, and the woods behind our homes (now bush hogged and bulldozed and paved over for a supermarket parking lot) were as deep and dark and haunted as any of the cobweb-shrouded castles I read about in tattered copies of *Famous Monsters* and *Monster Times.*

I never had brothers of my own, but Toby and Cozy came close.

I'd like to say I've stayed in touch with my childhood friends, but I haven't spoken to Toby in nearly twenty-five years. We never had a falling out. We remained friends throughout high school, as best we could all things considered, but we eventually drifted apart. I've heard he's now a music teacher somewhere in Tennessee.

Cozy never made it out of the woods that night.

The ghost was named Maddie Someday, although no one ever said her name aloud, at least not without spitting twice and making the sign of the cross. Maddie had been a witch of the cruelest variety, according to local legend, befouling crops, poisoning wells, and kidnapping children. She died long before I was born, but her ghost, some said, could still be seen wandering the forest near the lake after nightfall. Everybody knew somebody who had entered the forest after dark, never to be seen again.

I didn't really believe the stories, but sometimes I awoke from a nightmare of being chased through a black forest by a cackling, leering old crone.

They say she had witching eyes.

My grandfather, a superstitious and some said crazy old man, said people with eyes so pale in color as to be almost white were best avoided.

"They'll put a hex on you, boy," he said. "The devil boiled the color from their eyes when he made his soup, and now they have the witch's touch, just like that old woman. She was too damn mean to die."

But like I said, many people thought he was crazy.

Time had slipped away too quickly, I realized. We had spent the afternoon cutting down trees and lashing logs together to build a raft like the one I had read about in *Huckleberry Finn.* We were almost done, but it would be dark soon. I wasn't so much afraid of Maddie's ghost as I was of getting punished by my folks for staying out too late.

"It's getting awful late," I said. "Maybe we should be getting home. Help me with the raft."

We set what few tools we had brought with us on top of the raft. Together, we pulled the craft over to a makeshift lean-to Cozy had constructed from pine tree branches. When covered, the raft would be well hidden so no one was likely to spot it unless they were really searching. In the next couple of days we would push it into the lake's cool water and climb on board.

"I bet I could outrun her," Cozy said. "If I saw her, I'd take off through the brush quick as a squirrel, and she wouldn't be able to catch me."

"As dark as it's likely to get, you'd probably run smack into a tree," I said. "Of course, that might work out all right for you, because she'd surely think you were dead and leave you be."

We all had a good laugh at that.

But then Toby stopped laughing all of a sudden. He looked over his shoulder, as if he had heard someone … or something … creeping through the trees. He shook his head, stared at his sneakers, and kicked a few loose stones down the sloping bank. The water rippled out and the orange glow of the setting sun danced upon the surface.

"What's the matter, Toby?"

"I was just thinking. We're talking about that old witch like she might fly out of the shadows at any minute. We ought to be more worried about those other things…the things what killed her."

"You know those things never existed," I said.

"Who says? How do we know they didn't stay out here in the forest after they finished with her?"

Toby shivered. He was the biggest, strongest kid in seventh grade, partially because he had been held back a year in elementary. I had never seen him scared—really scared—before. I thought maybe he was pulling my leg, but if so he needed to pack his bags and head to Hollywood.

"W-what are you guys going on about?" Cozy asked.

"Well, most folks believe that old Maddie Someday was caught by an angry group of townsfolk and killed," Toby said.

"Right." Cozy nodded. Almost every kid in the county had heard the story. "She killed a little boy, used his skin to make herself a drum or something so she could play a tune for the devil. They caught her, tied stones to her ankles, rowed out to the middle of the lake, and tossed her in."

"Yeah, but that's only one of the stories." I gave the raft a once over, checking all the bindings one last time. "Others believe that she didn't get drowned at all."

"So what happened to her then?" Cozy's voice took on a whiny quality he used whenever he felt as though he had been left out.

"Some folks, mainly the old timers who had been kids back when she was alive, say how the townsfolk were planning on lynching her. But when they came upon her cabin, she ran out screaming and crying and begging for help … and she had something crawling on her … little creatures that looked like men, only their skin was as grey as river mud and their faces looked like shriveled apples."

Cozy gulped as his brother continued the story.

"Those little creatures were eating her alive, taking bloody chomps out of her arms and body and face and tearing away scraps of skin with their claws. The townsfolk were so startled they didn't know how to react, and they just watched as Maddie ran right past them, all the while screaming and crying and beating at the little monsters that were crawling all over her. She ran right to the lake and threw herself in, I guess thinking she might wash the creatures—"

"Goblins," I said.

Toby stopped, like I'd slapped him across the face, then started up again. "Yeah, she must have thought she could wash the goblins off of her or maybe drown them, so she dove down into the lake...but she never came up again. Blood billowed up from the water, a huge cloud of it that near about turned the whole lake red."

After Toby finished his story, the three of us sat quietly, not saying a word, for several minutes.

"Where did the ... goblins come from?" Cozy finally asked.

"I guess she called them up from Hell," Toby said, "only she must have done something wrong, because they turned on her."

"But even if the story's true, all that happened so long ago," I said, "those goblins aren't here anymore."

"We can't be sure," Toby said. "Heck, maybe those people that disappeared were attacked by goblins, not by Maddie's ghost."

With the sun setting, the orange afternoon glow had turned crimson, reflected off the lake's surface ...

Like blood.

Whether or not the goblins were real and still roaming the woods, I suddenly wanted to get out of there. I stood up, brushing my hands on the seat of my jeans. "You fellas ready to head home?"

Cozy nodded his head vigorously.

"You think the raft will be safe?" Toby asked.

"No one will mess with it." I nodded and smiled. "Not even goblins."

Toby grumbled under his breath as we started trudging through the woods on the way home. We didn't follow a path, but all three of us hunted and fished and explored the forest every chance we could get, weather allowing, so we weren't worried about getting lost. We had scurried down trenches and crossed over fallen trees with the skill of Indian scouts. We had played hide and seek and gone on snipe hunts. We had picked huckleberries until our mouths were smeared purple and plucked blackberries from the vine until our fingers were swollen from a dozen thorny stabbings.

We weren't scared of anything in those woods ... except for the witch's ghost, the goblins, and Old Rootbelly.

Toby and Cozy had both seen Old Rootbelly, or so they said, and they knew what areas of the woods were best to avoid if you didn't want to run afoul of the ancient, ill-tempered snake. I had never seen him, but I told the others I had on numerous occasions. We all three told harrowing stories of near-death brushes with the snake, a copperhead as long as three cars lined nose to tail, as mean as his venom was deadly. It wasn't uncommon for one of us to go take a leak and come back with a yarn about how Rootbelly had boiled up out of the earth with murder in his slitted eyes. Whenever we investigated, of course, we never found a sign of the creature, but Old Rootbelly was tricky, and he knew the woods better than any of us. Even though I had never seen the snake, something in the back of my mind told me he was real, more so than the ghost of Maddie Someday, and certainly more than the goblins.

"Our mom's gonna kill us," Toby told Cozy as we pushed through the woods. Soon, we would reach the pine straw-covered path leading out of the trees to the old dirt mail route that ran behind our houses. "You know how she is about us staying out after dark. I bet we're gonna miss supper tonight."

Cozy frowned and his stomach growled. Few things killed his spirit like the thought of missing a meal.

The sky grew dark more quickly than I thought it would, and the shadows in the woods deepened. Even though we were familiar with the woods, we stumbled and staggered in the darkness. The trees took on an unfamiliar and foreboding nature, strangers in the failing light. Color slipped away, and the forest was painted in blacks and grays.

Something snapped in the darkness behind us.

Toby whirled around. A slash of pale light crossed his face. His eyes were wide, his face sweaty.

"What was that?"

I looked in the direction of the sound, but saw nothing but darkness swelling between the trees.

"Must have been—"

I heard another snapping sound, followed by another.

"Somebody's out there," Cozy said, his voice dropping to a whisper.

The sound grew closer. It sounded like someone running through the woods, feet crunching twigs.

Closer.

"Who's that?" I called. "Who's out there?"

"Tate!" Toby looked at me as if I had rung a monster's dinner bell. "He'll hear you!"

"So? It's probably just—"

The rushing steps of another pair of feet joined the first, shuffling through the undergrowth.

I looked at Toby. My eyes must have been as wide as his own. Cozy was already rushing towards the trail up ahead. Without another word, we followed him.

Behind us, the pace of the footsteps quickened.

"They're following us!" Toby yelled.

I saw Cozy up ahead, racing in front of us, almost vanishing into shadow.

I heard a giggling sound and looked to my right. A figure dashed past a line of trees, keeping pace with us, a short, loping thing with skin the color of moldy

Swiss cheese.

Another joined it. And another.

Three squat figures ran alongside us. They moved through the forest with ease, clambering over downed branches and scurrying under briars and brambles in fluid motions. Their movement reminded me of monkeys, and they were about the size of chimpanzees.

They howled laughter.

"Who are they?" Toby cried.

I didn't answer. I just kept running. But I knew.

The goblins.

Up ahead, Cozy stumbled over a root, almost tripped. He slammed into a tree and leaned there for support. We caught up to him.

"Keep moving!" I said. "Don't stop!"

A rush of blood thundered in my ears. I panted for breath. I no longer heard the goblins, didn't see them racing through the shadows. But they were still out there.

Moonlight spilled onto a strip of matted earth and pine straw up ahead. The trail. We moved in that direction. We stopped.

A fourth creature squatted in the center of the path, waiting.

I looked around frantically. Where were the others? Where?

The goblin in the center of the trail rose to its full height. It was not even as tall as Cozy, but its body was wiry muscle. Its hands nearly drug the ground, and each finger ended in a curling claw that clicked against the others as the creature flexed its digits. Its face was shriveled, a shrunken apple head with no lips, but a razor sharp ridge of boney teeth leaked saliva down its gnarled chin. It cocked its head as it saw us, sniffed the air. Its eyes twinkled as it regarded us—

Its eyes, as cloudy and colorless and cold as thick ice.

Witching eyes.

Its weirdly wrinkled face contorted into a vile grin.

I stepped back. Toby and Cozy did the same. Cozy shook in violent spasms.

"W-where are the others?" Toby asked. "Do you see them?"

I shook my head. Even though the air was cool, a wash of heat rolled over me. Sweat beaded on my upper lip. The feeling made me think of sticking my hand into a woodpile nest of black widows.

I took another backwards step, then another.

The brush exploded and a small, twisted shape leapt onto Toby. He screeched and toppled to the ground. The goblin had both flat feet planted on Toby's chest and slashed at him with its hooked nails, flailing its arms back and forth as Toby screamed, and wicked, wavering, bleeding slashes opened along Toby's face, across the front of his shirt.

The goblin at the road threw his head back and laughed, spittle flying from his lipless mouth. From the trees, still unseen, the others joined in his mirth.

"Get off him!" Cozy shouted.

Toby's assailant looked up. Spattered blood dribbled from the folds of its dried-up face.

Cozy charged. He had snatched a broken limb, nearly three feet long, and he wielded the piece of wood like a baseball bat. He cocked the club and let fly with his best little league swing. The goblin ducked, but not quickly enough. The club struck it in the face, and even though the rotted wood splintered and broke, the goblin flew off of Toby and into the brush.

Home run.

The others continued to laugh for just a few seconds before they realized what had happened. Then they fell silent. Then they started growling.

"Come on!" I grabbed Toby and pulled him to his feet. His face was a mess of blood and shredded skin, dirt and snot and tears.

Cozy stepped towards the path again. He brandished the broken stick like a sword. He had tasted victory and was ready to wage war with the goblin on the road.

"No! Not that way!" I cried. "Come on!"

The goblins crashed through the brambles after us. The creatures panted and grunted like wild animals. I looked over my shoulder, but I didn't see them, only the bushes shaking as they gave chase.

In the years since, I have been a high school track star, but I never moved faster than I did that day, limbs and thorny vines snapping at my face, nearly tripping over roots and stumbling in old stump holes. The two brothers were close behind me, Toby bleeding and huffing and puffing, Cozy falling back, the bravery he had shown just moments earlier already draining away.

"They're right behind us," he called. "I can hear them!"

As I ran, I tried to keep a mental fix on the course of the trail, hoping for a break so we could catch it again. If we hit that trail, no goblin could possibly keep up with the three of us.

The memory of their witching eyes haunted me.

Sweat matted my hair to my forehead and dampened my T-shirt.

Cozy cried out.

I whirled around just in time to see him, now lying on his stomach, reaching out for us. Bony gray hands ensnared each of his ankles. He kicked, but could not shake the grasp of the goblins. I saw two of the creatures in the undergrowth behind him. Each tugged at his ankle. His frantic kicks shook them, but they held on.

"Help," he cried. "Toby!"

He clawed at the ground, tearing away the carpeting of dry straw and digging trenches in the black soil underneath. Tears cut streaks down his dirty cheeks.

And then he was gone.

The goblins tired of wrestling with him and took off into the woods, moving quickly, carrying Cozy as if he weighed nothing. His eyes snapped wide open, and his cries and tears stopped, just for a few seconds, before he was jerked away, the brush snapping and swallowing him up, the trails his fingers dug trailing off and vanishing into the foliage. His screams—and the goblins cackling—faded as they fled from us.

Toby called after his brother. He turned to me, his face a monster movie mask.

"We've got to go after them," I said.

We followed them. I heard the goblins snapping and crunching through the woods, heard Cozy's thrashing, his frightened sobs, just up ahead. I paused, just for a second, to grab up a stick, only hoping I could wield it as well as Cozy. I knew two more goblins waited somewhere in the shadow and in the darkness, waited, like spiders awaiting prey. I tested the weight of the stick in my hand. If they jumped us, they would have a fight on their hands. Using the trunk of a large tree for cover, I watched.

All four of the goblins now worked together to drag Cozy through the woods. Two held him by the wrists, while another had worked its claws into the tendrils of his hair. Sometimes, it stumbled, and tore out handfuls of the boy's hair by the roots. The fourth sat upon Cozy's chest, and it poked at him with a jagged stick every time he started to cry out. A half dozen nasty gashes covered his face.

Cozy's fingernails were dirty and bleeding.

The creature on his chest pointed the stick, and the others dragged the boy in that direction.

"What do you see?" Toby asked.

"I think they're taking him to the lake," I said.

"How do we stop them?" Toby's breath came in painful wheezes. "We're going to stop them, aren't we?"

"We're going to try."

We didn't move very quietly. I wondered if the goblins knew we were behind them, but were letting us follow, leading us into a trap. Still, when their pale eyes turned in our direction, we hunkered down quickly.

Cozy was quiet now, and I worried that his heart might have given out from fright. I didn't tell Toby my concerns, but I could tell he was worried as well.

The lake was still and quiet, and the moonlight seemed to make the water glow.

The goblins slogged along the muddy bank, dragging Cozy's still form. The big goblin leaped off of Cozy's chest, croaked a command, and pointed the pointed stick in the direction of the lean-to my friend had constructed earlier.

"They're going after our raft," Toby whispered.

"We've got to stop them now. If they take Cozy out on the lake, we won't ever stop them."

Toby nodded.

"We'll have to hit them quick. We can't give them a chance to attack us. I don't think they're much tougher than you or me, but they're a lot stronger than they look—"

I stopped myself, realizing with a wave of nausea, I was stalling.

The three goblins were already lugging the raft from the brush, leaving the big one all alone, standing guard over our friend.

I clenched the stick tightly and stepped towards the tree line.

Something uncurled from the weeds. It could have wrapped itself around our makeshift raft three times, maybe four. It stretched across our path and wound towards us, its pointed head as large and sharp looking as an Indian spearhead. Its black tongue flicked out, tasting the air as it approached.

I stopped. Toby ran into me.

"W-what is it?" he asked, but he caught his breath as he saw the snake.

Old Rootbelly.

I stepped away, pushing Toby back. I tried to move to the right, but the snake's pointed head slithered in that direction, blocking my path. I moved to the left, and the snake followed my motion, watching me.

Watching with its ghostly, almost human eyes.

Witching eyes.

I craned my neck and saw the goblins had now reached the shoreline. Furrows in the earth trailed across the ground where they had drug the raft.

In the instant I looked away, the snake struck.

Toby jerked me back just in time. The snake's head shot towards me, the mouth open, strangely distended. I could see the venom sluicing over the glistening fangs, felt it spatter my face. The fangs sank into the collar of my shirt, right along the neck, and the snake followed me as I stumbled backward, all the while looking up at me with those wild too-human eyes, and for a moment I feared it might fall on top of me, smothering me and biting me again and again. The shirt collar ripped. I stumbled and dropped the stick, and my fingers scrabbled of their own accord in a fruitless search for the weapon. My head struck a stump, and for a moment I saw only stars. I was distantly aware of Old Rootbelly hissing, sliding across the ground towards me with a rustle. More distantly, I heard the laughter of the goblins.

I couldn't move. My muscles wouldn't work. I thought maybe the snake had sunk its fangs into me after all, and now I was paralyzed, awaiting the time when Old Rootbelly would feast at leisure. A thought played through my racing mind—a thought that had not dawned on me yet, even with all the terrible sights I had witnessed.

I am going to die.

I felt the heavy, slithering weight of the snake as it crawled over my hiking boots.

I tried to pull myself onto my elbows, but my head spun and I crashed back down.

Toby loomed over me. His mangled face was twisted into a kind of fear and anger similar to the emotion that had danced across his brother's face when he had attacked the goblin. He stepped over me, a long stride—towards the snake. He raised the stick above his head, clutching it in both hands, and drove it down, planting it right between Old Rootbelly's unnatural eyes with a thick crunch.

He turned and helped me to my feet.

The stick stood from the ground. The snake's head welled around it like messy caulk bubbling from the earth. The serpentine body twitched and coiled and uncoiled in its death throes.

I touched the back of my head, and my fingers came away bloody. I felt blood tickling the hairs at the back of my neck. I felt unsteady, like I might topple over if I tried to take a step.

Toby clasped me on the shoulder and said, "Cozy!"

The goblins had already pushed the raft into the water. They were several yards away now, floating towards the center of the lake. Their eyes glowed in the shadowy folds of their faces.

Toby kicked at the ground, unearthing a large stone. He picked it up, pulled his arm back, and let the rock sail.

He hit one of the goblins square in the chest. It shrieked and toppled into the water.

I scooped up stones as well and started throwing them. The goblins chattered at us as the rocks started pelting them. I knew we must have been hitting Cozy, too, but hoped that the goblins took most of the damage. When a rock missed and splashed to the lake's surface, the water exploded like a depth charge.

Toby kicked at the edge of a buried stone. He fell to his knees and pushed at it. It came free of the earth. It was as large as a cinderblock, covered in caked mud and earthworms.

"You'll never be able to throw that," I said. "They're getting out of range anyway."

Toby nodded and dropped the rock into the mud with a thump that seemed to send a tremor across the lake. "We're going to have to swim it."

The last thing I wanted to do was get in that water. I knew at least one goblin was somewhere beneath the surface, and I imagined us trying to climb on board the raft while the remaining creatures beat at us and stabbed us with their weapons. But it was our only chance to save our friend. I pulled off my boots, threw them into the mud, and stepped towards the cold dark water.

Toby grabbed my shoulder.

"Look," he said.

Two more of the goblins jumped off the raft and dove down into the water. The leader beat upon its chest and started croaking, its throat swelling like a bullfrog's.

Even from the shore, I could make out almost every prunish wrinkle of the creature's face, every jagged tooth, the foul gleam of its eyes.

The three goblins surfaced. They brought something up with them, a bloated, waterlogged corpse. Stringy white hair trailed in patches from the scalp. The empty eye sockets. The lips peeled back from the crooked teeth.

The goblins clambered onto the raft and pulled the flabby, dripping, oozing body along with them. The fish had had their way with the corpse. Gashes of flesh had been chewed away, and the remaining flesh had the consistency of chewed hamburger.

The leader of the goblins tore out a hunk of the dead woman's flesh while the other three forced opened Cozy's mouth. He awakened then, and he started screaming.

We all screamed, I think, Toby, Cozy, and me, as they started stuffing the dead woman's flesh into his mouth, bits of her rotted skin and tissue smearing his face. His cries were muffled now. And then they stopped.

Cozy sat quietly now, next to the goblins and the dead woman. In the moonlight, his eyes reflected pale blue.

And I understood. The legends of Maddie Someday and the goblins were true … almost. The old witch had died, but somehow, she had lived on in the goblins when they fed on her, lived on in the creatures that had tasted her flesh. Like Old Rootbelly.

Like Cozy.

That old woman was too mean to die, my grandfather had said.

From the raft, Cozy stared right at us, his eyes glowing. The goblins followed his gaze, watching us. They howled and jumped, rocking the raft, the water sloshing up around them.

A horrible, bestial cry answered them. I flinched as Toby bellowed back at the monsters. He held the large, mud-caked stone again, hefting it above his head. He grunted, and I thought I heard muscles tearing in his back and arms. The veins stood out on his neck.

He threw the rock.

I would have never thought that rock would have gone for more than a few yards, but the missile sailed over the lake and for a moment I thought it might keep going forever, but it crashed into the raft, smashing one of the goblins flat and knocking another into the water. The raft seemed to collapse in upon itself with a brittle crack.

Cozy sank down beneath the water. The whole time, he stared at us.

We ran. We didn't look back to see if the goblins—or Cozy—emerged from the cold water to hound us. Even though our sides and lungs ached, we didn't stop until we broke free of the woods and saw the old dirt mail route that would lead us to our homes.

Toby didn't cry. I could tell, though, that he was fighting back tears, chewing at his lower lip, clenching and unclenching his fists. His brother was gone.

Of course, Toby's mother thought I was somehow to blame for what had happened, and Toby was forbidden to spend time with me. We still saw each other, eating lunch together, sometimes planning on doing something to put the ghost of Maddie Someday to rest once and for all, both of us knowing full well we didn't want to risk getting close to that witch or the things that served her ever again.

A wildfire destroyed much of the forest the following summer. No one really knew how it started, but most people suspected a campfire that had not been properly extinguished. I still have the old matchbook, although none of the matches remain. I keep it in a change jar on my dresser.

Toby's family eventually packed up and moved away. We tried to keep in touch, but eventually the letters stopped coming.

The year I graduated high school, I joined the Marines and moved away. My mother passed away in the fall of '82, and my father followed soon after. My sisters scattered across the country, but I still see them at least once a year. The house and land, along with nearly all the others, were sold to a development company. The area has really grown over the years, with fast food restaurants and shopping malls and movie theaters, but something must always be torn down to make room for progress.

I visited the area a week ago—the first time in nearly 25 years. I drove by my old school, now a closed relic, the kind of place I might have explored in search of phantoms as a kid. The fields where I picked tobacco to earn pocket money during the summer still stretch as far as the eye can see in places, but now massive combines, and not school children, harvest the crops. A large shopping center, complete with video store, Chinese restaurant, and discount department store sits not far from the area the woods once spanned.

I stopped in the store to buy some film for my camera. It was too crowded, I thought, the customers in too much of a rush. Strange. I've lived in much larger, much more fast-paced cities, but coming back "home," I hoped to return to the lazy afternoons, weekends, and summers of my youth.

"Did you find everything all right?" the cashier asked as I threw my purchases onto the rolling black conveyor belt and I fished my wallet from my back pocket.

"Just fine," I said, looking up, and my breath hitched.

The cashier—Meg, according to her nametag—looked back at me with pale

eyes.

Witching eyes.

I can't be sure, but she might have recognized me.

"I didn't think there would be any of you left," I said, tossing my money down, grabbing my bag, and striding away. "Keep the change."

I felt an unfamiliar wash of emotions flood through me. Nervousness. Excitement. Fear. When I walked out the door, I noticed a change in the air, a shift in the wind that brought with it the distinct scent of pine trees. I sat in my car for close to two hours, watching people walk past. I saw at least four people with witching eyes.

Another feeling lurked somewhere in the mix of thoughts and emotions, fleeting, but surfacing, just for a moment, like a jumping fish waiting to be snatched from the air.

Hope.

I think I'll be able to track down Toby's telephone number. I'm sure he still remembers what happened to his brother. Maybe now, after all this time, we'll finally put the legend of Maddie Someday to rest.

"Witching Eyes" was originally published in the anthology
BOOK OF MONSTERS (2004)

The connections to my middle-reader horror novel CROOKED HILLS should be apparent here. The two share some of the same inspirations – the backwoods, witches, strange creatures stalking the forest in the dead of night. I think even Old Rootbelly might show up in CROOKED HILLS at some point. When I originally wrote this story, it featured "goblins" but the editor of the anthology wanted me to change them to "ghouls." (Apparently, he already had a story featuring goblins, but he wanted to feature this one as well. I've changed the story back to its original form in this collection."

- CB

BLOOD FEUD: A VAMPIRE YARN
...WITH SPIDERS

I've got a story to tell—a story about how me and a couple of poker buddies squared off against the very legions of Hell … and maybe even saved the world. Like all good yarns, this one has its share of action, adventure, mystery, and romance. As for how it ends, though, you'll have to judge for yourself. I've always been partial to happy endings—the singing cowboy riding off into the sunset after rescuing the rancher's daughter—but I reckon that just ain't the way of the world.

This story's got vampires, too, loads of them, but not in the beginning.

It began, for us at least, with spiders.

In the fall, the tarantulas run, thousands of them, crawling in massive armies through the fields and across paved and dirt roads alike. You can't hardly drive across town without caking your Goodyears in the slimy carcasses of tiny, eight-legged speed bumps.

The tarantulas brought Sue Hatchell to Spider Creek.

And Sue dragged me into this mess, although I reckon trouble would have found me soon enough even if she hadn't interrupted my weekly poker game.

* * *

Not ten minutes before the screaming started, I was staring at four of a kind, all of them kings, and listening to my cousin Cecil babble about dead frogs.

"I've seen some strange things in my time, but this takes the cake and the ice cream." Cecil absently thumbed the worn edges of his playing cards. He removed two from the right side of his hand—he always shuffled his best cards to the left—and slid them face down across the table. I flicked two replacements in his direction, and he scooped them up to examine. "I was hanging around on Main Street, right? This was yesterday. Bought myself a Co-Cola at the Tastee Freeze and took a load off down by the beauty parlor."

Loitering outside the Spider Creek Beauty Parlor and Nail Salon—sounded like Cecil's style.

"So, I'm minding my own business, sipping my pop," Cecil said, "when I see old Roy Avrum strolling along the sidewalk. He's wearing these mud-covered rubber boots and toting a frog gig in one hand and an old paint bucket in the other. The bucket's slam full of big, fat bullfrogs, some of the biggest I've seen in a long while."

He cupped his hands and held them up to illustrate the size, the way a man does only when describing breasts or bullfrogs.

I glanced at Jack and raised my eyebrows. He held up three fingers and I passed him his cards.

"Anyway, I figured I'd invite Roy to play cards with us," Cecil said, "and maybe he'd bring some plump, juicy frog legs to eat."

"Some frog legs would taste good right about now," Jack agreed. "A whole mess of 'em, breaded and pan-fried."

My mouth watered. I grimaced at the bowl of stale pork rinds and cheese puffs on the table. "So where is he? He too good to play cards with us?"

"I was getting to that part if ya'll would quit interrupting," Cecil said. "So, we're standing there talking, and all of a sudden the bucket starts shaking and trembling, and the frogs start kicking and squirming and croaking. I swear, those frogs were deader than my Aunt Mami not a minute before. Saw them with my own eyes. But they woke up somehow and started floundering on top of one another and croaking like they were back in the mud. They knocked the bucket over, spilled out, and hopped down the sidewalk, heading in the direction of Black Rock Swamp, I figure. A couple of them had their guts near about ripped out, and they trailed behind them like wriggling earthworms."

"You're making this up," I said.

"No, sir. I near about shit myself. Shook Roy up pretty bad, too. He looked like he was fixing to puke up his lunch."

"Ask me, I'd say you and Roy both had too much to drink." I kicked back my own bottle of Cold Creek.

"I hadn't had a drop. Sadie Perkins saw it, too. She came stepping out of the beauty salon, all dressed up with her hair done up real high and pretty, and one of the frogs hopped right over her high heel shoes, leaving a trail of blood and guts over the patent leather. The roots of her perm damn near turned white. She swooned and almost fainted dead away, then started wailing on Roy with her purse, screaming about how he shouldn't bring such filthy creatures among 'civilized gentry.'"

Jack snorted. "I'd have liked to seen that. I'm surprised Sadie even noticed the frogs, what with her nose turned up in the air the way it always is."

"Dead frogs." I finished off my beer and set the bottle down. "Sounds like something outta one of those science fiction movies Jack likes so much."

I never considered myself the superstitious sort. I didn't jump at shadows or search for the ends of rainbows. But you don't grow up in Spider Creek, Missouri, without realizing some folk tales sprang from the truth. Every old house is haunted in some way, either by lonely ghosts or lingering memories. There's catfish in the deepest parts of the creek that'll swallow a man whole. And witches living in the darkest hollows are known to hex crops and hobble cows when their burlap panties rode too high and tight. Folklore, maybe, but—

"The Good Lord can be a mighty peculiar sonovabitch," my granddaddy used to say.

So I owed Cecil the benefit of the doubt.

Just chaffed my ass to give it to him.

"Been a lot of strange goings-on lately," Cecil said. "Carol Grimes told me she saw four blue jays sitting on her fence Friday morning."

Old wives' tales claimed you never saw a blue jay on Friday because that's the day they flew to Hell to get their orders from the Devil.

"Wonder what that means?" Cecil asked.

"Means there won't be enough juicy gossip for Carol to stick her nose into," I said, "so she pulled some nonsense out the back of her drawers."

"Damn." Jack shuffled uncomfortably in his chair. He held his cards up before his face and squinted at them, as if they might tell him something different than they had the last few times he examined them. "Now I got a taste for frog legs."

"Are we gonna talk about food and superstition? Or are we gonna play cards?" Eyeing the pile of money on the table, I grew a bit anxious to finish the hand and collect my rewards. If my luck held, I'd be a hell of a lot closer to getting my pickup out of the shop. I threw another five into the pot. "I'm gonna raise."

Across from me, Jack—Big Jack, we called him—frowned and folded, slapping his cards face-down to the table.

One down.

Cecil fanned his cards out before him, his beady eyes ticking from one to the next as he decided whether to fold or see my bet.

These boys were my best friends in all the world:

Big Jack Sutherland could have easily gotten a job in Hollywood as a stunt double for one of those muscle-bound action movie stars. As a younger man, he considered a career in professional wrestling, and the NWA even offered him a contract. Would have been something to see Big Jack (I always imagined that would be his fighting name) locking horns with Ivan Koloff, the Iron Sheik, or Nature Boy Ric Flair. But in the end he turned down the offer and ripped up the contract. He said a career in professional athletics would keep him away from home too often. I figured the decision had more to do with a certain Miss Cordelia Miles … but I'll tell you about her later.

My cousin Cecil was as small and wiry as Jack was big. Never could understand how a boy who ate as much as Cecil stayed so scrawny, especially considering he never worked an honest day in all his life, and near about broke out in hives at the thought of holding down steady employment. He got by doing occasional odd jobs around town and using his sly charm to wrangle free meals from the local ladies—usually the older, well-to-do, widowed ladies, mind you. When he wasn't making time with the aforementioned women, he wiled away the hours watching television, drinking, and playing cards.

Every Saturday night we got together at Cecil's place over on Old Mill Road for a few hands of poker and a few bottles of Cold Creek beer. The cabin reeked of mildew and dust and old chewing tobacco, and the roof sagged and leaked like a sieve when it rained, but I wouldn't have traded the place for any three of those fancy, noisy riverboat casinos like the ones in St. Louis.

"Aw, hell, R.F., why don't we call this a practice hand?" Cecil's whiskered face split open in a friendly grin.

"We've been playing for more than two hours, Cecil, so I'd say it's a little late for practice," I said. "Shit or get off the pot. You don't lay down some money or your cards … cousin or not, I'll take you out in the yard and whoop you right in front of your dogs."

Jack laughed.

Now, I've been known to be a terrible son-of-a-bitch from time to time, and I ain't afraid to whoop an ass when its deserved. But I had no intention of hurting Cecil. He moaned and complained and piddled about every time we played cards. All part of his routine. I was used to his antics by now and was only funning with him.

Tossing his money to the center of the table, Cecil said, "I'll call," shakily.

Outside, the dogs started barking.

A heartbeat later, someone banged on the front door. Hard. Sounded like it might come off its hinges.

Startled, Cecil hopped to his feet, knocking his chair over with a clatter. I jumped, too, and bashed the underside of the card table with my knees. Jack looked hopefully towards the door.

"You think that might be Roy with some more of them frogs?"

Cecil's a-frame sat just off a seldom-traveled dirt road meandering through hill, forest, and pasture country. Besides me and Jack, he didn't get many visitors, especially not roundabout nightfall.

"Help!" The scream—a woman's scream—came from outside. "Is anyone in there? I need help out here!"

Poker night pretty much went to shit from there.

* * *

"Guess we'll call this hand, right?" Cecil asked.

"Leave those cards and the money where they are," I said, "and answer the door. Or haven't you noticed there's a woman screaming on your front porch?"

The woman continued yelling and beating against the door. "Can you hear me?" she cried. "Is anyone home?"

Cecil went to the door—with Jack and me a half step behind—and threw it open.

Cecil's two mangy dogs stood at the foot of the porch steps, their red fur bristled as they growled at the pretty young woman at the door. She leaned with one hand on the doorframe and the other on her hip. Her tan skin glistened under a light sheen of sweat, and her olive-colored tank top was soaked beneath her arms. She stepped back and wiped her palms nervously against her shorts. As she caught her breath, her ample chest heaved, just barely contained within the top. I found myself staring right into the sweaty cleavage peeking out from the dipping collar. I shook myself from my trance and hauled my eyes up to meet her own. Heat washed across my neck, ears, and cheeks.

Her name was Sue Hatchell, and she studied spiders.

I recognized her, of course. In a town the size of Spider Creek, a young college girl from the city—especially one who came to study the local tarantula population—was the subject of quite a bit of gossip. From the moment she stepped off the Greyhound bus, the hens started clucking and the roosters, myself included, started strutting.

She had a head of fine, honey blonde hair (pulled back beneath a checkered red hippie bandana) and bright blue eyes, clear as a summer's afternoon down by the river. She was broad-shouldered, maybe a little big-boned, and she probably wouldn't ever grace the pages of a girlie magazine, but I liked her just fine, despite the fact that she had her nose pierced and sported tattoos on both her shoulder and ankle.

I had seen her around, sure, walking along the road, following herds of tarantulas, all the while scribbling notes on a pad of paper or recording memos into a miniature tape recorder she carried in the back pocket of her khaki safari shorts. Once I saw her step right out in front of Buzz Harley's beat-up pickup, stopping him cold so he wouldn't run over a slow-moving colony of spiders trundling across the road. That mean old coot pitched a red-faced, screaming fit, threatening to roll right over her and calling her every name in the book and a few brand new ones to boot. Sue wouldn't hear any of his ranting, though, and didn't budge until the very last poky spider skittered off the road and into the weeds. Word around town was she came from up Springfield way to research the tarantula population as part of her college studies. A lot of ladies would be terrified to work so close to even one of those big, hairy spiders, let alone a good two- or three-hundred, some as large as a man's fist. Spider Creek tarantulas were known for their ill tempers, and if one gets riled it can jump a good three feet and bite several times before satisfying its anger, but Sue would stand right out in the middle of them as they scrabbled around her sandaled feet. They seemed to have an understanding, her and the spiders. "We've all got places to be and jobs to do," the tarantulas might have said. "Don't get in our way, and we won't get in yours."

Got to admire her spunk.

I like to think that if Sue and I met under different circumstances—

But there's no reason to dwell on such things, is there?

Especially not now.

As my granddaddy always said, "if ifs and buts were candy and nuts, we'd all have a merry Christmas."

Cecil said nothing for several long seconds, staring at Sue's bosom like a starving man drooling over twin cuts of prime rib on the grill.

I pushed past and shrugged him back. "What's wrong, miss?"

"There's a man out here who needs help," Sue said between gasps. She pointed down the road. "He's hurt. Bad."

As she hurried down the steps, the dogs skedaddled out of her way, but threw a couple of quick barks in her direction to save face. She looked back, waiting for us to follow.

Quick as a whip, the three of us went after her.

Cecil's yard was a tangled, cluttered mess of old junkers, rusted swing sets, balding tires, and overgrown landscaping. The bulks of cars and trucks rose like craggy islands from a sea of weeds. (Cecil swore he didn't know where some of the cars came from.) Sue cut across the yard, paying no mind to the scratching weeds, even though she wore sandals and no socks.

The dogs woofed at us, whined a little, then followed.

Along the root-knotted hills on either side of the pebbled and rain-washed road, spindly shadows spilled from overhanging trees. Thick patches of dried weeds crawled along the slopes, and when a breeze blew through, the weeds rasped as if whispering secrets. Katydids screeched from the brush, their last hurrah before vanishing in the cold months ahead.

"He's right over here," Sue said.

"Who is he?" I hustled to walk by her side. "Your boyfriend?"

I winced, realizing how clumsy that must have sounded.

"Don't know him. He just stumbled out of the woods."

The road crested a hill, and Sue raced ahead of us.

"You said he needs help," Cecil called after her. "What's wrong with him?"

"I don't know. He's … messed up."

"What does that mean?" Cecil's voice peaked in his excitement.

"Messed up." She didn't glance back, but frustration edged Sue's words. "Like he was attacked or something."

I looked at Cecil and Jack. Both of them stutter-stepped and paused—just for a second—while they considered what she had said.

Attacked?

The dogs cocked their heads and sniffed at the air as if catching a whiff of something out of kilter. One of them whined. The other growled. Those two hounds were no account in most respects, and they were uglier and smellier than a week-old lard bucket full of armpits, but they had good noses on them. They smelled trouble.

On the other side of the hill, the road curved sharply, vanishing behind an outcropping of trees. Just before the bend, a figure lay in the middle of the track. Damp leaves trailed the man out of the surrounding brush and across the road to where he sprawled. Dark stains—mud and blood—covered his rumpled, tattered coveralls and threadbare T-shirt. He lay on his stomach, his arms stretched out in front of him. I saw no movement, and he might have been dead for all I knew.

"He came out of nowhere." Sue said. "Scared me half to death."

Sue and I hunkered down next to the man and gently rolled him onto his back.

Blood, dark and dry, spread in flaking patches across his face and neck. His wide, wet eyes stared up at us, and he choked out a cry. He was alive after all. His legs kicked in the dirt as he tried to scrabble away, but he collapsed again, blubbering and clawing at the earth with dirty fingernails. His eyelids fluttered and closed.

"It's all right," Sue said in a soothing voice. "I found help, like I promised."

Cecil and Jack sidled up behind me. The dogs remained a few feet back, dashing back and forth and snarling.

"Lord Almighty!" Cecil leaned over the injured man. "That's Seth Stubbs."

I had hardly recognized him for all the dirt and gore, but looking more closely, I noticed the tell-tale pimples and pockmarked flesh of the Stubbs family. Folks in these parts always said the Stubbs could make a lot of money with their looks, but not for being pretty. Every last one of them was as pimpled as a freshly plucked chicken.

"You know him?" Sue asked.

I nodded. "He lives on the other side of Prescott Ridge. Quite a ways away from here."

Sue cleared her throat, and her brow furrowed. "Should we get him to a doctor or something?"

Seth Stubbs.

Remember when I said I wasn't afraid to whoop an ass now and then? Well, Seth had been the proud owner of that ass on more than a couple of occasions. He wasn't really a bad fella, I reckon, but he got a little mean when he'd been hitting the bottle at the Stag Tavern, and I'd put him in his place a time or two.

But nothing I'd ever done compared to this.

Deep scratches crisscrossed over his face and neck, a violent connect-the-dots with his zits. Looked like he had tried to fend off the attack, too, and his hands and forearms were cut badly. At his throat, the skin plowed up and hung in loose, jagged strips down to the collar of his shirt.

"Whatcha think happened to him?" Cecil asked. "Think a bobcat got ahold of him?"

The way he was chewed up, it sure looked like a wild animal had made quite a bit of sport out of poor Seth. I touched him on the shoulder. "Seth, can you hear me, old son?"

His eyes snapped open.

Bloodshot. Wild.

"D-don't! Don't you touch me!" He squirmed in the dirt. "Don't!"

"We're not going to hurt you," Sue said. Sitting back on her haunches, she held her open hands out to show she meant no harm. "We only want to help."

"Ain't nobody can help me now!" Seth's voice was high-pitched and filled with pain. He took quick, shallow breaths. "Ain't nobody can help any of us!"

"Who did this, Seth?" I asked.

His eyes darted from me to Sue to the woods, as if he expected someone—or something—to come crashing out of the brush to snatch him up.

"Is someone out there?" Sue asked.

Seth swallowed, his Adam's apple bobbing, and nodded.

Sue and I both jumped to our feet and stared into the trees. Big Jack took a step towards the woods. Cecil took a step back.

"Who's out there?" Sue asked. I couldn't tell if she were asking Seth or calling out to the unseen presence possibly lurking nearby.

Tears seeped down Seth's ruined face. "T-they killed them, every last one. Every one..." His eyes closed again. Her skin was very pale.

"Who's out there?" Sue asked again, turning towards the injured man, sudden fear fueling her impatience.

The dogs, either sensing the agitation of our little group or catching the scent of something in the woods, started barking.

Seth didn't open his eyes. His answer came as a whisper.

"It's a feud," he said. "A blood feud."

Sue shivered and wrapped her arms around her bare shoulders to stifle a sudden chill. I reckoned she knew more than her fair share of gruesome stories about backwoods lunatics—banjo-picking, inbred rednecks with unspeakable lusts and mean streaks a mile wide. For all she knew, some maniac watched us with lust-filled eyes from the trees even as we tended to Seth.

"Let's get him inside," I said. "We'll call the doctor from there."

We helped Seth to his unsteady feet. Jack and I threw his arms over our shoulders and carried him down the road, his boots dragging behind us. He smelled of blood and unwashed flesh and shit—more than likely his own.

The dogs jumped and barked like they'd tree'd a possum as we hauled Seth's limp body past them. They followed us all the way back to the cabin, and deep growls rose from their throats as they crossed between us and the door. When we tried to go around, they nipped at our feet.

Seth moaned.

Cecil yelled and stomped his feet. The mutts tucked tails between legs and slinked into hiding among the wilds of the weeds and abandoned junk.

We got Seth inside, stretched him out on the couch, and covered him with a heavy quilt. Sue removed her bandana and used the cloth to wipe some of the blood away from his face. Exposed, the wounds looked even worse, ragged and inflamed.

I sure didn't want to meet the man or beast capable of doing such things to a living soul.

But somehow I knew I would.

Soon.

* * *

While the others looked after Seth, I grabbed the phone and called the sheriff. My fingers trembled just a little. I clenched the receiver tightly to steady myself.

A blood feud.

Big Jack looked at me from across the room. His thoughts ran the same course as mine. If a member of the Stubbs family mentioned a feud, it could mean only one thing.

The Whatleys.

The very thought of those strange old coots near about froze my blood.

On the other end of the crackling telephone line, Annie Tills, the dispatcher, answered.

"Well, R. F. Coven!" Annie's fingernails-on-the-chalkboard voice piped across the line. "Haven't heard from you in quite a spell. What have you been keeping yourself busy with? You know, you never did make good on that promise to take me line dancing, and—"

"Sorry about that, Annie, but I'm afraid this isn't a social call."

"Oh." I heard the hurt—about half of it for show—in her tone. "What can I do for you, then? You haven't gotten into another scrape, have you?"

"Reckon you best let me talk to the sheriff."

"It's Saturday night, R.F." I could hear her eyes rolling from across the phone line. "You know he ain't around."

Shit. How could I have forgotten? Regular as clockwork, Sheriff Hargrove played bingo at the VFW in West Plains every Saturday night.

Sue paced back and forth, stopping to peer out the window every few seconds.

A frustrated rumble danced in my throat.

"Listen," I told Annie, "I got a bit of a situation here. I'm over at Cecil's place with Sue Hatchell—"

"Who? Sue Hatchell? That weird city girl? What are you doing with her? And Cecil, too? R.F.—"

"Get ahold of the sheriff and tell him something's happened to Seth Stubbs." I lowered my voice just a hair. "Something bad, I think."

The hurt in Annie's voice bristled into snootiness. "Like I said, the sheriff's unavailable. He's playing bingo."

"I don't give a good God damn if he's been especially appointed to pluck the hairs from the governor's back. You get him back here. And while you're at it, call Doc Bishop and send him to Cecil's place."

"I'll see what I can do," she said curtly.

I thanked her and assured her I'd make good on the offer to take her line dancing as soon as possible. I hated being two-faced, but the little white lie lightened her mood and would hopefully make sure she did what I asked.

I put the phone back in the cradle, closed my eyes to clear my head.

So much for the cavalry.

Even if Annie got ahold of the sheriff, he'd likely be too loaded to be of any help. It was just getting to be sunset, but those Bingo games could get wild—and fast. Chances were the sheriff was already three sheets to the wind, and would wake up some time tomorrow morning with his patrol car parked in a ditch, his losing bingo cards spread over his potbelly like a sheet, little daubs of bingo marker ink covering his body like polka dots.

"Sheriff on the way?" Cecil asked.

"It's Saturday," I said. "Bingo."

My cousin's shoulders slumped.

Sue still clutched at her arms as if fighting off the cold. She leaned against the wall and looked at me as if to ask "what now?"

"He'll get here as soon as he can," I said, knowing full well we wouldn't see his sorry ass anytime soon. "Sent for the doctor, too."

Sue relaxed a little, but shot a glance at Seth and then at the window.

"What were you doing out here anyway?" I said in a clumsy attempt to make small talk. "If you don't mind me asking."

"I'm working on a paper about the local tarantula population," she said. "But I guess just about everyone has already figured that out, huh?"

I smiled and nodded.

"Really?" she asked. "People are talking about me?"

"It ain't like you've caused any juicy scandals." I shrugged. "At least not yet. But we're easily entertained."

"What are they saying?"

"Oh, I don't pay much attention to that sort of gossip."

"Right." She rolled her eyes. "Well, I'm heading back to Springfield in the next few days, so you'll have to find something else to amuse yourselves with. I was just trying to collect some final notes on a colony of spiders moving through here."

I hated to hear she'd be leaving so soon, but I tried not to show my disappointment.

She kept looking towards the window. I doubt she even realized she was doing it. She couldn't see much anyway, not with the curtains drawn.

"This whole mess has got you spooked, huh?" I asked.

"Guess so." She looked at her trembling hands, squeezed them into tight fists. "The funny thing is, right before Seth came out of the trees, the spiders scattered and ran for cover. One minute they were moving slow and deliberately, the next they were running in all directions, like they sensed him and were afraid."

Like I said, it started with spiders.

Sue went to the window and pulled the curtain aside for a better look. Dust motes swirled in the last rays of sunlight trickling through the glass.

"Cecil," I said, "Do me a favor and fetch a couple of flashlights, some guns, and ammunition."

Sue snapped her head in my direction, a question trembling on her lips.

"Be quick about it," I told Cecil.

As my cousin rushed off towards the back of the house, Sue crossed the room and cornered me.

"Flashlights?" she asked. "You're not seriously thinking of going out there, are you? Something in those woods almost killed a man."

"Reckon that's why we're taking the guns. If what Seth says is true, his whole family might be in danger, might be hurt, just like him, and there are children— lots of them."

I didn't like the idea of hiking through the woods, either, what with the twilight deepening to full-on, blacker-than-snuff-spit night and somebody or something meaner than a copperhead in a frying pan waiting in the dark. There wasn't much choice, though, unless I was willing to abandon the Stubbs family to the desires of whoever—or whatever—had gotten ahold of Seth.

I wasn't.

Like I said, Seth wasn't a saint, especially when he'd been walking on a slant, but what had happened to him was just wrong.

Downright inhuman.

"You're going on foot?" Sue asked.

"Hell, not a one of Cecil's old beaters has a working transmission, Jack doesn't own a car, and my truck's been in the garage for going on three weeks. A car wouldn't do much good anyway. The road winds through miles of hills before even coming close to the Stubbs place. We'll get there a lot faster as the crow flies."

"Maybe we should try to get to town."

"We barely got Seth onto that couch," I said. "I'd hate to lug him all the way into town. We're liable to do more harm than good. You're better off staying here and waiting on the doctor. We won't be gone long. If all's well, we'll bring some of Seth's folks back with us. Chances are Doc Bishop will be here and have everything under control by the time we get back."

Seth stirred on the couch fitfully. "Got to fight ... fight..."

"You don't need to be fighting anyone," I said.

I wouldn't understand until later what he meant.

Carrying a couple of flashlights, a shotgun, a box of shells, and a wooden cigar box, Cecil shuffled into the room. The flashlights—bought on special at Radio Shack in West Plains—were heavy and grey, with red plastic bands encircling five-inch lenses. I flipped the switches on both a couple of times to test them out. One glowed brightly, but the other dimmed and brightened and dimmed once again to a fitful orange pall.

"Batteries are going dead in this one," I said, knowing full well my cousin didn't have any extras lying around. "We'll save it for emergencies."

A chill raced up my spine. I hoped we wouldn't run afoul of anything even close to an emergency situation, but somehow I knew we would.

Jack cracked the double barrel shotgun open and loaded it, stuffing the remaining shells into his pockets.

From the old cigar box I withdrew a pistol and a handful of bullets. The pistol had belonged to Cecil's daddy, and to hear my own daddy tell it, had been involved in more than one sort of trouble during younger, rambunctious days. I flipped open the cylinder, loaded each chamber, and dropped the extra ammo into my shirt pocket.

The reflection of the shells glimmered in Sue's eyes.

I nodded toward Seth. "Keep him warm if you can. If it looks like more trouble than we can handle, we'll run on back as quick as we can. You'll be all right here with Cecil."

She offered my cousin another of her forced smiles.

"Do me a favor, will ya?" I pointed the shaft of the flashlight towards the card table. "Don't let Cecil mess with those cards."

"I won't." She smiled—a real smile this time. "Be careful."

Jack drew in a deep breath and opened the front door. "Looks like we're the cavalry," he said.

I grinned. "Some things never change."

* * *

This is Spider Creek:

Only one major highway, slicing and winding through the long shadows of the Ozark foothills, passes anywhere close to town, and only a handful of paved roads branch off from the main stretch like tributaries, leading past the Tastee Freeze and Andy's Bait & Tackle and the Outfitter Five-and-Dime before giving way to an overrun of dirt, milkweed, and wild onions. A "one horse town," maybe, and that suits me just fine. Way back in high school, before I blew my knee out and my dreams of playing football for a big university dried up, I wanted to get away to some place bigger and better. In some ways, my bad knee might have been the best thing to ever happen to me. A big city would have chewed me up and spit me out like old chaw, and I needed time to realize just how good I had it in this sleepy little community. You can get one of the thickest cheeseburgers you've ever tasted, along with fried potatoes and onions, for less than four bucks at the Red Eye Diner. Neighbors—and we're all neighbors—still have the common decency to wave when they pass you by, and most folks feel perfectly safe leaving doors unlocked and windows open at night, and dulcimer music echoes through the hills on crystal clear evenings. Fishing's good, and I've personally seen grizzled old fishermen pull fat, two-foot long catfish out of the river only to toss them back for "being too scrawny." No sir, I can't imagine wanting to live anywhere else. May not be Heaven on Earth, but it's about as close as you can get these days.

Except, of course, for the vampires.

* * *

Night gobbled up the last of the late afternoon sunlight.

We followed Crooked Hollow (Crook'd Holler, as the old-timers called it) past Brussell Branch and the Old Mill, heading to the Stubbs farm to find God-knew-what. The hollow had once been a winding cave system, but the roof collapsed thousands of years ago, before the first settlers stumbled upon what would eventually become Spider Creek. The whole area was riddled with sinkholes and cave systems, but Crooked Hollow was a winding canyon through the woods, crossed every now and again by a natural bridge—leftover portions of the cave ceiling. Come a storm, rainwater rushed through the Hollow like whitewater rapids, but on a dry night only a narrow band of water trickled along the path. The hollow was the quickest route to the Stubbs place.

Dark caves lined the rock walls here and there, and some descended deep into the earth.

The moon was a great red eye staring down on us.

A blood moon.

More omens.

Dead frogs jumping from a bucket. Blue jays on Friday. And now a plump, bright, full moon, glowing the pale red of homemade strawberry wine. Something bad was going to happen tonight, I realized. Something a helluva lot worse than the injuries inflicted upon Seth.

The Good Lord can be a mighty peculiar sonovabitch.

My fingers flexed on the extinguished flashlight in my right hand. We didn't need the light—not yet—but I would have preferred pitch blackness to the harsh glow of the moon. Tucked into my jeans waist band, the pistol rubbed against my thigh as I took a step. I was overly aware of the weight of the spare bullets in my pocket, the jangling sound of the casings clinking against one another. I hoped I wouldn't need the weapon, but somehow knew I would.

A blood feud.

The Stubbs and Whatley families had been at each other's throats for as long as anyone could remember, and they still hated each other—from Zebulon Whatley, the eldest of his clan, right down to the youngest of the Stubbs children. A Stubbs baby popped out of his mama hating the Whatleys, and the Whatleys taught their brood from a young age how to fling rocks with cruel accuracy if a Stubbs wandered too close to their property. No one remembered how the feud started, probably not even the two families involved. Some say many years back the heads of each household had been good friends. But an argument over land, money, women, or—as the more outlandish stories held—the secret of making gold, set them against each other. Every now and again a story made the rounds about a Stubbs who chased a Whatley with a wood axe or a Whatley who peppered a Stubbs' backside with rock salt.

The stale aftertaste of Cold Creek beer lingered in my mouth.

The Stubbs were a rowdy, troublemaking bunch, but the Whatleys—

Folks in these parts spoke of the Whatleys in hushed whispers.

"Them Whatleys," my granddaddy told me once, "they got the witch's touch, each and every one of them, and you don't never want them to turn their wicked gaze towards you."

According to local legend, the Whatleys ran naked in the woods, beating out strange tunes on deerskin drums, making animal sacrifices beneath the Old Gallows Tree on Summit Ridge, and meeting with the devil himself on pitch black nights.

But never on a Friday, I mused, the bluejay's day in Hell.

Eventually, when we had gone as far as the hollow would take us, we climbed the craggy hillside and continued through the woods. Stepping back under the blanket of forest shadow, I felt relieved to be out from under the harsh glow of the blood moon. The woods grew dark around us, as if a wash of runny black paint had spilled across the trees and stumps, the dry creek beds and jagged outcroppings of mountain rock. Some light trickled through the branches overhead, though, and we managed without the use of the flashlights for a while longer.

Jack cradled his shotgun in his arms. He had tucked the flashlight into a denim loop in the leg of his coveralls. He clenched a cigarette in his teeth, and as he drew breath, a flare of red illuminated his face like a devil's mask. He offered me one of the smokes, stick thin in his thick fingers, the trademark silver band between the filter and tobacco. A Millennium Red. My brand. Only I didn't smoke anymore. Cut back when Doc Bishop informed me I had the choice of either living to a ripe old age or choking on blood and lung tissue before I ever reached my golden years. The good doctor's bedside manner was for shit, but he presented a mean argument.

"You know I quit."

Still, he offered the cigarette. "You got to die of something."

Black as witch's milk, the forest rose up around us.

"Thanks for reminding me." I plucked the cigarette from his hand and took a deep drag.

Best damn smoke I've ever had.

"You reckon this is gonna be bad?" I asked Jack.

"A-yeah," he responded matter-of-factly.

I had known, even before asking, what his answer would be, but asked anyway just to make small talk and break the monotonous crunch-crunch-crunch of our footsteps through the leaves and twigs carpeting the hills.

I hoped Sue would be all right. Again I found myself wishing we had met under better circumstances.

"What's on your mind?" Jack asked. "You thinking about that girl?"

"Huh?" I laughed. "I reckon I got better things to worry about right now." I tried to turn my thoughts away from the pretty young college girl waiting for our return.

"I wonder if Cecil is putting the make on her," Jack said through a mischievous grin, "don't you?"

Warmth flooded up my neck and the back of my ears. Jack may have just been funning with me, but his jibes struck a cord. Cecil fancied himself something of a playboy—a tobacco-chewing, unemployed, weasly Romeo—and he wouldn't let an opportunity to charm Sue slip away. Sue, being a more sophisticated girl, wouldn't hardly fall for Cecil's pass, but it made my teeth hurt, thinking of him offering her a glass of home-brewed cherry mash, dimming the lights, and putting Don Williams on the record player.

Jack chuckled.

"You are one mean old bastard," I said, but I couldn't help but smile.

Our laughter raced off into the darkness, a good sound, but a sad sound, too. Final.

"How would you feel," I asked, hoping to give Big Jack a taste of his own medicine, "if it was Cordelia waiting back there with Cecil?"

Jack's laughter ended abruptly, and his smile turned to a frown. "That ain't funny."

Miss Cordelia Miles. I could almost hear Jack's heartbeat quicken at the mention of her name. The torch he carried for her had been burning for a long time, and while she let him take her out every now and again, she didn't really love him and he would never win her favor. Several fellas, from as far as sixty miles away, actively courted Cordelia. The prettiest girl in the county, she had her pick of well-to-do men, and a guy like Jack, who scraped his coins together by hauling junk for the auction barn same as me, simply didn't stand much of a chance. Still, Heaven help the man who hurt sweet Cordelia, because he'd have to go a few rounds with Big Jack, and nobody in their right mind and proper sobriety would want that.

Standing over six feet tall and built like a brick wall with prize hams for fists, Jack could pound fence posts into hard-packed earth with one swing of a sledgehammer and lift tractors out of mudholes without breaking much of a sweat. I myself once saw him rip a St. Louis phone book in half just to show how easy it was, and I'll never forget the night he whipped all three of the Dobson brothers, who had been drinking a little too much and running their mouths a little too loudly.

I hadn't seen anything, though, until we came across the bull.

* * *

Here's what happened with Big Jack and the bull:

As we reached the hill overlooking the Stubbs farm, we noticed three things.

First, the place was pitch dark. I turned the flashlight on and aimed the beam downhill, scanning across woodpiles and fenceposts, clapboard shacks and crumbling barns. Just out of the beam's reach, the dim shapes of other buildings loomed. No lights shone through windows. No sounds came from within.

Second, an awful smell, like a meat freezer gone bad on a summer day, clung to the air.

Third, somewhere in the darkness, the Stubbs' bull, Samson, bellowed like the devil himself was riding him bareback.

I reckon every small town has a bull like Samson, a creature of such ferocity

342

and meanness that it had become a legend—a monster who'd just as soon gouge and trample you as look at you. Foolhardy children dared each other to brave the pasture where Samson roamed. Men nodded solemnly and speculated in grim whispers about the day that bull might break out of captivity and wage war on every living soul for miles.

Maybe Samson had attacked Seth, I thought.

Maybe he had broken out of his pen and slaughtered the Stubbs family in his boundless fury.

Maybe he waited, there in the darkness, for Jack and me to approach.

Loose dirt and pebbles skittered from under our boots as we slid down the incline, making too much racket for my tastes. I felt as if we were approaching a graveyard haunted by an angry ghost, and I didn't want the specter to hear us coming.

I swung the light around. The beam played across dirt pathways, partially collapsed split post fences, and shoddy shed walls. I half expected for Samson to charge out of the darkness, snorting steam, blood in his eyes.

Jack must have been thinking the same thing, because he grabbed up his own flashlight and pointed its guttering beam into the darkness.

The bull bellowed.

Not a cry of anger, but of pain and fear.

"Over here!" Jack cried out.

I hustled towards the beacon of his flashlight. I almost ran into the thin grey wire of the electric fence separating the farm from the pasture. The wire trembled and wavered as a great force tried to tear it down.

Jack dropped his flashlight and shotgun at his feet. The feeble ray of light rocked back and forth before coming to a rest, spreading its glow over Jack.

Before him stood Samson, roaring and kicking and shaking his great horned head. The bull had jumped the electric fence, but only made it halfway. While his front hooves stamped at the ground and chopped up dirt and rocks alike on one side of the fence, his back legs were still planted on the other. The electric wire stretched beneath his hindquarters, buzzing right across his nut sack. Samson kicked and jumped, but every time his bulk descended, the sparking wire gave him a shock right to the nether regions.

My own balls shriveled at the sight.

"We got to get him off of there," Jack said. "He's going to hurt himself if we don't."

I put my own flashlight and firearm on the ground and looked for a length of loose board. Didn't take long before I found a section of two-by-four left over from an unfinished shed.

"I can knock the fence loose," I said, testing the water-swollen board. "But as soon as I do, Samson's gonna come after us."

I couldn't blame the bull for being angry, but I didn't want him to vent his rage on the two of us.

"When I say so—" Jack stepped towards the bull. "—do it."

I didn't know what Big Jack planned, but I cocked the piece of wood back like a baseball bat.

The wire sizzled and popped.

Samson roared and grunted.

Jack reached out and wrapped a massive hand around the tip of each of the bull's horns. The muscles in his forearms and neck popped as he started to push the bull back. Samson lowered his blocky head, and his front hooves dug into the ground. Despite the jolting fireworks crackling around his balls, the bull saw Jack's actions as a test of strength, and he wasn't backing down. Jack grimaced, holding the huge beast in place.

"Now!" he cried.

I brought the two-by-four down as hard as I could. The electric fence snapped with a metallic twang! and whipped past me, nearly slicing across my eye.

Free now, Samson put all of his weight into the shoving contest with Jack. As mighty as he was, Jack was no match for the bull's blistered-ball fury. He stumbled and fell, hands still locked like vices around Samson's horns. The bull kept pushing. He pressed Jack down towards the earth, like he wanted to plant him in the ground. Jack held on, because if he didn't Samson would surely trample him to death.

Snot oozed out of Samson's big, pulsing nostrils. Frothy spittle flew from his mouth.

"Get him off me!" Jack yelled. "Hit this ungrateful bastard!"

Drawing the two-by-four back once more, I took aim on the spot directly between Samson's eyes. "If I hit him," I said, "I'm going to kill him."

"I don't care!" All his compassion for the bull's plight had been knocked from him as Samson bore him to the ground. "Do it!"

I hated to kill him, but—

"Get him off!"

I readied to swing.

Just then, Jack let out a mighty yell, and he twisted the bull's horns like a NASCAR driver steering around a sudden curve. Samson screwed his head around to fight against the motion, but Jack was just too strong. The bull flipped off of Jack and crashed to the earth with a shuddering thud, all four hooves sticking straight up in the air. I might have seen a look of astonishment in the bull's eyes.

Jack scrambled to his feet.

I brandished the piece of wood, awaiting the attack.

Samson bucked and rolled onto his hooves, but instead of attacking, the bull shot off in the other direction, running for dear life. Still kicking his back legs to warn us from following, Samson vanished into the night.

"I never seen anybody flip a bull like that," I said.

"Well now you have," Jack said, wiping sweat from his brow. He struggled to catch his breath.

"Well, you sure scared the hell out of him, manhandling him like that."

"He won't be scared of me." Jack pulled a half crushed Millennium Red cigarette from his shirt pocket and lit up. "There's something else here. Something that made him try to jump that fence in the first place."

First the tarantulas had fled from Seth's approach, and now something had scared mighty Samson bad enough to risk his own dick jumping the electric fence.

"I don't feel good about this," I said.

Jack shook his head and leaned down to pick up his gear. "Me neither."

We started in the direction of the Stubbs' house, but stopped again.

Something moved through the darkness.

I pointed the flashlight towards the front porch. Several pale figures moved across the yard towards us.

Children.

The Stubbs children came out to greet us.

* * *

Each of them, from the smallest toddler to the gangliest, pimpled teenager, looked like living death—skin bloodless, eyes sunken and reflecting red like a wild animal's in the crimson moonlight. Their tattered sleeping clothes were bloodied and dried gore flaked upon their flesh, but no cuts or scrapes marred their flesh, at least not as I could see.

Haints, my granddaddy would have called them. Ghosts or monsters or devils.

Haints.

Their glowing eyes moved from Jack to me and back again as they lurched towards us.

"That's just about far enough," I said. My heart slammed in my chest. The hair on my arms stood on end. My flesh crawled, recoiling from the presence of the children. I couldn't bring myself to point a gun at a child, but my hand quivered upon the handle of the pistol, and my unsteadiness set the flashlight to trembling. "We came to check on you. Make sure everyone was all right here."

Wasn't that a damn fool thing to say? I knew by looking at them that they weren't all right. They were dead. Some part of me knew it, but I had a hard time wrapping my mind around the concept.

I quickly counted them. Nine children stood before us. I tried to remember how many children belonged to the Stubbs clan. Was this all of them? No telling. The Stubbs had been breeding in these hills for years, and it wasn't such a far-fetched notion that a kid might grow to adulthood without ever coming into town.

They took another step. Another.

A watery ball of ice grew in the pit of my stomach.

"He said stay back," Jack barked. He was still winded from his tussle with Samson. He hefted his shotgun, took aim.

One of the young'uns in the lead—a girl of maybe seven or eight—opened her mouth hungrily, revealing razor sharp fangs jutting this way and that from her gums. Her brothers and sisters and cousins did the same, as if eager to impress us by imitating her action. They reached out for us with clawed fingertips.

Snapping the pistol up, I said, "This is it."

"Huh?" Jack asked.

"When it gets bad."

The children hissed like angry cats, their mouths overfull of fangs, their breath a graveyard stink.

I fired.

God help me, I didn't want to shoot a child, but the things lumbering towards us were not children—not real children—but something else.

The bullet slammed into the little girl's shoulder. She whirled around and crumpled to the dirt. She didn't make a sound. I aimed the gun at the next target, a boy who was likely a couple of years younger. A curl of smoke drifted from the barrel.

He kept coming.

The little girl lifted herself off the ground, the bullet hole in her shoulder dribbling a thick milk-white fluid.

I fired again, twice.

The first bullet punched through the little boy's throat. His face wore an expression of sudden shock as he somersaulted backwards. The second shot struck the little girl again, this time in the stomach, and she doubled over and staggered, but she didn't fall, almost like she had grown accustomed to the feeling of being shot.

The thunderous flare of Jack's shotgun set the darkness alight. The blast tore through the group of children, knocking some from their feet but barely fazing others as the pellets sprinkled smoldering black holes in their bodies.

The little boy I had shot clambered to his feet again. The remains of his throat dangled in sticky, meaty flaps down the front of his pajamas.

I shot at him again, but he ducked to the side like he was dodging an annoying skeeter.

And then they were on us.

Despite their previous shambling stride, they now moved with the speed of mountain cats. One of them grabbed me around the waist, as if playing a game of King of the Mountain. Jagged nails dug through my shirt at the small of my back. I brought the butt of the pistol down between his shoulder blades once, twice, three times with little to show for my efforts. I drove my knee into his gut, but he didn't even flinch.

Another child grabbed my arm and knocked the flashlight to the ground in a spinning arc of light.

I cracked him across the forehead with the gun. He staggered and fell back, his forehead split open, a crooked gash, like a lightning bolt, ran from his hairline to the bridge of his nose.

But there was no blood. Not a drop.

I saw the gleam of his skull beneath the broken skin, but no gush of red spurted down his features. Instead, something white and thick as biscuit gravy oozed down the valley between his eyes. Strings of clotting goo stretched across his lips and clung to his teeth. His teeth were like knives in a messy cutlery drawer.

The boy with his arms around my waist dug his bare feet into the ground and pushed with all his might. He was stronger than I expected. Not as strong as Jack, but almost. Stronger than me for damn sure. Any minute now he would bear me down.

I pressed the gun to the back of his neck and squeezed the trigger. The shot near about deafened me. An explosion of snotty gunk spattered my shirt. Gun smoke filled my nostrils and burned my eyes. The boy flopped to the ground, kicking, flailing, screeching an ungodly sound. He clawed at his ruined neck. His head hung to the side, connected to the rest of his body by strips of shredded meat and gristle. A putrid vapor rose from the wound. It stank like rotten eggs.

But no blood.

I drew my foot back and kicked him right beneath the chin. His head ripped away and sailed into the darkness. His body slumped to the ground, still except for the foul-smelling gas rising from the neck stump.

"Jack," I cried. "Get them in the head! Take their heads off!"

Jack shrugged one of the leaping children away, kicked another as it charged for him, sending the little monster scuttling onto its rump in the dirt. He raised his shotgun and blasted away, taking the child's head off in an explosion of skin and bone fragments. The body fell, an oozing steam rising from the ruin of a face.

A pair of children threw themselves at me, each of them grabbing one of my legs just below the knee. They pulled this way and that, tripping me, and I toppled backwards and slammed into the ground. I heard the metallic clatter of my spare bullets as they flew from my pocket and spun into the dirt.

Jack's shotgun boomed. He cursed as he cracked open the weapon and hastily reloaded. He would be out of ammo soon.

The two children pinned me down and crawled up my body.

I fired the gun, destroying the head of one of the children. The body collapsed on top of me, spewing slimy puss and green vapor into my face. I almost puked up pork rinds and cheese puffs. The other child—a girl of maybe five years old—was still on me. I pointed the gun at her and fired.

Click!

Out of ammo.

I pulled the trigger again. The gun dry fired on empty chambers.

The girl pulled her lips away from her sharp teeth. Her nails dug into my cheek as she pushed my head to the side, exposing my throat. I tasted dirt. I blindly struggled with the girl. I tried to shove her away, but she was far too strong. She leaned close. Her icy lips and hard teeth brushed against my skin, but she pulled away before she took a mouthful of my flesh. She snapped her head up as an angry, train whistle sound resonated through the night.

* * *

A dark shape loomed over us. I wondered if the shadow of Death had come for me.

With all my might, I pushed the little girl off of me and rolled—

Just as a bull's hooves plowed into the earth, right where my head had been seconds earlier.

Samson had returned, pissed-off and out for revenge.

The girl hopped to her feet and spat at the bull, tried to ward him off with a swipe of her claws.

Samson stood between me and my attacker. He stomped the earth and snorted, swung his horns from side to side in a challenge. The smell of burned hair and skin clung to the air around the behemoth and vied for dominance over the smells of spoiled meat and the green vapor. A blast of steam gushed from Samson's wet, flaring nostrils.

I pulled myself to my feet, saw Jack using his shotgun and flashlight as clubs against two small figures. I called out to Jack, but he didn't answer. I didn't want to take my eyes off Samson or the little girl for more than a second.

The girl shrieked and lunged past Samson, trying to get at me.

But she never made it.

With a swipe of his engine-block head, Samson smashed into the little girl. A great, curling horn caught her across the midsection. Her body folded around it, then unfolded as she toppled through the air and thudded to the ground. She scrambled to her feet and backed away, vanishing into the dark.

Samson whirled and turned his attention towards me.

"Easy now, big fella," I said. "I'm the one who helped you get free."

But in the bull's eyes I might as well have set fire to his scrotum myself.

He charged.

I flung myself out of his way. Samson trampled the earth as he passed, then wheeled around for another stampede.

I hauled ass.

I felt Samson's hot breath at my back, urging me to run faster.

Straight towards Jack.

He still fought with two of the monsters. He punched one, staggering it, and when the little boy leaped at him again, Jack clotheslined him, damn near yanking his head off. He drove his knee into the other, raked his fingers across the boy's eyes, like a professional wrestler sparring with gruesome opponents in a no holds barred match. He didn't see me. Didn't see the bull.

"Look out!" I cried.

Samson rammed into the small of my back, and my feet left the ground. I somersaulted through the air, crashed into a wooden fence, tearing it down and bruising my ribs. I couldn't breathe, but I was lucky one of his horns didn't stab into me.

I called out to Jack again, but my voice came in wheezing gasps. Stars danced in my eyes. I tried to push myself to my hands and knees, but fell back to the dirt.

Samson continued his charge towards Jack.

The bull remembered his earlier humiliation and wanted to settle the score.

Jack wrestled with the two creatures, pushing them back in a desperate struggle to avoid their snapping teeth. He was slashed and bloodied in several places. He held a kicking, scratching, biting creature in each arm. If you didn't know better you might think he was just playing around with them. Jack's eyes grew round as saucers as Samson's dark bulk barreled towards him.

Jack was finished for sure.

But just as Samson blasted past, Jack dodged to the side, and now he moved less like a wrestler and more like a bullfighter, only instead of flapping a red sheet, he waved monstrous children. He hurled one of the boys at Samson, and the angry bull's right horn pierced the child through the chest. The boy shrieked as the tip of the horn emerged from his torso in a gout of smelly green and white spray. He went limp, still dangling from Samson's horn like a morbid decoration.

As the bull spun, the dead boy's slack arms and legs flailed.

Jack hurled the second boy at the animal's head, impaling him on the bull's left horn. The child twitched and sagged. He nearly matched the corpse of the first boy.

Samson shook his head, trying to free himself of the two dead boys. The bodies bounced, legs and arms flopping, like dancing puppets. When the bodies didn't come free, the bull only grew more angry. He stamped the earth, then lowered his head and charged Jack once more.

This time, Jack stood his ground. As Samson drew close, Jack pulled back a mighty fist and punched the bull right between the eyes. I heard a thump and the crack of bone. I didn't know if Jack's fist or the bull's skull—or both—had shattered.

Samson backpedaled on the wobbly legs of a newborn calf, then toppled over in a heap with the dead children still stuck to his horns.

Just then, the little girl jumped out at me again.

I snatched up one of the fallen fence posts and jammed the jagged end through her chest. She shrieked, spewing green smoke from the wound, and dropped like a sack of rotting onions.

Jack's hand was already swelling. I figured he'd busted it pretty badly when he knocked Old Samson cold. Around us lay the still-twitching bodies of dead children and the unconscious form of the meanest bull in the county.

Jack bled from a half dozen angry looking wounds, same as me. His hand was red and swollen, and he held it close to his chest. But we didn't insult each other by worrying over our injuries, at least not yet. There'd be time enough to bemoan our nicks and cuts and compare scars later.

I scrounged up a couple of the bullets I dropped. I looked for more, but had no luck. I grabbed the flashlight, too. Jack's flashlight was smashed to bits during his battle with the children.

"That," I said, "was a hell of a thing."

Jack shrugged. "Same old, same old."

We started to laugh, but a sound from the house stopped us cold.

An infant's gurgling cry.

"Oh, Jesus," I muttered.

Not a baby. Anything but a baby.

Still favoring his swollen hand, Jack squatted and grabbed another jagged piece of broken fencepost from the ground. "Bring the light," he said.

The baby's wail lured us deeper into the house. The sound was so much worse than Samson's furious cry, because my imagination ran wild at the notion of what we'd find when we reached the beckoning source.

The house was a wreck. Windows smashed—from the outside coming in, I noticed. Drying blood pooling on the hardwood floor. Some of the puddles looked partially sopped up and smeared, and the tiny handprints in the gore told me the children had gone on hand and knee to lick at the blood.

I loaded the last two bullets into the pistol. My fingers trembled, and I clenched my hand into a fist, my nails digging into my palm.

The baby's cry came from a dark room at the end of the hall. The walls were covered with crooked family portraits—pictures of pimpled, whiskered, cross-eyed men and women, pictures of gnarled old-timers, pictures of mothers and fathers ...

Pictures of children.

Big Jack stopped in the doorway to the infant's room. I shone the light past him, towards a crib and the moving form within.

The baby cried, a hungry sound.

Jack stepped toward the crib, blocking my line of sight. Leaning over, he raised the fencepost and brought it down in a swift motion.

The cry stopped.

Jack stood quietly with his back to me for several minutes.

"Jack," I said, breaking the silence. "Let's go home."

* * *

"You know what they were, don't you?" Jack said as we staggered through the woods.

"Like hell I do."

"Draculas," he said. "They were draculas."

"What—" I stopped myself. I knew what he meant. A couple of years back, Jack had taken Cordelia to the picture show in West Plains. The movie had been *Dracula* or *Dracula's Revenge* or *Son of Dracula* or something like that. To hear Miss Cordelia tell it, it was one of the most horrible things she had ever witnessed, full of violence, sexual innuendo, and gore.

"All that blood," she said. "It was awful. Ghastly."

But Jack loved it. Went to see it a couple more times and made special trips whenever a monster flick lit up the big screen.

"God damned draculas," Jack spat.

Vampires. He meant vampires.

Hell. Who was I to argue? If nothing else, thinking about them as vampires made it easier to live with what we had just done. They were only children. But they were something more. They were stronger than they should have been. Tougher too. Their eyes glowed. Their fangs.

I nodded. All right. Vampires.

"Here's the bad news," Jack said. "You become a dracula when you get bit by another dracula."

"I thought that was werewolves?"

"Them too. It works near about the same way. Anyway, somehow the Stubbs were attacked by a dracula, I reckon, and it just left those young'uns there to change."

"You didn't get ... bit did you?" I asked, hoping Jack was just reeling me in for another ribbing.

He sucked at his teeth and shook his head.

"So what's to worry about? They're all dead now."

"Not all of them. Something turned them, wouldn't you say? And that something may still be out here right now."

I was starting to like the vampire theory less and less.

"And whatever it was," Jack said, "it attacked Seth, too."

But that would mean—

We picked up the pace.

* * *

Before we reached the Hollow, I realized we were being followed. Not just followed. Stalked. I heard the soft crackle of twigs underfoot, a shuffling in the scrub. Someone kept pace with us. I spied movement beyond a line of nearby trees. Pale flesh. A glint of red.

My muscles tensed. I crouched down behind a tangle of branches and dry leaves, turning the flashlight off. I hoped we hadn't been spotted. I'm no coward, but I didn't want to run into another of those… things anytime soon.

A few hundred yards ahead, the forest floor would give way to the craggy slope of the Hollow. I was guessing the distance, but didn't dare turn on the flashlight to get my bearings.

Another dark shape loped through the brush. Between us and the Hollow. Coming closer.

I pulled my pistol and silently prayed my last two bullets struck true. The gun had been near about useless against the creatures at the Stubbs place, but it was something at least.

Jack still carried the wooden stake—the weapon he had used to kill an infant. No.

The Stubbs family was already dead by the time Jack and I arrived at the farm. We only laid them to rest. I sounded like a character from one of those Dracula movies Jack liked so much. But maybe that was easier—thinking of the children as something other than human.

"You don't suppose it's another of those…" Draculas, I almost said. "…things, do you?"

I heard the snapping again. Close. Too close. I flipped the flashlight's switch and pointed it towards the pitch black swelling beyond the trees. The light chased shadows away.

Three men stood in the thickets, two blocking our path and another behind us.

They leapt at us.

They were naked, and their faces were whiskered and covered in pimples near about ready to burst. Their shriveled peckers bounced from side to side as they attacked. Their eyes glowed like a blood moon.

Jack raised his leg and planted his boot in the chest of one, and the vampire sprawled back and crashed into the other. They tumbled over. I pistol-whipped the third and elbowed him for good measure. He fell. By the time they scrambled to their feet, Jack and I were making tacks.

We crashed through the woods. I heard the three vampires chasing after us, cackling like madmen. I felt as if my chest might break open, and my heart might jump from my body, yell out, "every man for himself!" and dash off into the darkness. My bad knee ached, but I didn't dare stop running.

Somewhere up ahead, I heard babbling water. A stream. Or maybe that was just piss dribbling down my leg.

We stumbled out of the treeline and splashed down into a shallow strip of creek run-off. Jack nearly fell over. I followed, and the icy water rushed into my boots and soaked my socks. The three vampires lurched out of the trees.

And they stopped.

"Why aren't they coming after us?" I asked.

Jack snapped his finger. "The water," he said. "Dracula can't cross running water."

The vampires growled deep in their throats. Their faces were masks of shadow lit by their red eyes.

"Go on back where you came from!" Jack shouted. "Git!"

His version of "Back, back, creature of the night!"

As if heeding his command, the three lumbered into the woods again, casting hungry, defeated glances back at us, like we'd hurt their feelings.

"What do you know?" Jack muttered.

"Something tells me they're looking for another way around," I said. "Let's not be here when they find it."

* * *

First thing I noticed upon stepping into Cecil's cabin was the soft hiss and pop of the record player. The needle had already reached the end of the last track, but I saw the sleeve of a Don Williams album beside the player.

My blood boiled.

Jack staggered in, exhausted, and near about collapsed into a chair in front of the poker table. He tossed the stake onto the table with a clatter, knocking a couple of cards to the floor.

"Are you all right?" Sue met us as we stumbled in. "You look like hell. What happened?"

"How's Seth?" I ignored her questions. I still didn't quite know how to explain what I'd seen, what had happened, not without sounding like I'd been sampling shine.

"He's sleeping."

"No sign of the doctor, either," Cecil said. "I thought he'd be here by now."

"Will somebody tell me what's going on?" Sue snapped. "What did you find? What happened?"

I pushed past her.

I strode across the room. I didn't mean to ignore Sue, but my mind spun in a storm of confusion and anger and fear. Seth lay upon the couch, still as a coffin nail and covered in a patchwork quilt, his hands crossed over his stomach.

"He dead?" Jack called after me.

"I can't tell."

"We didn't let him die if that's what you're wondering," Sue said, her feathers ruffled.

"Seth, wake up." I slapped him across the face. "Come on."

"Hey!" Sue snapped. "What the hell are you doing?"

"Careful." Jack stepped up behind me. "He might be turned by now."

"Turned?" Sue asked. "What are you talking about? Turned into what?"

"A Dracula," Jack answered.

"A what?" Sue asked.

Cecil laughed, but stifled his mirth when he realized Jack was deadly serious.

I smacked Seth again, harder this time. "Wake up!" When he didn't stir, I drew my hand back again, but Sue caught me by the wrist.

"I'm not letting you beat him like that."

Just then, it hit me. When we brought Seth in, his face had been cut up. The cuts were gone now. The faint ghosts of scars remained.

Seth opened his eyes.

His eyes didn't have any whites. They had turned blood red.

I jumped back, pulling Sue with me. She squeaked in surprise.

Cecil muttered, "What the hell?"

"You boys back already?" Seth chuckled as he sat up. His voice was hoarse, like he hadn't had a sip of water in days. His lips peeled away from jagged fangs in a cruel grin. "How's the young'uns?"

Like he somehow knew what we'd done.

The zits on his forehead and cheeks split open, oozing tiny, slow-moving rivers of puss.

Sue clutched at my arm, breathed, "Oh, God."

That tickled Seth, and he rocked back and forth on the couch, giggling. His red eyes bore right into mine. He clacked his razor-sharp teeth at me.

Jack had just about had enough. He pushed past me and grabbed Seth's shirt collar, yanking him to his feet.

"Hand me that stake," he said. "I'm gonna put it right through—"

Seth grabbed Jack's busted, swollen hand and squeezed. I heard the wet snapping of bone. Jack screamed and went to one knee like he was proposing marriage. Seth, looming over him now, twisted and squashed Jack's hand, like he was trying to wring water from a cloth. Tears ran down Jack's face.

"Let him go!" Cecil pulled at Seth's arm.

Seth released Jack, and the big man crumpled, laying on his side and drawing his legs up to his chest, clutching his hand. Seth backhanded Cecil. My cousin flew across the room, knocking over the card table, crashing in a shower of cards and dollar bills.

"I ain't no wet-behind-the-ears, snot-nosed brat," Seth yelled. "I'm stronger than they would be. Closer to the Master. Much stronger."

I didn't know exactly what he was talking about, but I believed him.

"Look, Seth," I said. "We ain't looking for trouble. Why don't you just go on your way and leave us be?"

"We can't just let him go," Jack rasped from the floor.

"You don't want trouble?" Seth flashed his fangs at me. "Is that what you told the children?"

"They attacked us, Seth," I said.

"What are you talking about?" Sue asked me. "What children?"

"Did they scream when you killed them? Did they cry for their mamas and daddies?" Seth shrugged. "Not that I care, of course. They were weak, not like me."

How could he know all that? It was like he had been riding on our shoulders the entire time.

He stepped closer.

"Stay where you are, dammit."

"No use fighting. I laid on the couch, fighting, for so long. The minutes seemed like years, you know that? And then I started to feel them...the children... screaming as you killed them. I still kept fighting, because I didn't want to be like them, and what did all that fighting amount to? Nothing. It would have been so much easier to just give up the ghost. I feel so much better now."

He didn't even sound like Seth anymore.

He flexed his fingers. His talons clicked together.

"And you know what?" he said. "I won't end up like the children, because they're dead, and me ... I'm gonna live forever."

He grinned. When he spoke again, his words were slurred, as if drool pooled in his mouth, even though he was bone dry.

"Who's it gonna be first?"

He looked at Sue hungrily, licked his dry lips.

"Naw, I'm gonna leave you for last. Best for last. Best for last."

He turned his gaze towards Cecil, who still lay under a covering of money and playing cards. "Hell, you ain't never been worth a shit, you know that? The Master would probably whip the skin from my bones just for bringing a no account like you over."

Seth didn't see Big Jack clamber to his feet behind him.

I did my best to distract the vampire. "The Master?" I asked. "Who's that?"

"I'm connected to him." He swept his arms out, as if welcoming us. "We'll all be connected to him."

Behind him, Jack was a tower of shadow. He inched forward, and as he passed the window, a beam of crimson moonlight swept across the mask of rage he wore for a face.

"What happened to you, Seth?" I asked. "I mean, who did this?"

Seth cocked his head. Either he didn't know the answer exactly or he didn't know why I would ask. His eyes snapped wide open as he realized I was stalling him. He whirled around.

Jack wrapped the thick fingers of his hand—his good hand—around Seth's throat. The vampire squeaked in surprise and wheezed, even though he surely didn't need to breathe, as Jack crushed his windpipe. Seth clutched at Jack's forearm, his curled nails digging into the big man's flesh up to the first knuckle.

Jack howled and flung Seth like a rag doll towards the window.

The glass exploded as Seth sailed out of the house, crashing to the porch in a hail of glittering shards and tumbling down the steps.

We rushed to the window. I grabbed one of the broken table legs and Jack's stake from the floor.

Cecil's dogs jumped to their feet, bristling and barking at the vampire. Seth stood, brushing himself off with one hand and massaging his throat with the other.

"Get on out of here," Cecil yelled.

"You damn fools!" Seth spat. "Don't you know what I was offering?"

Seth climbed back up the steps and moved towards the window.

I held up the two pieces of wood, placing one across the other in the shape of a cross. Seth howled, covered his red eyes, and jumped away. He scurried off the porch like he had a bad case of the green apple splatters.

"You had your chance, asshole!" Cecil let out a short whistle and yelled, "Sic him!"

The dogs launched themselves at Seth, snarling and snapping at his pants leg. Vampire or no, Seth fled from the nipping fury of the hounds. He kicked and stomped, and the dogs almost tugged him to the ground amidst the rust buckets and thistles. Seth skidded to a stop at the edge of the yard, bathed in the reddish light of the moon, and kicked at the mutts. Heads lowered, teeth bared, they circled him.

"I offered you eternal life!" Seth yelled.

The vampire held his arms out and threw his head back. He produced a series of short squealing sounds.

"Rhee! Rhee! Rhee!"

"What's he doing?" Cecil asked.

Seth's throat swelled like a bullfrog's.

"Rhee! Rhee!"

Throat puffed up, then shriveled.

"Rhee!"

Puffed up again.

"Call the dogs back," I told Cecil.

A shadow moved across the ground behind the vampire, flowed up to his feet, like a spreading oil slick.

"What the hell is that?" I muttered.

The dogs lunged at Seth again.

The crawling shadow took on weight and shape. The mass washed over the dogs, swarmed over their paws and legs, up to their bodies, and they yelped and howled in pain and fear.

The shadow grew, swarmed past Seth and stretched towards the house. It flooded from the trees, out from under wrecked cars in a skittering wave.

"You've got to be shitting me," Jack said.

Spiders.

A massive, chittering carpet of tarantulas spread across the yard. They crawled and hopped up the porch steps, scurried over the warped boards.

They clung to Seth's body as he continued to cry out like a hog caller from Hell.

"Get away from the window," Sue cried.

Cecil whistled for his dogs.

The hounds scurried back towards the house, still yowling and biting at their own bodies, only they weren't so much dogs anymore as much as dog-shaped masses of spiders, and they collapsed before reaching the porch, the tarantulas scurrying off of the steaming mess of bloated, chewed meat.

"We have to get out of here," I said. "Get to the back door."

Tarantulas leaped through the shattered window—first one, then another, then dozens at a time. They scrabbled over the sill and plopped to the floor. Dark, hairy shapes crawled up the glass on the outside of the good windows. They thumped against the front door again and again. It sounded like hail.

I felt a searing sting at my calf.

Then another.

Two or three spiders crawled up my pants leg. I slapped at the bulges beneath my clothes and felt their bodies mash against my skin.

Sue cried out. A half dozen spiders crawled across her sandaled feet and up her bare legs, leaving a trail of blistering bites in their wake.

Cecil started stomping. His boots rattled the loose floorboards. He looked like he was mashing grapes for wine or dancing a jig.

I dropped the makeshift cross and grabbed a straw broom from the corner and started sweeping, clearing a path. The straws of the broom impaled several tarantulas. One scurried down the handle and bit my fingers.

Jack swatted at the spiders with the comforter that had covered Seth. With a flick of his wrist, the blanket snapped out like a patchwork bullwhip. Each heavy thud of the sheet left a mess of spiders upon the floor.

Still more spiders invaded the house. They crawled through the window. They plopped down from the chimney, and I heard more of them scrabbling down the flue. I rushed to close the vent—crushing spiders with every step—and a half dozen leaped onto my arm, tearing at me with their tiny, stinging fangs.

The dusty floorboards bounced and vibrated, and tiny, hairy legs scrabbled out from between the slats. They were under the house, trying to push their way in up under the floor.

I've been a churchgoer all my life, but never thought of myself as religious. Still, I prayed under my breath as I swept sheets of tarantulas into crushed piles. I just hoped someone was listening. I looked across the room at the two pieces of the cross. Spiders swarmed all over them.

Great, writhing patches of tarantulas came at us, all fangs and glittering eyes and twitching legs. Every time we killed one, a half dozen raced in to take their place.

I could hardly imagine that many tarantulas in the entire county.

Cecil got a hammer from a kitchen door and duck-walked across the floor, pounding tarantulas flat with machine gun quickness, leaving a ring of hairy legs around circular splotches of spider guts.

The spiders piled around Sue, climbing her legs, getting in her hair, biting her face and arms. She cried out. Then she did something I never expected.

She started stomping.

She swore a blue streak that would have put Buzz Harley to shame as she ground her sandals down on the spiders, mashing them flat.

Cecil whacked spiders in rapid fire strokes. As he knelt down, his shirttail pulled from his jeans, and the crack of his ass peeked out. A couple of spiders jumped for the opening, and he straightened—"Youch!—and swatted at his own backside.

I was bitten in a dozen or more places. So was everyone else, though, some worse than me.

As I stumbled across the room, I noticed Sue's tape recorder lying upon the floor. Without thinking, I scooped it up. Not really sure why I bothered. A tarantula sunk its fangs into the back of my hand. With a flick of my wrist, the spider sailed across the room. I shoved the recorder in my pocket.

I stood in the middle of a biting, hissing, jumping storm of spiders—hundreds of them. One of them jumped at me and caught hold of my shirt collar. I felt its tiny legs at my throat. I slapped at it, but it scurried up my cheek and bit me beneath my eye.

We swept and swatted and stomped the spiders until the floor was matted with a soggy carpet that sucked at our feet when we took a step. Welts covered our bodies, and I felt as blistered as a boy who spent too much time inner-tubing down the river on a hot and sunny day. A few stray tarantulas still crawled through the house, but it looked like we had beaten the fight out of them.

Still rubbing his backside with one hand and swinging the tarantula-caked hammer with the other, Cecil ran to the window and looked out. "I don't see him!" he said. "I can't see Seth!"

Snarling, the vampire jumped into the window.

Seth crouched there for a second or two, perched like a bird of prey on the sill. He bared his fangs. He braced his arms on either side of the window, and his nails dug into the wood.

Cecil backpedaled, swinging the hammer wildly.

Seth leaped at him.

They fell in a tangle. The hammer clattered to the floor. Cecil beat at Seth as the vampire snapped at him. Tarantulas joined their master in the fight, crawling over Cecil and biting his ears, his nose, his hands.

Cecil reached for his weapon. His fingers crawled across the floor like one of the tarantulas. The spiders attacked the intruder, covering his hand in seconds. Cecil screamed, but his hand reached the hammer, and as he grabbed it, he squeezed spider guts out from between his fingers. He whipped the hammer against Seth's head. The claw punched through his skull with a gout of green vapor. Seth clutched at the wound and jumped back, slamming against the wall with the hammer still jutting from his temple.

"Got him," Cecil cried.

Seth punched him, right in the gut.

Cecil made a whooofing sound as the vampire's claws punched into his stomach. Blood spattered to the floor. Seth smiled and turned to face us. His arm was still submerged in Cecil's breadbasket, nearly to the elbow. Cecil's legs kicked in jerking spasms.

Jack came up behind Seth and wrapped his big arm around the vampire's neck in a choke-hold. Several tarantulas that had been nesting in Seth's hair leaped out and bit Jack's face, but the big man didn't let up.

Cecil slid off of the vampire's arm and fell in a drizzle of blood. He dragged himself away from the monster as even more spiders attacked him. He didn't seem to notice the bites.

Jack wrestled with the vampire, nearly pulling him off his feet.

"Somebody stake this bastard!" he cried.

Seth bit Jack's arm. Blood spurted up around his fangs as he tore through muscle.

I cracked Seth over the head with the broom handle. It snapped in two over the bloodsucker's skull. His teeth pulled out of Jack's arm, and the big man released Seth.

As Seth picked himself up, I planted my boot on his chest and shoved him to the floor again.

"You can't stop us!" he hissed through swollen, cracked lips.

I shoved a broom handle through his heart.

Seth writhed and grabbed at the shaft of wood and spat and cursed. His red eyes bulged, and he slammed his head against the floor again and again. A vented geyser of green vapor sprayed out from the flesh puckering around the broom stick. The point of the stake struck the floor beneath the vampire. Finally, Seth lay still.

For a few seconds, I kept my foot upon his chest, holding Seth down in fear that he might rise again. The rush of my blood thundered in my head, and my pounding heart hammered against my chest. All other sensations were gone. I heard only my own blood flow, felt only my rapid heartbeat, and saw only Seth's twisted face leering up at me.

Jack grabbed my shoulder, shook me. "He ain't getting back up," he said.

"You sure about that?"

He shrugged, but I took my foot away from the corpse and stepped back.

Every stick of furniture in the house was broken or overturned. Shattered glass and scraps of timber littered the room, along with the smashed remains of spiders on the floor, walls, and even the ceiling.

Jack was covered in sweat and mashed spiders. Blood soaked his sleeve, dribbled off his fingers, and puddled at his feet.

Sue stood upon a wet mat of crushed tarantula carcasses. Her sandals were covered in squished spider innards. The mess pulled at her feet like quicksand as she stepped away.

Somewhere in the house, Cecil moaned.

* * *

Following a smeared trail of dark blood across the floor, we found Cecil in a back room. He had crawled into the room, and now leaned against the wall, taking quick breaths. He clutched bloody hands over the gaping gut wound. His shirt was stained a glistening red, and blood pooled beneath him.

He wheezed out a laugh. "Reckon that wasn't so smart. I'm not cut out for vampire fighting. Ought to have left it to you and Jack."

"You did just fine," I said.

He coughed and winced.

Jack and Sue followed me into the room. A sad and angry grumble grew in Jack's throat, while Sue stifled a gasp and sob.

A few straggler tarantulas crawled around Cecil. I pressed one beneath my boot heel and enjoyed the crunch.

"Just rest easy there." I hunkered down next to my cousin, trying to keep a calming smile upon my face, trying not to look for too long at the yawning, bloody hole in his stomach. "You're gonna be just fine."

He smiled, but it slipped away quickly.

"He killed my dogs."

"We'll get you some new dogs, all right?"

"You don't think I'll come back, do you? I mean, not like Seth."

"What are you talking about? You ain't gonna die. You're too damn annoying to die."

"Ain't worried about dying. I'm worried about coming back."

I glanced over my shoulder at Jack. He shook his head.

"No." I fought to keep my voice steady, but my eyes burned. "You won't be coming back. You weren't bit."

Cecil looked past me. "Jack—"

"Don't worry about me." Big Jack's voice hitched just a little. "I'll be all right."

"You big dumb asshole, getting yourself nipped like that trying to help me."

"I'll know better next time," Jack said.

Cecil's eyelids fluttered. "I'm so tired."

"You just go ahead and sleep then," I told him.

He closed his eyes.

I rested a hand on his shoulder. Sue wept behind me. The house creaked, settling.

Cecil opened his eyes again.

I half expected to see red orbs staring back at me, but his eyes were normal.

"Did I win?" he asked.

"Yes, sir. You got him."

"That's not what I mean. The cards. I had a straight. Did I win?"

"That's right. You beat me. Won near about all my money."

Cecil smiled. "Liar." His eyes slowly closed again. His final breaths came in rattling gasps.

"Ain't gonna be no next time," he muttered.

And he was gone.

Silence. No one dared speak. We all held our breath until we were sure he wasn't coming back.

* * *

"What do we do now?" Sue asked.

"We could just wait here until morning—until the sun comes up," I suggested.

"And what happens if another of those creatures shows up?"

None of us wanted to consider the possibilities. I couldn't shake the memory of the tiny, hairy legs of the tarantulas on my skin.

"I hate to piss on the parade," Jack said, "but I don't think I'll make it until morning."

He rubbed his shoulder just above the spot where Seth had chomped away a good part of flesh.

"I'll stay with you as long as I can," he said. "Sooner or later, though, I'll have to take my leave of you."

Sue said. "But if there's a chance you might change—"

"This isn't about chances. I've been bit. There's no changing that now. Sooner or later, I'm gonna change. I'll let you know before that happens, and I'll finish myself off if I have to."

I tried the phone. "It's dead."

"One thing for sure," Sue said. "We can't stay here. It isn't safe. Maybe we're no safer outside, but I'd rather risk it."

"The next closest phone would be at the Miles place," Jack said. "We can call for help, maybe reach the state police."

I should have guessed he'd be eager to suggest the Miles place. That way, he'd be able to check on Cordelia. He was right about their phone being the closest, though, and they owned a working car.

"That's still quite a walk in the dark," I said. "I'm not saying we can't make it, but we're all worn out and scared already, and I want everyone to know this might not be easy."

Sue nodded, and I knew Jack had already made up his lovesick mind.

"All right, then." I yanked my broomstick out of Seth's corpse. The stake tugged Seth right along with it, then the body flopped back, the stake making a slurping sound as it pulled from the meat. "For what it's worth, we have a plan. Let's get moving."

"What will we tell the state police anyway?" Sue asked.

"Anything," I answered, "as long as it gets them here."

We stepped out into the night again.

Only this time, it was darker. Colder.

The dirt road stretched out before us, a stripe of pale stone and gravel cutting through the shadow. If I'd walked the trail once, I'd walked it a thousand times, but it seemed more unfamiliar. Trees I had seen since I was a boy now looked strange, and each footstep felt uncertain, as if the whole world might give out and fall apart beneath my feet.

Looking back, I could no longer see Cecil's place. It was lost in the night. With every step, I felt as though I was leaving my life—the life I'd known for so long—behind, never to return. No more funning with my cousin. No more weekly poker games. No more Cold Creek beer. No more—

"A car!" Sue gasped and dashed off.

Sure enough, a car sat on the side of the dirt road. The extinguished globes of the headlights winked at us as we approached.

"Shit," Jack said. "That's Doc Bishop's car."

The outside of the car was beat up, the trunk, roof, and hood crumpled, the doors battered in. The windows were smashed, the glass broken in spider web designs. The inside looked as if someone had let a souped-up chainsaw loose upon the seats, the dash, the floorboards, and the driver. The seat cushions were slashed, the dash busted. Blood coated the windshield and soaked into the upholstery.

"He must have encountered another of those creatures," Sue said.

Poor Doc Bishop.

As we searched the car, a high-pitched cackling noise echoed through the darkness. Another eerie cry answered. Then another.

"What's that sound?" Sue asked. "It's awful."

"Coyotes," I said.

The yipping of the coyotes erupted from the brush again, closer now, as the coyotes inspected our presence.

"If those vampires can control spiders," Sue asked, "what's to stop them from sending coyotes after us?"

"She's right," Jack said. "In the movies, Dracula controlled wolves. Hell, he could turn into one. Maybe those draculas turned into coyotes."

"I don't reckon a vampire can control a coyote," I said. "Way I see it, coyotes are about the oldest tricksters in the world. They may be animals, but they ain't dumb, and they're too crafty to let themselves be controlled by anyone."

My companions seemed satisfied by the answer, but from the shadows, the coyotes laughed at my reasoning.

* * *

In another ten minutes, we reached the home of Cordelia Miles and her parents, Arthur and Rebecca. Lights shone through the windows, but the car wasn't in the gravel driveway. A knot of ice in my gut told me we wouldn't like what we found, but I mouthed a prayer as I trudged across the yard.

Funny. I became more and more religious as the night wore on.

Jack shuffled past me like one of his matinee monsters on a rampage, hunched over and clutching his hand, covered in dried blood, grunting as he climbed the steps to the front porch, calling for anyone to answer him. He wrenched open the screen door, and it almost came loose from its hinges. The front door trembled as he pounded his meaty palm against it.

"They've been here, too," Sue said, too quiet for Jack to hear, but her words were like cannon fire in my head.

Jack rushed through the door without a care as to what dangers awaited.

Shit. What could I do but follow?

In the front hall, I found the phone. I picked the receiver up and held it to my hear. Static caterwauled at me.

We found Arthur Miles in the living room. A pool of gore spread around the rocking chair where he sat. His eyes were half open, and he sort of smiled when he saw us. Most of his teeth had been broken, and bits of bone and grit clung to his bloody gums. His throat was a ruined mess.

"I thought … at first … you were one of them come back to … finish me."

Sue and I rushed to his side.

"Try to relax," Sue said. She looked around the room for something to stop the bleeding. "Help me find some towels or something."

"Too late for that," Mr. Miles said. "I'm a goner. Surprised I made it this long."

Jack stomped through the house, shouting for Cordelia. I wanted to call for her, too, but I knew it would do no good. Jack threw open every door, checked every possible hiding spot. Finding nothing, he returned and asked, "Where's Cordelia?"

"Gone. Her and her mother both They got away while I held those … monsters back." Mr. Miles grabbed Sue's arm. "I tried to stop them, but I couldn't. It was the Whatleys."

The Whatleys?

"I recognized their oldest boy. Only they were … changed. And . . . and I think I saw some of the Stubbs with them!"

So that meant they'd been afflicted with the same ailments the Stubbs had suffered. And they had the Stubbs with them. The Stubbs and the Whatleys working together—maybe the world was coming to an end after all.

With a trembling hand, Mr. Miles pulled a crumpled chewing tobacco pouch from his shirt. He took a dip and savored it. "Wife didn't like me doing this … but no sense in worrying about it … now." Tears welled in his eyes. Tobacco juice oozed from between his lips.

Jack approached the dying man. "R.F., why don't you take a load off your feet for a couple of minutes. I want to talk to Mr. Miles a bit." He squatted next to the chair and spoke to Mr. Miles in a whisper.

I slouched down next to the wall. I just needed to rest. Five minutes. No more.

"I'm sorry about your friend," Sue said. She glanced over at Jack. "About your friends."

"I am too."

She sat down next to me. Close. She smelled of fresh sweat.

"And I'm sorry about the way I acted when you returned from the Stubbs place. It … it must have been awful, what you saw there … what you had to do. I just didn't understand."

Words seemed to jump out of my mouth. I was so tired, I hardly thought about what I was saying. "I understand. I jumped to some conclusions, too. I saw that record and I wanted to snap Cecil in two." Too late, I realized what I said. Suddenly wide awake, I looked up at Sue.

She tilted her head curiously. The corner of her mouth curled. "What do you mean?"

"Oh, nothing," I said, blushing. "Forget it."

"Oh, come on. After all we've been through tonight, you might as well tell me."

I sighed. "It's just that Cecil always played Don Williams music when courting a lady."

"And that upset you?"

"Yeah," I said, "I guess it did."

She nodded and looked away. Rosy circles colored her cheeks.

"Reckon it shouldn't have bothered me none," I said. "A girl like you wouldn't consider going out with one of us country bumpkins anyway."

She drew her legs up and looked at me. "This is probably something we should talk about later. I think it's just the wrong time to even think about such things, you know?"

"You're probably right," I said.

Wasn't a "no" at least.

"You planning on taking them back to that fancy college as part of your research?" I said, looking at the bottom of her sandals, where the crushed remains of several tarantulas still clung, despite the hike. "I doubt your fellow spider scientists will look kindly on such reckless tarantula stomping."

She smiled. "Screw you, okay?"

"Promises, promises."

We left it at that, pulled our lazy asses up, and checked on Mr. Miles. Jack squeezed the old man's hand, whispered something else, and stood up. Mr. Miles' eyes were red and watery as he looked at us.

"We're going to try to get to town," Sue told him. "Try to get some help."

For some reason, when she said that, it sounded like a bad joke.

Mr. Miles hacked like he was coughing out a piece of gristle lodged in his windpipe.

"Go get my guns. You'll need them. They're in the hall closet."

In the hall closet, we found a hunting rifle, two pistols, and a shotgun.

"You fellas take my guns," Mr. Miles said. "Just leave one here to—" He shot a glance at Jack. "—defend myself."

Something bumped and thundered above us. Footsteps. On the roof.

"There's one of them out there," Jack said, looking up.

Brandishing my pistol, I rushed out, just in time to see a figure leap from the roof of the house and into the trees. I heard the swooping and shuffling through brush as the figure ran off into the night.

Jack and Sue joined me outside, watching the trees.

Inside, a shot rang out.

* * *

When we reached town, we discovered a nightmare.

If I'd heard the popping of machine gun fire and the rattling grind of tank treads, I wouldn't have been surprised. Main Street looked like something straight out of newsroom footage of a third-world country invasion.

Overturned cars. Broken storefront windows. Trash littering the street.

Bodies.

And there was the difference. On the news, the footage of war-torn cities showed strangers, but like I said, in Spider Creek we're all neighbors, and each mauled body wore a familiar face.

Nothing moved, except for fleeting banks of night fog.

A ghost town.

Usually, this time of early morning, the smell of cooking griddlecakes and sizzling bacon from the Redeye Diner wafted through the street. Instead, the stink of death loomed over the place like a big top tent of some madhouse circus.

The street was littered with spider carcasses. The phone lines had fallen, heavy with spiders, and power lines sizzled and writhed across the street, sparkling like electric serpents. Blood smeared the pavement, glistening. More than a couple of badly-mauled bodies lay upon the street.

At the intersection of Main Street and Lee, my heart sank. Lee Street ascended a hill beyond the Post Office and family store, directly into a residential area.

The people of Spider Creek would have been asleep when the vampires attacked.

The houses were dark and quiet. More than a couple of doors stood open, some ripped right off the hinges, even though I doubted they'd been locked in the first place.

"If they were attacked by vampires, they're going to come back as vampires themselves, right?"

Jack said nothing, just stood there, chewing his lip.

"Right?" Sue asked again.

He snapped out of his daze and looked at her with watery eyes.

"Jack," she said, "are they going to come back, too?"

He nodded. "I reckon they might."

The vampires were spreading like a disease. If we didn't stop them somehow, who would? What stood between them and the entire world?

"What do we need to do?" Sue asked.

He didn't need to answer. We all knew what needed doing.

We climbed the steps into each house, and in almost every house, we found a horror. By the time we finished, we were covered in blood as heavy as syrup, the salty taste on our lips.. Not a vampire or soon-to-be vampire remained.

Except for Jack.

"It's so dark," he said, looking at the crimson stains upon his hands. "Not like the movies."

The front of the Presbyterian church was defiled with splashes of blood, but the doors were intact, the stained glass window unbroken. The sign out front read XXXXXXX. I crossed the lawn, climbed the steps to the front doors, and put my ear against the wood.

"They wouldn't be able to go in there," Jack said. "Holy ground."

But I heard sounds within. Voices. Crying. I pulled open the door—

And stared down the cavernous barrel of a .45.

"Don't fucking move," a high-pitched voice commanded.

Holding my hands up, I tilted my head and looked around the barrel. "Evening, Annie. You want to get this gun out of my face?"

"R.F.?" the frazzled police dispatcher said. "What are you doing here?"

"Right now I'm wishing you'd put this gun away."

She reluctantly lowered the pistol. Without the threat of a bullet between the eyes taking all my attention, I saw several kids in the church, huddled together and scared, but alive.

Behind the woman holding the gun, a child's voice whispered in the dark. "Did you hear what she said? She said the F word."

Living children.

"They attacked not too long after you called," Annie said. "I was able to get a few of the kids rounded up. One of them came up with the idea of hiding in the church. Said we were being attacked by vampires."

"Smart kid," Jack said. "May have saved your ass."

"W-what's happening?" Annie asked. She sagged against me. Her body trembled.

A screeching cry echoed through the hills.

"What the hell is that? It sounds like the noise Seth was making when he called the spiders… only worse."

Jack had broken out in a cold sweat. His flesh was pallid.

"It's him. The master. He's calling us … all the others to him. To him, we're nothing but lower creatures, like the spiders were to Seth."

"How do you know?"

"Because I can feel him. He's afraid. He's afraid of us. He knows what we've done to the Stubbs children and to Seth. He's connected to us. He's never had anyone destroy one of his brood before. He's powerful, but he's not foolish. He's scared of us."

"Jack," I said, "are you saying he's called all the vampires to one place?"

He nodded.

"And you know where?"

"Yeah." He licked his lips and swallowed. "He's calling me, too."

"The sun will be up soon, and we'll have daylight on our side," I said. "If we stop them now, we'll be able to get them all at one time. Where are they going?"

"The Whatley place."

I turned to Sue. She must have known what I was about to ask, because she started shaking her head before I even got the words out.

"No," she said. "I'm staying with you."

"You can't. I need you to find a way to West Plains to get help. There's bound to be a car you can use around here somewhere."

"What about her?" she nodded to Annie.

"The children need her here."

"Come with me then."

"If this thing keeps spreading, we're looking at Hell on Earth. Jack and I are gonna try to put an end to it by killing the Master. You've got to get help, though, in case we don't make it. Besides, there might be other survivors."

"So why not wait to kill this master vampire once we get help?"

"Because we can't even be sure the authorities will believe you. Besides, we don't have time to wait."

I knew a thing or two about vampires, too, although I never put much thought into it. Hell, you can't hardly turn on the TV late at night without seeing a vampire movie. If Hollywood was right, we might be able to save Jack. If we could kill the master before Jack turned, maybe he wouldn't turn at all.

"And if the movies are wrong?"

"Then at least I'll be able to get a little payback for Cecil. We got these vampires scared. That means we can hurt them. We can kill them."

Suddenly, Sue grabbed hold of my shirt collar and pulled me to her, planting a kiss on me that damn near blew the boots off my feet. I ain't ashamed to say I felt as warm and tingly as a school boy sneaking his first kiss beneath the bleachers, and when she pulled away, I just sort of stood there, still puckered up and stammering.

"Make sure you come back alive," she said.

* * *

Hardly a word passed between Jack and me as we made our way through the hills, this time heading to the Whatley place to kill a master vampire.

"If I turn," Jack said, "you kill me."

"That ain't gonna happen."

"If it does, though, you kill me. I'd sure as hell do the same to you."

"All right, but it ain't happening, because we're gonna kill the Master."

An uncomfortable notion nagged at the back of my mind. "Those people back in town," I said. "Maybe we didn't do right by them."

"How do you figure?"

"If we kill the Master, they wouldn't turn, at least that's what we're hoping, but we drove stakes into every one we found. We—"

"They were already dead. If we kill the Master—and that's a pretty big if—all we've done is drive a few wooden posts into corpses. There's no coming back from the dead, unless it's as one of those things."

Jack shielded his eyes from the glare of the rising sun.

"You all right?" I asked.

"I think so. Just burns is all. We need to hurry."

I looked at him.

He wiggled the fingers of his broken hand at me.

* * *

A collection of sagging, rotting shacks, barns, and chicken coops made up the Whatley farm. The chicken coop doors stood open, some hanging loose on the hinges, and tufts of feathers littered the rocky path. The feathers danced in a light breeze that carried the stink of chicken shit. Looked like a coyote had a heyday in the coop. A whole pack of coyotes. I spotted the ripped remains of chickens in the weeds. The carcasses looked like they might have been there for thirty years. They were withered. Dry. Drained of blood. The hogs, too, were withered husks, grey and brittle, eyes sunken, sprawled in the pig pen. Not a drop of blood pooled in the stinking mud and shit.

The farm reeked of the all too familiar rotted meat stink, but there was another smell, too, something like sulphur, lingering in the air.

Under the protection of the sunlight, we tromped through the grounds without fear of a vampire attack. We knew, though, as soon as we entered one of the shuttered houses, we'd be in danger, possibly from every vampire in the county, and there was no telling how many that might be.

We rounded a corner and heard a furtive movement, a weak moaning.

Curled up like a dying spider, an old man squatted next to a weed-choked woodpile. With his arms wrapped around his knees, he shivered, rocked back and forth slightly, and sobbed, his head hung low. He flinched, but did not look up, as we approached.

"Who's there?" he asked, his voice low as if he both wanted an answer and was afraid someone might hear. "Who's there?"

I recognized his grizzled, raspy voice.

Ezekiel Whatley.

"It's R.F. Coven and Jack Sutherland, Mr. Whatley," I answered.

"What are you boys doing here?" he asked. His head quivered from side to side, but he did not look up. "You shouldn't be here. Bad things are about."

"We know, sir."

"You seen them?" He moaned—a defeated sound.

"Are you all right, Mr. Whatley? Are you hurt?"

I smelled the stink of burning coal and brimstone.

Now I noticed dried blood upon his hands, tracing the outline of his wrinkled skin, staining his fingers brownish red.

"Mr. Whatley?"

He raised his head.

Where his eyes should have been, only gaping holes remained. Blackened tissue puffed along the interior of the sockets, and oozing blisters clustered upon the surrounding skin. Tears of dirt, blood, and puss snaked down Ezekiel's cheeks.

Someone had taken a hot poker to his eyes, I thought.

"Who did this?" I asked.

"He was so bright." His breath hitched. "So terrible to look upon. But I couldn't turn my eyes away."

His fingertips lightly touched the seared flesh, and he flinched and snapped his hand away. The corners of his mouth spasmed, but instead of sobbing again, he told us how his family sought to bring their long feud with the Stubbs to an end, and how they damned themselves in the process.

"We shouldn't have called up what could not be put down," he said. "We conjured the devil. Called him up to help us end our feud once and for all."

I thought about the bluejays Cecil mentioned. If the devil had been called up in Spider Creek, they would have had no reason to make their Friday trip to Hell. Dead frogs coming back to life, the blood moon—all side effects of whatever witchcraft had been used to summon the devil.

"We asked him to give us a weapon," the old man said, "something we could use against them. He ... he promised to give us a weapon. He gave us—"

The Master, I thought.

"A thing straight out of hell," the old man whispered. "One of his brood crawled up from a festering hole in the ground."

A dracula.

"What did you do?" Jack asked.

"We should have known better, because his words were soaked in just enough honey to cover the taste of the poison. I never wanted them to take my own family, to make them like—"

"You old bastard!" Jack reached down with both hands and hoisted Ezekiel off the ground like a rag doll. "You know what you've done? You know how many people died?"

The old man trembled. He brought his gnarled hands to the ruins of his eyes.

"The whole town!" Jack spat, shaking the wizened sorcerer. I heard the old man's bones snapping with each shake. "All of them dead, because of you!"

I grabbed Jack's shoulder. "Let him go. He's done for already. No use in killing him now."

Big Jack looked to be on the verge of tears, his eyes ringed with red as he stared into the eyeless face of the man who had called a vampire into our world. The large man's hands flexed at the sorcerer's scrawny neck, and if he wanted to, he could have ripped him in half. Instead, he dropped him into a squirming, sobbing pile in the dirt.

I leaned next to him, and he coughed up a glob of blood and spit.

"Ezekiel," I said, "we come to kill that thing. Where is it?"

His crooked finger wavered in the direction of a pair of bulkhead storm cellar doors.

"That's it then," I told Jack. "That's where we'll find him."

"Time's a wasting."

As we turned away, Ezekiel coughed, "It'll take more to kill it than it does the others." He collapsed into a wet hacking fit, then rasped, "Drive a stake through his heart, but you'll have to take off his head, too."

He started coughing again, each whoop racking his spindly body more forcefully than even Jack's manhandling. We walked towards the storm cellar and threw open the doors. A smell like roadkill rotting in the sun rose from below. Just then, I realized the old man had stopped coughing. I looked back, and saw him laying on his side, dead like the rest of his family, but staring after us with those hollow eyes.

We set fire to each and every one of the houses. The desiccated wood went up like paper. Screams came from inside. When the barn went up, a pair of figures broke out, and as soon as the sunlight touched them, they exploded in a cloud of green smoke.

Took less than a half hour, but we were covered in sweat, and Jack looked as pale as could be.

"You all right?" I asked.

"Don't feel good, but I'll be fine as soon as we finish this."

All that remained was the Master.

Throwing open the storm cellar doors, we leaned down and peered into the shadows.

"How do you reckon we're gonna get him out of there?" Jack asked.

"Think he'd come out if we asked nicely?"

"Why don't you stick your hand down there and wiggle your fingers?"

"Not hardly." I knew some old boys who fished for catfish by sticking their hands beneath rocks and using their fingers for bait. When a catfish nipped them, they grabbed a hold and yanked the fish out of the water. I thought they were about crazy as Hell for trying something like that with a fish, let alone a vampire. "Guess we'll have to go down and get him."

"You go first," Jack said.

We descended into the cellar.

* * *

The storm cellar was damp and dark. A single, catawampus wooden support beam kept the whole place from collapsing. Like stored food reserves, several people lay in the dirt—people I recognized, even—

"Cordelia!" Jack cried.

The pretty young woman and her mother lay in the dirt. They must not have made it out of town after all.

"She looks all right," I said. "Leave her be and let's find the Master."

Spiders by the hundreds crawled around the chamber. They scurried around our feet, but did not approach.

"Why aren't they attacking us?" I asked, but Jack didn't say a word.

The spindly, desiccated thing came into view. It nested in a tangle of roots along one of the dirt walls. His face was vaguely human, but sunken and twisted into something demonic. A couple of bodies, dry as termite-eaten wood, lay at his feet.

So this is the bastard who's been causing all the trouble, I thought. Doesn't look like much to me.

The master raised his head, bared his wickedly curved fangs, and hissed. In the darkness, his bulging eyes gleamed like miniature blood-colored moons. Flecks of rusty brown freckled his face, and a curdled beard of thick gore clung to his lower lip and chin, dribbling down to his breastbone and chest.

My fingers tightened around the stake. My nails dug half-moon gashes in my palms.

A fine rain of dust trickled from the ceiling and stirred in the air between me and the monster in a ghost-like veil.

My muscles coiled like wire. Tension rushed up from my toes, through my legs, my stomach, and my arms. My jaw clenched so tight I thought my teeth might snap at the gumline.

"Hold him down, Jack," I said.

Jack—

A dry cackle from the master set the hairs at the nap of my neck on end. I was suddenly aware that Jack no longer stood by my side. Stepping back as my confidence drizzled away, I looked for my friend.

I somehow knew where I'd find him.

Big Jack—my best friend since childhood, the strongest and toughest man in the county, the man who had knocked Old Samson flat with a single punch—crouched over Cordelia's unconscious form. He scooped her into his arms and held her close. His fingers flexed, kneading at her like the paws of a kitten nursing at the teat.

The slurping noises were the worst.

Cordelia's body sagged, her head lolling back to reveal the ragged wound at her throat, blood still pumping in slowing spurts to the earthen floor. Jack's baleful eyes met my own as he dropped his victim and rose to his full height. His head almost brushed the ceiling, and I reckoned he could have brought the whole place down around us if he set his mind to it.

"Aw, shit."

Jack slammed into me with the full force of a runaway locomotive. My feet left the ground and the wind blasted out of my lungs in a grunt. My back smashed into the single support beam, and I heard either the wood or my spine give way with a splintering crack. I hit the ground with Jack pressing down on top of me.

The large man let out a long, weary groan, and his muscles went slack. A rotten egg smell assaulted my senses.

When he charged, my friend impaled himself on the stake I had intended to drive into the heart of the Master. The wooden point ruptured his heart, and Big Jack was no more.

I like to think he threw himself on the stake on purpose.

Pain overwhelmed me then, and I slipped into unconsciousness.

* * *

Sometime later, I awoke, thinking Big Jack could damn sure hit hard when he wanted to. A shame he passed on his wrestling career. I lay with my eyes closed, half dreaming of being in my bed, sleeping off a Cold Creek hangover and mentally counting my winnings from the poker game. In another hour or so, I'd drag my sorry butt out of bed and slog through the day. Maybe later I'd ask Sue to go out to a honky-tonk with me and light up the dance floor and—

I remembered where exactly I was. My senses sharpened, focused on the smell of dirt and blood; the ache of my bruised ribs and back; and the angry pain at my throat.

My throat.

I almost brought my hand up to check the wound I knew must surely be there. I scrambled to my feet, trying to calculate how long I'd been out, looking around for any sign of the Master.

I felt his will pushing into my mind, digging in like a tick. For several horrifying seconds, I wanted what he wanted. My thoughts weren't my own, and I longed for endless darkness, endless suffering, and endless rivers of blood.

He was in my head!

Hammering in my chest, my heart sounded like a tribal drum. My blood thundered like whitewater rapids.

I was still alive. I was not a—

A dracula.

My eyes strayed to Jack's body.

I might have a chance, but only if I killed the Master before I changed.

I grinned, but it more likely looked like a snarl.

I spotted the Master, nesting again in the roots and runners and dirt of the cellar wall. His sunken eyes were closed. His arms were crossed over his chest, protecting his heart.

Weak daylight still trickled in from the bulkhead doors. The ceiling seemed to sag and creak, and the rain of dust was steady. Pieces of the support beam lay scattered about the floor.

I stepped over Big Jack's body and grabbed a two-foot shard of the beam.

I approached the Master, and he did not stir.

His thoughts invaded my mind.

I raised the stake, and he did not stir.

The psychic seed tick of his will suckled at the core of my being, and I fought with all my might to remain in control. I was not a vampire, not yet, and if I killed this bastard I could be myself again.

I rammed the weapon into his chest, cutting through his crossed wrists, pinning them in place, into his heart, and out of his back and into the dirt wall behind him.

He woke, screeching.

He threw himself at me, but the stake held him in place. He kicked, and his arms trembled, but he could not free himself to scratch at me.

I pulled out my pocket knife and flicked out the blade.

Mental commands battered at my brain, but I blocked them out. I thought of the look on Cecil's face as he died. I thought of Jack drinking the blood of the woman he loved. The Master insinuated his will upon me, but all I felt was rage.

Grabbing him by the hair, I pushed his head back against the wall.

He screeched "Rhee! Rhee! Rhee!" but no one was left to listen, except me, and I honestly didn't give a shit.

Suddenly, a tarantula jumped onto my hand and sunk its hangs into the meat between my thumb and forefinger. Another jumped onto me. A third. Another landed on the back of my neck and scurried under my sweaty shirt collar. I ignored the pain from the bites.

I stabbed the knife into the side of his neck and started to cut. The vampire thrashed his head left to right, his eyes filled with anger and terror, his teeth snapping fruitlessly as I sawed. My knuckles brushed against dead, flaking skin. The blade rasped against bone, and I leaned into the cut, tearing through his neck.

He sensed his fate and stopped struggling. His face fell slack, and he said, "But you belong to me," or some such shit.

"Ifs and buts, asshole. Ifs and buts."

I ripped his head from his body. I felt his soul, like an ice-cold wind racing through the chambers of my heart, as his soul fell back to Hell. I touched Hell, I think, in that moment, and it was one of the most chilling things I have ever experienced, because I felt something greater, more terrible than even the Master, watching me. Instantly, the Master started turning to dust. His skin shriveled down to his bones, his bones deteriorating like termite-eaten wood. Green vapor billowed from the cancerous holes opening in his flesh.

I watched, then drew in a deep breath, despite the rancid decay clinging to the air.

Over.

But I felt no different.

I hung my head and coughed out a laugh. Movies can't be right about everything, I reckon.

The spiders, free of his control, scurried away.

The ceiling groaned. I looked up and saw the timber start to come apart, the stress of the missing support post finally too much for the sagging floor to bear.

I didn't even have time for an "oh, shit," before the ceiling crashed down upon me like fifteen tons of pain.

* * *

So that's my story, true as I know how to tell it.

I feel right awful about what happened to Cecil and Jack. They deserved better. They were my best friends, and I'm proud to have been there with them when the fires of Hell breathed down our necks. Of course, it goes without saying I'm glad Sue made it out alive. I only hope she's able to go on with her life and achieve her dreams ... if she can forget the nightmares she saw in Spider Creek.

Ifs and buts, my friend, ifs and buts.

As for me, my job wasn't finished when the building collapsed in a flaming heap upon me and the Master. As the darkness and the dust and the smoke plumed around me and the ceiling crashed down in a wash of heat and pain, I thought for sure my life had come to its end. But even the crushing weight of the timber did not kill me. I awoke sometime later, waves of pain lapping at me as if I lay with my feet submerged in an ocean of agony. My legs and lower back were shattered and twisted, but I still drew breath, and my heart still beat.

If I kept still, the pain wasn't so bad.

I lay there for what seemed like forever, waiting for death to finally take me.

I grew cold. My breathing grew short and quick. My heartbeat slowed.

Thin beams of daylight pierced holes in the wreckage around me. The settling debris creaked. Dust motes swirled in the rays.

I was not afraid.

There in the dark, waiting, I touched my fingers to the wound at my throat. My blood was as thick and sticky as jam.

I reckon I should have guessed what would become of me, having been bit by that thing, but surviving, just as poor Seth Stubbs had survived for a time, before the hunger for blood overcame him.

My mouth was as dry as cotton.

The movies were wrong. Killing the master vampire didn't save those who had been … infected. Most of the day had slipped away. Nightfall was approaching again. And I was still alive, even though I was busted in a dozen places.

The cowboy has no happy song to sing as he rides into the sunset.

The sunset.

I nearly passed out from the pain as I crawled from the rubble, pulling myself towards the last rays of failing daylight filtering in from above. I tore my fingernails down to the quick. I dragged my crippled legs behind me, sacks of quivering muscle and crushed bone. Shivering from the strain, stinging sweat running into my eyes, I reached a small opening in the debris. Through the hole, I saw clear blue sky, marred by columns of smoke. I smelled smoke and blood … but, distantly, I smelled fresh air and pastures, too. I placed my trembling hand upon the mass of wood and stone and soot blocking my path. With a shove, I widened the opening so I might fit through.

I pulled myself into the open and that's when my strength or willpower finally gave out. I collapsed in the dirt with the stink of ash and smoke and blood filling my nostrils and warm, wet tears rolling down my cheeks.

So, again, I wait.

I haven't changed yet, but it's only a matter of time.

I remembered Sue's little tape recorder—the one I picked up off the floor during the tarantula attack—and pulled it out of my pocket. Since I don't expect to be around for much longer, I reckon it can't hurt to record this account of what happened, so maybe—just maybe—it won't happen again.

My legs are starting to knit themselves back together. I can even move them a little. It's a strange feeling. Warm and cold at the same time. Painful and soothing. I figure in another hour I'll be able to stand and walk away from here. But if I'm lucky I won't make it that long.

I don't want to be no vampire.

Listen real close. You hear them? Coyotes. Six or maybe more. Showed up just a few minutes ago, scrounging around for an early evening snack. They're yipping and snarling nearby—and coming closer. They sound mighty hungry and there's blood—my blood—in the air.

Like I said in the beginning, you'll have to judge the ending of my story for yourself.

I can hear the coyotes rustling in the trees.

I'm going to turn the tape off now, because I don't reckon anybody wants to hear what's coming next.

All I have to do is wait.

"Blood Feud: A Vampire Yarn... With Spiders" first appeared in the anthology THICKER THAN BLOOD, Tigress Press (2005).

This, along with CROOKED HILLS, ranks among my favorite work. It is dedicated to my father, who was called R.F. by friends and family. Some of the elements – the bull, the tarantulas – are drawn from actual events. Spider Creek, I think, is just up the road from the town of Crooked Hills. The two have a lot in common.

This novella has been adapted into a graphic novel, BLOOD FEUD, from Oni Press.

- CB

SLAVES TO THE WHEEL

The painfully bright glow of headlights flooded through the rear window of the car. Sarah clutched the steering wheel tightly and watched the approaching vehicle - a truck? - in the rear-view mirror. A bead of sweat trickled down her face. She turned the key in the ignition for what might have been the hundredth time in the past hour. She knew it would do no good, but she hoped, prayed, the car would start. The engine screeched, coughed, and fell silent.

Sarah's father used to say, "We're slaves, you know. Slaves to the wheel. Our fancy cars break down, and we're helpless." She had laughed at him for saying that at one time, calling him a crotchety old man, but now she understood what he meant all too well.

The vehicle slowed as it passed, and Sarah's mounting panic gave way to relief as she recognized it as a tow truck. Painted words on the door read APPLETON AUTO REPAIR. Brake lights flashed. The truck pulled onto the shoulder in front of Sarah's car and rumbled to a stop.

The door swung open, and a large man in filthy coveralls emerged from the truck. The red glare of the brake lights illuminated his face as he approached and peered at Sarah through the window.

Her anxiety returned briefly, coldly. She tried the key again. A SERVICE ENGINE SOON light pulsed weakly. How could she know this man meant no harm? How could she know he wouldn't --

"Stop it," she told herself through gritted teeth.

"You all right?" the man called, puffing plumes of frosty breath and tapping at the driver's side window with his stubby fingers.

"Good thing you came by when you did," Sarah said as she unrolled the window a crack -- just a crack -- to greet the man. Cold, damp air stung her cheek. "I thought I might be out here all night."

"Broke down, did you?" The man, whose grease-stained name tag identified him as Bud, offered a grin that was more gums than teeth. "Bad luck on a night like this."

Even though she used her thick coat as a blanket, Sarah felt frozen down to the bone and she shivered uncontrollably. "Do you think you could take a look?"

"Guess so. Pop the hood for me and sit tight while I see what I can do."

Sarah pulled the release lever and sat back, bunching the coat tightly around herself, as Bud walked around front to lift the hood and examine the engine. She hoped the problem was simple and easy to repair -- a loose wire or the like -- because she wanted to get moving as soon as possible. She glanced at her watch and sighed.

She'd been driving home from college for the weekend and was eager to arrive, because her brother from Colorado and sister from Texas were also visiting. If she hadn't been in such a hurry, she would have heeded the advice of her roommates and waited until morning to leave. Now she was stuck in the back of beyond, at night, with a four hour drive still ahead and no one to blame but herself.

The town of Appleton looked different at night, she decided. She had driven through the place a dozen times, never paying much attention. She never realized how much the area around the town -- with the twisted trees clawing their way out of the bare, rolling hills; the dilapidated and rotted houses; and the tangled, overgrown brush -- made her uneasy.

Waiting in the car, too frightened to get out and walk to the nearest phone, she could have sworn she saw several pairs of gleaming, almost human eyes staring at her from the surrounding forest.

She shook her head at her foolishness.

Still, when Bud slammed the hood down, Sarah yelped and jumped in surprise.

"Didn't scare you, did I?" he asked.

"A -- A little."

"Sorry." He looked towards the hood, then back to Sarah, sheepishly. "Well, I'm afraid there ain't a whole lot I can do here. Can't even tell what's wrong, really. Must be something with a computer chip or something. Something's always wrong with the computer chips in new cars like this."

"Oh." Sarah clenched her hands into tight fists. Her fingernails bit deep into her palms. "So there's no chance of me getting back on the road again tonight, is there?"

"I was just now going home," Bud said, "but I can't rightly leave a pretty thing like you stranded out in the cold, I guess. Tell you what, why don't I tow your car back to the garage and see if I can't get it running again?"

Something about the way Bud looked at her almost persuaded Sarah to turn him down. She glanced at her watch again. She wanted to get home and she certainly didn't want to spend the night out here in the cold.

"You mean you'll work on it? Tonight?"

"Sure. Why not? I wasn't going to do much anyway, except maybe watch the late show, and there's a TV in the shop."

"I really appreciate this," Sarah said, getting out of the car and stepping into the cold night air.

* * * *

Bud spent the next few minutes hooking Sarah's car to the tow truck. He glanced up every now and again to eye Sarah, who paced nearby, watching nervously as the mechanic clamped the heavy chains in place.

"You can wait in the truck if you want," Bud said. "Nice and warm in there."

"I'm fine," she answered, even though the frigid wind sliced through her coat and sweater. "Don't worry about me."

She noticed for the first time the terrible condition of the tow truck. Dents and scratches, like scars and bruises, covered almost every inch of the metal body. A crack spiderwebbed across the front windshield.

"What happened?" she asked, nodding towards the truck.

"You mean how come my pride and joy's so banged up? Damn kids. Last Halloween a bunch of them decided it would be right funny if they tore up my truck. I have to keep it locked inside nowadays. Soon as I get the time, I'm gonna fix it up."

"Nice kids."

"That's all right. They'll get what's coming to them."

Something stirred in the woods, scurried through the dry pine straw and fallen leaves. A pair of glistening eyes winked for an instant in the darkness.

"Did you see that?" Sarah pointed towards the woods. "Something's out there!"

Bud looked up, squinted, and shrugged. "Probably nothing. A raccoon or squirrel." He stood and brushed his hands on his overall's leg. "Anyway, we're all set."

Sarah took one last look into the woods before climbing into the tow truck. Cigarette burns and spilled coffee stains covered the frayed fabric seats. Crumpled gum wrappers and empty chewing tobacco packages littered the floorboards. An open fruit cocktail can, serving as a spittoon, sat on the dashboard, almost overflowing.

A pistol lay beside the can, gleaming in the moonlight. Sarah scooted away from the weapon instinctively.

"Don't mind that," Bud said, climbing into the seat beside her and turning the key in the ignition. "I just keep that around for protection."

The truck rumbled to life. Static and country music hissed loudly through the radio speakers. The truck rattled and shook as if the frame would fall apart as Bud drove along the desolate stretch of blacktop. Sarah looked out the back window to make sure her car was all right. She thought she saw a thin, stooping figure scurry across the road. A startled gasp escaped her throat.

"Your car's fine," Bud said. "Not a scratch on it. Besides my shop's the best in the whole county."

The only shop in the whole county, Sarah guessed and she slid an inch or two away from Bud when she thought he wasn't looking.

* * * *

With a heavy ring of keys, Bud unlocked the scarred wooden door and escorted Sarah into the front lobby of Appleton Auto Repair and Body Shop. A long, cluttered counter filled most of the room. Crumpled paperwork covered the countertop. A television, with a twisted clothes hanger serving as an antennae, sat on one end of the counter. A cash register sat next to the TV. The lights were off, but a soda machine cast a flickering glow into the room. A few seats, which looked to have been torn from an old car, were pushed against the wall, facing a large, fingerprint-smeared window.

"You wait here. Make yourself at home." Bud clicked on the television. The fuzzy, black and white picture faded into view. "Might want to watch TV. Late show's supposed to be a good one."

"Thanks," Sarah said.

"Need a drink?" Bud started to dig in his pocket for change.

"No, thanks. I'm fine."

"Okay. Phone's over on the wall if you need to give your folks a call. I'll get to work out here. Shouldn't take too long."

Bud exited through a side door leading back to the garage. Sarah dialed her parents' number on the rotary phone, which smelled of stale beer and cheap aftershave, and waited until her father answered sleepily. She explained the situation to him, listened to him relay the information to her mother, and assured him that she would be all right.

"With any luck," she said, crossing her fingers. "I'll be on the road again in no time."

"You just be careful," her father said. "You know how some of these mechanics might try to take advantage of you."

"I know, Daddy. I'll be careful."

Hammering rang out from the garage -- metal against metal. Sarah winced at the sound, unsure of what damage Bud might be inflicting on her car.

"I have to go now, Daddy. See you soon."

"Sarah -- "

"Daddy, I'm a big girl." She hung up quickly, before her father had a chance to respond.

Listening to the hammering, she tried to open the door leading to the garage, but found it locked. She knocked, doubting Bud could hear over all the racket. Shrugging, she walked across the room and collapsed into one of the ratty car seats. She hoped Bud knew what he was doing. Not that it mattered. Good mechanic or not, Bud was the only person available to do the job at such an hour. He was her only chance of getting her car running again tonight. Sarah figured she was in for a nasty surprise when it came time to pay, but she had no other choice.

Sarah stared out the window at the tall, chain-link fence surrounding the garage. The fence, she thought, looked better suited to a concentration camp than a repair shop. She felt a wave of weariness roll over her. She stared at the tiled ceiling, and listened to the sounds of repair from the garage and the monotonous dialogue and deep pipe organ music from the horror movie on the television. Before long, she found herself struggling to keep her eyes open.

* * * *

The sounds in the garage invaded her dreams.

She found herself alone in an industrial nightmare. Massive, steel pipes rose out of a vast plane of concrete. She saw Bud, smiling, wiping his dirty hands clean. Sticky oil dripped from his hands and pooled at his feet. She saw her car, covered in rivulets of the same dripping oil, only she thought it wasn't oil, wasn't oil at all. She saw a red glow illuminating the interior of her car, where a gaunt, ghoulish face, a face which contorted into a vision of anguish, screamed and screamed and screamed.

Sarah awoke, nearly jumping to her feet.

On the television, a hapless victim screamed as a vampire stalked towards her.

Rubbing her eyes, Sarah laughed at herself.

A sound -- a soft scratching -- drew her attention towards the window. She blinked. With a sudden movement, an emaciated figure staggered out of the shadows, naked and covered in dark streaks of dried blood, staring at her with bulging, white eyes.

"Bud!" Sarah shrieked.

The thing at the window leaped back and scrambled away on its hands and knees.

Bud burst into the room, looking back and forth, a large wrench clutched in his hands like a weapon. "What? What is it?"

"A man!" Sarah gasped. "There's a man outside!"

Bud peered out the window, pressing his dirty hands against the glass, then shook his head.

"Do you see anything?" Sarah asked.

"Not a thing. Whoever it was must have gotten out of here pretty quick. Probably just some kid looking to cause trouble."

"He--"

On the television, the pale, grotesque vampire, crept closer to its victim.

"God," Sarah said, slapping herself in the forehead. "I must look pretty stupid. I think I must have been dreaming. The movie . . . ."

"Too much of the late show can do that to you. You'll be all right. You see anything else, just give a holler."

"Any idea how much longer?"

"Not long now. Another hour or so."

A lot of work for a computer chip, Sarah thought. Then again, Bud probably couldn't tell a computer chip from a potato chip.

This time, when Bud entered the garage, Sarah heard the distinct click! of the door lock.

* * * *

"All done."

Bud stood in the door, smiling broadly. Sarah followed him into the garage. Slick patches of oil covered the concrete floor, as did dozens of discarded and scattered tools, an engine twisted into a tangled mass of metal in a pool of leaking fluid, and -- strangely -- bare footprints. Had Bud walked across the filthy floor without shoes?

"You're gonna be surprised at how well this car runs now. Probably runs better than ever."

"What was wrong with it?"

"Like I said, something's always going wrong with the computer chips in these new cars. Problem is, manufacturers nowadays don't care about quality. They don't care about putting hard work into their cars."

Sarah could feel the price tag for the repair job growing as Bud spoke.

"How much do I owe you?"

"Well -- " He licked his lips as he thought it over. "--Why don't we just say a hundred dollars for parts and call it even?"

"That's all?"

"Sure. I ain't greedy or nothing. I just like to work on cars." The overhead light glimmered in his eyes. "I'm what you might call a slave to the wheel."

Sarah stepped back.

A metallic crash from a room marked STORAGE startled her. She jumped and spun on her heels. She held a hand to her chest, tried to catch her breath. "What was that?"

"Oh, that ain't nothing. I just don't know how to stack oil cans I reckon."

Sarah quickly fished through her purse and handed Bud five twenty dollar bills. "Thanks for fixing my car. I really appreciate it."

"No problem." He stepped towards her and took the money. A sticky syrup-like red liquid covered his fingers. "You have a safe trip."

Sarah stared at his hands. Transmission fluid, she told herself. What else could it be?

"I-- I better be going. Don't want to keep my family waiting any longer than I already have."

Had to be transmission fluid.

"Sure thing." Bud's smile faded. He stuffed the money into his pocket and wiped his hand clean on his coveralls, smearing the inky redness across the cloth. "Let me get the door for you."

Walking past her, he hoisted the garage door open with a rattle and the screech of metal against metal. Cold air rushed into the garage.

Sarah glanced from the car to the mechanic and back to the car again. She opened the door and jumped in, making sure to press the automatic lock button once she was inside. The key dangled in the ignition. Sarah whispered a soft, "please," before starting the car. The engine purred. She threw the car into reverse and backed out of the garage.

As she passed Bud, he waved for her to stop. She rolled the window down as he approached. He leaned against the door and said, "Don't stop until you're well away from Appleton. It ain't safe to be out there alone at night. All right?"

"Sure," Sarah answered.

She rolled up the window, waved a quick good-bye to Bud, and headed on her way.

The spot where Bud's fingers had rested on the car was smeared red.

* * * *

After driving about two miles, Sarah had to admit that the engine ran more smoothly than ever. Her parents -- especially her father -- wouldn't believe the repair job cost so little. But she didn't think she would tell them too much about Bud, the mechanic, because just thinking of his toothless leer, his eyes glimmering in the shadow, chased a shiver down her spine.

Suddenly, a figure appeared alongside the road, perched like a bird atop a crooked fence post. Sarah turned to get a better look at the strange, malformed man, just as the front window exploded.

Shards of glass showered her. She hit the brakes. The tires smoked. The car skidded off the road, into a deep ditch, and lurched to a stop.

In the confusion, Sarah's chest and forehead slammed into the steering wheel. She sat back in the seat, dazed, covered with tiny cuts from the glass, gasping for breath. When her head stopped spinning and her vision cleared, she saw dozens of thin, silhouetted figures approaching the car slowly, slowly, like dreams.

A large rock lay in the seat beside her.

The strange figures hissed to each other. Sarah heard but did not understand the words. They staggered and crawled and hopped along the banks of the ditch. They were naked, and their bones protruded sharply just beneath their skin, which was covered with crisscrossing scars. They regarded her with curious and bulbous eyes which were afire in the glow of the headlights.

They surrounded her car, tapped at the windows, scraped at the glass with splintered, dirty fingernails. They reached through the remains of the shattered windshield to clutch at her.

A trickle of warm blood seeped from a gash in Sarah's forehead, stinging her eyes, blinding her for a moment.

She hit the gas, but the tires only spun in the dirt.

"What do you want?" she asked.

Several of the figures grabbed the hood of the car and wrenched it open with a strength beyond their withered muscles. Sarah tried to see what they were doing, but could not, as the car rocked and the suspension squeaked.

One of the creatures screamed -- painfully.

The engine sputtered and died. The headlights faded into blackness. The heater spat out the last of its warm air.

A cry erupted from the crowd, and they started to wander away, sinking back into the darkness, one by one, watching Sarah with their curious eyes.

Two of the creatures supported a third, whose body was covered not by scars, but by open, bleeding wounds.

Then they were gone.

Sarah sat motionless for several minutes before trying to crank the car again. The engine wouldn't even turn over. She watched the surrounding darkness, saw no sign of the strange creatures, and cautiously opened the door. It did little good to stay in the car for protection with the window broken out. She walked around to the front of the car. The bitter chill clawed at her.

Wet footprints trailed across the dry blacktop, leading away from the car. Kneeling, Sarah touched the liquid. Blood -- or transmission fluid.

Standing, she looked under the hood of the car and gasped. The engine was gone. The area beneath the hood was almost completely empty. Only a few twisted wires snaked across the empty space which should have been filled by the engine.

How had the car been running?

Coating it all was a sticky film of blood, steaming in the night air.

Slowly, Sarah started walking away from her car. She shivered in the cold, but she didn't want to stop, not until she got far away from the town of Appleton. She prayed that the next light she saw -- if she lived to see another light -- would come from the sunrise and not from the headlights of the APPLETON AUTO REPAIR tow truck.

Once upon a time, by truck broke down on this deserted dirt road. I have no mechanical know-how. In fact, vehicle repairs are one of those things that just stress me out to no end. I started walking in hopes of finding help, and this old guy stopped to give me a hand. He laughed at my plight, saying, "Ain't we all just slaves to the wheel?"

- CB

SOMEDAY DOLLS

"Isn't that Tina?" Justin asked. "What's that she's doing over there?"

His sister, Katie, shrugged.

Folks usually avoided the old Pritchard homestead. Justin and Katie almost never walked this way themselves. But Katie had begged her older brother to take the long way home after Sunday school. It was a beautiful day, after all, and the dirt road wound through lush forests and past creeks of clear water. They didn't really expect to see another soul, especially not Tina, especially not at the Pritchard place. The girl sat in the overgrown yard before the dilapidated shack. Crouching among the weeds, she chopped at the earth with a rust-speckled hand spade. Every couple of minutes, she put the spade aside and scooped away handfuls of dirt clods and pebbles.

"Hey, Tina," Justin called.

The spade plunged into the ground.

"What are you doing?"

She looked up, smiled, then continued to dig.

"Why won't she answer?" Justin asked Katie. "She's your friend. You have any idea what she's up to?"

"We're not really friends," Katie said. "No one else talks to her much—"

"That's because she's touched in the head."

"Maybe so, but it makes me feel bad, so I talk to her every now and again." Katie shook her head. "But I don't have a clue what she's thinking."

"Guess I'll go take a look."

Justin took a step, but Katie grabbed him by the arm. The abandoned property was a minefield of rusty nails, broken glass, and spider nests. One wrong step might mean a trip to Doc Regis, and that old sawbones didn't have one whit of sympathy for careless children. Parents warned children to stay away from the place for other reasons—restless haints and baby-snatching goblins. But Justin didn't believe in ghost stories, and his curiosity was riled anyhow.

"It's all right." Justin pulled free from his sister and took another step. Dry grass crunched underfoot. He looked up, letting the bright sun wash across his freckled face. "It's broad daylight. No ghosts here now."

Katie stood at the edge of the property for only a few seconds before following her older brother.

Tina wore a frilly white dress, probably what she'd worn to church this morning. She had not bothered to change, and her clothing was caked with soil. She didn't seem to care, even though her parents would more than likely take a switch to the back of her legs for ruining her best dress. She busily gouged at the earth with the rusty spade.

"You shouldn't play here," Katie said. "It's dangerous."

Tina looked up, squinting in the sunlight, and wiped her hands upon her dress.

"What are you doing, anyway?" Justin asked. "Digging a hole to China?"

Ignoring the question, the girl scrunched up her nose and stood. Dark, loose dirt fell from the folds of her dress. "Would you like to see my doll collection?" she asked.

"What on earth are you talking about?" Justin asked. "I don't care nothing about dolls."

"You'll like it."

Tugging at her older brother's sleeve, Katie asked, "Can't we see it, Justin?"

"Come with me." Tina turned and skipped across the yard. Thistles pulled at the hem of her dress. She was barefoot, and her ankles and feet were covered in fresh scratches. She climbed the rotten, sagging steps of the Pritchard house and threw open the front door. The hinges screeched like a skinned cat. "Hurry up, slowpokes!"

Termite-eaten planks creaked underfoot as Justin and Katie followed Tina onto the porch. Wouldn't take much, Justin thought, for the weakened wood to give way, and they might fall through into whatever dark, vermin and snake infested hole waited beneath. For that matter, the entire house looked like it might fall in upon itself at any moment. Justin had a bad feeling about the house, but he didn't dare say anything. He didn't want to look like a coward in front of his baby sister. Instead, he muttered, "Seems like a weird place to keep dolls."

"Not really," Tina called from inside. "You'll see."

Old newspapers, rusted cans, and bits of plaster carpeted the floor inside the house. No one had lived here since before he was born, but Justin knew all about the people who used to live here. Kids still talked about the Pritchard clan, the stories being passed down through the years. Stories of kidnappings and murders in the dead of night. Stories of squealing, squirming things locked away in dank root cellars.

"Where are your dolls?" Katie asked.

"Right through here."

Approaching an open door, Tina tucked the spade under her arm and grabbed a filthy oil lantern from a peg on the wall. A half dozen wooden matches had been stuck into the door frame. Tina plucked one up and struck it against the wall, leaving a dark score upon the plaster, along with several others. She lit the lantern, grabbed the spade from under her arm, and motioned towards the door. Beyond, stairs descended into darkness.

"After you," Tina said.

Justin and Katie went down first. Before following, Tina pull the door shut behind her. Justin looked back at her.

"We don't want anyone else to see," she said. "Do we?"

The warped wooden steps groaned as the three children descended. The splintered glass of the lantern's hood cast odd-shaped shadows along the walls, ceiling, and floor. Darkness recoiled from the approaching light. Below, Justin saw a patch of earthen floor.

"Dad says we shouldn't play here," Katie whispered.

"We'll be all right." Justin's voice was shaky.

"You afraid?" Tina asked.

"No," Justin blurted. He took a breath, then said again, "No."

"Most kids think this house is haunted."

"I don't believe in ghosts."

"You should."

Justin stepped onto the floor. The dirt was softer than he expected.

"I know what everyone says about this place." Tina brushed past. "But they've got it all wrong. My grandma told me the truth about the Pritchards, about how they were God-fearing folks, but cruel and mean-spirited, too, the men most of all. A bunch of years back, they found out a coven of witches were meeting in the woods late at night. These women weren't hurting anyone, leastways not anyone who didn't deserve it, but do you know what the Pritchards did to them? They burned them, hanged them, and drowned them in Miller's Creek. And when they were done, they buried the bodies on their property."

"I-Is that what you were digging up?" Justin asked. "The bodies?"

The glow pushed the shadows back as Tina swung the lantern around. Six figures leaned and squatted along the basement walls. The light spilled across their withered, leering faces. They were wormy, desiccated things, their skin flaking and peeling away, patches of dirt, like flesh upon their bones.

Justin and Katie gasped. Justin took a single steps backwards, towards the steps.

Tina waved at the bodies, showing off her prized possessions.

"This is Audrey Mason. She was stoned to death for poisoning a farmer's crops. See how her skull is caved in?"

She moved towards the next figure.

"This is Ester Hayden. They say she smothered her own baby so she could create a—." She searched for the right word. "—a familiar to do her bidding."

"What's a familiar?" Katie asked.

"It's a demon," Justin said. "At least I think that's what it is."

Smiling proudly, Tina thrust the lantern towards a third figure.

"And this one—" She motioned to a grinning, blackened thing. "—is Maddie Someday. She's my favorite. When they tied her to the stake and lit her on fire, she promised that she'd return and gather her coven once again."

Katie pressed close against her brother.

"Someday," Tina said, and it was not a name, not exactly, but the designation of some future time and event. "She said she'd bring her sisters back together again. And the people who killed them—the men who killed them—couldn't do anything to stop them."

Justin stepped in something wet and slippery.

"What's this?"

The puddle was black in the dim light.

"Ewwww . . ." said Katie.

Justin knelt and touched the puddle. His fingers came away red and sticky. "It looks like—"

"Of course, silly., Tina giggled. "My girls have to eat if they're going to grow up big and strong."

Justin turned and saw Tina hold the lamp close to her face. The flickering light cast pools of shadow under her eyes. She grinned playfully, drew in a breath, and blew out the flame.

Blackness.

"Hey!"

He whirled around.

Where was Katie?

"If you're trying to scare me, Tina, it's not working."

How could he feel so lost in such a small room?

A room that seemed to be getting smaller, pressing in on him.

"Katie?"

He thought he heard the bodies of the witches move, the bones creaking, the rotted teeth chattering.

Something brushed past him.

"Katie!"

She did not answer.

He heard the padding of feet.

A shuffling.

He wished he hadn't let Katie talk him into taking the back way home after Sunday school.

"Katie," he hissed. "Katie!"

No answer.

"Katie, be careful!"

A hand gripped his. He jumped, thinking one of the decaying things had reached out and grabbed him. The fingers were warm, though, and squeezed his own gently.

"I'm right here," Katie said.

"Where is she?" Justin asked. "Where's Tina!"

"I don't know."

"We've got to get out of here!" He pulled her in the direction he hoped might lead to the stairs. "Come on. Hurry."

Katie tugged against him.

"Katie, please!"

His heart felt like it might explode from his chest. He couldn't believe his sister was resisting him. For a split second, he thought of leaving her there in the darkness.

With Tina.

Tina, collecting dead bodies like dolls.

Tina, chopping up dirt with that—

A knot of ice roiled in the pit of his stomach.

"Katie! Be careful! I think Tina's still got that spade!"

"That's all right," Katie grabbed his wrist, her nails digging into his skin. "I've got one too."

Another story that has some connective threads to CROOKED HILLS. I think I have issues with root cellars. Maybe I watched EVIL DEAD II one time too many.

- CB

GALLOWS

It had been more than fifteen years since he last visited the Gallow's Tree, and the old paths were overgrown with treacherous weeds and briars. Val worried he wouldn't remember the way through the tangles of crooked oaks and pines. But as he trudged along the shadow-dappled carpentry of leaves and pine needles, he started to notice familiar landmarks—the rotting remains of a great stump, a jagged outcropping of rock with peculiar red markings—though they be concealed by moss and brambles.

"This way," he said, pushing aside a grasping, thorny vine. "I can almost make out the trail."

David followed. As he ducked beneath the vines, a thorn snagged his sleeve. He cursed and tugged his sweater free.

"Let me get this straight." He laughed. "You used to live here?"

Val nodded. He had been expecting David's sarcastic streak to bloom at any moment.

"Here," David said again.

"In the vicinity, yeah." Val glanced over his shoulder and cocked an eyebrow. "You find that hard to believe, I take it?"

"Well, yeah. No offense, man. Me of all people—I'm not judging you, but I just can't imagine you growing up in a place this … I don't know … rural."

"Eight years of my life," Val said. "My family moved here around the time I turned nine. Remember the house we passed at the edge of the woods? I grew up there."

"That old ruin?" David laughed again.

"It was in better shape back then."

"I can't imagine anyone ever living there, let alone the great Val Winters, cosmopolitan playboy."

"Houses rot," Val answered, "and people change."

With every step, Val felt the day-to-day pressures of boardroom battles and grueling conference calls and scandalous media attention. He had wondered if returning after all this time would be a good idea. Now he wondered why he had waited so long.

"Val Winters!" David's voice rang out through the forest. A flock of agitated black birds took flight from nearby branches. "King of the Wild Frontier!"

Up ahead, wiry vegetation with inch-long thorns swallowed the path. To the right, dense grey trees formed a nearly impassable wall. To the left, the path descended toward a dry creek bed. This Val remembered, only water flowed through the channel when he had last seen this place, and he had used stepping-stones to cross. He skirted down the bank and climbed the other side. David tripped when he reached the creek bed, falling to his hands and knees. He regained his footing quickly, brushing feverishly at his slacks.

"We never discussed the matter of my dry cleaning bill," he said. "And my shoes are ruined."

"Should have worn something more suited to the woods."

A snide smile curled David's lips. "Like I have anything like that."

"Haven't you ever been camping?"

"You're kidding, right?"

Offering a hand, Val hoisted David up the other side of the bank. David's palm was clammy and sweaty.

"You all right?" Val asked.

"Fine. Fine. But tell me again what we're looking for. I mean, I understand wanting to take a walk down memory lane as much as the next guy, but this—"

"We're not far now," Val said.

The path was even more overgrown on this side of the creek bed. If not for Val's memory of the route he had taken on so many occasions, they might have quickly lost their way. As they proceeded through the forest, the twilight shadows grew longer, the darkness between the hollows of trees deeper. Soon, the trail broadened, exposing a shaded clearing.

Before them loomed a massive, gnarled old tree.

Val stopped.

"This is it," he said.

The trunk of the tree was gray, and runners, like veins, threaded along the craggy bark. The limbs stretched in all directions, reaching to the edges of the clearing and forming a crisscrossing net overhead, a web ensnaring the darkening sky. The bends and knots of the branches reminded David of the arthritic arms of retired muscle builders.

"This?" David asked. "This? You drug me all the way out here for this?"

"You don't know what you're looking at."

"What did you call it?" David asked.

Val's gaze danced over the tree.

"The Old Gallows Tree," he said.

David shrugged. "Sorry, man. I was expecting a little more, I guess."

"This spot was used during lynchings," Val said. "From the branches of this tree—the Gallows Tree—criminals were executed. A lot of people believe many of the men who were killed here were innocent, victims of an overzealous lynch mob. At night the ghosts of the hanged men appear, still dangling from the branches, whispering their pleas of innocence to anyone who will listen."

"You've got a real morbid streak, Val. Did I ever tell you that?" David shook his head, but his laughter caught in his throat. "Wait a second. You're not going to tell me that you believe the stories, are you?"

"Of course I do," Val said.

A gust of wind rushed through the clearing, and the old tree limbs swayed.

"When I first heard the stories about the Gallows Tree," Val said, "I was fascinated. I always loved monsters and ghosts. They terrified me, but I loved them."

"Sounds vaguely like a co-dependent relationship," David mused.

"Smartass. You know what I mean. Then I learned that this tree was just a short hike through the woods from my house, so of course I had to check it out. I snuck out of the house one night and followed the trail back into the woods. Got lost so bad at least once that it's amazing that I ever made it out. I found the tree, though … and the stories were true."

He approached the tree, ran his fingertips along the trunk.

"The tree hasn't changed much in all these years," he said.

"So if it's true," David said, "where are these ghosts?"

Val backed away from the tree, still looking up at the crooked boughs, and sat down upon the ground. "We wait," he said.

"What? For how long?"

"As long as it takes. You don't have to stay if you don't want to." He fished the car keys from his pocket and tossed them to David. "Go on back to town, check into a motel. I'll catch up with you later."

"As if I'll be able to find my way to the car." David threw the keys back. "I guess I'm waiting with you, although I hate the idea of fueling your delusions."

As night settled around them, the air grew cold.

Val continued his story.

"Here's the thing. When I was a kid, I felt like no one wanted to talk to me. No one wanted to listen to me. We had just moved to the area. You know how it is—being different. I didn't have any friends."

"Everyone feels that way at one time or another," David said.

"Yeah, I guess so. I know it's going to sound crazy, but the tree became something of a friend to me. Not the tree. The spirits. I listened to them and they listened to me."

"Val, if you're not pulling my leg with all this, the first thing we have to do when we get back home is get you a therapist. Sitting out here in the middle of the woods, waiting for … ghosts to appear—it's crazy. We don't even have jackets, and it's freezing out here."

"It always gets colder before they appear."

"Oh, come off it, will you—"

The tree groaned and creaked.

Val turned and looked up at the tree. A pale luminescence washed across his face. David followed his gaze.

From each of the heavy branches descended a ghastly figure. Coarse, knotted rope dug into the flesh of their throats. Their bodies sagged, limp beneath outstretched and distended necks. Their faces were bloodless, frozen in painful leers. Their eyes bulged in the sockets. They swayed back and forth as they glared down upon Val and David.

"Oh, Lord," David choked.

The whispered voices of the ghosts joined the unremitting creaking of the ropes.

"Innnoocccceennntt …"

"I did not do this thing."

"Please. Innocent. Please."

Each horrific spirit gibbered of its innocence.

"Val, let's go. I believe you, OK? You've proven your point. Let's just go."

But Val stepped towards the tree. He raised his arms towards it. "Do you remember me?" he asked.

"Innocent," the spirits hissed.

"I used to come out here." Val's voice sounded almost childlike. "To talk with you."

"Mercy! Mercy! I have committed no crime!"

"Please," Val said, "you remember, don't you?"

But still the spirits ignored him, instead crying out to the unseen lynch mob that had killed them so long ago.

"Let's get out of here," Dave said, grabbing Val by the shoulder. "They … they don't remember."

"No!" Val shrugged his hand away. "They know who I am."

The spirits gibbered incessantly, and it was impossible to tell where one plea for mercy ended and another began.

"They remember," Val said. Spittle flew from his lips. "They just want me to prove myself."

"What are you talking about? I'm leaving. You hear me, Val? I'm leaving."

"You'll get lost in the woods," Val said. "You said so yourself."

David stepped away.

"Funny thing about these spirits," Val said. "They hang there professing their innocence. But they aren't innocent, David. They committed the crimes. Only they won't admit it, except to one of their own."

"One of their own?"

"I found out quite by accident, you know? And they demanded so little. A favorite pet. Then they started asking for more and more, but it was worth it, because they listened, really listened. They understood me."

Val jangled the car keys in his hand. He wrapped his fist around the keys, leaving the point of one protruding from his fist.

"I just have to remind them. That's all."

He took a step towards David.

"What are you doing?"

Val drew closer.

As if sensing Val's intent, the tree spirits started convulsing and howling, only this time they did not plead for clemency, did not weep for their disavowed innocence confessions, but instead cackled and hissed the most awful stories—stories of murder, theft, rape, and worse—all the while trembling and bucking and swinging back and forth—back and forth—on the decaying, creaking ropes.

Val's hand flashed out.

Once again, spooky trees play into this quick and bloody little tale. This is the kind of story I would write very quickly in one sitting.

- CB

www.ingramcontent.com/pod-product-compliance
Lightning Source LLC
Chambersburg PA
CBHW060220030726
47499CB00004B/1127